Indigo Children

A.K.Biggins

This is a work of fiction. Names, characters, businesses, places, events, locales and incidents are either the products of the author's imagination or used in a fictitious manner. Any resemblance to actual persons, living or dead, or actual events is purely coincidental.

For my family – Thank you.

Indigo Children

Dreams

Last night I walked up the drive to Sunny Bank again. There were no locked gates or security barriers to stop me and I was transported back into a warm, sepia tinted past. The new housing estate wasn't even an idea and the garden with its long winding drive was still intact. Stepping happily along the gravel path, I held my breath until I reached the turn and on rounding the large plane tree, I caught sight of my childhood home again. As I neared the sanctuary of this happy place, I had the dreamers knowledge that it was the same yet different, familiar yet strange. The large white rose bush was in full bloom around the stone archway that protected the heavily glossed, red front door. Smiling, I reached out to touch the black iron knocker but it moved away from me as the door swung open. I woke up. I could still feel the house around me, the smell of Mum's cooling apple pie on the window ledge next to a bowl of setting jelly. A happy memory bubble in my austere and chilly bed. Sighing I rolled on to my back and my sensors jarred. The images shattered and panic hit me as I became aware of dark eyes watching me from the corners of the room. Waiting for my heartbeat to steady itself, I rubbed my temples and took a deep breath, allowing the morning light to settle around me, accepting that it was just another vivid dream, a trick of the darkness and relaxation of my mind.

No matter how many times I trace the steps towards my past in these nocturnal outings, I know I can never go back. The past is gone and I cannot get back what was lost. But sometimes in my dreams I manage to catch a glimpse of the life I had in that South Yorkshire village, of the child that I was...and it breaks my heart.

Indigo Children

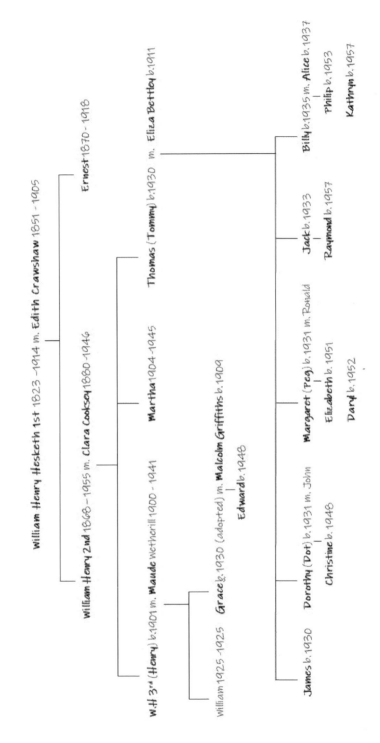

Hesketh Family Tree

Part One

Indigo Children

Chapter One

Kathryn

It's hard to know where the story really starts, where the rot first set in. Maybe it was always there. In hindsight there was always something a bit off kilter in my childhood, although no one else seemed aware. Even those closest to this strangeness seemed oblivious to it, not seeing the malevolence lurking just out of peripheral vision, for such a long time. Or perhaps they were all enthralled in a spell of acceptance. Whatever the reason there were few clues and I doubt an outsider would have noticed anything amiss or the long shadows hovering over my family.

My brother claimed it started on the morning of Uncle Jimmy's funeral in 1967 but Mum insists it started long before then, her cataract-impaired eyes always giving the impression that she was looking directly into the past.

As a child I remember there was invariably sharpness in my Granny Eliza's voice whenever she spoke about the past, particularly when referring to Burntwood, the family's ancestral home.

"There's always been badness in the big house, lurking in every room; you were not safe anywhere in there for long," she pronounced when I again asked her what it was like on the day before the funeral. Dad rolled his eyes at me before admitting with a sigh, "It's certainly a dark and creepy old place, that's for sure."

"Never mind dark and creepy, it's a horrible place, full of spite," Granny insisted and now, in the hindsight of what happened, I smile at the irony of Eliza's prophetic statement.

I never heard Gran refer to it as anything but the big house, but the big house had a name. It was Burntwood Hall and was the family home of the Heskeths, my forbearers, for 125 years.

I suppose then that this is a story of two houses; Sunny Bank, a spacious, beautiful and welcoming seven bedroom family home with an inside as well as outside toilet - bought by my great grandfather and given as a gift to my Grandad Tommy and Granny Eliza in 1933 - and Burntwood Hall, a twelve bedroom, dark, cold, gothic looking Manor house built in 1730 and acquired by my Great Great Grandfather William Henry Hesketh in 1846.

However, my story is disjointed, as indeed my life has been. I have to divide it up into parts and even these parts will not be linear – sorry. It starts long before I was born and the cast is quite large but I am sure it won't take you long to work out who the significant players are. It has taken me years to make sense of what happened and perhaps I will struggle to make you understand why, but the writing of this has been as cathartic as I was told it would be. In the latter years of my life I have been studious, or as some have said obsessive, about my family history. Well to be fair, I did have a lot of time on my hands.

To keep the story as straight as it can be and to set the scene a little, I'd better start with the manor house. Situated on the edge of Great Houghton, Burntwood had previously been owned by the Marsden family, who were prominent and influential people with a self rumoured connection to minor aristocracy dating back to Henry VIII. This noble bloodline dried up in 1835 with the death of the last surviving son Francis Marsden, a pious and solitary man. The Hall had fallen into disrepair during his tenure and in the subsequent years it lay empty allowing the first William Henry, ever the business man, to buy it at a low price with his 'new money' and establish his own nobility. To say that he had a large chip on his shoulder about being looked down on by the real aristocracy, would be an understatement. It was a massive chip, a solid block of seething resentment by all accounts which made him hard and cantankerous, traits that remained in the family for generations to come. I never met him of course, he was dead nearly ninety years before I was born – neither did I meet his son, also a William Henry, my great grandad, but I do know lots about them. Their lives were held up over the years by subsequent generations as the foundation stones of our family's social climbing and self-important status.

Even though I only went to Burntwood twice, and to my knowledge there are no surviving photographs of it, I still feel that I know exactly what it looked like. My recollection is solidly encased in what happened on those visits and tarnished with the horrors of it.

On both occasions the whole of the Hesketh clan were together. The first time was for the funeral of my uncle Jimmy and I think that would be a good place for me to start to tell this tale of my close and crazy family and their downfall. As predicted by my mother, who had not wanted me to go, the funeral did not go exactly to plan and there were, again as she predicted, tears before bedtime.

At 10 years old I was excited and deliciously frightened at the prospect of seeing a dead body. The dearly departed was to be in an open casket in the drawing room of the big house, as was the Hesketh way. And so the family gathered at Burntwood, two hours before the procession was to leave for the church, on the morning of Tuesday 21st November 1967.

It was cold and the sun was a bleary shape behind bleak grey clouds as we got out of the car. My new, shiny black patent shoes crunched on the gravel as I walked towards the door. The booming voice of Great Uncle Henry made me raise my head quickly and fear wrapped itself around my shoulders as I saw him framed in the doorway. I stopped abruptly. Mum turned and took my hand roughly, her patience already tested by the car journey.

"Come on Kathryn don't start your nonsense." I shrunk into my new big coat, stepping quickly to remain as close to her as I could. Dad was shaking hands with his uncle as we passed through the doorway while my fourteen year old brother, Pip stood miserably at his side. Mum let go of my hand to begin her pretence at an affectionate family greeting and I moved quickly towards the window to wait for my sibling and protector.

The hall was dark and cold and a strong smell of something sweet and acidic hung in the air. I could feel my eyes starting to sting as I glanced around at the formally posed portraits aligning the oak panelling. All my ancestors were placed strategically so their unsmiling faces could witness the comings and goings. Taking a few steps towards the stairs, I felt a shudder of excited fear. It looked like something from 'House of Dracula' a hammer horror film Pip and I had secretly watched a few weeks before. The bare stone wall to the right of the wide staircase was adorned with large ostentatious oil canvasses favoured by the first William Henry, mostly of him in various poses and family groupings. The massive reproductions showed him formally dressed and standing stiffly in postures intended to look commanding. His cold hard eyes seemed to look right at me and, as I stepped back, they followed me.

"What are you doing?" Pip asked as he touched me on the arm. Startled, I let out a small yelp for which I was admonished with a sharp beam from my mother's vivid blue eyes. Philip pulled me back towards a small door at the left side of the hall.

"I was looking for Eliza," I whispered. Dad had driven Granny and Grandad Tommy over while I was eating my breakfast so that they could be here to greet the family but I couldn't see either of them.

"She's with Uncle Jimmy," he said giving me a meaningful stare, "Uncle Henry says we have to keep out of the way and go to the kitchen and see if Aunt Grace needs us to do anything." He was opening the door as he spoke.

"Really?" I whined but my voice was barely a whisper, "Do we have to?"

"Fraid so. Come on, it'll be alright."

Behind the small door was a narrow staircase that led down to the kitchen. In grander days the family had 'staff' to look after their needs, never to be referred to as servants, Eliza had told me. There had been a house keeper, a cook, a driver and two girls who came in every day to help with the cleaning. When the last cook died in 1958 the driver, her husband went to live with their daughter in Scarborough. The housekeeper lasted another year before taking a much better paid job in a larger house near Harrogate. Since then the family had managed with a cleaning lady who came twice a week and cooked them a roast dinner on Sunday. Since Great Uncle Henry had become the head of the family and he saw no need for entertaining at the Hall, they 'muddled on nicely'. Uncle Henry saw no reason to pay out good money when there was a woman in the house with time on her hands. The funeral tea however, was a different matter. It was being catered by a team of ladies from the Women's Institute under the supervision of the said woman of the house, Aunt Grace - Great Uncle Henry's adopted daughter and one of the scariest women I had ever met.

"You boy, stop skulking in the doorway. Come here where I can see you!" Grace's sharp voice cut through the muted mumblings of village ladies. I grabbed my brother's hand as he stepped forward and edged myself behind him as we shuffled into the room. "Ah, you're Billy's boy. Philip isn't it?" Pip nodded. "Oh yes and your odd little sister, Karen or Christine?" She shook her head slightly and looked at me, unsmiling. I shrank back further, pressing my face into the back of my brother's smart coat.

"It's Kathryn." Pip's voice sounded small and tinny and I could feel his thinly suppressed fear, "And she's not odd."

Grace tilted her head slightly, her cold eyes on his, but Pip returned her gaze. The kitchen went silent and peeping from behind my brother, I could see a lady in a pink cardigan holding a half shelled boiled egg, frozen in the moment, waiting for Grace's reaction.

"Well time will tell on that one," she snorted with an unfriendly smile and dismissed us to the back corner of the kitchen, "Go over and help Edward fill the dumb waiter and don't break anything."

Edward was Aunty Grace's nineteen year old son. We knew of him although had only seen him once or twice over the years at family events and we had never spoken to him. He had his mothers glower and I stayed behind Pip as we shuffled towards him.

"I have a system here and I don't need you two messing it up," he hissed at us.

"Well we'll go back upstairs then," my brother answered quickly and turned around to steer me back towards the door. Feeling relief I needed no encouragement and moved forward. Putting my hand out to open the door a bolt of electricity shot through me and I shrieked before falling limply back into Pip's arms. Aware of voices around me, I couldn't move or respond and dense smoke was filling my nose and throat. I could hear the crackling of burning wood all around me and just before it all went black I saw Aunt Grace smiling in delight through the flames.

The next thing I knew someone was stroking my face gently and calling my name. I had been carried back up to the sitting room and was lying on the musty old sofa. Opening my eyes, I could see Mum crouching in front of me holding a glass of water.

"The fire..," I tried to say but my voice was raspy and low and I could still taste the smoke.

"Really Alice, this is the last thing we need today. Can nothing be done to control this child?" A dark shadow appeared behind Mum blocking out the light as Grace's displeasure seethed around the room. I tried to look around for Pip but my eyes wouldn't focus. I was about to cry but the noise of the door banging into the large oak writing desk as it was flung open stopped me in my tracks, and in rushed Eliza.

"Go back to your catering, Grace, and leave the child alone," she said, edging her small frame to block everyone out of her way, "I can see to her Alice, you get back to Billy." Although she addressed Mum with a softer voice, the firmness left no doubt that this was an instruction. Both women left the room, Mum dutifully handing the water to Eliza first. I felt dizzy and sick but said nothing as I watched my Granny place the glass on the small side table before pulling me into a sitting position and lowering her face to take a good look at me. Once she seemed satisfied that I was properly with it, she retrieved the glass and held it to my mouth. After a few gulps I felt the fear, along with the sickness, subsiding as my senses returned.

"What happened Kitty?" She asked gently.

"Fire, there was a fire, it was here, this house...just like...," and the tears came back.

"Hush my love, it's alright, there's no fire, it was just one of your little turns. Nerves I expect with all this emotion flying around." She stroked my cheek and smiled, "Your Aunty Grace is enough to put anyone's nerves on edge. Now come on lets me and you go outside and have a little walk round the garden and get out of this stuffy old house."

Holding my hand we went out of French windows, down the crumbling stone steps and crossed the lawn towards the small rose garden, the furthest place away from the house. I was worried about my new shoes but she said in the scheme of things they didn't matter and I felt suddenly bad as I remembered Uncle Jimmy. We sat down on the bench looking over the green algae coated birdbath, frightening away a collared dove.

"I am sorry that Uncle Jimmy died, Granny," I said, meaning it, "I really liked him."

"Yes love, I know you did, everybody did. He was a good boy my Jimmy, my first born." Sighing deeply, she stared across the garden of neglected rosebushes and I felt her tense as she added, "He was too good for this family. I should never have let him come back here."

"You never liked it here did you, Granny?" A fact she had stated many times. She looked at me and smiled and raised our enjoined hands.

"No, I did not. It's not a nice house and the folk that live here are not very nice either," she chuckled, "And they've never thought very much of me either."

We sat for another half an hour or so, sucking on sherbet lemons,

13

while she told me about her first impressions of Burntwood and what life was like in the three and a half years she had lived there after she'd married Grandad Tommy.

I remember clearly the coldness of that day both inside and out of the house but in that short time sitting in the garden I was somehow warm and content. The story Eliza told me was clearly one sided and her perspective heavily clouded with the animosity she felt towards the family she clearly loathed. Years later, when I did the research into our family history, I filled in the gaps to get a better rounded view of my ancestors but even then my view would always be tainted with Eliza's propaganda.

"They claimed I married above my station," she said, "that I wasn't good enough, well look at them, their high and mighty stuck up ways got them nowhere. They'd have no real family left if it weren't for me."

The big house was a lot more luxurious than anything she was used to but, although it was very grand, it was never a happy house and she had known that from very first moment she crossed the wide dark threshold. I often heard her say the only good thing about Burntwood, not that she ever used the name, was that there was space to hide herself and her babies from the sharp tongues and frosty glances of her in-laws.

I had just asked her to tell me again about how she and Grandad Tommy had met when Pip appeared running across the lawn towards us.

"Grandma, it's time to say goodbye, you have to come in now."

She got to her feet and, still holding my hand, pulled me lightly to walk beside her. I was confused and asked,

"Why are we saying goodbye, don't we have to stay for the funeral?" She stopped and turned towards me, putting her hands on my shoulders, her dark brown eyes looking right into mine.

"This is where you have to be very brave, Kitty. I want you to watch very carefully what happens as we all say our own goodbyes to Uncle Jimmy."

Chapter Two
Eliza - 1925

Eliza's mother married for love. Eliza knew this because her mother told her and her siblings over and over as she scrubbed and scoured their tiny back to back house. She performed this task daily after doing similar chores at the big house where she was considered indispensable, according to Eliza's father.

Eliza also thought that her mother could perform miracles because her father repeated this every day when he came home from work and sat down to his dinner.

She was the love of his life and he had met her at a local dance when she was seventeen and about start work as a teacher. He was nineteen and had been working down the pit since he was fourteen, like his father before him.

"He fair took my breath away, soon as I saw him I knew he were the one," her mother often proclaimed. She was smiling wistfully as she boiled up potatoes peelings.

Eliza never knew her mother's parents although they only lived a mile away. They hadn't approved of the love match. Their daughter had married beneath her, against their wishes, so they had washed their hands of her.

"But it didn't matter, when you love each other that's enough." Eliza noticed that as the years went by her mother said that less and less.

It might not have been so bad if the love Eliza's dad had for his bride had not been quite so carnal. In the 15 years of their marriage, she had 9 pregnancies to full term but, as were the times, only four survived, all girls. Eliza came to realise even the survival of her and her sisters was probably another of her mother's miracles, given their abject poverty. Luckily for her, Eliza wasn't the eldest of her siblings. She was third in line and so as her mother faded, her two elder sisters took up the mantel. At 15 and 14 they became mother's little helpers as well as taking on her work at the big house. Their mother deteriorated rapidly and just before Christmas that year, at the age of 33, the effects of her harsh and selfless existence took their toll. Eliza had just turned 13 and the only one of her siblings that headed their mothers dying words,

"Never marry for love."

Chapter Three
Kathryn - 1967

Back in the house the whole family was assembled in the hall. Great Uncle Henry and Grandad Tommy were standing by the door of the front parlour waiting for Eliza. Tommy and Eliza's twin daughters were standing in their own satellite family branches. Aunty Dot and Aunty Peg were accompanied by their respective husbands, John and Ronald, and between them their children, all older than me. Christine was the eldest and offspring of John and Dorothy, Elizabeth and Daryl were Peggy and Ronald's children. Great Aunt Grace stood at the bottom of the staircase looking like she had a bad smell under her nose. Great Uncle Malcolm, her husband, looked dishevelled and fed up as he always did and Edward, slightly behind them was messing with his tie. Mum and Dad were furthest away from the door with Pip. Eliza led me towards them and patted my hand as she let go before moving to the front of the line, brushing Mum's arm and nodding as she went. Mum turned and took my hand and bent to say something but stopped as everyone's attention turned back to the large front door. The sound of car tyres crunching up the drive and stopping outside took everyone by surprise. Mum straightened as Uncle Henry stepped forward, muttering about it being too early for the hearse as he strode towards the door. The engine remained running and we could all clearly hear two doors being opened and slammed shut and a man's voice calling out thank you before the car drove off. Everyone seemed confused and Great Uncle Henry had his thunderous face on as he yanked open the door.

"For God's sake, Jack! What on earth are you doing here?" he exclaimed. Eliza let out a yelp and ran to the door to hug her prodigal son.

"I've come to see my brother off. Hello Mum." He smiled warmly at Eliza and hugged her while smiling over her shoulder at his uncle.

Dad moved to the door and held out his hand. "Hello Jack, long time no see. How are you?"

Jack ignored his hand and locked him in a bear hug, slapping his back enthusiastically. "Hey Billy Boy, look at you." Grinning widely, he pushed him to arms length before his attention wandered over Dad's shoulder. Moving Dad aside, he stepped forward and grabbed Mum, "Alice, aren't you a sight for sore eyes. My god, you are still the most beautiful woman I've ever seen. I bloody wish I'd had the sense to ask you first!" He laughed out loud, bellowing in the pleasure of his own words but never took his eyes off Mum.

"Jack, please remember where you are!" Henry snapped sternly, "This is your brother's funeral."

"And Jimmy would be more than happy that his brother is here," Eliza said, taking Jack's hand and leading him towards Grandad Tommy who only nodded and mumbled his son's name in greeting.

"Granny!" I called, "What about the boy?" I pointed to the frightened looking boy standing in the open doorway. All eyes turned to notice the child.

"Oh yes," Jack walked back to the door, "Come on in Raymond and meet your family." The wide eyed, dark skinned boy stepped forward at his father's request.

"Mum, this is your grandson Raymond. He's just turned ten and it might not look like it but I promise you he has Hesketh blood flowing through his veins."

"And where is the child's mother?" Grace asked pointedly.

"Delores died last year I'm sorry to say." He lowered his voice and cast his eyes to the floor, "So it's just been me and young Ray here since then."

"Hello Raymond." Eliza smiled at the frightened looking boy, touching his dark curly hair. I looked over at Grandad Tommy who wasn't looking very happy but his annoyance was nothing compared to Great Uncle Henry's. He'd gone all red in the face.

"Jack, this is outrageous; to just turn up like this," he boomed, "And this child..."

"This child," Eliza cut in, "Is my grandson." She took Raymond's hand and held out her empty one to Jack, gesturing for him to slot into the line behind Mum and Dad, who stood in front of Grace and Malcolm, before leading Raymond to a chair at the far side of the hall.

"You never met your uncle Jimmy so there's no need for you to banish the bad dreams. You just sit here quietly while we say our goodbyes."

A panic hit me as Granny mentioned bad dreams. I had been plagued with night terrors for as long as I could remember. I grabbed mum's coat sleeve.

"Mum," I said, shaking her arm.

"Hush, Kathryn!" was her only response, made without looking at me, but she did find my hand with hers and squeezed it tight.

Great Uncle Henry opened the door, leaving his arm on the brass handle and bowing his head slightly to Eliza and Tommy as they stepped inside. After a meaningful glance at the rest of us, he followed them into to the parlour. I swallowed hard; this was the moment I had been waiting for with ghoulish and fearful excitement. The line of family began to move slowly forward, filing past the coffin and pausing in turn to say goodbye to Uncle Jimmy. My nervous fidgeting received a sharp pull on the arm from Mum as I leaned and twisted to try and see ahead. It seemed to be taking ages and I could hear sobbing amongst the muted speech and whisperings. Just before I crossed the threshold into the room, I glanced back at Raymond. He was sitting straight backed on the chair. His feet were a good six inches above the floor were still, as was his body, but his eyes were flittering nervously all around the room. I caught his eye and we exchanged tentative smiles before I was pulled through the doorway. The room was in semi-darkness with the curtains closed, a small table lamp provided a yellowy 30 watt glow near the far side of the room. I stood up on my tiptoes to try and see what was happening. Aunty Dot was bending forwards. Uncle John passed her a handkerchief and she dabbed her nose before balling it in her hand and leaned even further in.

"Goodbye big brother, rest in peace."

A sliver of cold fear tingled at the back of my neck as I thought for a moment that she must be expecting Uncle Jimmy to answer as she leaned in further.

"Mum!" My loud involuntary cry provoked a sudden stiffness in my mother before she bent to speak to me. I readied myself to say sorry.

"It's alright Kathryn, we're all here and there is nothing to be scared of. You just need to be brave." The unexpected softness in her voice and echoing of Eliza's words compacted my fear into a hard ball that lodged in my throat. I held out my free hand to touch Pip. He turned and tried to hide his fear with a smile, but I saw it.

"It's ok, Kitty," he whispered.

Behind me, I heard an irritated sigh and Great Aunt Grace asked, "For goodness sake, what's wrong with the girl now?" My eyes brimmed over as I tried to sniff down the dread along with a snivel. Three more paces forward and we were almost in front of the casket. I could see Uncle Jimmy's shoes. My eyes followed the line of his body and Aunty Peg, standing by his shoulder, her hand inside the coffin and resting on Jimmy's prayer hands, head bowed slightly, looking down at him sadly. My attention was distracted by a movement just behind her, it was Eliza, standing slightly back from the head of her first born with her eyes fixed on me. I looked away quickly and back at Aunty Peg just in time to see her dip her head into the coffin and kiss the cold blue lips of her dead brother. I squeezed Mum's hand and pulled her down towards me.

"Mum, I don't want to do it, I want to go home," I pleaded.

"Hush, Kathryn, you have to, it's important. You need to kiss him goodbye then he won't haunt your dreams." Her voice was soft but it was firm. "Come on Kitty, be a good girl and don't make a fuss."

I moved forward along the line in silence, trying to reign in my fear. After Dad kissed his brother, he stood back slightly to wait for Pip to do the same. I watched as his white fingers gripped the side of the casket and he closed his eyes before performing his kiss. Mum next. She let go of my hand and muttered a goodbye, patted her brother-in-law's hands and leaned in. She only moved a few inches away and turned expectantly to me, her eyes meaningfully wide. I swallowed hard and gripped the dark oak side, my fingertips sinking into the white satin of the lining and I suddenly felt calm.

"I'm sorry you died, Uncle Jimmy," my words came from nowhere, "It wasn't your time." I looked into his lifeless face, his closed eyes, and remembered what a lovely uncle he was and the sadness almost overwhelmed me. I leaned in and kissed him goodbye and as my ten year old lips touched his waxy bloodless ones his coldness seeped through me and I stepped backwards quickly. Mum's arms came around me and pulled me slightly around to where Eliza was standing. She had something in her hand and waved it under my nose.

"Come on Kitty," Eliza was saying, "You stand here with me now." She held me from behind so I could watch as Great Aunt Grace bent into the coffin. Just before my legs gave way and everything went black, I saw Uncle Jimmy's eyelids flicker.

Chapter Four

Eliza - 1926

Two months after the death of her mother Eliza was sent to help keep house for the childless Vicar and his wife. Her two elder sisters were still working at the big house and she had been keen not to skivvy for anyone but once inside the vicarage she knew fate was on her side. The vicar's wife was immediately taken with the child and was impressed at her keenness to improve herself with her reading and writing. Eliza saw her chance and told this kind middle aged woman of her mother's plight and her change of circumstance, embellishing the tale with a death bed promise to try to become a teacher herself. She had no qualms about presenting her father as the hard hearted villain who had little love for his daughters. The couple were horrified and vowed to help Eliza escape the life she had been born into. It's not known if any money actually changed hands but within six months of her starting at the vicarage as the paid daily help, she was promoted to live-in companion and protégée with barely a backward glance at her father or siblings.

The big house where her sisters worked was, in fact, Burntwood Hall, an imposing dark stone mansion at the top of Elder Hill and home to the Heskeths, a wealthy family who had made their fortune in the manufacture of glass. This was the big house that Eliza's mother and then her sisters had cleaned and tendered, curtseying and bowing and making it clear that they knew their place. Eliza had never been inside and never wanted to but she knew all about the family from her mother and sisters chatterings when she had lived at home.

William Henry 2nd was a nasty old man who seemed to do little else but grunt and smoke cigars. His wife who Eliza had been told was the real head of the family was Clara, a large woman with a sharp tongue who counted out the coins carefully when paying for their services. William and Clara had three off spring, Henry, Martha and Thomas. Henry was like his father and referred to them as 'you girl' when he bothered to acknowledge them at all. He was married to a very strange and jumpy woman called Maude. She cried a lot and shouted at the girls that they were good for nothing and told them to stop looking at her, even when they weren't. Martha was a queer one, they said and very quiet. When they did see her she would be mainly in the garden or cowering in corner of a room looking like she wanted to blend in with the wall dressings. Thomas was the favourite of both Eliza's sisters. He was a proper gentleman, even though he wasn't that old and always spoke nicely to them and said please and thank you.

When Eliza took her step up to live in the Vicarage that summer the sketchy caricatures of the inhabitants of the big house was all she knew about the Hesketh family and she was not really that interested. She had her new life with the kindly couple who treated her as their daughter and for the first time in her life, Eliza was happy.

Chapter Five
Kathryn - a little more Family History

Uncle Jim was my Dad's oldest brother, only by seven years though and his sudden death at 37 was a great shock to the family. Eliza, my Granny, was deeply upset and expressed most of her pain through anger at the family. Grandad Tommy was no less affected by the death of his eldest son but he was still a Hesketh and emotional displays in public were not their way, or so Mum said. The death of James Albert Hesketh had also been a massive blow to Great Uncle Henry. With no son of his own he had taken a shine to James, his nephew, giving him a job and training him in how to manage the company.

When his brother Thomas, my grandad, left the family firm decades previously, Henry had been desperate to father an heir of his own but it was not to be. Henry's only son had died within days of his birth after which, his wife's health had deteriorated and she had been unable to have any other children of her own. Henry had somewhat reluctantly but eventually decided that the family business should be passed on to Thomas's eldest son and so Henry had made James, Uncle Jimmy, his protégé and next in line to run the family business. What Grandad Tommy thought of that I am unsure but I know there was never any noticeable affection between the two brothers. Maybe this would be a good time to tell you a little more about my gnarled and twisted family tree.

The Hesketh Family Fortune was created from the manufacture of glass and their understanding of its adaptability and usefulness, not to mention their shrewd business decisions. My great-great grandad did the equivalent of winning the lottery when he purchased a small glass manufacturing factory from a bankrupt family in South Yorkshire eight months before the abolition of the Glass Tax in 1845. The Heskeths already had a small scale operation in Dewsbury which was by no means successful, making very little profit.

Great-great grand-pops, William Henry was only twenty-one years old when he went against his father's advice and bought the new operation but was proved right within twelve months. To celebrate, the young entrepreneur purchased Burntwood and began his plan to turn the rundown and neglected manor house into a house of substance, worthy of the family's new found fortune and standing.

Not long after this, Hesketh Glass was very profitably involved in the construction of London's Crystal Palace for the Great Exhibition in 1851. Although there is no documentation or public record of this anywhere, it is an absolute sworn true fact – according to Great Uncle Henry - providing another boost for the family fortunes and demonstrating glass as a viable building material. William Henry was an amazingly shrewd business man. He developed and extended the new plant with facilities to manufacture plate, decorative leaden glass and bottles. He understood the need to diversify and to invest in the new technology; Hesketh Glass was the first factory in Britain to use a semi-automatic machine capable of producing 200 bottles per hour, three times quicker than the previous process. From what I gather, this William Henry was a force to behold and, standing no nonsense, was totally ruthless in his quest for power and status. After proving his father wrong with his big plans for expansion, he quickly pushed him aside, taking total control of the company by the age of thirty. He married a year later and when his first wife died in childbirth, along with the baby; he married her sister, after a not very decent period of mourning. The sister also died in childbirth but not before giving him three daughters. He remarried a third time at the age of 49 to the 16 year old daughter of a one of his glass blowers. She finally produced two sons in quick procession, William Henry junior and Ernest Albert. Her reward for this was to be given her own set of rooms at Burntwood and then almost totally ignored by her husband. There is not much known or recorded about what happened to the three little girls. In my recent research, I have managed to find records of their christenings; they were named Edith, Ida and Vera and there is a further record of Vera's death at the age of seven. What happened to her sisters remains a gap in the family tree although one of the church archivists suggested that perhaps they were sent back to their mother's family; perhaps to make up for the two daughters they had lost.

The two little boys though were in evidence from their birth. Doted on by their mother who was young and healthy enough to care for them, along with a nanny and governess. They were also idolised by their father who could hardly bear to be apart from them. He often took them to the factory, making sure they understood the importance of family and their place, as he saw it, in society. He was the worst type of snob – a self-made man with a grievance against the world built on his own insecurities.

Whether it was nature or nurture, luck or good management, William Henry's son, William Henry 2nd, had his father's business acumen and took the successful company onwards and upwards. His slightly younger brother Ernest was also clever and, perhaps because he had always been aware that he was the spare to the heir, lacked any real passion for the company - his interest instead was in local politics. Much to his father's delight, Ernest became an MP shortly before the outbreak of the First World War.

William Henry 2nd remained the apple of his father's eye and proved to be the perfect, dutiful son and heir. He married Clara, a 19 year old from a good and wealthy family in 1898 and secured the linage within a year with the birth of William Henry 3rd, who to prevent confusion, finally, was always known as Henry, my Great Uncle Henry no less. It was, by accounts a difficult birth and Clara was confined to her room for sometime afterwards but understanding her duty to the Hesketh family, struggled back to health in order to produce her second child two years later. Although a much easier birth, Martha's arrival was a massive disappointment to both parents who did little to hide this fact. However, fortune or something shined again for Clara and she produced her spare a year later in the form of Thomas Stanley – my grandad, Tommy.

The first William Henry did not live to see how the Hesketh fortune was increased or the contribution the business he had founded made to the Great War, as he died peacefully in his sleep in the summer of 1914 at the incredibly grand old age of 90. Nor was he around to see his very shrewd and head strong daughter-in-law, Clara, who, after fifteen years of being married to the heir to the business and providing the required heirs, showed her full potential as the family matriarch.

She had been quick to understand the family, a slightly head strong girl who had instinctively known when to keep her powder dry, she had fitted in well. Clever and calculating, she had learned how and when to speak and act, subversively letting her husband believe he was in control. She was a master of manipulation and brilliant puppeteer. Quickly becoming the power behind the Hesketh throne with her quick mind and calculated ambition, she provided the boost the family needed at the onset of the Great War.

When William Henry was terrified of what the shortage of able-bodied men would do to production, Clara stepped up to the plate and astounded him. No less a social climber than her father-in-law she was way ahead of her time with her understanding of networking. She joined committees and worked tirelessly to promote and sustain the family within social and important circles. She invited the great and the good to dinner and to weekend parties and wrote and corresponded daily with anyone she thought might prove helpful to the family and/or business.

Ernest spent most of his time in his London flat but often brought his political friends to Burntwood, referring to it pompously as his country seat. Clara encouraged him to cultivate a friendship with Arthur Bramshaw, Minister for Supply. He and his wife became regular visitors and great friends to the Hesketh family, although Clara referred to him in private as that silly little man and his ridiculous wife.

On one particular weekend, Clara was keen to take the ridiculous Mrs Bramshaw for a walk around the grounds and endured her endless chattering about nothing, just so the men could discuss the predicted hostilities. The family had been well aware of the advances made in Germany with optical glass and its importance in the technology of warfare and lost no time in pointing out the significance of this. The advent of superior optical glass would make an incredible mark on military ordnance. "In short," William told a well fed and slightly drunk Arthur Bradshaw, "warfare has evolved to the point where the side with the best optics will have a clear advantage." The family received both financial and preferential support throughout the conflict and were therefore able to feather the family nest considerably and the business went from strength to strength.

Ernest, however, did not do quite so well. His very unremarkable and slightly tarnished career came to an abrupt end in 1919 when he became one of the 50 million victims of the Spanish flu. No one else in the family was affected by the pandemic but no one else had celebrated the end of the war by spending their days and nights like Ernest, in his London flat with a recently returned solider called Colin.

There was no scandal of course, friends in high places saw to that. The family name would not be tarnished. Instead, it was mentioned with reverence and praise for the good work performed during hostilities and the surviving Heskeths were allowed to bask in the post war glory, where they found themselves in even more improved financial circumstances.

The next generation of Heskeths grew up with this affluence and in the important glory. Henry was a serious child who listened carefully to instruction. He was very much a chip off the old Hesketh block. Martha was quiet and timid and was seldom seen around the house. She grew into a shadowy figure, appearing in company only when Clara insisted, which was not often. Although she was not seen much about the house, Martha spent a lot of time wandering the grounds, particularly at night.

Thomas, the youngest and the only one of the three with Clara's fair hair and complexion, was given a much easier passage through his early years. Always his mother's favourite, his easy-going nature and humour also charmed his father, much to his brother's annoyance. This annoyance only increased when Thomas joined the family firm at sixteen to work alongside Henry. The main issue was that Thomas never took anything seriously enough and wasn't remotely interested in the business, making it clear he didn't want to be there. He couldn't settle into any role or task his father gave him and Henry resented the fact that while his parents were obsessed with finding a role for his brother, they failed to notice how well he was doing. He had been brought up with stories of his grandfather's business prowess and the money he had made at an early age and had been determined to replicate this success. He worked hard and listened and learned, always thinking of the business and wanting to keep the Hesketh name prominent in the community.

At the factory, the brothers constantly clashed and the discord between them grew daily. Henry was a shrewd businessman with an eye to the future and could not bear Thomas's time wasting and perceived laziness. Although far from being a philanthropist, Henry understood it was important to keep the workforce happy and started his tenure in management with a sense of fairness but he was driven mad by the unfairness of his position. Always desperate for his father to acknowledge and appreciate his hard work he constantly felt taken for granted, while Thomas remained the golden boy despite his many failings.

At 22, Henry married Maude Wetherill, the daughter of a business associate from Leeds, at the suggestion of his father. Maude was a plain girl and almost five years older than him but came with a dowry that provided a welcome boost to the company. In fact, Neville Wetherill, a textile mill owner, was so relieved to find a husband for his 27 year old only child that the settlement he made was unbelievably generous. But even this sacrifice for the good of the company, and marrying Maude was indeed a sacrifice for Henry, was not enough to incite the emotion Henry craved from his parents.

It wasn't that Henry disliked Maude or that she annoyed him more than any other woman in his life. If he were honest, he found her less annoying than his ghost of a sister and far easier than his domineering mother, but she was irritatingly clingy and he had no idea how to handle her. Maude's cosseted and privileged life as a much loved, only child of wealthy parents was swept away with the few handfuls of confetti thrown at her wedding. It was made very clear to her the moment she arrived at Burntwood as the new Mrs Hesketh, how things worked in the family. Her new mother-in-law was quick to let her know who ruled the roost and that Maude's place in the hierarchy was at the very bottom. Clara was in charge and as long as Maude created no problems and carried out her wifely duties, producing the required heir and spare, she would be tolerated.

Maude struggled with Clara's coldness towards her but took her cue from Henry and did everything she could to stay in her good books and earn favour, but life was hard. After two early miscarriages in the first two years of marriage, she finally carried a son to full term, only to be heartbroken when he died after only a few days. Another miscarriage followed the following year and Maude's physical and mental health deteriorated to such a degree that she was not expected to see the Christmas of 1928. She managed to pull through physically, if not mentally, but the doctors warned Henry that another pregnancy would probably kill her and her mental fragility became a major concern. Henry was furious. He wanted a son and if Maude couldn't give him one, he wanted rid of her. There was even a suggestion of sending her to an asylum before divorcing her but Clara wouldn't hear of it.

Chapter Six
Kathryn - 1967

The day after the funeral, I was hoping everything would be back to normal. Our small family unit, Eliza, Grandad Tommy, Mum, Dad, Philip, me and Pal, our lovely Alsatian dog, living happily at Sunny Bank, like it was before Uncle Jimmy died. I had thought that the funeral would be the end of it but as it turns out it was just the start. After breakfast, Mum took me to see the doctor about my funny turns. I had never had two in one day before and I was apparently still looking pale and pasty. Dr Freeman, our local GP, took my temperature, listened to my chest and looked into my eyes and mouth. He concluded that I did look a bit pasty but couldn't see much wrong with me. He patted Mum's hand and said there was nothing to worry about. I was a healthy growing lass and maybe I was just a bit run down, probably the funeral had been a bit much for me. Mum reminded him that I had been having these occasional fainting spells for years now and she was worried they were getting worse. He looked a bit cross at this and called Mum 'My dear' as he told her that I would grow out of these funny little episodes, I just needed fattening up a bit. Mum didn't look particularly reassured so he suggested I have a day off school and that she bought me a bottle of Lucozade to give me a bit of energy. Mum said I was taking my eleven plus the next day so I was not having a day off school, but she would buy me a bottle of Lucozade. She smiled her thin smile at him, took my hand and led me out of the small surgery. I knew she was in a bad mood as she set a brisk walking pace and muttered under her breath all the way to the school gates.

My long lost uncle Jack and his son stayed with us the week after the funeral before going back to their home to sort out their affairs. There had been whisperings and speculation throughout the wake about Raymond's 'exotic' looks and where Uncle Jack had finally settled after his wanderings. The truth was he had been in Wolverhampton the whole time. He had married Delores, a West African woman, and the two of them had started a removals business which had done well. He needed to make up with Eliza and Grandad Tommy he told me and Philip. He had been headstrong and had let that 'bastard Henry' and Grace, his 'witch of a daughter', get to him and hound him out of the family. It was the morning of the eleven plus and we were sitting in the kitchen at the big old farmhouse table. Eliza was at the cooker frying bacon and eggs, Pip had a bowl of sugary cornflakes and I was eating toast and Eliza's homemade jam. I'd been up extra early as I was feeling a bit scared of the day ahead. I glanced towards the cooker when Uncle Jack said the word bastard but Eliza continued with her task, seemingly unfazed. Raymond sat silently next to his Dad, breaking his jammy toast into little pieces on his plate but not attempting to eat them. Pal was standing expectantly just to the side of him.

"Family is everything and you two should remember that. Us Heskeths have got a heritage and we're not going to let some bloody cuckoo take it from us." He picked up his cup of tea and practically gulped down the entire contents in one mouthful. I took another bite of my toast and chewed slowly as he went on, "Your granny's right, there's badness in that big house, I knew it back then and I could still feel it at that farce of a send-off they gave our Jim. We've got to stick together, it's the only way we can put a stop to it!" He seemed to have made himself cross as he spoke, waving his finger at us. Unsure what he meant, I nodded, thinking I would ask Pip about it later. Eliza turned holding a hot plateful of breakfast in her tea-towelled hand and placed it in front of Uncle Jack. She looked so happy.

"Now then Jack, get that on your chest and you won't take much harm," she said, her smile getting bigger as she stood there just looking at him. Then suddenly she turned her gaze to Pip and me, "Now you two take on what your Uncle Jack just said. You have Hesketh blood in you and we're not going to be cheated out of what's ours." I was even more confused by this statement and Pip had that look on his face he always had when he wanted to be somewhere else. I finished chewing my breakfast, looking round for a distraction.

"Why are you doing that with your toast, Raymond, don't you like it?" I asked.

Raymond looked flustered and his dark skin became a little darker as he muttered,

"Yes, I just ...yes, thank you," without looking up from his plate. I laughed and said he didn't have to thank me for asking him a question. He squirmed in his chair and looked at his Dad.

"Kathryn, your cousin is a guest here!" Eliza said sharply, glancing from the plate to me, "Please show him some manners. Anyway, shouldn't you two be off to school. It's a big day for you isn't it?" her tone softening a little. Pip put down his spoon and stood up, wiping his mouth on the back of his hand.

"She's going to ace it aren't you Kit?"

"Maybe..." I answered getting up to wash my hands and trying not to smile. I noticed Raymond still secretly balling his toast into his hand under the table and trying to give it to Pal.

My big day was the culmination of lots of extra school work over the last few months. Pip had passed four years earlier and was now comfortably in his fourth year and working towards his O'levels. The grammar school was in Normanton, which had initially been a fifteen minute train ride away but, thanks to Dr Beeching closing our local station, was now a forty minute bus ride. I had been really upset at this bit of economical progress. Getting two train rides a day had seemed a wonderful prospect but Pip said the bus ride was equally good so I was mildly consoled as everyone, including me, expected that next year I would be doing the same.

Pip hurried into the hall to get his things together for his quick five minute dash to the bus stop. As I moved to follow him, I saw Raymond turn slightly to hold out his hand under the table for a waiting Pal to take it. At the same moment, Eliza drew up a chair to sit with them, shooing the dog away while animatedly continuing the conversation on the badness of the folk in the big house with her prodigal son. Raymond stood up and surreptitiously dropped the balled sticky mass in the bin before washing his hands. As he turned back he caught my eye and I smiled with a little nod, letting him know that I had seen him but wouldn't tell.

"Good luck, Kitty!" Pip called as he went through the front door realising he would need to run to catch his bus. I went upstairs to brush my teeth and was just leaning over the wash basin to spit out the tooth paste when I suddenly felt dizzy. Panicking, I grabbed at the porcelain and steadied myself, I mustn't have one of my funny turns today. I sat on the side of the bath for a few minutes, feeling my heart thudding in my chest, before using Grandad's false teeth glass to get a drink of water and thankfully, I started to feel a bit better. I wondered if I should tell someone that I wasn't feeling well but Mum had gone to the betting shop with Grandad, Dad had already left for work and I could hear Eliza talking and laughing with Uncle Jack so I decided I would probably be alright. Taking a deep breath, I stood up and went downstairs and although my heart was still thudding and everything seemed a bit over bright, the dizziness had gone. Carefully, I padded down the stairs holding tight to the banister and took in another deep breath before letting go and reaching for my coat. I was just putting it on when Eliza dashed into the hall and gave me a big hug. Hugging her back, I felt her stiffen as she whispered,

"I know you saw something at your Uncle James' funeral and once the dust has settled here we can have a talk about it." I tensed at the prospect of revisiting what I did and didn't see at Uncle Jimmy's funeral but managed a small smile before escaping out on to drive of Sunny Bank, my head swirling and blood rushing in my ears.

Pip had got a new bike when he passed the eleven-plus and Dad had said I would get one too. Weeks before, I had picked mine out in expectation of my success. It was shiny, blue and had a basket on the front and blue and white ribbons hanging out of each side of the handlebars. I had picked it out one day while shopping with Mum and every day since then, on my way home from school, I had crossed the road by the park to stand in front of Perkins shop window to look at it. I usually spent a good ten minutes or so just standing there smiling as I imagined myself riding around the village on this beautiful blue machine. However, on that day, the day of the exam, I came out of the school gates and I did not cross the road, I just walked quickly home.

Christmas that year was as lovely as all other Christmases had been and I tried hard to enjoy it but there was a shadow of dread hanging over me. Two weeks after the exam, on Christmas Eve, Pip asked me what was wrong.

"I don't think I did very well in the tests," I answered flatly.

"Well they are hard, they have to be to make sure only the clever people go to the grammar school, but you're not stupid. You'll have passed don't worry, you'll get your bike." He punched me lightly on the arm, "So stop looking so miserable and come and help me put the trimmings up in the front room. I got up and followed him, trying to agree with him, telling myself it would all be ok and the little flashes of memory I had of that day were just bad dreams.

On the day of the results, the shadow was still hovering as I walked slowly to school. My two best friends, Lynn and Cheryl were standing in the porch over the entrance to Royston junior girls. They smiled at me as I approached.

"Hiya, Kathryn," Lynn beamed at me, "Cheryl says we'll probably have to stand up in assembly when they read out who's passed. Do you think we will have to?"

I shrugged and stepped up to stand with them, leaning on the side wall.

35

They were so excited they clearly didn't notice the dark foreboding cloud just above my head, but I knew it was there and I knew before long it would burst and wash away any hopes I had of wearing the Grammar school uniform.

No one had to stand up in assembly but twelve names were read out at the end. Twelve very clever boys and girls, who had passed their eleven-plus exam and in September were going to be travelling on the school bus every day to their new school. Lynn and Cheryl's names were amongst them but mine was not.

I groaned silently, it was as terrible as I thought, but there was worse to come. Not only had I failed but I had failed so badly my teacher, Mrs Thackeray, was furious. She saw my failing in such a spectacular fashion as an affront to her teaching. She had worked so hard with me and would not have done this if she'd suspected for one moment that I would so deliberately throw away any chance I had of getting a good education. Mrs Thackeray had a very poor opinion of the local senior school. She gave me a letter to give my parents at the end of the school day telling them in no uncertain terms her thoughts about how I had not only let her and the school down, I had let my parents down and I had very much let myself down. She hoped that they would see to it that I was suitably punished.

I could smell the baking when I walked into the kitchen and Mum was just lifting a sponge cake out of the oven. She smiled over at me, distracted no doubt by the heat coming through the tea towel. I tried to smile back but the sob I had been holding in all day finally forced its way out of my mouth and brought with it the well of self pity and disappointed tears. Mum tried her best to be kind about it but was in a complete state of shock. She read the letter as I sat at the table, pacing out her confusion on the kitchen lino. I was snivelling and whaling, unable to control myself. Eliza came in from the garden with Pal trotting behind her. She looked from me to her daughter-in-law and asked,

"What on earth's going on here?"

Mum handed her the letter and moved across to the kitchen sink. She clearly couldn't look at me or the celebration cake she had been making. Eliza read the letter and sighed loudly before sitting opposite me at the table.

"So what happened, Kitty?" She asked reasonably and I knew I should answer but how could I? How could I explain what I didn't understand myself? I looked up at her and felt my tears run down my cheeks before dropping off onto the table. I glanced back down at the wet patch and instinctively tried to rub it with the cuff of my school cardigan.

"Kathryn!" My mother turned back to us, "Answer your Granny and tell us what on earth happened?" Her sharp voice forcing more sobs to evolve through my chest.

"I, I don't...I don't know," I managed to stammer.

"Your teacher says you didn't try," Granny said, holding out the letter to confirm her words, "She thinks you didn't want to pass because you knew some of your friends wouldn't and you wanted to go to Royston Seniors instead. Is that true?"

"Well it must be," cut in Mum, "She could have easily passed, everybody said so, even the bloody teacher says so." I could hear her anger growing as she spoke, "Well you're not getting that bike now that's one thing for sure!" she finished and turned back to the washing up.

"Is that true, Kitty?" I could feel Eliza's eyes on me and I looked up at her hoping she would see my devastation, "Didn't you want to go to Normanton?"

I didn't know whether to nod or shake my head so I did both and rubbed my eyes with my cardigan sleeve. "Yes I wanted to go. I don't know what happened. When I got into the hall and sat down it was really quiet at first but then I could hear a funny noise," I said miserably.

"What sort of noise?" Mum snapped.

"Hush, Alice, let the girl speak." Eliza was the good cop.

37

"I don't know," I pleaded again, "I looked round but everyone had their heads bent over the desks...the noise just went on getting louder and then...." I trailed off as I knew I was going to make Mum even madder.

"And then what? Kitty, what happened then?"

Eliza reached across the table and held on to both my hands. I glanced over at Mum leaning on the sink, now watching me, before looking back at Granny. She had her soft smile, the one that made her eyes twinkle. "Come on love tell me, you won't be in trouble."

"It was making my head hurt and ...." I paused and looked deep into Eliza's soft eyes, "I thought... I thought I could hear Uncle Jimmy. He was trying to talk to me but there was too much noise for me to hear what he said."

Mum, as predicted, was furious and told me to go upstairs and get washed and changed and then stay in my room until Dad got home. Eliza said she was being hard on me. The funeral had clearly upset me and I was probably still overwrought. Mum should go to the school and ask them to make allowances - if she explained, I could probably still go to the grammar school. I could hear all this from my bedroom as I sat on my bed hoping she was right. Mum's response soon dispelled any expectations of a happy ending.

"Well you knew my thoughts about her going to the funeral. I knew it would be too much for her but no, Eliza, I will not go up to the school and use Jimmy's death as an excuse for what she has done."

"It was important for her to be there, I needed to see if she felt anything," Eliza said firmly.

"Oh for God's sake please don't you start all that stuff again, she is just an ordinary little girl and you have to stop this. I should never have let her go." Mum's voice was shrill with a mixture of emotions.

"Alice, I have to know what really happened, you know this," Eliza said sharply, "We all need to know."

"Oh for crying out loud Eliza, this has got to stop. I have been stupid to indulge you in all this mumbo jumbo and now it's affecting Kitty. This has got to stop; I'm not letting Kitty use all this nonsense that you are filling her head with as an excuse. Nor am I letting her get drawn into these stupid family feuds."

"She needs to know the truth about her family." Eliza's voice was raised, something that didn't happen that often.

"Jesus Christ *NO*, Eliza! No, she doesn't and neither does anyone else," Mum shouted back. There was a brief silence before she went on, "All this fainting and stuff...I don't know what to think. The doctor says there's nothing wrong with her; he more or less said she's doing it for attention, just playing up, but now this!"

Eliza said something I didn't catch but Mum's anger flared again,

"You've seen what the teacher wrote and why has she waited 'til now to tell us, eh?". She didn't wait for an answer, "Because she is lying. She deliberately failed that exam and she will now have to live with the consequences."

I lay down on my bed and sobbed into my pillow in wretched frustration as the evening drew in around the house and my room filled with shadows. Then I heard a familiar voice,

"Come on Kitty, it's not the end of the world." I rolled over on to my side and there he was standing by my wardrobe, with his lovely Uncle Jimmy smile, almost six weeks to the day after we had buried him.

Chapter Seven
Eliza - 1929

Eliza met Thomas in St Michael and All Angels on Christmas Eve. He had stormed out of Burntwood after a trivial disagreement with his brother. The boys had been talking about the factory with their father who was enjoying a cigar and encouraging them both to discuss the future of the business. Henry had become angry when Thomas suggested that they come out of the agreement they had with their competitors to keep prices high. Tommy suggested that the Pilkington brothers, who were their biggest rivals, were probably going to reduce prices since they had been working with a French company to develop a new type of safety glass. Henry said this was a ridiculous idea but William seemed to be taking the suggestion seriously. Henry became incensed and the discussion escalated into a massive row which wasn't helped by Clara chipping in and telling Henry not to be so pompous. Henry retaliated saying he might be pompous but at least he wasn't a failure who had to keep going to his mother to cover his gambling debts.

It was uncharacteristic for Thomas to lose his temper, normally he would have ignored Henry's snipes and personal remarks or laughed them off but on this occasion a line was crossed. Clara covering her younger son's debts was supposed to be a secret and the fact that Henry knew, and had brought it up in front of William, stunned her into silence. Not Thomas though - the worm finally turned. He crossed the room and punched Henry in the face, breaking his nose. Momentarily, the family froze in a shocked tableau. It was Thomas that broke the scene with a stark realisation of what he had done. He hated violence and had never intentionally harmed anyone or anything before. Trembling, he strode from the room and grabbing his coat from the hall, marched out of Burntwood and towards the village.

After tramping through the empty streets for a good half an hour Thomas was feeling the cold but it was not cooling down his anger. He had no idea how Henry had found out about the debts but he knew that calling him out in front of his parents was just another of his spiteful attempts to usurp him. Turning onto church lane, he saw St Paul's ahead of him, glistening in candlelight and the sound of 'Hark, the herald angels sing' drawing him towards the congregation. He shuffled into one of the back pews just before the song ended and was handed an order of service by a smiley woman who was already there. As he sat, he felt relief to be off his feet and out of the freezing night air. The vicar spoke about how God's love was unchanging and how they should all open their hearts and be kind and generous to each other as they met to celebrate the birth of Jesus Christ our Lord. Thomas attended church regularly with his family and he would be back there the next morning in the regular Christmas day show of the family largesse; but he could not remember ever listening to any sermon before. He glanced around the parishioners, some familiar faces of employees and trades people and saw they were all listening, really listening to what the Reverend Hoyland was preaching and they all looked happy. The Rev concluded his sermon and blessed his listeners who responded with a hearty 'amen'. Smiling broadly he asked that the congregation remain seated as he invited Miss Eliza Bettley to come to the front. Thomas watched as Eliza rose from one of the front pews to stand at the front. She smiled at her audience, took in a deep breath, and began to sing, a cappella, 'O little town of Bethlehem'.

It was his Damascus moment, the moment he knew he had reached a turning point in his life as this voice of an angel floated around the almost silent church. He could not take his eyes off her, having to dab them occasionally. As he gazed at this beautiful young woman in the decorated, candle lit church, despite his 'manly tears', he was smiling broadly and he knew he was in love.

Chapter Eight
Kathryn - 1968

My first conversation with my dead uncle was cut short by my brother bursting into my bedroom. I sat up, startled, opening eyes that I hadn't realised had been closed, in startled confusion.

"What's going on? Mum says you failed."

"Yes, I have and they all think I did it on purpose." I swung my legs off the bed and sat up. Pip sat next to me.

"That's rubbish."

"I know but it's not the end of the world," I replied, trying out the phrase.

"Mum says you're not getting your bike now."

"Oh well." I didn't really know what else to say. We sat quietly side by side on my bed as I struggled to find the words to tell him about Uncle Jimmy.

"So..." He looked at me with his eyebrows raised.

"I tried to tell Mum what happened but that only made her madder," I said, dropping my gaze as I continued, "I had one of my funny turns but not like normal. It was all a bit fuzzy in my head and I felt a bit like I was floating, then I sort of, well, I could hear Uncle Jimmy's voice."

"What... oh Kitty, why did you say that? You know what Mum thinks about all that stuff."

"Because that's what happened. I'm not making it up. It was like everything faded away and I was just on my own and I heard Uncle Jimmy talking to me."

"So you saw a ghost." Pip sounded annoyed now.

"No, I didn't see him, well not then, I just heard him saying my name. He was saying other stuff as well but I was all dizzy and there was someone else talking. Then the time was just gone and I'd hardly written anything." I looked at him willing him to believe me. If he wasn't on my side, no one would be. I sniffed and wiped my nose on the back of my hand. "Uncle Jimmy is worried about Mum and Uncle Jack."

"Uncle Jimmy is dead and we saw him buried, Kit. You're making Mum really mad saying stuff like this." Pip stood up. "You'd better go and wash your face, Dad'll be home soon and Mum says you should come back down and explain yourself." He walked to the door but before opening it, he said, "Better not tell him that Uncle Jimmy made you fail." He shook his head before going to his own room.

Dad was disappointed but not quite as much as Mum. I took Pip's advice and when Dad asked me, I said I'd been nervous and couldn't think properly. Grandad Tommy said that these things happened sometimes and I would just have to make the best of it. I was suitability ashamed of myself and tried to look as sorry as I felt, hoping to quell any further anger from Mum. Dad said that at least they wouldn't have a uniform to buy which would save a bob or two and Grandad agreed.

"Well, what's done is done," Grandad said and ruffled my hair.

Mum remained tight-lipped, her annoyance at Grandad's philosophical stance illuminating around her like an all over halo. When I went into the kitchen to help carry the plates and dishes to the dining room, she didn't look at me, she told me to go and sit at the table, she didn't need any help. Philip was already at the table doing his homework. He looked up as I walked in and screwed his face slightly before whispering 'don't worry she'll get over it' in my ear as he packed his books back into his satchel. I could hear Dad and Grandad in the sitting room talking. The news finished and they didn't notice that Voyage to the Bottom of the Sea was starting; Mum's voice was almost as sharp with them as it was with me as she yelled from the kitchen doorway,

"Will you turn that bloody television off now before the tea is ruined!"

"Now Alice," Eliza said, with a sharpness of her own, "There is no need for that."

The set was switched off just before the final bar of the theme music and

43

Grandad coughed loudly. They came into the dining room and I bowed my head, trying to hold back my tears.

"Z Cars is on tonight, Kitty," Grandad said, ruffling my hair again as he passed behind me. I nodded but daren't speak.

"I love Z Cars," Pip said enthusiastically, trying to keep the conversation going.

"Me too," Dad said with a smile.

"No you don't," began Pip, "You always complain about how rubbish it is."

"Well I think we might enjoy the distraction of it tonight," he replied, winking at his son. There was some further hushed but heated discussion between Mum and Granny in the kitchen ending with Mum saying quite loudly,

"Enough!"

They both appeared carrying in the evening meal silently, meat and potato pie, carrots and two pints of gravy in Eliza's blue and white striped jug. Dad said how wonderful it all looked and Grandad asked if the carrots were from the garden. Eliza said they were shop bought as she hadn't had the time this week and it had been too wet to spend much time there. Dad seized on this as a prompt to talk about the weather. After tea we congregated around the TV and the subject of my failure was, thankfully, closed.

At 8pm, my bedtime, I could still sense the remnants of Mum's displeasure as she said goodnight but Dad seemed to have retained the same pragmatic view as Grandad. Eliza had hardly spoken throughout the whole evening, which was in itself highly unusual, but I was too wrapped up in my own misery and assumed there had been further exchanges about the circumstances of my failing. When I came out of the bathroom she was waiting for me and, following me into my bedroom, she closed the door and leaned against it.

"Now Kathryn, I want to talk to you about Uncle Jimmy and I want you to tell me the truth."

"I'm sorry Granny, I didn't mean to upset you..."

"I'm not upset but it's important that you tell me exactly what you saw and heard."

"Do you believe me?"

"Of course I do, I've always known that you were special." She came over and sat next to me on the bed and took hold of my hand. "You just need to learn how to use your talents. I know your Mum gets upset, she's always been a doubter," shaking her head to make clear her disappointment, "Even though she knows, deep down, its real. Sometimes she forgets where she came from." I glanced over at the wardrobe as Granny rubbed the side of her temples like Dad did when he was upset. "Anyway," she went on, in her confident tone again, "That's just something I need to remind her about, but you and me, we know the truth."

"She's really mad with me," I said, simply latching on to the one solid thing that I understood. There was a large part of me that wanted Eliza to leave me to my misery; much as I loved her there were times when she made me feel uncomfortable and this was one of them. I felt like I was on a precipice and she was about to pull me over the edge. She patted my hand again and nodded, taking in a deep breath.

"Yes, she is but she'll get over it, I'll talk to her again tomorrow and she'll come round to you not going to Normanton and Grandad Tommy and me will get you that bike so don't worry about that." She smiled at me and I felt a warm slither of hope spark up in my tummy.

"So first of all, let's go back to when we said goodbye to Uncle Jimmy. You tell me everything that you saw." And so I did. I told her about seeing Uncle Jimmy's face move as Aunt Grace bent to kiss him, about hearing his voice as I sat in the school hall and then about him being there in my room. I told her he had said he was worried about Mum and Uncle Jack and said we all needed to be careful around *her*.

"Is that exactly what he said? 'Be careful round her'?" she asked, holding up her hand. I nodded solemnly trying to be as sure as I can.

"He didn't say a name, which 'her'?"

"No," I shook my head, "But I think he meant Aunty Grace," and as Eliza smiled, I had a sudden burst of surety. My Granny beamed at me and I felt the relief of getting it right. Her eyes gleamed and she stood up.

"I knew it, I knew it from the first moment I laid eyes on her. Rotten!" She paused and I sat very still. She looked down at me and smiled, "You are a good girl Kathryn and you have a gift but we have to be careful. Don't tell anyone else about this – no one, not even Pip. Do you understand?" I nodded and she smiled again.

"It will be our secret and if you hear or see or even feel anything again I want you to tell me, only me." She tilted her head slightly and raised her eyebrows as she looked directly into my face.

I nodded again, "Yes Granny, I will."

"That's good, and even if it's something you don't understand or doesn't make any sense, you must still tell me."

I was looking down at my knees trying to ignore my peripheral vision. The warmth of the hope Granny had given me had gone completely and I could feel myself starting to shake as the chill of the room and overwhelming emotions crept through me. Eliza stood up, still smiling, and I raised my head slightly and parted my lips. I was about to speak but as Eliza turned away, I dared a glance over towards my wardrobe. Uncle Jimmy, who had been there throughout most of the conversation, raised his finger to his mouth and with a quick glance at his mother, shook his head and put his finger to his lips.

"Night night, Granny," I said and Uncle Jimmy smiled and nodded as his shape blurred slightly and faded into the walnut grain of the wardrobe.

Chapter Nine

Eliza - 1929

In the three and a half years she had lived at the vicarage, Eliza had become the daughter they had longed for. Vera Hoyland, the vicar's wife, enjoyed helping the girl with her continued learning. She had recognised Eliza was bright from the outset and taken great pride in her academic success. As a member of the local education board, it had been easy for Vera to arrange for her ward to take up a position as a teacher in the small village school. This was a real step up for the daughter of a miner and daily help and Vera enjoyed taking credit for making something out of the pauper child. On that Christmas eve, she glowed with pride as her protégée sang with the 'voice of an angel' while Eliza beamed her good fortune out to the congregation, with a warm and satisfying feeling, knowing she alone was the master of her improvement in circumstances. Although I think even as ambitious as she was, she could not have suspected how much more those circumstances were yet to be improved.

After the service, people were milling around inside the church exchanging Yuletide greetings and Christmas cards, mainly in a reluctance to leave the festive, warm building for the cold streets and in most cases their cold homes. Eliza stood with the Reverend and his wife by the doorway as people slowly moseyed back out into the cold. Thomas held back to almost the end of the line and as he approached, Vera's face lit up.

"Hello Mr Thomas, how wonderful to see you and a merry Christmas to you." Her face flushed with pleasure. "I hope your parents are both well, and all your family of course." Vera was so busy tugging her forelock to the lord of the manor's son that she didn't notice his eyes were completely fixed on Eliza. However, her husband and Eliza herself were perfectly aware where his attention lay. Eliza, head slightly bowed as she pulled on her gloves, gave him one of her practiced demure glances and the merest hints of a shy smile. Reverend Hoyland shook his hand enthusiastically,

"So good to see you here, Thomas, and I trust you enjoyed our service?"

"Very much." Thomas was still engaged in the handshake but could not force his eyes away from Eliza. Vera finally caught up with the mood of the group and burst out with a giddy pride,

"Oh, but you haven't been introduced, this is Eliza Bettley, our ward. Eliza, this is Mr Thomas Hesketh."

Finally letting go of the vicar's hand and with a smile that was verging on manic, Thomas turned fully towards Eliza,

"You have a beautiful voice Miss Bettley."

"Thank you, Mr Hesketh," she replied quietly, treating him to a flutter of her eyelashes.

"Eliza has recently taken up a position of teacher at the local school."

"That is wonderful!" Thomas's immediate and over enthusiastic response rendered them all to silence and a cough from the Verger who had appeared in the doorway reminded the Vicar of the time and place.

"I trust we will see you tomorrow at the service, along with the family?"

"Yes, yes of course." Thomas still seemed reluctant to take his gaze from Eliza, "My mother is very much looking forward to it, as am I."

Eliza smiled and with a slight nod stepped towards the verger who was holding a large pile of hymn books.

"Goodnight Reverend, Mrs Hoyland," Thomas said, with a smile that was a little more contained and stepped out into the churchyard.

Chapter Ten

Kathryn - 1968

It took a few days for Mum's coolness towards me and the rest of the family, but mainly me, to thaw. But as the bitter coldness of February was displaced by a mild but overcast March, things did seem to start and look better. As the weeks went by the debacle of my exam failure faded and after a suitable gap of three weeks, Grandad Tommy took me to the bike shop and bought me the shiny new blue bicycle with the pink basket and blue and white ribbons on the hand grips. Uncle Jimmy was not mentioned again even though, when Mum was not around, Eliza would widen her eyes at me in a questioning way. I always responded to this with a quick shake of the head, even when Uncle Jimmy was actually sitting across the table from me.

Uncle Jack and Raymond came for another visit but only stayed a couple of days. There was a hold up with the sale of the business but Raymond had his name down to start at Royston juniors in September. There was a lot of discussion about where they would live. Eliza said that of course they should be there at Sunny Bank, there was plenty of room. Uncle Jack wasn't sure it would work, he said he and Raymond would probably be happier in their own house. Grandad Tommy agreed with him which made Eliza really mad. Mum and Dad kept quiet and Pip followed suit. I'm not sure what made me offer an opinion when I had only just got back in the good books but there you go, I don't know why I did lots of things at that time.

"You should get your own house, Uncle Jack, I don't think Raymond likes being here. He never eats anything or laughs or even smiles," I offered. We had been sat at the table and as I spoke, Raymond stopped pushing his food around his plate and looked quickly at his dad with large worried eyes. I saw Dad roll his eyes and mum shake her head slightly.

"Kitty, what on earth is the matter with you?" Eliza snapped, "Of course Raymond likes being here and is looking forward to living here properly." She raised her hand to stop Uncle Jack from contradicting her, "He is younger than you and has not had the benefit, as have you, of having his family around him so I would expect a little more consideration from you."

"Sorry," I mumbled and the subject was dropped. Eliza believed that Uncle Jack and his boy would be moving in with us in at the end of the summer. Pip heard Grandad Tommy and Dad talking a few days later. Uncle Jack was buying a house on Alfred Street, which was only just round the corner form Sunny Bank, but it was a secret and no one wanted to be the one to tell Eliza.

Most of the summers of my childhood, I remember as being hot and sunny but that particular year, 1968, I remember as being fun and Eliza being in an exceptionally good mood for most of it. She took the news of Jack and Raymond living in their own house much better than anyone had expected. Jack was savvy enough to ask for her help and advice in furnishing his small three-bedroom house and was, in the first few weeks, a constant at our dining table at Sunny Bank. But Raymond remained detached, his thoughts and feelings a mystery with his large eyes full of doubt. He spoke only when he was spoken to with one or two word answers and, despite Eliza's many offers and requests, he never came to Sunny Bank without his dad. Even on those occasions, he never strayed far from his side. Uncle Jack brought him up to the attic playroom a couple of times and once asked him if he would like to stay and play with us while he went back downstairs. This question was met with such terror in Raymond's face that no one dare suggest it again.

After Pip and me broke up from school at the start of July, Eliza threw herself into planning a series of days out with walks and picnics in an attempt to lure Raymond to join us but he could not be tempted. Uncle Jack didn't have a job but he did have 'business interests' in Leeds and drove his big green car over there most days. Raymond was always in the passenger seat beside him so Eliza finally gave up asking. The novelty of Eliza wanting to take us anywhere, ulterior motive or not, had been a wonderful bonus for me. Pip wasn't too impressed and sulked a bit sometimes but all in all, that summer started off really well.

As well as the Eliza outings, I did lots of lots of riding on my bike with and without Pip; I even rode over to call for Lynn and Cheryl one day, although that turned out to be a low point of that summer. Our friendship had cooled quite a lot since the day of the results. They had gone through the stages of shocked, sympathetic and finally, indifference. On the day I called for Cheryl, she had said she wasn't feeling very well and so didn't want to come out and she wasn't allowed to ask me in. I cycled round the corner to Lynn's and she was just coming out of her house. She frowned when she saw me and when I asked her if she wanted to come for a ride round the back lanes with me. She shook her head and said she was going round to Cheryl's to play with her new painting by numbers set. I said ok and see you later and managed not to let my hurt show as I rode back home.

The next day I went to the park with Pip. I had wanted him to come bike riding with me but he said he was going to meet some of his pals and play football. Eliza was in a frosty mood and Mum was not feeling very well so I said I would go with him and just play on the swings. We rode our bikes and he didn't speed off like he normally did. I told him about Cheryl and Lynn and he said not to worry about them. I would make new friends and there were lots of people I knew who would be at the senior school. He was always great at making me feel better. He gallantly accompanied me as far as the slide and after telling me not to talk to strangers and to come and get him if anybody bothered me, he rode off to his friends. I got off my bike and was laying it down on the grass when I heard someone call my name.

"Kathryn, hey Kathryn!"

Turning round, I saw Beverley Haigh, a girl from my class, on the

51

swings waving and smiling broadly at me. I walked over to her and sat down on the swing next to her.

"Hiya." I smiled back and pushed myself off. Within seconds we were swinging in tandem and chatting away. She lived on Calder Avenue which wasn't too far from Sunny Bank and although we had been in the same class all the way through school, we didn't really know each other much. I knew she had been best friends with another girl called Gillian who had passed her eleven plus. Gillian had then told her that there was no point in them being friends anymore as now they would be going to different schools. There would be nothing for them to talk about and Gillian's mum had told her that she shouldn't waste her time with the girls who'd failed.

"But I didn't fail," Beverley said matter-of-factly, "I didn't take it, my dad says I wasn't clever enough so there was no point"

"Everybody said I was clever enough but I failed it," I admitted, "Mrs Thackeray and my Mum were really mad. They think I failed it on purpose."

"Did you?"

"No, well I don't think so." I suddenly wasn't so sure.

"Anyway Royston Seniors is alright, we can be friends if you want."

"Yeah, I'd like to be friends." We swung higher kicking out or feet and smiling. My spirits lifted and we stayed in the playground for a couple of hours until Pip came back to get me. We had instructions to be home for half past four to help Grandad with his pigeons.

Later that night, after tea when I was drying the pots with Pip, I realised I hadn't seen or heard Uncle Jimmy since I had broken up from school and Eliza had stopped coming into my bedroom quite so often to talk to me about him. My little episodes seemed to have stopped too and I had this sudden thought that I might at last be starting to be normal. I turned away from Pip to hide the smile on my face as I realised I was secretly looking forward to starting at Royston Senior School; even if I wasn't smart enough to pass my eleven plus I was smart enough not to say that out loud.

On the second week in August, Eliza took Pip and me into Leeds on the train to the Majestic Cinema for a matinee screening of 'You Only Live Twice'. Pip was a massive James Bond fan and could hardly contain his excitement on the way there. I was excited too but mainly about going on the train. Leeds was always held up as the big metropolis in grown up discussions in our house, Mum was from there but as her parents had died before she married Dad we had never been.

We had to leave really early as Grandad Tommy was driving us to Wakefield Kirkgate Station to get the train before he opened up his betting shop. Dad worked in Barnsley and got the bus to work. Eliza and Mum couldn't drive but even if they could Grandad was a bit funny about anyone else driving his car, which was why it was generally always parked on the drive of Sunny Bank.

"It will do it good to have a bit of a run out," Eliza told him two days before when we were all in the kitchen, "I sometimes wonder why we have a car at all when we never go anywhere."

"We have a car for convenience," was all he said before going out of the back door and down the garden to see to his pigeons.

He dropped us off at half past nine before going back to open up and Eliza reminded him of the time of our return train before slamming shut the door. There were no pleasantries exchanged and Eliza wore her tight lipped, watchful expression as her eyes followed the car as he drove away.

"Right you two, let's get on with our day shall we?" her smile back in place as she turned towards the station entrance and the three of us walked briskly up the steps. The train journey was wonderful; the smell of the diesel and roaring, rhythmic noises of the massive metal beast had me enthralled the moment I saw it charging down the tracks towards us. As soon as we were comfortably in our seats and the train left the station, Philip launched into his favourite subject of the previous James Bond films he'd seen and the books he had read and how brilliant it all was. Eliza let him talk, without pausing, for a few minutes before holding up her hand to silence him. Then she asked me,

"Is everything alright, Kitty?"

"Yes, I'm alright," I smiled at her, "And I really like being on a train." I gave her my biggest smile and she nodded slightly but I could see disappointment on her face. I was sorry that Uncle Jimmy's eventual resting in peace caused her to be sad and felt that I was letting her down but my guilt over this was nowhere near as great as my relief.

"How many times have you been to Leeds, Granny?" I asked, as a distraction.

"Oh I've been to Leeds many times Kitty, yes many times." She got that look in her eye and I knew one of her tales from the past was coming. Pip and I knew most of them off by heart but the one she liked to tell best was the story of how we came to be. I loved hearing it, Pip not so much.

"The first time was during the war of course, after the terrible bombing."

Recognising my cue, I knew the right thing to ask and was fully aware that Pip was put out that we'd stopped talking about James Bond and was not going to join in.

"Was that when Aunty Maude, Uncle Henry's wife was killed?" I asked, knowing the script well. Pip looked out of the window with a resigned expression. Neither of us were strangers to the importance Eliza has put on her version of the family history and knew it was best to let her tell it, no matter how many times we had heard it.

"Yes that's right, poor Maude never had any luck. She'd gone to Leeds to celebrate her Mother's birthday and show off her little princess, Grace." She made the loud huffing sigh noise she used to signify her annoyance and contempt. "Wrong place, wrong time and in my opinion, wrong person killed." Philip and I looked at each other. She had never been quite this free with her hatred of Aunt Grace.

"Mr Granger, our history teacher says it was one of the worst attacks of the war," Philip announced into Granny's reflective silence.

"Well the German's certainly went to town. Leeds was hit bad, no doubt about that. They were mainly after the railway station, the one we're going to. it were hit quite bad an' all but not as badly as some other places."

"Where was Aunty Maude when she was killed?" I asked, knowing the answer.

"She was at her parents' house, it took a direct hit." I knew Granny loved to tell this story.

"How come Aunty Grace wasn't hurt?" I asked and Philip gave me one of his wide eyed looks which I knew meant I should shut up.

"Because the devil looks after his own," she replied, shaking her head, "Everybody in that house was killed except her; she came out of it without a scratch on her!" I got another look from my brother, stopping me asking or saying anything else and the three of us sat in silence as the clickerty-clack of the train allowed Eliza's words to settle. I looked down at my red, plastic sandals but made a few sly glances to watch her far away gaze. She was lost in the rich seam of her incredible life history. It was several minutes before she spoke again, her voice softer and full of a different emotion.

"We knew that the city centre had been hit hard but nothing prepared us for what we saw. There was glass and rubble everywhere and so much grief, it was heartbreaking. The ones that weren't crying were subdued, stunned by the horror of it all and so many dead." She shook her head and the hardness returned to her face, "But when I saw her, sat on that camp bed in the hospital, waiting for your Grandad and me to fetch her back, when I saw her smug little face, I knew then that I'd been right about her."

"Wasn't poor Great Aunty Maude expecting a baby when she died Granny?" I prompted.

"Yes she was and Henry was devastated. I'm convinced that baby would have been the son he wanted so badly but Grace wasn't going to let that happen."

"But she was only eleven and she could hardly have arranged the Luftwaffe to target that particular house," Philip said slightly impatiently, repeating what we had both heard Mum say.

"Maybe." Her reply was soft and she remained still in her seat, moving and re-classifying the files of memories around her always active brain. Pip and I exchanged a brief glance and before giving me the flicker of a scowl, he looked out of the window.

"But the really good thing that came out of that terrible time was that you met Mrs McLean and her little girl Alice!" I announced showing I had listened carefully to this favourite anecdote of Granny's. In response, I was treated to one of her lovely warm smiles, snapping her out of cross mood. She took my hand.

"Yes that's right Kitty. It was a wonderful thing that happened out of all that carnage. Poor Mrs MacLean's house was also hit and her Albert was killed outright." She shook her head and looked down slightly to show her respect but then the smile came back. "Luckily her and your Mum weren't in the house or they would have been killed as well and then you two wouldn't have been born."

"Did she take Mum out because she knew the Germans were going to bomb the house Granny?" I asked ignoring Philip's hard stare.

"She probably did," She answered with an over dramatic nod.

Eliza always referred to Mum's Mum as Mrs MacLean whenever she talked about her. I'd asked years before why she did this and she gave me one of her looks, letting me know that I was being ridiculously dense and said because that's what everyone called her, she was the famous Mrs McLean. Mum would roll her eyes and change the subject if ever she was around and I knew better than to annoy her by asking about it.

Immediately the train pulled into Leeds City station, Eliza sprang to her feet and hurried us off the train. As I trotted along slightly behind her, I was completely mesmerised by the vast metallic structure and the hypnotic echoing tones of the engines, announcements and bustling travellers. Trying to have a look, I was suddenly jolted out of this fabulous new world as Eliza took my hand and with a "stop dawdling, Kitty", pulled me out into the bright sunshine. My disappointment at not having a proper look at the station for signs of the bombing was soon forgotten as we crossed the road into Leeds City Square. The buildings were massive and ornate and I saw more people around us than I had ever seen in my life.

"Hurry up and keep close, Kitty," Granny said as my steps slowed and my head took in the scale of the architecture. Pip was at her other side looking around and pretending not to be impressed when he caught sight of the front of the cinema and the massive poster of Sean Connery proclaiming he was James Bond in Ian Flemings 'You Only Live Twice'.

"Look!" he cried, pointing with his arm right across Eliza, forcing her to stop. He looked like he was going to explode with excitement and Eliza glanced from him up towards the Majestic.

"Me and your Mum came here to see South Pacific about ten years ago. I loved that film." Eliza's face softening, "We made a night of it and went for a meal at Jacomelli's afterwards before getting the train back. Aye, it was a lovely night that, you were only a baby at the time and it was good for your Mum to have a night out, she really enjoyed it." She had her wistful expression again, "Maybe I should take her out again, just the two of us, that'd do her good." She nodded letting us know she'd made up her mind. I was still gazing around and full of questions. We were next to a huge statue of a man on a horse.

"Who's that, Granny?"

"That? It's the Black Prince," She said matter-of-factly, like I should know.

"Was he from Leeds?" I asked, having to lean my head right back to see the top of the statue.

"No love, course not. He had nothing to do with Leeds. Just some pompous pen pusher wanted a big statue and the name probably appealed to him. Anyway you two, come on let's get inside and get our tickets bought." The three of us crossed the road out of the triangular shaped square and into the Majestic.

Two hours and forty minutes later, we did the reverse journey; out of the darkened cinema, my eyes blinking in the still strong sunlight, walking briskly back across the square and two roads. Philip talking excitedly with lots of "What about the bit when..."and "Wasn't it great when...". Eliza smiled a lot and assured him that it was indeed great but I didn't agree. I wasn't in the least bit impressed with James Bond and the whole film seemed a bit silly. I asked Eliza why all the girls walked about in bikinis and she just shook her head and said because they lived in a man's world. I was thinking I would much rather have walked round Leeds and seen more of the amazing buildings than watch that silly film.

"Do we have to go straight home Granny?" I asked hopefully.

"Yes we do. Don't you spoil a perfectly good day out with your whining, Kitty." The finger she pointed at me as she spoke left me in no doubt that there was no more to be said; I tried not to sulk but I was hot and restless. During the interval, Eliza had produced sandwiches from her large Mary Poppins style bag. We ate them quickly and washed them down with fizzy dandelion and burdock, poured from a big bottle into two plastic cups from Grandad's thermos flask. Then she treated us to choc ices which she bought from a lady with a big tray. I was starting to feel a bit sick but Pip was insisting he was still hungry. Sighing, Eliza shook her head in the way she did to pretend she was cross before saying,

"Come on then," striding off towards the railway station, "Hurry up!" and we briskly trotted after her towards the kiosk at the side of the cafe. As we drew up behind her, she was fumbling in her cavernous bag and not looking at us.

"I'll get you some crisps to eat on the train," She said, pulling out her purse.

"Can we have some fizzy orange as well please Gran?" Pip asked. I thought he was pushing his luck but Eliza gave another sigh and with an 'I suppose so' turned to the man behind the counter. While she performed this transaction, I wondered away from her side, taking in the wondrous surroundings. I could still see the Majestic Cinema building through the entrance; it seemed to shimmer slightly in the warm afternoon light. My eyes were wide with wonder and my mouth open as I turned around, stepping across the concourse. I felt dizzy with the vastness of it all. My eyes like a camera shutter blinking hard to help me to focus as my brain recorded what I was seeing. I was mesmerised by the eerie dimness of the platforms and being drawn towards them, taking small floating steps. I looked up, taking note of the dirty glass and steel roof that reminded me of Pip's Meccano set and I smiled at the familiarity of it. The beauty of the sparkling slithers of sunlight heightening the dust particles and making them dance in the diesel fumes. I was caught within the scene, feeling my breath catching with excitement and a gravitational pull towards the edge of the platform, unaware of anyone around me.

"Hey there, look out, careful, little girl!" A deep male voice broke my trance and a uniformed man grabbed my shoulder. I blinked hard trying to squeeze the odd feeling out of my head as the man was pulling me back. He turned me around and I just caught a glimpse of Eliza and Pip running towards us before I was sick all over the man's shiny shoes.

Chapter Eleven

Eliza - 1929

It was three days after Christmas when Thomas Hesketh called at the Vicarage. He made no pretence that it was Eliza he had come to see and was disappointed that she and Mrs Hoyland were out. However, he was heartened when the Reverend invited him back to have tea the following day. The Vicar and his wife were beside themselves at this turn of events, fussing about the house and chattering anxiously about what Clara and William Hesketh would make of their son's interest in their protégé. Eliza watched them with a quiet detachment she had been mastering over the previous months, knowing very well the advantages of keeping her thoughts and feelings deep inside her and invisible. She was well aware of her prettiness and enjoyed the importance her newly found status as a teacher, along with the respect that living at the Vicarage had brought her. She had heard the Hoylands talking about a suitable match for her with boys from the village and had, herself, been watchful of eligible males, considering each for her next step up. Unlike her guardians, Eliza had a broader field to consider as age was not a barrier to a favourable partnership to her. There were three fairly wealthy widowers in the parish who she'd noticed let their gaze linger on her curvy young body at every opportunity. She had not, however, considered this scenario. The son from the big house! Well this was a turn up for the books and never let it be said that Eliza Bettley ever looked a gift horse in the mouth.

Thomas was so besotted with Eliza that he proposed after three afternoon teas and two walks in the park. He asked Rev Hoyland the day before and having reassured him that the Heskeths would be as happy as he was, received his blessing. Eliza said she would be delighted and Thomas gave her a ruby and diamond engagement ring that he had bought two days before and Eliza treated him to her most radiant of smiles, followed by a very passionate kiss, before they went back to the

Vicarage to celebrate on the Hoyland's sweet sherry. Later that evening, using parish business as an excuse, the Reverend and his wife left the young folk alone to talk about their future. Once they were alone in the house, Eliza turned her coy flirting up a notch and in no time, they became intimate. Afterwards, Eliza cried softly. She was afraid, she told him, that now he had had his way with her he would cast her aside. Thomas became alarmed and pulled her into him. Holding her close, he began stroking her hair and telling her how much he loved her and how marrying her was going to make him the happiest man alive. She melted into him and their gentle caresses turned again into an intense intimacy. As he unleashed his desire, Thomas passed his seed and genetic makeup on to Eliza and in that moment she knew she had him. Running the tip of her finger over her fiancé's face as he lay beside her on the vicarage hearth rug, she asked a question she already knew the answer to.

"Have you told your parents that you are going to marry me?"

The contentment left his face briefly but he forced the smile back as he turned to face her.

"No, I haven't told them yet but there is a lot going on just now. My brother's wife is unwell and there is a bit of a family fallout about it."

"Oh I'm sorry to hear that. What's wrong with her?" Eliza asked, although she knew full well about Maude Hesketh's health problems; about her wanting a baby and her husband wanting an heir. According to village gossip 'the poor cow' had gone insane through grief at her loss and inability.

"She's suffering badly with her nerves and the way my brother treats her doesn't help. Anyway, don't you worry about them, I love you and we are now engaged so unless you throw me over, we will be getting married."

"Well that sounds wonderful but I can't say I'm not worried what will happen if you parents decide I'm not good enough." Eliza affected a slight catch in her voice and she sat up.

"Not good enough? Good grief Eliza, it's me who's not good enough for you." He sat up and put his arms around her, "There is nothing they can say, or do, that will stop me marrying you."

"I really hope that's true," she said, relaxing in his arms.

Chapter Twelve
Kathryn 1968

I was poorly for three days after the trip but the upside was how nice everyone was to me. Mum called Dr Freeman in the morning as I was still pale and floppy and feeling like I was going to be sick, even though there was nothing left inside me. Over the phone, he said to leave me to rest in bed and try and get me to drink something sweet to build me up and he'd come round after his surgery. I felt horrible and did a fair bit of crying in-between my dozes. Mum and Eliza were in and out of my bedroom constantly touching my forehead and stroking my hair. The room was hot and stuffy and the curtains were drawn making everything even more unreal. It was the middle of the afternoon when Dr Freeman arrived; the whisky on his breath alerting me to his presence as he leaned over me. Opening my eyes I saw him very close to my face and his slightly bloodshot eyes peering at me.

"Any diarrhoea?" he asked the room.

"No, I don't think so, just the sickness," Mum said.

"Now Kathryn, can you stick out your tongue for me?" He leaned in closer to me and I obliged. "Right," he muttered and squinted, "Let's look at your eyes." He frowned as he pulled the skin under my eyes down, made a humming sound before pulling the eyelids up. "Hmm," he observed again, standing up to retrieve his thermometer from his bag. Still peering at me he shook it violently before saying, "Open wide," and, pushing it under my tongue, he added, "Close your mouth but don't bite it," and picked up my hand by the wrist, holding two fingers over my pulse while he casually looked round the room. Mum and Eliza edged a bit nearer.

"Just a slight temperature," he murmured, glancing briefly at the thermometer before giving it another shake and dropping it back in his bag. He gave me one last peering glance before asking, "Do you have any pains in your tummy?"

"Yes," I croaked, my throat painful from the retching. He pulled the covers back and asked me to put my hand where it hurt. I wanted to say that that it hurt everywhere but the dry soreness of my mouth wouldn't let the words out. My eyes filled with tears and I saw Eliza's worried face just behind him. I moved my hand down to the middle of my belly, moving it he started pressing with two of his fingers.

"Does this hurt?" I nodded, "What about this?" He pressed hard and I yelped. He withdrew his hand, smiling.

"Right, I think what we have here is grumbling appendicitis. Nothing too serious. We'll see how she is in a couple of days but if it hasn't cleared up by then, we'll get her into St Helen's and have it whipped out."

They went downstairs, leaving me to my discomfort. I heard some mumbling and the clinking of china as Granny rewarded the doctor with his usual tipple of a cup of tea strongly laced with whiskey. Pip came in and sat on the side of my bed.

"Are you feeling better?

"No." I shook my head to reinforce my reply, "And I might have to have my apple licks whipped out," I whispered, trying to blink away the tears.

"Only if you're not better in a couple of days," Pip clarified, proving my suspicion that he had been listening outside the door.

Mum came up with a glass of water after the doctor had gone and sat with me while I sipped at it. Once I was better she and Eliza would take me and Pip to Scarborough on the train for a day out and maybe we would look at going on holiday with Dad and Grandad to Morecambe or even Blackpool! She kissed me on the forehead and smoothed my covers before she left and I settled into an easy dreamless sleep.

The next morning, as I lay in bed reading a comic, I heard Mum and Eliza arguing in the kitchen. Mum was speaking quite loudly as she told Eliza that it was serious, she'd been talking to Mrs Fretwell at the chemist's and she said that my apple licks could have burst and killed me. Eliza reminded Mum that they hadn't and I was getting better but Mum said that they still could have and Eliza should have let them call an ambulance. I got out of bed at this point, my interest aroused, and crept to my half open bedroom door. Mum was really cross and I could hear something else in her voice too; she sounded a bit like she was crying. Eliza wasn't saying much, which was really quite odd, but then as I shuffled out of my room and closer to the banisters, I heard Eliza say very clearly, in a tone I had not heard her use before,

"I know Alice, I should have and it was wrong of me not to let them but I just wanted to get her home. I am really sorry and shouldn't have taken the risk, it's just that I thought they might take her to the War hospital." Her voice cracked and I realised she was crying too, "I'm sorry," she finished, before letting out a sob. I could tell from Mum's muffled voice that they had hugged and Mum would stop being cross with Eliza. Mum was probably as shocked as I was to hear Eliza saying sorry and that she was wrong.

"Anyway, if she does have to have her appendix out, she'll be in St Helen's, here in Barnsley," Mum said, "Which will be a bit easier for us." I didn't hear any response from Eliza, but feeling that Mum wasn't so cross now, I relaxed and quietly returned to my bed, settling back to reading about The Four Mary's in my Bunty comic.

I didn't remember much of what had happened inside the railway station or of the journey home, other than a lot of pain and confusion. Pip had been in to see how I was that morning and after telling me I looked loads better, he went on to fill in some of the blanks for me.

After regurgitating my sandwiches and choc-ice over the feet of the station guard, Granny had taken me to the ladies lavatories to clean the residuary sick out of my hair. I was doubled up holding my tummy and she had to almost carry me.

"You were crying and there was a long trail of snot mixed with all the

65

sick round your mouth," were his actual words. Eliza had gone into a bit of a panic when she had seen me being sick, he said, she'd been annoyed at first when she'd realised I'd wondered off but when she heard the guard shouting, they had both seen me wobble before I keeled over. By the time they got to me, a little crowd had gathered and lady in a brown fur coat was saying someone should call for an ambulance.

"There's no need for that," Eliza had snapped, bending down to take hold of my head, "She's just having one of her turns, she'll be alright when I get her home."

"Well I don't like the look of her; she's clearly not very well," the lady insisted.

"I said she will be fine thank you. If you would all just leave us alone, I can sort her out." I was unaware of any of this, only coming round as Eliza pulled me roughly to my feet. Philip followed us to the ladies toilets and waited outside hearing the guard complaining about his shoes and trousers to the fur coated lady.

"She was still insisting that you should be taken to hospital and telling the guard he should go and tell the station manager," Pip said, "She said she would go into the Ladies and explain that an ambulance was on its way. The Guard looked a bit unsure but she was insisting. As he walked off, I saw her stand up straight and throw her shoulders back before walking toward the Ladies waiting room."

My memory of the time in the station toilets was a bit sketchy. I remember being sick again and Granny was trying to get me to drink water from the tap but in between retching and sobbing, I couldn't do it. She'd wet a hanky and kept wiping my mouth and telling me I would be alright in a few minutes and that I had just eaten my ice-cream too quickly. She was actually trying to force my head under the running tap when I heard another voice and she let go and turned round. I put my hands under the water and tried to splash my face. As the nausea abated a little, I raised my head and I heard Eliza speak.

"She's fine and does not need to go to hospital." I knew that tone, Eliza was very cross.

"Well she certainly does not look fine. The guard has gone to ask the station manager to call for an ambulance," the voice said, but I could see the shape of a lady backing towards the doorway. Eliza followed her through the door and she strode after her. I gripped hold of the sink and started to cry again but Eliza was back within seconds.

"Come on now Kathryn, we have to get our train," she said as she rinsed out her hanky and wiped my face again. As we got back on to the platform, Pip came running up. Eliza had told him to go to the manager's office and tell them I was fine and we were getting our train.

We made the journey home in silence and I sat snuggled up to Eliza while Pip sat opposite looking out of the window. I don't remember getting off the train, I know I had felt dizzy and hot but the next thing I knew, Grandad Tommy was carrying me across the station car park. I could hear some conversation but I couldn't open my eyes. Apparently, I slept for the twenty minute car ride but then threw up all over the back of the car as it pulled up outside Sunny Bank. Pip said he felt bad that he had told Grandad and Mum about the lady wanting to call an ambulance, which had got Eliza into trouble with both of them.

On day three, I was allowed to get up and sit in the dining room with my cut-out paper outfits and cardboard dolls. Mum was singing along to the radio while she pottered around the house and I could see Granny out of the French doors checking on her plants and picking flowers to put in her wooden garden basket. Pal was lying on the lawn watching her.

"Why didn't Granny want me to go to the War hospital Mum?" The words were out before I remembered that I hadn't been in the room when Eliza had said this. Mum looked over at me and tilted her head slightly, probably considering telling me off for listening in. She took a deep breath and then sat down next to me and picked up one of my paper dolls.

"There is a hospital in Leeds that some people still call the War Hospital because that's where most people that were hurt in the war went. It's the hospital where your Granny and Grandad Tommy went to fetch your Aunty Grace from, after the bombing." Mum wasn't looking at me, her attention focused on the doll in front of her. I glanced through the glass and Eliza saw me and waved. I waved back.

"That's where she first saw you, when you were a little girl," I interrupted, hoping for a smile or a less serious expression from Mum. She blinked hard like she was batting my comment away with her eyelashes and took a deep breath.

"She saw a lot of bad things there. People, some of them children, really badly hurt and it stayed with her for a long time." Mum wore her false smile again and as she put the doll down, she nodded to the window. Eliza was walking towards the door.

"Please don't ask her anything about it Kathryn. In fact, don't encourage her with all her tales of the family, it's not good for any of us and it's about time she learned to let it go." Mum got up and went to unlock the door, "I was just coming to ask you if you were ready for a cup of tea," she said, as she opened it to let her mother-in-law in.

Chapter Thirteen

Eliza - 1930

Thomas invited Eliza to the house to meet his parents the following week, arranging to come and collect her after she had finished teaching on a wet Tuesday afternoon. Vera Hoyland was disappointed not to also be invited but cheered up when Thomas said there would be a proper engagement party once his mother had time to arrange it.

Eliza had known it would not be an easy meeting but had prepared as much as she could to gain some approval. The day before the meeting, as she was getting ready to go to school, she engineered a quiet conversation with the vicar's wife. Explaining that she was worried about what the Heskeths would think of their son marrying the daughter of their cleaning lady, she had dabbed her eyes before bowing her head. Vera sighed loudly and agreed that Clara Hesketh might find this unacceptable at first and may be a little difficult to begin with but once she had met her she would see what a wonderful and delightful girl she was. Eliza wondered out loud if the Heskeths would even know who she was or where she came from as she had been resident at the vicarage nearly four years. Her guardian immediately perked up at this as if she had just thought of it. Neither of her sisters still worked at the hall, both of them had married themselves and had moved away, so there was a good chance that Clara would not be aware of her birth family. In all the time she had been with the Vicar and his wife, they had always referred to her as their niece or ward.

"And," Eliza broke in enthusiastically, "I don't feel like I belong to them, I never did. You and the reverend have been my only real parents." These words were just what Vera Hoyland had always longed to hear and she hugged her with tears in her eyes. Eliza softened in her embrace.

"Do you think the Lord would forgive me if I don't tell them the whole truth?" she asked with a catch in her voice. Vera kept her in the hug for a few more seconds as she made up her mind.

"I think the lord helps those that help themselves," she replied.

We only have Eliza's testimony about the welcome Clara and William gave her when their favourite son introduced her as the girl he was going to marry but from all the other bits of Hesketh family stories I have heard, it is probably fairly accurate, even with Eliza's bias. They were cold and tight-lipped as they held their saucers and sipped their tea, eyeing her with open distaste. When Clara asked about her parents, Eliza politely told them the lie she had prepared and already tried out on Thomas.

"I never knew them; I was orphaned at an early age and brought up by an elderly Aunt. When she died, almost four years ago, the Hoylands adopted me and I have been with them ever since."

She had decided on this story as the safest and as the words fell from her mouth she watched them carefully for any sign of disbelief. She saw none and her confidence grew. She commented on the beautiful room and kept her head raised and her back straight and, even though the atmosphere remained frosty, Eliza felt hopeful. That was until Thomas said that they were thinking of June for their wedding. Clara raised herself, without leaving her seat, her long neck taught and her steely eyes wide in unconcealed horror.

"Oh no that is much too soon," she barked, "You haven't known each other nearly long enough and we don't really know anything about this girl yet." Her voice was full of the authority she was used to enforcing. "You shall have a long engagement, two years at least and then we will see," she finished. With a forced closed mouth smile and nod of her head, she sat back in her seat.

"Oh I don't think so, Mother," Thomas spoke with a smile at Eliza, "I know that I love Eliza and that's enough for me. We are getting married in June and I hope you will be happy for us." Eliza smiled as Thomas stood up and walked towards her, holding out his hand, "Come on my love, let me show you our wonderful garden." She kept her smile as they walked around the formal, heavily manicured grounds. Clara's reaction had been a disappointment but had not surprised her. She sighed slightly as she thought of how upset Vera Hoyland would be to learn there would be no engagement party.

Chapter Fourteen
Kathryn - 1968

When Pip got home after an afternoon in the park, I told him what Mum had told me. It had turned into a hot day and Eliza had put a blanket out on the lawn for me to lie on. She and Mum had sat with me for a bit on the old stripy deckchairs but had soon got bored and hot and gone indoors. Pal had placed himself on the blanket turning in a circle several times before settling down in the semi-shade of one of the chairs. Even though I hadn't eaten anything, my stomach still hurt and I was mainly just drinking water and Lucozade. Pal seemed content to be my companion and lay semi-alert and panting and occasionally licking my arm as I stretched out. He stayed there for well over an hour, leaving only when Pip arrived and flopped into one of the empty deckchairs.

"I think it's probably about the workhouse thing," Pip said with a nod of his head to let me know he knew a good deal about this subject and what he didn't know he was confident enough to make up. I knew my required response.

"What workhouse thing?"

"You know Eliza's family were really poor?" lowering his voice and leaning closer. The poor circumstances of Eliza's birth family were not exactly a secret but Eliza's angry reaction to anyone mentioning it was also no secret. I nodded. Pip glanced towards the house.

"Well before he sold her to the Vicar and his wife, her dad had said he was going to send her there."

"What's that got to do with the War Hospital?"

"All the big hospitals started off as workhouses so Eliza's scared of them. That's why she wouldn't let Mum go to hospital to have us."

"That's rubbish," I said, a bit louder than I meant to. Pip shushed me and I repeated in quieter voice, "That's rubbish, why would anyone be scared of a building? And anyway, Mum says that I will probably have to go into hospital, into St Helens, to have my apple licks out and Granny wasn't bothered about that. I think it's just all part of the Grace thing and what she saw there, like Mum said."

"Well you have it your way but if you do have to go into hospital to have your *appendix* – not your apple licks – out, Eliza won't come and visit you." He gave me a knowing tight lipped smile. "Grandad Tommy once told me one of her sisters got taken to St Helen's and they kept her locked up in a room there till she died!"

"Oh that's awful!" I said, with the relish that belied my words, "Which sister?" I sat up and leaned a bit further towards him. He leaned back, happy at catching my full attention.

"If I tell you what I know you have to promise not to let Eliza or Mum know that I told you anything. Grandad got into trouble off Eliza for talking to me about it."

"I promise," I whispered, feeling the thrill of being allowed into a secret.

"I think it was the youngest one, I don't know her name, and neither did Grandad. It was before you were born. The Vicar came to see Eliza, here at Sunny Bank to tell her that her sister was a lunatic and had to be shut away. He asked her to go with him to see her." He paused for dramatic effect, "She said no, there was no way she was going anywhere near St Helen's and that she didn't owe them anything."

"Then what happened?"

"Nothing, that's it..." I frowned in disappointment and Pip smiled, "But Grandad Tommy told me that when he met her, he thought she was an orphan, said Eliza lied about her family; it was last Christmas when he'd been on the Rum and Peps and I went down to help him shut up the pigeons." He pushed himself out of the deckchair on to the blanket and gave another quick glance over to the house before going on,
"He said Eliza had tricked him into marrying her, he said she's a witch!" My eyes must have been like saucers as I gawped at him.

There was lots of little trinkets of forbidden information that Pip and I had learned about our family, most of them from Eliza who was more than happy to dish the dirt on the Heskeths, although always very cagey about her side. We knew her family had been poor and we knew that Grandad Tommy's family thought he had married beneath him, even when they thought she was the adopted child of the local Vicar. They had assumed, no doubt on Eliza's sketchy details, that her real parents had been from the skilled working classes.

Two years before Pip and I learnt that Eliza's dad had sold her to the Vicar and we had been thrillingly appalled at this knowledge. We became privy to this juicy bit of family history via our cousins, Lizzy and Daryl, on one of the monthly visits with their parents, Aunty Peg and Uncle Ron. Aunty Peg was Eliza's oldest daughter, only by about five minutes but this title was something she always declared as soon as she arrived. Her twin sister, Aunty Dot, would roll her eyes and say,

"You might be her oldest daughter, but I am her favourite one. Hello, Mother." Both sisters would roar with laughter at this. Eliza never responded to either of these remarks and generally treated both her daughters with indifference, although there were occasions, generally when alcohol was being consumed, that her manner towards them could be construed as thinly veiled dislike. Peg and Dot seemed to be oblivious to this. Their response to Eliza's coldness towards them was to talk constantly about themselves and their own family units as if it were a competition to impress their mother. Grandad Tommy did a better job of hiding his feelings, smiling a lot and even asking the odd question, but he always said 'those bloody girls drove him mad' and 'did they have to come every month?' as soon as they had gone.

On this particular visit though, he was actually looking forward to the seeing them. He was in a particularly good mood as it was his birthday and they had come to help him celebrate. It was a Sunday afternoon and the grown-ups had set up a card school in the dining room and Pip, Lizzy, Daryl and me had been sent up to the attic to play and keep out of the way. Aunty Dot's daughter, Christine, was allowed to stay for a while and watch. She was nearly 18 and would also be leaving early as she was now courting (a boy with a desk job and prospects) and was being collected by the young man in question to be taken to the cinema up on Midland Road.

"Our Christine knows how to behave and is a very sensible girl." Aunt Peg said this as she pointedly looked at fifteen year old Lizzy and fourteen year old Daryl when they asked why she got to stay.

The attic was a massive room that spanned the whole of the house. It was mainly used as storage but was the favourite place to be when the cousins came. There was an old leather settee and two upturned tea chests that were placed in a semi-circle around a large wooden rocking horse called Coolean. Grandad Tommy had bought the horse shortly after he and Eliza had moved in. He had named it after a racehorse that had been a heavily backed favourite in some big race but had lost. This made Grandad a lot of money and even though it had been years and years ago it still made him smile. Coolean had been well loved and much rocked by all of Eliza and Tommy's children and was still popular with my generation, even the teenage boys. I saw Daryl push Pip out of the way as they reached the top of the stairs so he could get onto her first. Daryl was only six months older than Pip but he always tried to boss him around.

"Bet you didn't know that Eliza's got a secret family," he declared as he adopted a jockey's stance and started the rocking motion. Pip was instantly dismissive, telling Daryl he was talking rubbish but Lizzy interrupted him and confirmed that it was true. They had heard their Mum and her sister talking about it after the funeral. Lizzy had got more information from Edward when she caught him secretly drinking sherry out of a bottle in the back garden while his mother was overseeing the bun-fight in the best parlour. She threatened to go tell Aunty Grace what her son was up to but promised not to if he told her what he knew about Eliza.

75

Everyone in the family thought that Eliza was an orphan who had been adopted by the local vicar and his wife but soon after the wedding, they discovered that she'd lied and she had a father and three sisters living in the next village.

"And even better..." Daryl went on with relish, "Her sisters were cleaners at Burntwood!"

"Great Granny Clara went mental when she found out and there was a really terrible row. That's why Tommy and Eliza had to move away," Lizzy finished.

"So what happened to her dad and sisters? Why don't we know about them?" Pip asked suspiciously.

"Edward said they were sacked and then this right scruffy old man came to the house demanding money, he said he was Eliza's dad. When he wouldn't go away, they called the police." Daryl had slowed to not much more than a sway on the horse and leaned back, "Edward said that Great Grandad went mad with the Vicar. He said that he found out that the Vicar and his wife had bought Eliza from this scruffy old man for two pounds!"

"That's rubbish!" Pip said.

"No, it's not," Daryl snapped

"But what happened to them?" I asked.

"Dunno anymore," Daryl said, getting off the horse, "Why don't you ask Eliza?"

"Edward didn't know what happened after that. He only knows about it because his grandad told him. He said Eliza was a jumped up parlour maid!" Lizzy said, "Anyway, it was years ago, they're probably all dead."

After they had gone, Pip and I discussed this new bit of information at length and decided we needed to get it verified. The best way to do this, Pip informed me, was for me to ask Grandad Tommy. We had no loyalty to Daryl so it was perfectly alright to tell him that Daryl had told us this. We both agreed that this conversation should happen well away from Eliza's earshot. It was nearly a week before I got a chance to help Grandad clean out the pigeons.

"And who told Daryl this?" he asked as I passed him the bucket of bird seed.

"He said Edward told him," I dobbed.

"Right, well I've no need to ask who told him. No love lost between your Granny and Aunty Grace." He said as he began filling up the feeding trough along the coop, "Pass me that other bucket."

"He said it was his grandad, Great Uncle Henry that told him." I wanted to keep the provenance of this Chinese whisper as accurate as I could.

"Well even less love lost there!" Grandad muttered, with a shake of the head.

"So is it true, does Granny have some sisters, three of them and a dad?"

"Well her dad died years ago and probably her sisters by now." He stopped and tilted his head slightly as he seemed to be thinking.

"Were they really poor?" I prompted.

"Yes they were, your Gran was just a girl when her mum died and her dad struggled to feed and look after her and her sisters. So he had to find homes for the two littlest ones. The vicar and his wife took your Granny."

"Did Great Granny Clara sack her sisters when she found out?"

"No," shaking his head smiling a little, "They'd both left a few years before, I think they both got married and moved away, so that little bit of the tale is made up."

"Daryl said the vicar bought Eliza off her Dad for two pounds."

"I don't think it was as much as that," Grandad said sadly, "It was very hard times, Kitty, and the poor man did what he thought was best for his children but it was hard for your Granny too. I don't think she ever forgave her dad. "

"Was she mad at him for selling her?" I asked, holding out the second bucket. Grandad didn't answer straight away, instead he busied himself sweeping the dirty straw from the bottom of the coop. I was trying to think of something to say to prompt him when he finally spoke,

"No, she was just mad at him for being poor."

Chapter Fifteen
Eliza - 1930

It was actually the end of June when Grandad Tommy married his seventeen year old bride Eliza Bettley, in a hurry, her pregnancy fairly evident despite the generously cut, white lace dress. They didn't wed at the local church, at the request of the bride, but instead travelled the eight miles to St John the Evangelist in Carlton for a small private ceremony conducted by the Reverend Swansworth. Reverend Hoyland gave her away and there were no other guests other than Vera Hoyland on the bride's side. The wedding had been arranged quickly and Eliza's guardians, both complicit in the fabrication of Eliza's past, were at pains to keep the news from spreading in the village.

Clara and William were furious about the whole affair, considering Eliza a poor match and not bothering to disguise their disapproval. They were however, aware of the scandal that their son not marrying her would cause. She was carrying his child and her condition seemed to become visible extremely quickly. Thomas had completely ignored his mother's instruction to keep the whole business quiet and had practically been shouting from the rooftops about his engagement to Eliza. So realising that the union could not be stopped and her son could not be dissuaded, Clara decided that it would need to be managed instead. The day was warm and sunny and went as planned with the small gathering eating a cold buffet lunch after the ceremony, back at Burntwood Hall. A broadly smiling Thomas claimed to be the happiest man alive as he stood beside his serene and beautiful bride while the vicar and his wife smiled and nodded throughout the day, pretending not to notice the silent fury in Clara's eyes.

Beginning their married life together in the dark sandstone family home, Eliza tried hard to fit in but, as she had suspected, it was never going to work in the long term. Accepting that she would never win the family over and understanding the importance of having allies in a

79

hostile climate, Eliza made friends with Mrs Turton the housekeeper who was a rich source of information and gossip.

It wasn't just William and his domineering wife that disapproved of her. Henry and his ailing wife Maude were equally vicious, although for different reasons. The grounds for their objection to the union increased when, scandalously soon after the marriage, Eliza gave birth to a healthy little boy, James William. Although happy to finally have a grandson to carry on the family name, Clara was incensed that Eliza seemed self reliant and able to evade matriarchal involvement by Clara in the care of the child. It came as a great shock to her that her coldness and domineering manner had no effect whatsoever on Eliza. She seemed to be able to smile through it and worse still her manner seemed to be rubbing off on Thomas who constantly sided with her. Eliza possessed endless reserves of tenacity and determination along with a strong will and sense of herself. They all assumed that she was an ignorant chit of a girl without substance. Her prettiness and outwardly docile countenance hid her guile and protectiveness and the hostility just seemed to bounce off her. She was playing the long game.

Henry's jealousy of his brother was multiplied by his choice of bride and his parents allowing it, albeit reluctantly. Why had they not thrown him and his common little whore out? He could not understand their continual support for him despite what he saw as his lazy inability and now this, a terrible marriage.

Maude's misery was compounded even more by Eliza becoming a part of the family. After James's birth, her mental health deteriorated and her raging and sobbing echoed throughout the old sandstone walls. Things got worse in the lead up to Christmas that year; Maude was literally out of her mind with despair and self pity. Clara was on the verge of relenting and allowing Henry to send his wife to a place where she would be 'looked after' when a family crisis threatened another scandal and the solution to this predicament brought Maude back from the brink of madness.

Martha, the Hesketh's 27 year old unmarried daughter, who barely spoke, was discovered to be pregnant and at quite an advanced stage. When Clara was told she refused to believe it. It was impossible – the girl never left the grounds but the evidence was right in front of her and becoming more evident by the day. Martha never revealed who was responsible for her condition, maintaining until her death that she had never had any physical relationship with any man.

Maude agreed with Henry that they would take the child and bring it up as their own. Martha was promptly confined to her bedroom where she gave birth six weeks later to a baby girl, helped by a well paid midwife from out of the area. As Maude had been housebound for over a year, the deceit was easy to pull off. Only the other occupants of the house knew the real mother of the new baby, born just three months after James. Henry was disappointed it was a girl but Maude was delighted and named her Grace after her maternal grandmother.

To the rest of the family, it seemed that Martha took no interest in the child and became even more withdrawn than before. The whole experience seemed to have made her more ethereal as she moved silently and almost invisibly through the house and grounds, lost in her own world and completely detached from her family's Machiavellian ways.

Chapter Sixteen

Kathryn - 1968

The rest of the summer holidays went without incident and my grumbling appendix gave me no more problems. At first, mum was convinced that the minute she let me out of her sight, it would rupture and I would die of peritonitis. She mentioned this most days for the first couple of weeks but when there were no further episodes or symptoms, after a while, she calmed down. Eliza was unusually quiet, choosing to spend most of her time on her own in the garden, and even when she was in the kitchen, making jam or baking, she didn't encourage me to help anymore, instead shooing me out to get some fresh air.

I called for Beverley a couple of times and she introduced me to a whole new world of adventure. We recreated scenes from *The Avengers* and *Lost in Space* as we wondered around the old tracks that came off the muddy back lane just off East End Crescent. There were plenty of things to see which spurred on our imagination, creating exciting subplots to our playtimes. We explored all the places we knew we weren't supposed to go near; the canal, the railway line, the old double-decker bus yard (we called it the bus graveyard), the dykes and streams and the colliery sewage works. We skirted around all of these forbidden sites, climbing the fences or ducking under hedges for dares with the excited surety of our youthful infallibility. Our favourite place was the murder bridge. No one really knew why it was called the murder bridge, nor could anyone remember who, if anyone had been murdered, but the name stuck. I knew Pip went down there sometimes with his friends and there were generally some older kids hanging around smoking or just loitering which made it even more attractive. Beverley had two older brothers and an older sister, Julie, who wore green eye-shadow and a bra. After hearing Mum and Granny telling my brother he shouldn't be hanging around with certain types of boys, one of these I knew to be Beverley's brother, I was pretty sure they wouldn't approve of Beverley's sister and so, by association, Beverley so I was evasive about her surname. In fact, I actually lied and said it was Smith. The first time I saw Pip down there he was a bit funny with me and hardly spoke. That night he said he didn't want me hanging around down there and I said,

"Well I don't think Mum and Dad or Eliza would like you hanging about there either but we're not doing anything bad, just going there sometimes to see what's going on."

He recognised the threat in my voice and shrugged before agreeing that we would both still go there sometimes but never ever let Mum and Dad, and definitely not Eliza, know even though we weren't doing anything wrong and – he wanted to make it very clear we were only going there to hang out with our own friends and not with each other. As it turned out we only ever saw each other down there once more before the end of the school holidays.

It was on Saturday, two days before the new term started. Beverley and I had met up with another couple of girls she knew who lived near her; Pauline and Joy. They went to the church school so I didn't know them but they seemed alright and not at all stupid like Eliza said churchy people were. There was no one around when we passed the old air raid shelter so we continued down under the first railway bridge, chatting about what the senior school was going to be like. Feeling a bit disappointed to find no one under the murder bridge either, we pressed on in search of entertainment, subconsciously veering left until suddenly finding ourselves close to the old bus graveyard. With the usual childhood bravado, we climbed through the broken fence and picked our way carefully through the wreckages and shattered glass to get onto one of the busses that wasn't too badly damaged.

"It must be great to drive one of these around," Beverley said, climbing onto the torn leather driver's seat, "If I had one of these, I'd take all my friends to Scarborough every Saturday."

"I'd go to Blackpool," I ventured, "To see the laminations."

"What's laminations?" Pauline asked.

"You know, the lights; they light all the streets up with coloured light bulbs."

"Oh yeah, I'd go to Blackpool an' all." Pauline smiled at me.

"The only place you lot of little vandals will be going is to borstal!" A man's voice boomed at us as a face appeared at one of the glassless windows.

"Bloody hell!" Beverley yelled, climbing through the back of the cab into the body of the bus at impressive speed, "Leg it!" she yelled. I tore after her as did Joy and Pauline, but I caught my foot in something and tripped a good ten feet before the fence, crashing down into a mangled bit of bus panel. Fear soared through me as I lifted my head to see the other three almost over the fence and I pushed myself back onto my feet, ignoring the stinging pain in my hand and the wetness of my knees.

"I'll have the police round all your houses, you bloody little sods!" I daren't look behind me to see how close the man was as I struggled up the fence, practically throwing myself over and landing heavily at the other side. Beverley sprang up from her crouching position in the bushes and, grabbing hold of me, pulled me into the undergrowth.

"He weren't chasing you," She informed me a few minutes later as we made our way back to the path, "He just stood there watchin' you. Have you hurt yourself?"

"I've cut my hands and I think my knees are bleeding," I said as I turned round to see the man walking away towards the front of the yard, "Do you think he knows who we are? He said he was sending the police to our houses."

"Nah, he were just trying to scare us. You can come to our house before you go home and we can try and clean off some of that muck before your mam sees you." When we got to the murder bridge, Pauline and Joy were talking to a group of other kids and behaving very un-churchy as they smoked their players No 6.

"What happened?" Joy's question echoed around the curved brick work, "Did the old bastard catch you?"

"Course not," Beverley said with a mock outrage in her voice, "Any road, some mates you two are, leggin' it and leaving us."

"You told us to leg it," Joy blew out smoke as she spoke. Stepping under the bridge, my eyes were adjusting to the light when someone struck a match to light another cigarette and in the brief flash, I saw Pip.

He wasn't having me going to Beverley's house, he said he needed to get me home and sorted out before Mum or Eliza saw the state of me. He practically marched me all the way back to Sunny Bank. My leg really hurt but I daren't say anything. He kept going on about how I was going to be in right trouble and it would end up somehow being his fault that I'd got myself into this mess. I just tried to keep up with him and not make him any crosser with me, although I was smarting with the unfairness of Pip being cross with me when I had clearly seen him smoking!

As we got to the gates of Sunny Bank, Great Uncle Henry's car was just turning slowly out of the drive and up the hill. I am sure he didn't see Pip or me but Aunty Grace who was sitting in the passenger seat did. She was looking out of the window and her eyes locked onto mine. I stopped dead and felt, rather than saw, her gaze take in the whole of my appearance and I shuddered with a cold feeling of dread as I saw her lips part in one of her funny smiles. Pip had also stopped a foot or so ahead of me.

"Did you see that?" I asked, with a tremor in my voice.

"Yes, thank goodness they didn't see us. Wonder what they came for." His voice had lost its crossness and I didn't want to make him mad with me again by telling him Grace had definitely seen me, so I didn't say anything.

"Anyway, come on, the front door might be still open so we can get in there and get upstairs without Mum or Eliza seeing us." Great Uncle

Henry and his evil daughter would never use the back door.

The heavy red front door was open but as we walked into the hall we could see Eliza in the kitchen. For a minute, I thought that Pal would give us away as he instantly trotted towards me, ears raised and sniffing suspiciously at me. Pip stepped in front of him and gave him a stroke before pushing him gently to the side. Pal looked from Pip to me then turned around and padded back to the kitchen to Eliza and her cooking. Pip gave me a shove towards the stairs before turning away and following the dog. I didn't hesitate but had to grab the banister after my first step sent a jolt of pain through my hurt leg. I gritted my teeth and ran up the rest of the stairs and into the bathroom. Ten minutes later, Pip knocked on my bedroom door. I had changed my clothes and washed off the dirt and blood. My cut and bruised leg was covered by some thick tights and my grazed hands would just be a testament to my clumsiness.

Pip said Mum was out and Eliza was busy jam making and had barely looked round when he had gone into the kitchen. He'd told her we were going up the attic to play and she had just nodded. My trousers were ruined and Pip put them in his school satchel, saying he would 'lose them' on the way to school. Once we were safely in the attic establishing our cover story, Pip's bad mood was completely gone.

"Do you think Eliza is alright?" he asked after a half an hour of companionable silence. We were sitting at the small desk, me with my Spirograph and Pip with his Macarno.

"What do you mean?" I asked, head bowed and tongue out in concentration.

"She's just been a bit different lately, you know, not so... well not so like she normally is."

"Well if she's just had a visit from Great Uncle Henry and horrible Aunty Grace, she's bound to be in a funny mood," I said as I changed the red pen for a green one.

"I don't just mean today but I wonder what they wanted, they never visit here."

"Aunty Grace looked so scary and she had a horrible smile on her face." I stopped drawing and looked into the distance at the memory.

"Aunty Grace is scary and she can only do horrible smiles." Pip treated me to one of his big brother smiles, "But Eliza's been a bit odd for a while now."

"Well she's not been coming into my bedroom asking about Uncle Jimmy for ages." As soon as I'd said this, I panicked and glanced over at Pip. I was expecting him to get cross again but he was busy with a spanner and his focus seemed to be on the long arm of the crane he was making, so I went on, "It's probably cos it's her busy time with the jam making and baking."

"Yeah, maybe but she just seems a bit different. Mum and Dad think so an' all. I heard them talking about her last night."

"What do they think is wrong with her?"

"They don't know but Mum says it's since we went to Leeds that day, she says she's not been herself since then. I think it's something to do with her secret family." We speculated wildly about what might have happened. Had she seen someone in Leeds, the posh lady maybe could have been one of her sisters, or had the row with Mum upset her, or maybe someone had been to the house. Pip suggested that she might have gone out to meet someone but I reminded him that Eliza never went anywhere except the library. The rest of her time she was either in the garden, the kitchen or asleep in bed.

"Well she could have said she was going to the library," he said sulkily, not wanting to give up his theory.

Mum called us down a little while later. Grandad wasn't coming home for his tea and Dad was back from work a bit early as he was going to the betting shop to help Grandad with important stuff, so we were eating early. As I helped Pip set the table, with all our musings germinating in my head, my eyes kept wandering over to the serving hatch where I could see Eliza plating up the food. Pip poked me hard and hissed, "Stop staring!" Jolted out of my reverie, I went out into the hall to see Pal laying on his side on the mat by the front door. Deep in sleep, his legs jerkily moving as he let out a little string of yelps.

"Pal's chasing rabbits in his dreams again," I said as I went into the kitchen to get some squash for Pip and me, "Is there any pudding?" I edged round to the side trying to look round Eliza to see what else was on the cooker.

"Jam roly-poly and custard for anyone with a clean plate," Eliza answered, without turning round.

Mum followed me back into the dining room, glancing at Pal as she passed the salt and pepper pots to me and tutted.

"Why is the dog laid there at this time of the day?" she asked no one in particular, and no one answered her. Shaking her head she went over to the hatch to take the filled plates through from Eliza. Dad strolled in and sat down as Mum put his tea in front of him, like a perfectly timed bit of theatre, and then spoke his usual line.

"Ah this all smells good!"

It was shepherd's pie with carrots and peas, one of my favourites, well except for the carrots and peas. Once she'd passed the other four plates through the hatch, Eliza came round and sat down next to me with a smile on her face.

"So what have you been up to today, Kitty?" she asked, with a smile in her voice that made me instantly nervous.

"Just playing at my friend Beverley's house for a bit. We went to the old air raid shelter at the end of East End Crescent but there were some older kids there and I didn't know any of them and they were smoking so I came back." I thought I did well with the story Pip and I had rehearsed but from his expression I could see I hadn't got it right.

"Goodness, that's a very detailed answer Kitty." There was a dangerous tone to her voice so I kept my eyes on my plate and concentrated on trying to mash my carrots into the potato topping.

"Stop making mud pies with your food, Kathryn, and get it eaten," Mum said, sharply. I turned my fork sideways and scooped up a large mound of the mush and shovelled it in my mouth.

"What about you Pip, did you go to the air raid shelter where the older kids, who your sister didn't know, were smoking?" I knew without looking that Pip would have coloured up. I wondered if Eliza had super-human powers and could read minds. She was certainly good at detecting lies or half truths.

"I was on the green in front of it with Alan and Pete Gregory playing football. I think there were some other kids in the shelter but I didn't go in."

"Is that it?" she asked, "You didn't go anywhere else."

"The others were on about going to the park when I saw Kitty so I came home with her instead." I wondered if it was the grammar school that had taught Pip to lie so convincingly. I scooped an even bigger forkful into my mouth.

"So, no one went down to the murder bridge today then?" she asked, putting her fork down.

At that moment, three things happened very quickly; I began to choke on the minced lamb and vegetable mush I'd failed to chew before swallowing; Pip knocked his orange squash all over the table as he stood up quickly and the rabbit that Pal had been dreaming about must have turned into some kind of vicious monster and he let out a blood curdling yelp.

Chapter Seventeen

Eliza -1931

Life at Burntwood was exactly as Eliza had known it would be and she was fully prepared for the everyday battles and attempted bullying; a lot better prepared than Maude had been. Although her health was much improved since the arrival of baby Grace, she still struggled to understand the tone and emotional turbulence inside Burntwood. William and Clara's initial disappointment at their favourite son's choice of bride had been dampened with the arrival of James and when Eliza's second pregnancy was confirmed, Clara's attitude, not quite an acceptance of her new daughter-in-law but certainly a thawing, made poor Maude confused and upset. She knew Henry didn't love her and that he resented her for her inability to produce the son he craved. She felt the heat of his jealousy and anger over his brother's good fortune and she also noticed the way he looked at Eliza. The happiness she had felt when she had been given baby Grace was diminishing daily with Henry's coldness and his complete disinterest in the baby. She tried to take her unhappiness out on Eliza with spiteful jibes and tale telling but all this did was make Clara and Henry more dismissive of her, while Eliza seemed amused. Maude's pettiness had no effect on Eliza at all. She continued to play the perfect wife and mother, biding her time.

Baby James was just over a year old when Eliza gave birth to twin girls, Dorothy and Margaret, and her confidence in her situation had reached a point that she felt it was time for the next move. She told Thomas that she was worried about the way Maude seemed to be reacting to James and the twins. She had not seen her directly hurt them but had found her in the nursery twice when she had gone in, alerted by James's crying, and found red marks on his arms and legs. Had Thomas noticed the way she looked at their son? Eliza let him know that now she had the twins to look after she was terrified that she could not keep him safe in that big house. Thomas had gone straight to Clara with what he thought had been his own suggestion that he and his wife should have their own home. Clara had immediately vetoed the suggestion and instead decided on a course of action that almost ruined everything for Eliza and all her plans. Almost.

It was just before Christmas in 1932 and Clara told Eliza that she had decided to engage a nanny to help her with the care of the children. This was not the solution that she had wanted but Eliza decided it was just one more small challenge she would need to overcome. Unfortunately, Clara had not mentioned that the person she had engaged to perform this role was one of the village girls. Eliza sat on the sofa in the drawing room with Clara when the candidate was ushered in by Mrs Turton the housekeeper who then retreated to the back of the room. Clara told the girl to sit in the chair opposite them, which she did. Placing her hand on her lap, she looked up for the first time and across at the two ladies of the house. Eliza watched colour burn the cheeks of the girl as she felt it drain from her own. Eyes like saucers, the girl looked from Clara to Eliza then down at the rug in an attempt to control her confusion. Eliza took a deep breath and closed her eyes as she exhaled, waiting for the storm, but it didn't come. The girl answered the questions Clara put to her politely and calmly and listening to Clara's descriptions of what was expected of her. The girl then explained, with a sly side glance at Eliza, that her Mother and her sisters had worked at Burntwood in the past and that a job as a nanny was a step up for her and she would not let them down.

"Eliza?" Clara's sharp tone brought her back from her hidden panic, "Is there anything you would like to say?" Eliza shook her head and Clara told the girl she could start the following day before nodding at Mrs Turton, an instruction to see her out.

Although the twins slept well that night, Eliza did not and the next morning she was up and dressed well before anyone else in the house. She had decided that as soon as breakfast was over, she would go to the vicarage and enlist Mrs Hoyland's help. Unfortunately, she didn't get the chance. The whole family were assembled in the dining room and she had just finished feeding James when there was a loud thumping on the front door. Eliza froze as she heard the broad South Yorkshire vowels of her father. He had come, he said, to see his daughter.

Chapter Eighteen
Kathryn - 1968

Grandad Tommy said there was no need to call the vet, Pal must have had a stroke or something and it was very sad but there it was. I was hysterical and Mum shouted at me to stop it and go upstairs but I knew it was only because she was upset too. Pip was really nice to me and although he didn't cry like me, his eyes were watery and when we went upstairs he was in the bathroom a long time and I could hear him sobbing. I lay on my bed wailing but when I heard Pip's bedroom door close, I sat up and instinctively looked over at the wardrobe. The door was slightly open and warily I wiped my sleeve across my eyes, got off the bed and moved towards it. I held my breath as I peered inside half expecting Uncle Jimmy to jump out but saw only my clothes.

I went back downstairs a little later and sat next to Mum on the sofa. Dad and Grandad had gone down to the betting shop and I noticed she looked really tired and I knew she wasn't watching the TV. She put her arm around me and said,

"Oh Kitty, I know you're sad but it's better this way than he lived in pain isn't it?"

"I know but he wasn't that old and I didn't know he was poorly."

"He was twelve my love and that's a good age for an Alsatian," she sighed, "Grandad's going to bury him in the morning, make a proper grave for him by the cherry trees." I immediately had a flash of him running around the fruit trees and started crying again.

"It's alright to be sad for a little while and we'll all miss him but we should be happy for having him in our family and all the lovely memories we have of him."

"Yes, I know, but I really miss him already. Where is he now?"

"Grandad has taken him in his bed down to the garden shed. He'll be safe there 'til tomorrow." She hugged me closer to her and I felt a warm sensation rushing through my body as we sat snuggled up on the sofa.

We sat like that for a little while, not speaking, but somehow just being that close to Mum made me feel better.

"Where's Granny?" I asked, suddenly noticing her absence.

"She's gone out for a walk, well that's what she said, but I think she's probably gone down to The Ship for a couple of gin and bitter lemons. I bet she'll probably go to the shop and annoy your Grandad and Dad as well after she's had a few." The small chuckle in Mum's voice was a like warm hug and made me smile too. She kissed the top of my head, "Shall I go and heat up the custard and get us both some of her jam roly-poly?"

"Yes please," I jumped up, "Shall I go and ask Pip if he wants some?"

"Yes you go up and tell him," standing up too, "We can eat it in here on our laps and watch the TV while Eliza's not here."

I knocked lightly on Pip's door. I would normally have gone straight in but seeing Pip crying was something I wasn't strong enough to deal with just then so I paused and waited for him to open the door. His eyes were red but he managed a smile and a nod when I asked him about the roly-poly, then he mumbled something about needing the toilet. I sat on the top stair outside the bathroom and heard him splashing his face and blowing his nose and wondered why it was so wrong for boys to cry. We exchanged a glance as he came out but there was no need for us to speak. He followed me down to the kitchen where Mum was pouring hot custard into two dishes.

"I thought we were having roly-poly." Pip peered into the dishes as pieces of chopped banana disappeared under the sweet, yellow sauce.

"Yes, well, for some reason Eliza has put all the pudding in the bin!" When Mum called Granny Eliza in front of us we knew she was cross. "Thankfully," she said crisply, "She saw fit to leave the custard."

"Why would she do that?" Pip asked, going over to the bin and lifting the lid. I moved across to see the big roll of suet and jam half broken and covered by the scrapings of cottage pie, peas and carrots.

"Why does Eliza do anything?" Mum said tetchily, "Anyway come on, Tommy Cooper's on in a minute."

Shortly after nine, Mum went out for an hour to meet Dad who she said would be ready for a drink at The Ship. Pip and I settled down to watch The Avengers with the strict instruction to go to bed as soon as it finished. Pip could read then if he wanted but I had to go straight to sleep as Mum didn't want me having one of my funny turns, what, with the day we'd all had. I loved The Avengers and although I didn't like Tara King as much as Emma Peel, I was still transfixed, laying on my tummy on the rug watching Steed and Tara rid the world of villains. When it had finished, I went into the kitchen and immediately felt the absence of four paws padding in behind me. Pip was already in there poking about in the bin.

"Ew, what you doing, you're not going to eat that are you?" I asked as I watched my brother lift out a big piece of the roly–poly. He looked at it wistfully and wiped a chunk of mashed potato off it before shrugging and dropping it back on top of the residue of our disturbed meal.

"Course not. Are you going to bed now?"

"I suppose so," I said as I went over to Eliza's baking cupboard, "Aren't you?" I was hoping he would play a board game with me but there was still something off-kilter with him and I didn't like it. I moved the tin where she kept her jam sugar and retrieved the jar of strawberry jam I had seen her hide two days before. I took the top off as I moved to the cutlery draw and took out a teaspoon. Pip was washing his hands but he turned to look at me just as I had put the heaped spoonful in my mouth.

"What are you doing?" snatching the jar from me. I took the empty spoon from my mouth.

"It's alright, it wasn't full, it's just the bit of jam she keeps for herself. She won't know we've had any." I went to get another spoon for him but he shook his head.

"Where was this?" he asked. I showed him and he told me to put it back exactly where I had found it and not to touch it again. I did as he said. He seemed so odd so I said I'd better go and brush my teeth and left him snooping around the kitchen. When I came out of the bathroom he was sitting on the top step.

"I need to go through my last year's school stuff and get things ready for Monday but you can come and sit with me for a bit if you like."

"Yes please. I'll bring my comic and I won't bother you," I began, "I just don't want to be on my own." I gave him my biggest thank you smile and he smiled back.

"I'll go and turn the TV off and get us some pop. I think they might be a bit late tonight so we can have a quick game of Ludo if you want."

I have no idea how late my parents and grandparents were out that night. Pip was a bit too obvious in letting me win at Ludo for me to enjoy it and so I refused a second game. I went to my own room just before eleven, insisting I wasn't tired but fell asleep almost immediately. I have a vague memory of waking to hear Grandad singing 'I'll take you home again Kathleen' but that could have just been part of the lucid dream of family gatherings I was having. It was dark and cold and someone was shouting at me to run. I woke up with a start just before dawn, full of panic with the image of Aunty Grace's menacing face looking at me out of the car window burnt on the back of my eyes. The bedroom door flew open and Eliza burst in.

"Kitty, what's the matter? Are you poorly?" she shouted, her eyes wild as she sat on the bed and tried to get hold of my flaying arms.

"Kitty! Keep still, you're hot, does your belly hurt?" Mum was on the other side trying to feel my forehead. I was confused and frightened. My bedroom was suddenly crowded as Dad and Pip came in. Before I'd woken with a start, I had been screaming and shouting for a good five minutes, waking everyone else in the house.

"Shall we call the doctor Alice?" Dad asked, leaning a bit more into the room.

"I'm not poorly; I was just having a bad dream." I sat up properly and Eliza got to her feet and turned to leave. "Granny, did Aunty Grace come round yesterday?"

"Really Kitty, now is not the time to start talking about that," she said curtly, "It's five o'clock in the morning. We all need to get back to bed."

Mum stayed and tucked me in, asking again if I had any pain, which I didn't. As she left I saw her glance at my wardrobe and noticed her tense a little.

"Mum?" I said.

"What, are you feeling sick?" she asked, turning back to me.

"No, I'm alright now. I'm sorry for waking you up."

"Never mind, you can't help it. Try and get back to sleep now and think about all those nice memories of Pal." She brushed my fringe off my forehead then kissed me lightly and left the room. I lay in semi-daylight, letting the silence of the early morning close in around me. I fixed my eyes on the ceiling, trying to conjure up happy times of playing in the garden with Pal, keeping my gaze fixed and not daring to look over at the wardrobe where I knew Uncle Jimmy was standing watching me.

It was nearly seven before I heard Pip moving about in his room so I got carefully out of bed and knocked on his door. He still had his pyjamas on but was sitting at his small wooden desk looking at a pile of school books. I closed the door behind me and blurted out,

"Do you think that Aunty Grace did something to Pal when she was here yesterday?"

"Why would she do that?" he snapped, glancing round briefly to look at me with his furrowed brow before turning his attention back to his books. I shrugged and moved from foot to foot trying to find the words to tell him how frightened I was. I hated him being cross with me and my tired frustration felt tight in my chest as I struggled not to cry.

"Because she's horrible and she doesn't like me," I tried, "Eliza says she's evil and she killed Uncle Jimmy."

"Kitty, come on you have to stop saying things like that."

"But Eliza says…"

"Shush!" He raised his hand in the air to stop me then got to his feet and came round his bed towards me. "Eliza says a lot of things but you shouldn't take so much notice." He moved me sideways and gently pushed me down to sit on his bed. "Pal was old and I loved him too but he's gone now and nobody did anything to him." He sat down next to me. "You mustn't say that you think anyone hurt him to anybody else and definitely not to Mum or Eliza."

"I know but…"

"I mean it, Kit, don't." He stood up and walked to the door. "I'm going down to get my breakfast and then I'm going to the park to meet Barry and Pete. I'll take your trousers from yesterday and get rid of them. You should go out and play for a bit and not think about Pal."

"OK," I got up "Thanks for not telling on me."

"Yeah, well, thanks for not telling on me for smoking," he smiled.

"Do you think Grandad is right about Eliza being a witch? She always seems to know things?"

"Course not!" he said sharply, "She could probably smell the cigarette smoke on me when I came in and you always go red when you're lying." He shrugged. "I don't even like smoking, I only wanted to try one and see what all the fuss was about."

As we walked down stairs, Pip touched my arm slightly and said,

"Shall we ask Mum if we can have boiled eggs and soldiers?"

"You mean you want *me* to ask Mum if she'll make us boiled eggs and soldiers." I laughed and ran down the last few steps. I got a real shock when I darted into the kitchen. Mum was standing by the sink and she had the tea towel up to her face and she was crying.

"Mum what's wrong?" I ran to her but then started to cry myself realising I'd been laughing and forgotten all about Pal. Mum gave her face a wipe and threw the tea towel on to the floor before reaching down to me. I had looked away to the empty space where our dog should be. Mum pulled me to her and gave me a brief hug.

"Come on now Kitty, we have to pull ourselves together. Grandad is down at the pigeons. He was waiting for you and Pip to come down. He's dug a hole."

We didn't bother with the dippy eggs and soldiers after that.

I did go round to call for Beverley later that morning but had been told I had to be home to help Mum with our Sunday roast. Eliza was going to The Ship with Grandad and Dad which meant that we wouldn't be eating until after closing time. I told Beverley about Pal and managed not to cry, although I did have to wipe away a couple of stray tears. We were playing in her bedroom with her dolls, sitting on the rug along with the four Sindys, two Pauls and all their clothes and paraphernalia strewn all over the floor. She looked down, pretending she hadn't noticed me wiping my eyes and nose on the sleeve of my cardigan. She said it was really sad and let me have a go at dressing her newest addition to her collection, a horse riding Sindy.

When I got back, the kitchen door was open and as I walked towards it, I heard Uncle Jack's deep voice.

"Oh well, I bet they bloody loved that, I can't believe Dad even asked them."

"It was Eliza, she said he had no alternative, he'd got to ask them and they'd got to help. If he doesn't find the money there'll be a lot more trouble." Mum sounded really fed up. I decided to wait a bit and see what else was said.

"I can't believe Dad was so bloody stupid." Jack's voice changed slightly so I thought he must have stood up, "I can help him out with some of it..." he was saying as Pip came up behind me. I was just about to shush him but he nodded his head slightly to the left and I saw Raymond standing by the dustbin watching me. I followed Pip into the kitchen and Raymond stepped in just behind us. Uncle Jack stopped mid sentence,

99

looking a bit cross before his familiar smile lit up his face again.

"Hello you two...ah and Raymond as well, just in time for a slice of some lovely Sunny Bank baking," he said jovially, sitting down again at the table and gesturing to the cooling array of pies on the table before him.

"They are having nothing 'til after their dinner," Mum said giving him one of her looks, "Go and wash your hands the three of you and then you can come and mash the potatoes and set the table, Kathryn."

"Kathryn?" Uncle Jack began, "Getting your Sunday name eh love? Are you excited about starting at the big school tomorrow?"

"Yes, I am a bit," I answered quickly, then panicked that this might set Mum off again but she didn't seem to have heard as she was back at the cooker. I went over to the sink as I heard Pip ask Raymond if he wanted to go up to the attic.

"Yes Ray, why don't you go up to the attic with Pip, he'll show you his Macarno and maybe let you have a go."

Raymond looked from his dad to Pip who was nodding. I watched his naturally worried expression soften into what, with a bit of cultivation, could eventually become a smile, and smiled myself as he nodded his acceptance of the invitation.

The roast beef and Yorkshire puddings were eaten in bit of a stilted atmosphere, I think mainly due to Eliza being in a really bad mood and snapping at anyone. Grandad Tommy was really quiet and hardly managed a smile, even when Pip told us all his new joke about an Englishman, an Irishman and a Scotsman. Uncle Jack roared with laughter though and said he knew a better one before Eliza glared at him and said he could keep it to himself. Raymond seemed to be actually eating his meal instead of just pushing it round his plate, although he did still look worried every now and then his gaze would dart around the room. I just wanted the meal over and was almost thinking about saying I didn't really want the apple pie and custard but, as I knew that I would still have to stay at the table anyway, I didn't. As soon as I'd helped carry things back to the kitchen, Mum told me and Pip to go back up to the attic with Raymond.

"Are you playing cards?" I asked, seeing Grandad Tommy opening the big old bureau where they kept the playing cards.

"No love, we've just got some things to sort out," Dad said in a really sad voice, giving my hair a half-hearted ruffling. I had been watching him while we had been eating; he looked really sad, like Mum and Grandad. I hadn't realised before how much Pal meant to us all.

Chapter Nineteen

Eliza - 1932

The fallout of the Heskeths finally learning the truth about Eliza's real family origins was not as big or devastating as Henry and Maude had hoped. They were, of course, beside themselves with glee at the revelation but if they'd thought Eliza would be cowed, they were to be disappointed. She maintained her poise, saying little other than that she remembered nothing of her life before the vicarage and she had never intended to deceive anyone.

William summoned the reverend and his wife to the house demanding to know why they had been complicit in the deception. They too remained contrite, pointing out that Eliza was a model daughter-in-law and a good, sensible girl, well educated and an excellent wife who had already provided them with three healthy grandchildren. Thomas rallied behind her too, pointing out that she was indeed a well educated girl and maybe his parents should be more aware that the Heskeths were not as perfect a family as they would like people to think. After some consideration and discussion with her husband, Clara decided that the best way to deal with the problem was money and threats. It was made clear to Eliza's father that the consequences of him or any of his other daughters coming near Burntwood again would be grave. This threat was delivered to him, along with ten crisp pound notes, by the local police sergeant on William's instructions.

Thomas and Eliza managed another year of living together under the Burntwood roof before Clara and William finally accepted that there was a need for some change. During this year, Eliza produced another healthy baby boy, almost as if using her fertility in retaliation and to prove her worth. The arrival of 9lb Jack, as the spare, provided a balm to the family disquiet and concern about her heritage. However, the hostilities between the two brothers continued and in the autumn of 1933 another fierce argument ended with Henry having his nose broken for a second time, this time at the factory and in front of half of the work force.

It was decided that Thomas should be allowed to pursue his own career path. Starting off with racing pigeons at the age of eight, he had always realised the potential for making money from other peoples' betting habits. His hobbies had extended throughout his teens with dog and horse racing. So when Thomas showed his father the information, facts and figures he had collated on exactly how much profit could be made, William was delighted. At last, his youngest son seemed to be showing some business acumen and he was only too happy to set him up with his own track-side betting stall at Doncaster races. At last he had found his vocation in a field that interested him. In addition to this, his parents bought him a house, for him and his family. Not too far away from Burntwood but far enough for the two brothers to be able to pursue their own careers. Although neither Clara nor William wanted their son and grandsons to leave Burntwood, they accepted that it was a necessary move and assumed that little would change.

Thomas and Eliza's new home was a six bedroom detached house on a good sized plot of land in the small mining village of Royston. It was originally called Bankside Manor but Thomas renamed it Sunny Bank, claiming that the sun would always shine on his family. He paid a gardener to come round once a week and keep the lawns and boarders tidy in the beautiful garden he had promised Eliza. There was a small orchard, eight apple, four pear and three cherry trees and small vegetable plot which was to be Eliza's personal project, a large garden shed where the children played that was like an Aladdin's cave of tools, rugs and boxes and, at the very bottom of the garden, a large fenced off square yard, wherein a large hut was installed for Thomas to keep his racing pigeons.

The sun did shine on his family on the day they moved in and as Eliza, in the early stages of her fourth and final pregnancy, surveyed her new surroundings, she smiled. Finally, she had her own home and could live the life she should have been born to. She had chosen wisely by marrying Thomas. She had known from the first moment she met him on that cold Christmas Eve that he was a man who would always take the easy option. He was weak, spineless and malleable and although the previous four years had been a learning curve for her, she had thrived. By trial and error, she had tested her influence and guile and was now perfectly placed for anything she wanted. It didn't take long after this move for it to dawn on Thomas that his wife was not the meek, compliant woman he thought he had married.

Chapter Twenty
Family History

Shortly after 9pm on Friday, 14th March 1941, around 40 bombers began to drop incendiaries onto the city of Leeds, igniting fires to light up the targets and aiding the Luftwaffe. The assault was merciless as they dumped their high-explosive bombs on and around the city throughout the night and well into the next day. Targets hit in the centre were Leeds New Station, the Town Hall, Kirkgate Markets and the Hotel Metropole. One hundred houses were completely destroyed and more than four and a half thousand others were damaged. It was a miracle that not more people were killed under the onslaught but there were 65 souls lost during the attack and hundreds more injured during what has come to be known as the Leeds Blitz.

It is one of those terrible ironies that Mrs Blanch Weatherill, Maude Hesketh's mother, died on the anniversary of her birth. She had been born on 14th March 1878 and on the night of the bombings was celebrating her 63rd birthday at home with her husband, her brother and sister-in-law and two nephews. Maude had travelled up earlier in the day with eleven year old Grace who was always subdued on these visits but seemed particularly sulky, to Maude, on this occasion. Henry never made the visits with her, always insisting he could not leave the business to go flitting around the country. Maude's parents, Neville and Blanch did not make any secret of the disappointment they felt about how the marriage of their only daughter had panned out. They had also been extremely vocal in their opposition to Maude taking the 'bastard child' as Neville had once called Grace, as her own, even though this very act had saved her from insanity. As the years had gone by, they had learnt to tolerate the girl although Neville still referred to her as 'the foundling' in private. There was never any affection shown to Grace by anyone other than Maude.

Almost as soon as they had arrived at Stockbridge Hall, Maude blurted out the news she had been bursting to share with her parents; she was expecting a child. Her father coughed and he and the other men present at the assembled gathering lowered their gaze as she went on to say she had missed three of her monthlies already and could feel a small swelling in her stomach. Blanch clapped her hands in delight and Maude was congratulated by all in the room as Grace edged her way towards the back of the room, forgotten by the family group. Blanche announced that it was now a double celebration and Neville, tears in his eyes, striding over to hug his darling daughter, agreed. Both parents chose instinctively to hide their concern that this pregnancy might end as her others had and commented instead that she looked well and had a glow about her, convincing themselves that her thinness and the dark circles under her eyes were probably down to her tiredness and the travelling. Her father poured everyone a drink and proposed a toast to Maude and her baby, her real child and his first Grandchild.

No one noticed the effect this comment had on Grace who quietly opened the French windows in the far corner of the room and escaped out into the garden. She was feeling confused. She had been aware of the swelling in Maude's stomach for some time but was sure from the dark haze that seemed to emanate from it, that it was not a baby.

Grace sauntered glumly across the lawn to the summer house at the bottom of the garden. She had been sulking there, her emotions swinging between upset and anger and she had just wished them all dead for a third time when the sirens went off. Hearing Maude calling her to come in and go with them to the cellar, she had crept out and moved into the long grass where she crouched, remaining still and quiet until she heard Blanch saying to leave the silly girl out there. She had to look after herself now and her father would go and look for her once the family were in the cellar. But of course, he didn't.

Waiting in the dark, she heard the planes before she saw them. Standing up, she moved a little closer to the house when she heard the high pitch of the bomb that was to wipe out the entire Weatherill family. Falling to the floor, she flung her arms up holding her head as the house exploded in front of her, smashing the debris through all four stories of the building. Her terror was compounded by the bang and as the shock wave reverberated through her young body, she thought her head was also going to explode. She remained laid on the grass, aware that the planes were still circling above. She watched as more fury fell from the skies but could only hear a dull ringing in her ears. She had no idea how long she stayed, laying in the damp debris strewn grass, but it was still quite dark when she saw the thin beams from the torches of the rescue party. Getting to her feet, she walked carefully through the wreckage towards where the house used to be.

The team of air wardens and fire fighters were astonished at the sight of the child standing in the wreckage and carefully got her to safety. The story of the miracle child would be told numerous times over the next few weeks and used as a morale boost and small crumb of comfort and hope throughout the rest of the war. The girl was unhurt but seemed unable to speak as she stared blankly at her rescuers, hearing nothing except the surging of her blood through her arteries and an eerie dull ringing sound. She was taken to St James's Hospital where she stayed for two days until her hearing recovered and the kindness of the over-worked hospital staff eased her out of her trauma so she could finally tell them her name.

Eliza volunteered to go to Leeds to bring Grace home. Leaving her five children at Burntwood early on the Monday morning, she and Thomas made the difficult and fragmented journey through the fresh ruins to get to the war hospital. The sights they saw on the way of the crumbling devastation were nothing to prepare them for the scenes inside the hospital. Trying desperately to keep his emotions in check, Thomas reached for Eliza's hand as they waited in a corridor full of walking wounded. His wife had moved her gloved hand away and she patted her hair slightly. As Thomas attempted to blink back his emotion he could not help but notice her cool and appraisive gaze as she looked around her.

While waiting for someone to take them to the overflow ward, a well-dressed woman wearing a smart, blue hat on her beautifully coiffured black hair touched Eliza's arm with her co-ordinated blue leather gloved hand. It was a chance meeting, the woman asking the time but it was the start of close and unlikely friendship.

The woman was Barbara McLean, a celebrated medium in the West Leeds spiritual community, although at that meeting all Eliza knew was that Barbara's husband had been killed and house destroyed in the same onslaught that wiped out the Weatherill family two nights earlier. Alice, her four-year-old daughter, had not been in the house but had sustained cuts and bruises and a nasty bump to her head. Thomas watched as his wife chatted amiably with Mrs McLean, seeing an Eliza he had not seen for a long time. Grace and Alice were both in a small corridor, used as an overspill for one of the wards and filled beyond capacity from the preceding days. A nurse took the three of them part of the way, pointing down a large badly lit corridor, before turning and hurrying off in the opposite direction.

The friendly and smiling version of Eliza remained for the whole time they were in the hospital but there was no warmth in her demeanour as they walked toward the subdued and fearful looking Grace. In fact, Thomas could clearly see her struggle to hide the loathing she felt for this child as she spoke sharply, telling her that they were taking her back to Burntwood now but did not know what her father would do with her now that her mum was dead. They had to wait for the nurse to come and bring the doctors note and Eliza turned her back on the child to continue her discussion with Mrs Mclean. They exchanged addresses; Barbara would be living with a friend in the short term and Thomas felt a jolt of surprise as he heard Eliza invite a woman she had only just met to come and stay for a day or two at Sunny Bank.

Thomas patted Grace gently on the shoulder and felt her tense beneath his touch. Eliza scowled at him as she turned and he dropped his hand back by his side. The nurse told them that she was in a state of shock but would be fine once she got home to her family. Grace didn't utter a word and the three of them left the hospital in silence.

Barbara and her daughter were frequent visitors to Sunny Bank in the years that followed. Eliza and Tommy's children grew used to having little Alice playing with them in the gardens and large attic playroom. Billy, the youngest and just two years older took a special interest in the dainty little girl and a bond of friendship was formed that lasted right through their formative years.

After the war ended, Mrs McLean was in great demand. She was being asked to speak at spiritualist churches and ministries all over the country. So it was decided it would be best for Alice, who had just turned thirteen, to go and live at Sunny Bank, for a while. This suited Barbara very well, enabling her to travel and socialise without her quiet and sometimes sullen daughter in tow.

Alice and Billy, with no small amount of encouragement from Eliza became close and were often found walking around or just sitting together. Their romance blossomed quickly and it came as no surprise when just after the Christmas of 1951, Billy proposed. Barbara had come to stay for a few days to welcome in the New Year with them and was more than thrilled, claiming she had foreseen this happy union many years before. It was a happy occasion for the whole family and, with Eliza's encouragement, a wedding was planned for later that year, as soon as Alice turned sixteen. Unfortunately, Barbara's untimely and ironically unpredicted death the month before the arranged date put the dampers on things a little. However, Eliza quickly began to manage everyone's emotions to match her own. She had not so much lost a friend as gained a daughter.

Indigo Children

Part Two

Indigo Children

Chapter One

Pip

When she was thirteen, my sister Kitty fell down the stone steps of my great uncle's garden and broke her arm in three places. This is the thing I hold on to, the fact that I cling to; she got hurt running away. She was not a part of, or in any way responsible for, the terrible things that happened that night, the things that put our family on the front pages of the papers and on the television news during that winter back in 1971.

I know I must bear some culpability for what happened and I feel certain that if I'd done or said something, spoken out, well maybe things might not have ended in the same terrible way. Because, although I wasn't actually there on that eventful night, I had known for some time that there was something very wrong in my family, I just hadn't worked out what. When you are really close to something, all the background stuff goes out of focus.

A long time ago my family were wealthy and influential people but over the generations, their fortune and reputation was lost, partly due to the changing times but mainly because of their stubborn and defiant attitude to accept any type of adjustment to either business or family life. This dwindling of fortunes started happening long before Kathryn and I were born, so the diminished living standards didn't affect us in the same way they did my parents and grandparents. Being at the trailing end of our family's considerable fortune in the late 1950's wasn't actually that bad. In fact, for us children, it was a good life. But we were oblivious to problems around us in the grown up world as the family lost its place and reputation, along with the cash. And although it was a time of hardship for the whole country in those years following the conflict, there were some in our family that found it much harder than others.

The Hesketh fortune, made from the manufacture of glass, had been considerable and the family's self-built reputation and affiliations made my ancestors important people. There was a hereditary entrepreneurial

113

gene, passed down through three generations, ensuring good business decisions and partner choices. These enabled Hesketh & Son's and family members comfort in their self-importance and worth. The opulence and substance began to diminish very quickly after the Second World War, although there has been a more recent school of thought to suggest that things really began to change for the family when my Grandad Tommy met Eliza.

Grandad Tommy and his brother Uncle Henry never got on. Even as children, there was never any brotherly love. The reason for this, according to our main source of information; Eliza herself, was that Henry was jealous of his younger brother. Thomas had been the favourite child and was indulged by his parents whereas Henry was expected to bear the responsibility of the family name. Henry's dislike of his brother strengthened as they got older and even though the Hesketh family home, Burntwood Manor, was a large house, it was not large enough for the warring brothers. Eliza told us that she was the one that made Grandad realise that he did not have to stay at Burntwood or in the family business. She made him understand that, with her help, he could start his own business doing something he loved and have his own family home; his parents were wealthy enough to set him up and bank-roll him. She made him see that they could have a much better life in a home of their own. She painted a picture of the idyllic future they could have, away from the dark grey mausoleum of the house of his forefathers, a new house where they could start their own dynasty. When Kitty, who would have been around twelve at the time, asked her why she hated Great Uncle Henry and Aunt Grace so much and never visited them at Burntwood, she gave a really bitter reply.

"It was a deal we struck. Your Grandad had his family money behind him to make our own fortune and I had the babies to make our future. I fulfilled my part and did above and beyond, I even sacrificed my first born when your useless Grandad needed more money to bail him out. I let my Jimmy go back into that snake pit and work with that devious swine Henry and his bastard daughter and you know how that ended."

I was born in 1953 in the front room of Sunny Bank, the home of my Grandparents Tommy and Eliza. My dad, Billy, was the youngest of their five children and when he married my mum, Alice, Sunny Bank became their home too. My sister, Kathryn Elizabeth, was born four years later and we existed as one happy family unit and the sun always shone, well that's the way it seemed for a long time. With the value of hindsight, I think those childhood memories are all tinged with something much darker.

Dad was Eliza's favourite child; she never made any secret of it and the others, Uncle Jimmy, Aunty Peg and Aunty Dot didn't seem to mind. Tommy and Eliza had another son, Uncle Jack, but he moved away when I was baby so I didn't know him or what he thought until he came back thirteen years later. Conversely though, there was an incident, one Christmas, when I realised that maybe the 'not minding' had worn a bit thin and that Eliza, sometimes, went too far. I think I was about seven or maybe eight and Uncle Jimmy, who never married and had until recently lived with us, was there, along with my aunties, their husbands and children. We were sitting round the big fireplace in the sitting room amongst the debris of wrapping paper and boxes from our individual piles of presents. Eliza was in her chair smiling at me and my cousins as we sat on the rug marvelling at our presents. Kathryn was setting out her new tea set on the side table for her imaginary friends and I was trying to get my cousin Daryl to play Ludo. The rest of the grown-ups were scattered around the room having just swapped their token gifts which had been given and received with polite but understated enthusiasm. The final gift was from Mum to Eliza and was a brightly wrapped parcel tied up with a green ribbon. Eliza smiled as she pulled the bow on the ribbon, carefully unwrapping the gift, a woollen turquoise jumper.

"Oh Alice, this is lovely, thank you," she said, reaching to Mum with her arms outstretched. Mum, in response, bent to kiss her lightly on the cheek.

"You are welcome, Eliza; I think that colour suits you. I'm glad you like it."

"Yes, it is my colour and I love it. You are such a thoughtful girl, really. You are like the daughter I never had." I could see tears in her eyes as she smiled up at Mum. Aunty Dot and Aunty Peg both shot to their feet, as twins they often did or said things at the same time but this time it was only Aunty Dot who spoke, loudly enough for both of them.

"Mother! That is such a hurtful thing to say."

"Why?" Eliza turned her head towards them with a look of confusion. "Why is that hurtful?" Her eyes narrowed and she had that look on her face, the one we all dreaded. "What?" Pausing, she looked directly from one daughter to another. "You two have never given me anything but grief and boxes of cheap and nasty soap and bath salts." Turning her attention to Mum, her voice got softer as she said, "Alice has been more of a daughter to me than either of you two."

"It's only a bloody jumper," Aunt Peg muttered.

"Oh no, it's much more than this jumper, Alice has given me something much more precious." Eliza looked at Mum with a funny half smile before adding, sharply, "Now sit down the pair of you." She turned to Dad, her smile now complete,

"Go and open the sherry, Billy, I've got time for a small one before Alice and me get back to the dinner."

Mum looked really pink and stood up saying that Kitty was looking tired and she would take her upstairs to see if she needed a nap before dinner. I think she was really embarrassed; well it wasn't a very nice thing for Eliza to have said. Aunty Peg and Aunty Dot had been buying her the same sets of soap and bath salts for the past few years and she'd never said before that she thought they were cheap and nasty and I didn't think they were.

Dad went into the dining room, followed quickly by the two aunts and Grandad Tommy. When they came back they all had glasses in their hands and the flush in Peg and Dot's cheeks suggested that they were on their second very large sherry. I don't recall any other incident that day but I suppose that was the moment I began to realise we weren't quite the happy family I had thought we were.

There had always been a massive feud between Grandad Tommy and Eliza and Uncle Henry and Grace. There was never any love lost between Eliza and anyone at Burntwood. Although she was happy when Uncle Henry, in lieu of not having a son of his own, gave Uncle Jimmy a management job at the factory and announced that he would be groomed to take over the family business. But she was horrified when she realised the full extent at what this job would mean. Eliza's initial delight at her eldest son being the heir apparent of Hesketh and Son's long established quality glass manufacturing business, radiated from her like sunshine. Even so, she still insisted that it was rightfully his inheritance anyway and Henry had not done it out of any favour but because of his failure to produce a son of his own. Mum later told me that Eliza's pleasure was more about Grace being slighted rather than anything else.

When she was seventeen, Grace had married Malcolm Griffiths, a man twenty years older and a business associate of Uncle Henry's. Within a year, she had produced her son, Edward. It would not be too much of a stretch to assume that in Grace's eyes, Edward would be the rightful heir to the family business. So in 1962, when Henry made it clear that he was training Jimmy to be his number two and subsequently take over the reins when he retired, Grace was furious.

Uncle Jim had been working at the factory for just over two years, starting in the autumn of 1960. Eliza had not been too happy about her son working for Henry and her reaction to the news was immediately hostile. However, it was a surprise to everyone that Grandad Tommy intervened and Eliza was swayed into acceptance. We were half way through our Sunday roast dinner when Uncle Jimmy said, in an exaggerated matter of a fact way, that he had been to see Uncle Henry about a job at the factory and was starting work there, the next day. Eliza started to say something but Grandad Tommy raised his arm in the air and spoke loudly over her, telling her not to interfere. The rest of us at the table looked from him to her in silent stillness, waiting. I remember the clock ticking away several long seconds before Grandad picked up his knife and fork and, cutting through his roast beef said,

"The lad needs a proper job Eliza. You know our circumstances and it will be good for him to learn more about the business." The clock ticked away a few long seconds and no one spoke. So Grandad went on, "Of course Grace is furious as she thinks it should be Edward being groomed to take over."

Eliza kept her gaze on Grandad for a few more heartbeats before picking up her own utensils, glancing across at uncle Jim and with the slightest nod and a grimace of a smile she conceded,

"Well I suppose it will be good for you Jim, after all you are clearly a much better choice than Grace's stupid son." Her smile moved further up her face as she spoke and she left the briefest of pauses before pointing her knife at Grandad and adding,

"But I will be keeping my eye on that brother of yours."

We all recommenced eating and Eliza's next comment seemed to be aimed at her own roast beef and Yorkshire puddings,

"In fact, it could turn out to be to our advantage; Jim can keep an eye on what he's up to and what he's planning. After all, we still have an interest in the family business."

There was the briefest exchange of looks between Grandad and his eldest son and as Eliza had bowed her head to continue with her meal, she was unaware of Grandad closing his eyes and shaking his head. It was years later that I learnt the significance of this little gesture in our on-going family dispute.

Eliza didn't know that Tommy had been bailed out by Henry twice already following some disastrous decisions he had made since buying the local betting shop. In fact, as we all learned much later, Grandad Tommy made lots of bad judgements and did not have any real business acumen whatsoever. On the second occasion Uncle Henry had helped him out, it had been at a cost. Grandad Tommy had signed away his shares in Hesketh Glass. In this third crisis, in 1960, of which Eliza didn't know the half of, it looked like Grandad might lose the business completely. When he asked his brother again if he would help, Henry agreed a small loan, just enough to fend off the main creditors, on condition that Jimmy came to work at the family business. Jim had been happy at the prospect. Up to that point, apart from his two years national service, he had drifted in and out of jobs and had spent the previous year helping Grandad at the bookmakers but only for pocket money. The offer of a good, regular job with Henry seemed like a godsend to both Tommy and Jimmy and neither of them were about to let Eliza spoil it for them. That night I heard Mum say to Dad that at last Grandad Tommy had stood up to Eliza and not let her interfere. I had noticed that when she brought the pudding in, she gave Grandad and Uncle Jimmy the biggest slices of apple pie and swamped them with deep yellow custard.

Two days later, Uncle Jimmy announced that he was moving to Burntwood as it made more sense for him to live there, through the week anyway. Kitty and me were in the kitchen and although Mum turned up the radio, I clearly heard Eliza scream that it made no sense whatsoever and under no circumstances would she allow him to move back into that house. A lot of raised voices and banging echoed though the house, ending with Uncle Jimmy shouting that, at 32, he was old enough to make his own decisions about where he lived and he should have got away from 'this house' a lot sooner, like Uncle Jack had done. His words created a sudden silence, broken only by the slamming of the door, as Eliza left the room before stamping upstairs. Mum turned the radio down

119

and muttered to herself,

"Well that went as well as could be expected," she sighed loudly before walking into the hall, hands on hips and said to me, "It'd be a good idea for you and Kitty to play out in the garden for a bit; keep out of Eliza's way." I nodded knowing full well that this was more than just a good idea.

Uncle Jimmy moved out the next day, Dad driving him and his two suitcases over to Burntwood after he'd hugged Mum and Kitty and shook hands with Grandad and me. Eliza was not around to see him off, choosing to get a bit of gardening done while the weather stayed fine. She was in the kitchen as we ate our breakfast that morning and seemed scarily calm and quiet. She poured herself another cup of tea but didn't drink it. Instead, she went out of the French window as soon as Uncle Jimmy came downstairs, without a word and her head bowed to avoid eye contact.

Later that afternoon, when Dad had got back from Burntwood, I overheard him saying to Mum that he was pleased that Eliza had now accepted that Uncle Jim's leaving was for the best and decided to let it go. Mum answered so quietly I really had to listen hard at the door to catch her words.

"Don't be fooled Billy, she's never going to accept decisions about the family that she hasn't made. She's just biding her time now and working out what to do. You mark my words; this isn't going to be easy; there's a lot more trouble ahead."

Chapter Two
Alice - 1941

When she was six years old, Alice's already unusual world became even more unorthodox. It was a sudden change and happened at ten-thirty on the night of Friday 14th March 1941 and perhaps it was her abnormal lifestyle that saved her life. Normal six year-olds would have been in bed fast asleep at this time and although the sirens might have woken her parents, the Luftwaffe gave scant notice of their assault. Had the MacLean's been a normal family, they would all have been killed in the devastation that was inflicted on Model Road, Armley. Instead, Alice was several streets away at the West Leeds Spiritualist Church on Theaker Lane attending the weekly meeting with her mother who was the well known medium and channel to the departed, Barbara McLean.

There was little warning as the Germans flew low over the Leeds suburb that night, filling the air with smoke and noise. The unsuspecting residents that were at home had only minutes to react before the planes dropped their payload, wiping out the three houses in the middle of the terrace. So it was some sort of a miracle that it only resulted in two fatalities and another three of the populace badly injured.

As the incendiary scored a direct hit in the middle of the terrace, houses 33, 35 and 37 were reduced completely to rubble. Eerily though, numbers 31 and 39 remained half intact, like giant bookends to the devastation. As the Friday night passed into Saturday morning, Alice sat, wrapped in a thick grey blanket, looking over at the precarious structure of number 31 that had been her home. The street was full of fire fighters and upstanding members of the community who had rushed to help once the sirens had signalled the all clear. Mrs Gaines who lived on the even numbered side of the terrace was sitting with Alice on her knee on a small wooden stool that Mr Gaines had brought out of their kitchen. Alice watched as her mother argued with three men who were blocking her way to their amazingly intact front door. She heard her mother's stern voice insisting that she had to get inside, she had to find her Bert and she watched her mother being led away by two men with hats on. She blinked away the upsetting images that were drifting back into her recent memory and lifted her head to see her parents' crimson bedroom curtains blowing about in the dust-filled breeze. The remains of the adjoining wall obscured the downstairs but the whole of the upstairs of their home was on full display. The bold design of Albert and Barbara's red and blue striped wallpaper looked overpowering next to the pastel shades of the daisy and buttercup decorated smaller room. She smiled, noticing her best pink dressing gown hanging on the back of her closed bedroom door but the nasty images pushed their way back into her head and she felt her eyes fill with tears.

"Not there," she tried to say but her voice was lost in her sobs.

"There, there, love," Mrs Gaines said, giving her a squeeze, "Don't you go getting upset. You're alright and your mam'll find your dad once all this dust settles. He's probably helping down the road so don't you worry."

Alice glanced down at Pearl, her favourite doll, lying across her lap and saw the glistening tear drop on the pink china face. She unfurled her index finger from her bawled left hand and touched the droplet causing it to run down Pearl's cold hard face. Alice didn't look up or contradict Mrs Gaines. Instead, she scrunched up her eyes, blinking away her tears and the picture in her head of her father's broken and lifeless body among the debris of the destroyed homes.

Chapter Three
Pip – Early 1960's

It's hard to pin down when my opinion of Eliza changed. She was a constant in our lives and, although I think I was always quite scared of her, I know I loved her very much. When I started school, I was surprised that most of my friends just lived with their parents and siblings. That's not to say that there weren't other families that had three generations in one house but none of my friends had anyone like Eliza in their family.

The fact that Kitty and I called her by her first name was always a surprise to our friends and for someone so small and gentle looking she could be unpredictably stern sometimes. She was always sharp with Grandad, who seemed to mostly just take her hostility in his stride, but she was the one who dictated the atmosphere in the house. She loved us, Kitty and me, and even if she didn't seem to like most of them, she had a fierce loyalty to the family, often claiming that family was everything. Growing up at Sunny Bank, I was taught that we were an influential family and that our lives should always be private. Outsiders were not usually welcomed into our little world. Eliza talked a lot about our standing in the village and the importance of family allegiance. I was never really sure what she meant until it was tested, causing me to fall out with my best friend, John Rogers.

John and I had been friends since our first day at Royston Infant School when we'd been given pegs next to each other to hang our duffle coats on. We then filed shyly into the classroom, choosing small chairs next to each other, risking a small smile as we sat down. I have clear memories of us filing into the school hall in the morning assembly to a piece of classical music, which I learned much later was called 'Trumpet Voluntary', to sit cross-legged on the polished parquet floor trying not to giggle and fidget. After trying to be good through long boring assemblies and then concentrating hard, as we were told we must, through lessons, we finally got the chance to run around the playground being fighter pilots and cowboys.

John told me his Dad was a major in the Salvation Army, which I thought sounded really important. I asked Eliza about this when she collected me from school after my first day. She told me the Salvation Army was like church but they had a band and they used this to lure children in, encouraging them to play tambourines. I was confused at this.

"Why do they call it an army then?" I had asked.

"Because they are an army and they've declared war on people enjoying themselves and so if this boy's dad is a Major, he'll not be a very nice man," she'd responded before adding, "Anyway, I'm sure you'll make lots more friends but this one's probably not right for you."

This worried me a little and so while Eliza was in the garden with a toddling Kitty, I told Mum about John and what Eliza had said. Mum laughed and said to take no notice. Eliza had funny ideas and opinions about lots of things and if I liked playing with John that was fine.

The next day I asked John if he had a tambourine and he said no of course he didn't, tambourines were for girls.

Our friendship became established and saw us through our two years at primary school and then the further four at the juniors. Eliza was never openly friendly with anyone outside the family but on the rare occasions John came to Sunny Bank, she only just managed a pleasant civility that could have, if you squinted your eyes, been mistaken for warmth.

However, any feelings of discomfort John experienced in those early years were never mentioned and any concerns I might have had about grownups in my family being unfairly harsh disappeared when I first encountered John's dad.

I was invited to have a bit of tea at the Rogers' house a couple of times in that first year of school. It was always arranged a couple of days in advance and John and I would be collected by his mum and escorted to their house while she chatted nicely to us both and seemed to smile all the time. Once at their house, we played in their small garden if it wasn't raining or on the rug in front of the coal fire if it was. Mrs Rogers was lovely although she seemed quite a lot older than my mum and was quite a large woman who smelled of the soap Eliza and Grandad always used to clean the garden off their hands. She baked a lot of cakes, which she was always keen for us to fill up on, but they were generally a bit dry and left a funny taste. I was far too polite to ever say that or to refuse to take one when the plate was held in front of me.

John had a passion for model cars and had loads of them, all in pristine condition and kept in their original boxes. His collection was then kept in three shoeboxes which he stored under his bed but his mum had always brought them downstairs and put them on the sideboard for when I had come round. John's idea of playing with them was just taking them out and placing them in neat lines, either on the fireside rug or the old garden blanket. Holding and looking carefully at them a while before putting each one carefully back in their packaging and closing the lids on their entombed resting place. Then we would have tea; usually fish fingers and chips followed by some jelly and Carnation milk and a piece of cake.

Mrs Rogers always referred to Mr Rogers as Daddy when she spoke to John. "Daddy say's, you know what Daddy thinks about that, let's not tell Daddy..." and often mentioned that he was doing his good works and saving souls. These good works took him all around the area and so he was seldom home before John went to bed. John said he didn't mind this as his dad was a very important man and it was important not to bother him with silly things. So Mr Rogers never featured in my consciousness until I had my first encounter with him eighteen months later.

It was just before Easter and John was having a party to celebrate his seventh birthday. Mum had taken me along on the Saturday afternoon to their house on Kirkfield Crescent. She had spoken briefly with Mrs Rogers before leaving to walk back home. I had run into the garden with John, who was tearing the paper off the small box containing a light blue Corgi Ford Anglia I had picked out for him that morning, as his mum shouted after him to calm down. Peter and Steven, two other boys from our class, were already on the lawn, standing by a tent made from a wooden clothes horse on its side with a stripy sheet draped over it. I ran towards it to see a girl I'd never seen before sitting inside. Her flowery dress, stretched over the knees of her crossed legs, was full of model cars that I knew were John's favourites. At that moment John, saw them too.

"Mum!" he wailed, in a mixture of horror and desperation. He loved his cars and treated them with care when he played with them. I felt my eyes widen at the sight of them all out of their boxes in a jumble on the little girl's lap which would surely mean scratches and dents from metal against metal. Mrs Rogers clearly had not heard his cry and, in his frustrated panic, John launched himself into the makeshift tent, trying to snatch the cars from the child.

"Help me Philip, help me get them off her," he called as he disappeared under the sheet. I got on to my knees to crawl forward and Peter and Steven went to the back of the structure. I saw the girl was struggling to bundle up the toy cars to stop John taking them back but couldn't see her face. I could see the pile of boxes she had discarded as she taken out the cars being crushed by the wriggling and pushing. John must have noticed them too as he started to shout at her and her response, opening her mouth wide, was to let out the loudest ear-piercing scream I had ever heard and then start crying and shouting for her mummy. I felt like I might cry myself and started to pull back out of the tent as a big hand got hold of me by the shoulder and hauled me to my feet.

"What on earth are you doing you nasty little boy!" Mr Rogers boomed at me. Three things happened then, all at the same time, creating a painfully scratched memory in my young mind that can still make me shudder today, more than fifty years later.

First Mrs Rogers appeared, quickly placing herself between me and her husband but not before he had given me a rough shake and lowered his head so I could see the rage on his face and smell his horrid breath. Secondly, John started to shout that I had not done anything and that Tracey had spoiled his party and broken all his cars and he pointed to the girl in the tent who had now stopped screaming. And thirdly, I felt a warm patch of urine grow on the front of my underpants and shorts.

John told me a few days later that Tracey was his cousin and had been staying with them while her mum was in hospital. It was years later, I heard that in actual fact, Tracey was John's half sister and Mr Rogers had lived a double life for a number of years before being found out but of course by that time, John and I were no longer friends.

I don't recall much of the party after the tent incident but I have a ghost of a memory of Mr Rogers saying something about me being a sinful child from a blasphemous and wicked family before taking Tracey's hand and leading her through the house and out of the front door, neither to be seen again that afternoon.

The only other thing that has stuck with me over the years was Mrs Rogers being really kind to me, asking if I'd come inside and help her with John's present. Once in the house, she took me up to the bathroom and gave me a pair of John's clean underpants and shorts to change into. She then somehow managed to get mine washed and dried in the following three hours before giving them to me to change back into just before the party ended. When Mum arrived to pick me up, Mrs Rogers looked like she might cry at any moment and although she had not requested it, I knew she really didn't want me to say anything to Mum about what had happened and so I didn't.

I went to John's house again many times over the next five years, while we were still friends but I never saw his dad again and John and I never spoke about 'the incident', not even the very next week as I helped him Cellotape some of the boxes of his precious cars back together.

Chapter Four

Alice - 1941

Mr McLean's body was not found in the rubble of his house and so it was assumed he had escaped and gone to a different shelter. So Barbara agreed to go to the hospital to have her bleeding leg stitched and let the nurses check over the cuts and bruises on poor little Alice. That was how Mrs Gaines and the other neighbours kept referring to her and Alice supposed that was who she was now but didn't comment on this acceptance. in fact, she didn't speak at all. She did not tell them they were looking in the wrong place and that her father's body lay three houses down. He was fatally injured when he and the lady of the house had fallen, along with the double bed they'd been in, right through to the stone flags of the kitchen, followed by the roof and the rubble which covered their broken bodies. Instead, poor little Alice retreated into herself in pain and despair.

Early the next day a nurse brought Mary Williams, one of Barbara's friends from church; over to the small camp bed, in an overcrowded corridor, being used for the walking wounded. When she'd first woken, sometime earlier, she had been confused opening her eyes on the stark darkness filled with noises of suffering and pain. Her mother was sitting on the edge of the bed speaking softly to someone in the next bed. Alice leaned forward as the panic rushed through her and reached for Barbara who immediately stopped mid-sentence and turned to stroke her hair. She told her not to worry, they would go home soon and her daddy would be waiting for them. Alice felt her eyes start to prick at the mention of her daddy as the recollection of events flashed behind her eyes but the strangeness of her surroundings gave her hope. Her memory of the day before had become blurry, mixing with traces of her night terrors. She sat up fully and her wide eyes took in the surroundings as they adjusted to the dimness and more people began to stir. She pulled Pearl from underneath the dark grey blanket, placed her carefully on her knee and leaned forward as a dim electric light, right above the makeshift bed, instantly dissolved the shifting shadows with a stark jaundice yellow flash. There was a girl in the next bed, laying on her side, her eyes open and staring back at her. There was a pretty lady in a black coat standing at the bottom of her bed, talking to Alice's mum.

So perhaps what had happened on her street had just been a bad dream. This wasn't so strange; she was often in different places with her mother and the lady was asking about the church. Her mum was in full flow, talking about the spirits and her gift and so Alice was starting to believe she had made a mistake. Then she saw Mary Williams and she knew why she had come. Her father had been found and it was sad news. She spoke with her eyes cast down and murmured words that Alice did not understand but she didn't need to. Her father was dead and would never be able to hold her again and tell her everything was alright. He would never read her anymore fairy stories that ended happily and would not be able to save her from the greyness that surrounded her mother or from the dense shadows that inched longer and closer each day.

As Alice started to cry, the girl in the bed sat up and looked across at her and the woman in the black coat turned her head as if she had only just noticed her. Alice paused, mid sob, and her breath caught in her throat as she felt these two new pairs of eyes on her. She clutched Pearl to her chest and closed her eyes to hide from the shadows as they edged their way closer.

Chapter Five

Pip – early 1960's

I am sure my parents loved me and Kathryn equally but I am also sure that they loved us differently. My sister had the prime childhood spot in our family, the angelic baby girl who was loved instantly by everyone and I was no exception. She had something of the ethereal about her, not that I knew it as that back then, but she had an aura of frailty that made me fiercely protective of her. Although I think I always felt like this about my little sister, I may just be remembering things in a different order because of what happened but I feel I was always watchful of her whenever we were away from our little world, or exposed to other people, and I feel sure I felt this way even before she started having her little turns.

The very first time it happened was horrible and what made it worse was, for a long time, I was terrified I might have caused it.

It happened on the afternoon of her fourth birthday, a hot Sunday in July. Eliza and Mum had arranged a family tea party at Sunny Bank. Things were already off kilter well before anybody arrived and it seemed that everyone, except for Kitty, had got out of the wrong side of the bed. A row erupted between Eliza and Grandad in the middle of the kitchen while Mum was baking. I was sharing my toast with Pal in an attempt to get him to like me as much as he liked my sister. Since Uncle Jim had gone to live a Burntwood, it didn't take much to set Grandad and Eliza off but this particular morning's onslaught seemed exceptionally vicious and centred on Aunty Grace and Uncle Henry having been invited to the tea party.

The arrangement had been made the weekend before and Aunties Dot and Peg, along with their spouses and offspring, had also been asked – Mum was always keen to include them, despite Eliza's indifference. Eliza had insisted that Uncle Jimmy came, and kept saying it was going to be a proper family party. It was clear she had plans for one of her card school evenings where they would all sit in a nicotine and alcohol fug around the dining room table into the early hours. Grandad had said, most probably out of mischief, that if it was going to be a proper family party, then Uncle Henry, Grace and her husband and Edward should also come.

"They are not coming!" Eliza had stated quite firmly. She had then changed the subject but I had seen the way Grandad narrowed his eyes and I knew he would invite them to spite her' and he did. He had not mentioned it again until that morning as he drank his tea. Eliza had reacted exactly as predicted and battle commenced. Dad had tried to calm things at first by mentioning his missing sibling.

"Well for it to be a proper family party, we'd need Jack here and as no bugger knows where he is, it's not likely he'll turn up." To be fair to Dad, the mention of Uncle Jack did usually send Eliza off in a more reflective direction and calm her down a bit - but not this morning.

"Jack is family, our family, and don't think I haven't worked out who it was who drove him away!"

"For goodness sake!" Mum shouted after ten minutes of needling. She was looking really hot as she retrieved a tray of buns from the oven, "Can't you two manage to be civil to one another for one day? It's Kitty's birthday in case you have forgotten and...," pausing to take off the oven gloves and point at Eliza, "You were the one who wanted it to be a family party so it would be nice if you could give me a hand getting it ready." Turning back to the oven she told Dad to go out and keep an eye on Kitty and as soon as he opened the door, Pal shot out ahead of him.

"I didn't mean Henry and his bastard daughter, I meant OUR family!" Eliza stood up and banged her hand on the table.

"Well hard luck!" Grandad shouted back, "They are coming and they are part of our family. What I want to know is why you have invited that toothless old crow Fanny Freeman. You know she frightens the kids, the wizened up old bag, and she stinks to high heaven."

"Miss Freeman is my friend and the children are only frightened of her because you call her these terrible names." Eliza took a deep breath in an effort to compose herself, "After the sacrifices that woman has made in her life I think she deserves a bit more respect, especially from people like you!" Her eyes were flashing as she tried to raise her small frame up in front of Grandad who suddenly looked furious.

"People like me?" his voice deep with anger.

"Yes, people like you!" She spat the words at him and for a few long seconds no one moved or spoke. The impasse was broken as Eliza let out a sigh and in a much gentler voice stated that she would go and spend some time with Kathryn in the garden.

Kitty had been out there since she had been given her big present. A three-wheel bike with a large red bread bin boot which she had filled with her dolls. When I went out a few minutes later, she was riding up and down the drive under the watchful gaze of Pal who trotted back and forward on the lawn, vigilantly on the lookout for any danger or hazard that might befall her. Although Dad was out there too, he was really just keeping out of the way of his parents and their ongoing hostilities. He came back in as soon as Eliza went out and he and Grandad went to the dining room to look at some work papers together.

"Mum, what's a bastard?" I asked without looking at her. She tapped my head with the wooden spoon she was holding.

"Don't try and be smart Philip, I am not in the mood for it today. If you really want to play that game, go and ask Eliza."

"Sorry," I muttered and wiped the jam off my mouth with the back of my hand, "Can I go and call for John and see if he wants to come round?"

"No you can't. There will be enough people here and you heard Eliza, it's a family party."

"Old Fanny Freeman's not family," I said sulkily before I could stop myself. Old Fanny Freeman the doctor's sister was even scarier than her

133

brother.

"*Miss* Freeman is Eliza's friend and I don't want to hear you call her that again. And...," she raised her hand quickly to stop my predictable interrupting, "Sunny Bank may be our home but that is only because Eliza and Grandad are kind enough to allow us to live here. This is their house and if either of them wants to invite people to come round, that is up to them." She turned back to the sink and picked up the tea towel. "Now are you going to help me make a cheese and pineapple hedgehog or what?"

Half an hour later, Kitty came running into the kitchen asking for a birthday biscuit. Mum told her she could not have one and to stop dashing around and making herself hot. She gave her a beaker of orange squash that she gulped down before dashing back out and peddling fiercely around the driveway on her new three-wheeler. Once we had finished making the party food, Mum told me to go and get Kitty and take her up to the playroom and read her a story to calm her down.

"Can't I just go out for half an hour and have a ride on my bike?" I asked but was given one of Mum's looks as a reply so I got up truculently, taking another jam tart with me, and went to get my little sister.

Our attic playroom was an idyllic place. I know that now but back when I was nearly nine, being told to go up there on a sunny day when I would much rather be out with my friends felt like a punishment, an unfair and undeserved punishment. Kitty was not keen to come inside either and would only come willingly when I promised to read her favourite book with her; The Tale of Peter Rabbit. This was always an easy but boring chore for me. She loved the book so much and had memorised the story, well her version of it, and would sit on the old sofa with me and animatedly respond to each turned page.

I have always loved my little sister but there where occasions during our early years when I felt the unfairness of being the elder and assumed more responsible child. That Sunday morning was one of those occasions. After getting through the tale of Flopsy, Mopsy and Cottontail the obedient triplets and their naughty elder brother, Peter's, escapade in Mr McGregor's vegetable patch, I was feeling rather fed up with everybody, including Kitty.

"Let's read it again!" she beamed at me.

"No, let's read a different story. I know, let's have a look at one from Mum's special book." I went over to the high shelf in the corner of the eaves where the very old books were kept. The ones we were only supposed to look at when a grown up was there. Taking down the large dark brown volume of Grimm's Fairy Tales, I brought it back to the settee and carefully opened it.

"Will we be in trouble?" she asked.

"No, of course not – it's your birthday. Anyway, I'll just read you one story then I'll put it straight back and no one will know." She smiled at me and cuddled up as I turned the pages to find the story of Hansel and Gretel and nightmarish illustrations of the nasty old witch who ate children.

I had to promise to read Peter Rabbit again at bedtime to get her not to cry when I had finished what really must have been an Oscar winning rendition of the children's ordeal with the cannibalistic old woman. I also had to say that I would sneak one of the butterfly buns that Eliza had made, and Mum had hidden in the pantry, to her so she wouldn't tell on me for getting the book down and scaring her with it.

We went back down to the garden after flitching one of the cakes with pink butter cream without getting caught. I passed it secretly to my sister. She ate it quickly with her head inside the bread bin trunk on her new bike, spilling crumbs on her dollies and teddy bears. I had just given her my handkerchief to wipe her mouth when I heard the noise of a labouring engine from an approaching car. Glancing across, I saw it was Dr Freeman in his funny little round car. Despite the cloud of black smoke, I could clearly see him sitting bolt upright, nose close to the windscreen and his terrifyingly ugly sister beside him.

"I'm off back inside now Kitty; you stay here and play but don't go riding round on your bike now as the gates are open and cars are coming in." She was sat on the lawn and was cuddling the old china doll that used to be Mum's. She didn't answer but gave me a brief smile before giving her full attention back to Pearl.

From my bedroom window, I watched Dr Freeman drive out again a little while later, no doubt after his obligatory tot of Grandad's best whiskey which would not have been his first drink of the day. There was a screech of brakes just after he had narrowly missed driving into the gate posts followed by a furious honking of horns. Seconds later, Great Uncle Henry's dark red MG Magnette, driven much more elegantly, came down the drive and up to the front door. I glanced down at Eliza, still on the lawn, and watched Fanny Freeman plonk herself in one of the stripy deckchairs a few feet away with Eliza in the other one. Kitty was sitting on the grass, her new trike at the side of her, chatting away to her dolls as she made them comfortable in the bread bin boot. She was oblivious to all around her but I could see Pal a couple of feet away at the other side, lying on his belly with his head high and his eyes and ears set to vigilant. Eliza had been nodding and old Fanny talking and clutching a round black handbag on her lap while they both followed the progress of the car as it swept down the drive. Eliza stood up and gestured to Miss Freeman to stay where she was before striding towards the front door to allow entrance to Uncle Henry, Grace and Edward. Grace's husband was unwell apparently and so couldn't make the party and Uncle Jimmy was coming later as he had to see a man about a dog. I'd heard Dad telling Mum this and they had both laughed before she said he probably wanted to come late and leave early and who would blame him. I could not help but wonder if anyone was going to enjoy this afternoon tea party.

Eliza called upstairs to me to go down to the sheds and tell Grandad he needed to come in now. Dad said he'd go down and get him but Eliza wasn't having any of it, knowing full well Dad just wanted to get away a bit too and would take his time coming back. I ran down through the back garden toward the pigeon sheds but Grandad was already walking back to the house.

"Uncle Henry and Aunty Grace are here," I managed to say, just before the noise of Pal, barking loudly and consistently, made me stop, turn and run towards the side of the house. As I rounded the corner, Kitty started to scream and Pal was snarling as well as barking. Kitty was crouched at the side of her trike with her arms over her head and Pal was bouncing around ferociously at the dark hunched figure of Fanny Freeman who was backing away, clutching her hand and muttering what sounded like swear words to me. Dad, who had rushed over from the front, got to Kitty first and scooped her up, glaring at the old woman.

"What the bloody hell's going on here?" he asked sharply.

"What's going on is your dog just bit me for no reason," she answered, holding out her hand on which the skin was clearly broken, "I was just asking the girl about her dollies and he went for me."

"Dad," I called quickly, "Pal wouldn't have gone for her if she hadn't been trying to hurt Kitty..."

"You be quiet you nasty little boy," she snapped at me, her wrinkly yellow skin round her toothless mouth making her look terrifying. She turned to look at Dad who was stroking Kitty's hair, "That dog wants putting down, where's your Mother? Don't just stand there, go and get her!"

At this point I thought I would cry but I managed not to as I saw Mum, followed by Aunt Grace and Edward striding towards us. Mum took Kitty in the house and I followed, calling to Pal to come too. I couldn't hear what was being said but I heard the high crackly sound of old Fanny yelling and thought she might be arguing with Aunt Grace. As we stepped into the house, Eliza emerged from the kitchen.

"What on earth is the matter?" she asked, glancing at the grouping on the lawn.

"Old Fanny Freeman tried to hurt Kitty so Pal bit her and now she's telling Dad he has to have him put down." My words came out in a sob and Kitty started crying more. Mum carried her into the hall and put her down on the floor, crouching down to face her, placing her hands on her shoulders.

"Is that true, Kitty? Did Miss Freeman try to hurt you?" she asked.

"Of course she didn't!" Eliza snapped, "Why on earth would she want to hurt Kitty?"

"She did, she hurt me," Kitty said through her tears, "She hurt me and she was going to eat me." Her eyes rolled before her head flopped backwards in a faint.

Chapter Six
Alice - 1941

Alice and her mother, now homeless and with barely anymore clothes than they stood up in, had gone to stay with Mr and Mrs Williams after their night in the hospital.

"Just while we get things sorted," her mother had said.

Alice did not like Mr Williams. He was a sharp little man with a very hairy face and he looked at her without saying anything. Alice was sure he wasn't a nice man. She did not like the back bedroom of their house either. It was tiny and barely big enough to house her mother's personality, let alone her large curvy body, which rolled into Alice every night on the small single bed, pushing her into the wall. The sorting themselves out seemed to be taking a lot longer than they had thought it should. Alice heard her mother say there was some irony in the insurance company not paying out on the life policy on her Albert as he was their local premium collector. She did not know that most people were citing the bigger irony which was that, not only had the famous spiritualist medium, Barbara McLean, not predicted her husband would be killed that night, it seemed she had no idea that he had been spending a lot of time in the bed of Mrs Colbourne from three doors down.

A few days after the bombing, Barbara announced that she was going round to Model Road to see the extent of the damage to her home in daylight and to see if there was anything that could be salvaged. Alice begged to go and Barbara was so taken aback by insistence in her normally compliant child that she agreed. Mrs Williams had started to suggest perhaps Alice should stay with them and do some drawing on the kitchen table, producing some sheets of yellow paper from her husband's work. But Alice had been implacable in her determination to accompany her mother. Mrs Williams, also being a little taken aback by the child's forcefulness, had yielded and stepped back.

By this time, Barbara was cross with everybody. Alice heard her use words like 'humiliated', 'deception' and 'harlot' and so had become barely visible, hiding in the shadows of her misery, until her dad whispered in her ear on the second night she lay squashed against the wall with her Mother snoring beside her.

Alice left Pearl on the kitchen table in Mrs Williams' care as she accompanied her mother on the walk back to the bomb site that had been her home. Once there she did not spend anytime surveying the devastation as her mother did. Instead, as soon as she was free of her mother's hand, Alice stepped quietly towards the still intact door, closed as if to defiantly protect the threshold, and crouched down just to the right, to look at a small pile of rubble. Barbara was busy in conversation with Mrs Gaines and so did not see Alice lean into the sooty and gritty residue and pull something out. A few moments later Alice was again standing with her mother, with the dirty but undamaged copy of Grimm's Fairy Tales clutched to her chest.

Chapter Seven
Pip – Early 1960's

Pal had stopped snarling as soon as Dad carried Kitty into the house, but he stayed by the front door watching the continued arguments on the side lawn. Grandad called him in and shut him in the dining room but we could all clearly hear his out-of-character whining. I could see Mum trying not to cry as she sat on the hall floor beside Kitty, gently stroking her cheek. Grace came in and pushed me out of the way, crouching down next to Mum.

"I think she has fainted, she's breathing alright…"

"No need for you to get involved," Eliza interrupted, stooping down beside Grace and slotting herself slightly in front to edge her away from Kitty, "We just need to leave her be for a few minutes. Philip, get a glass of water."

Grace gave Eliza one of her evil looks but got back to her feet saying, "The girl has some nasty marks on her arm, looks like the old woman really grabbed hold of her. She probably frightened her so much it's made her faint."

"Rubbish!" Eliza yelled and we all jumped, "Frances would not have hurt Kitty in any way."

"Well I'll tell you one thing Mother, that woman better not come anywhere near her again or I'll be putting some bloody marks on her," Dad said in a voice I had never heard him use before and certainly not to Granny.

"Has she gone now?" I asked in as even a voice I could manage, as I filled the glass at the sink.

"No," Grace began, "We told her she should go but she says Eliza invited her and she's not leaving unless Eliza tells her she has to."

"We'll see about that," Grandad said, moving towards the back door.

"Tommy!" Eliza yelled, leaping to her feet, knocking the glass of water I was holding out to her out of my hand and dashing over to grab

141

Grandad's arm, "I'll go and speak to her." She finished with a deep breath and, smoothing the sides of her tied back hair, calmly left the house.

"We're not having Pal put down Grandad, are we?" I asked as he bent down to pick up the broken pieces of the tumbler.

"Of course we're not, don't you worry about that. Pal's done nothing wrong. Although if he did bite the old witch, maybe I should take him to the vets to check he's not caught rabies off her," he answered with a smile and then, glancing down at his granddaughter, said, "Pick her up Alice and let's put her on the sofa in the front room."

Mum got to her feet and leaned in, hooking her arms under Kitty's neck and gangly legs just as her eyelids flickered open and she started to murmur something. Dad was suddenly at Mum's side and bent down to take Kitty from her. Mum's face was crumbling with concern and I saw her quickly wipe away a tear. Grandad clearly hadn't seen how worried Mum looked as he said in a cheery voice,

"Looks like Kitty's coming round. Come on Grace, let's go and fetch Henry and Edward in then we can make a start on the lovely spread Alice has put on for us all."

"Her eyes!" Mum's high voice created a new panic that surged up to my throat. I tried to see Kitty's face but Dad, Grace and Grandad had all moved forward.

"They're black," Mum was sounding really upset now.

"Give her a drink of water and splash her face a little bit," Aunty Grace said in her normal authoritative way. Dad moved towards the door to the hall and Mum and went over to the sink. Grace started to run the tap as Kitty started to cry.

"Shall I fetch the doctor?" Grandad asked the room.

"I think she's alright Uncle Tommy, we just need to get her to drink some water and let her come round properly," Grace began, holding a new glass of water to Kitty's mouth, "Come on young lady, have a few sips of this."

Grandad decided I should go down to check on the pigeons with him to get out of the way for a bit. We took Pal with us and went out of the French doors in the dining room so we didn't have to pass anyone. I knew he meant Eliza. I wanted to go with him but I was worried about what my sister would say when she came round. As the events of the previous half an hour had unfolded, I had been filled with fear that this was entirely my fault. I had frightened Kitty with the story and I may well have pointed at the evil witch and remarked on how much the drawing looked like old Fanny Freeman – in fact, the wicked old witch could actually be old Fanny Freeman. Well everybody knew she was a nasty old woman who did actually eat children. It had just been a joke and something I thought would be funny. I never meant for it to make Kitty poorly or Pal get in to trouble or for Eliza and Grandad to fall out even more.

"Come on Pip, cheer up, no need for tears, you're a big lad now." Grandad handed me his handkerchief and I took it and blew my nose. I hadn't realised I'd been crying as I stood in the porch to his shed, lost in my guilty thoughts. I was just considering telling him what I'd done when Edward came down to tell us Kitty was alright now and Uncle Jimmy had arrived and we should come up to the house.

The rest of the afternoon was filled with the same family tensions. Aunty Dot and Aunty Peg arrived together with their separate broods and despite the fact that it had been billed as Kitty's birthday tea, once the candles had been blown out by my little sister; the kids were banished up to the playroom while the adults cleared the dining table for a game of cards.

Kitty was a bit quieter than normal that afternoon and I remained concerned about my part in her fainting becoming common knowledge, so I was doing my best to keep her happy. She had sat on the sofa with her old doll and I noticed she kept glancing warily at the high book shelf. Daryl had made a bee-line for the rocking horse and even though it annoyed me, I let it go. His sister Lizzy picked up Kitty's new Etch-A-

Sketch that Grandad and Eliza had given her and I went over to the big table with Macarno on it. Our eldest cousin Christine, who was thirteen going on thirty, asked Kitty if she'd like her to read a story to her.

"Don't like stories," she answered, shaking her head and looking like she was about to start crying.

"You don't like stories?" A male voice boomed from the stairs and Uncle Jimmy's head appeared as he dashed up the last few steps. He snatched up Kitty, giving her a hug before tossing her lightly in the air and then sitting on the sofa with her on his knee, "Well I am not sure I believe you Kitty Kat. I think you *love* stories, especially ones about Flopsy, Mopsey and Cottontail", and he picked up 'The Tale of The Flopsy Bunnies' from the small book case.

Uncle Jimmy read with such excitement and animation that all five of us listened and enjoyed his array of voices as he drew us into the story. The dark cloud that had been following me round for the last two hours seemed to dissipate with Kitty's squeals of delight as Uncle Jim tickled her while he acted out the story, and pulled her cardigan over her head at the bit where Mr McGregor catchers the sleeping bunnies in a sack.

Later that afternoon, Uncle Jimmy came down to the pigeon shed with me to top up the feed and water and, for some reason, I was compelled to confess all to him. I told him about how I had scared Kitty with the story from Mum's special book, the book that we weren't allowed to touch, and what had happened afterwards. I had started to tell him as we'd walked and had not dared look at him as I spoke. We were inside the shed as I finished my confession and I waited see what he would say. After a few seconds of silence, I glanced up at him and he let out a massive laugh. He had been holding his hand over his mouth but when he saw me looking like I was going to cry, he tried to pull himself together.

"Sorry, Pip, really I shouldn't laugh but bloody hell it's funny."

"It's not funny. I don't trust old Fanny Freeman not to make

Grandad have Pal put down. I didn't mean to make Kitty scared of her but she is scary and Grace says she must have grabbed Kitty so it's not all my fault."

"Well yes she is a bit scary but I think Eliza is right. Frances Freeman, Miss Freeman to you, would not intentionally hurt anyone. She was a nurse years ago and she was also a very brave woman, a bit of legend really." He sat on the bench at the back of the shed and I sat down next to him.

"Really? How was being a nurse brave?"

"She went to Spain with her brother to help look after children that were injured in the civil war there. Her brother, Dr Freeman, came back after three months but she stayed on, driving ambulances and organising other groups as well as doing her nursing."

"What, old Fann...." The words had just started to jump out of my mouth but I managed to stop myself, "I mean, Miss Freeman was in the war?"

"The Spanish Civil War. You'll learn about when you get to the big school." He ran his fingers through his hair, "She went off to Spain not long after the fighting started and I'm sure she saw some sights. It were too much for their Bernard, your Mum says it's probably the things he saw out there makes him drink as much as he does."

"So she stayed there on her own then?"

"Well there were others of course, from all over the world. I have heard that she took up with a foreign feller, was going to marry him and go and live with him in some far flung place," he said, smiling as he passed on the snippets of local folklore but then his smile vanished, "He was killed helping her get children out of France as the German's invaded – one war running into another. She came back a very different person."

"Were her and Eliza always friends?"

"Not particularly, I don't remember her coming round here much when I were a lad but, apparently, it were Eliza got her to start leaving

145

the house again. Shame she couldn't get her to have a wash now and again," he laughed. I didn't say anything as I sat trying to picture the bent over, wrinkly old woman being a war hero and having someone wanting to marry her.

"Come on, let's get back in and see if everybody's calmed down. No need to mention your story reading or getting your Mum's book down but you might want to try and be a bit nicer to Kitty in future, and maybe let your friends know that Frances Freeman hasn't always been how she is now."

Later that evening, long after my bedtime, I came out of my room to visit the bathroom and saw Uncle Jimmy coming out drying his hands on the sides of his trousers. When he saw me, he put his finger to his lips and smiled before stepping quickly towards the attic door. Opening it, he quietly stepped up the wooden stairs. I could hear loud voices and laughing downstairs. Henry, with Grace and Edward, along with Aunties Peg and Dot and their offspring had left before I was sent to bed and it was Dad and Grandad who seemed to be finding something hilarious.

All thoughts of emptying my bladder completely gone, I crept up the stairs behind my uncle. As I emerged through the hatch into the Attic, I saw he was over by the high book shelf reaching for Mum's special book.

"I remember this book," he said, smoothing his hand over the cover, "When your Mum first came here, she was only a very little girl, not much older than Kitty is now. This book and that old doll that Kitty's forever carrying around were the only things she had from her old life, before the bloody Germans bombed her house." He carefully opened it and smiled as he looked down at something before bending down a little to show me the inside of the cover, "It's special to your Mum because her Dad gave it to her and he wrote her this message inside."

Fairy tales are not meant to frighten you with dragons and demons and bad people. Children know that dragons and demons and bad people exist. Fairy tales are here to remind you that dragons and demons can be beaten and that bad people will never win.'

I nodded sagely with the reverence I felt I was expected to have. Uncle Jimmy held my gaze for a second with a searching look before saying,

"Your mum's dad, the grandad you never met, was a very clever man and he read to your Mum every night before she went to bed. He was the only normal bit of her life so it's amazing that she's turned out as well as she has. But it's not been easy for her living here." I could almost feel the gaze from his deep brown eyes locked onto mine and I nodded, not really knowing what I was supposed to say or even what exactly he was telling me.

"Keep an eye on Kitty while she's dealing with her demons and don't let Eliza fill her head with all her nonsense." I nodded again and he smiled before finally blinking and unlocking my gaze. I watched his lips move and he seemed to be reading the books inscription again as he nodded to himself. Then he closed the book and put it carefully back on the shelf. Even though I really had no idea what it was he'd been trying to share with me, I was keen to show him I had listened properly to all he'd said.

"Come on, you need to get to bed, it's late."

"Are you going back to Burntwood?" I asked.

"No, I thought I'd stay here tonight, your dad and grandad have started on the whiskey so I think I'll kip here and keep an eye on things, just in case."

"Just in case what?"

"Just in case Eliza winds them up again and it all kicks off. Your mum'll need a hand to calm 'em down."

I nodded, not having witnessed but having heard several explosive arguments between Grandad and Eliza, which had been super-charged by alcohol. I was glad Uncle Jimmy was going to stay. Like Mum, he didn't drink, claiming he had never liked the effect it seemed to have on people and that he didn't need alcohol to have a good time. He ruffled my hair as we went back down the stairs to the first floor landing and he quietly closed the door.

"Night, Pip," he whispered as he turned to go back to the adults.

"Night, Uncle Jimmy," I responded and suddenly remembering my full bladder I dashed into the bathroom thinking about dragons, demons and bloody Germans.

Chapter Eight
Alice - 1941

It was three weeks later that Alice first saw Sunny Bank. Eliza and Tommy had driven over to Armley to collect her and her mother, along with a small brown suitcase of donated clothes. Mrs Williams had also given Alice one of her old shopping bags for her to use to transport her two most precious belongings. Her treasured story book had benefited from a wipe over and buffing of the leather cover by Mrs Williams, who had admired such a proper looking book. Mrs Williams had also given Pearl a good wash and provided Alice with a new outfit; a clean dress and cardigan that had once belonged to her grown up daughter.

It was a crisp and chilly April day and Alice sat quietly in the back of the car clutching the large bag and looking out of the window as her mother chatted away for most of the journey. It was the first time Alice had been in a car and she was mesmerised by the passing scenery. The background noise of her mother's confident conversation phased out as she saw the image of her father, his head almost touching hers through the car window.

"It's going to be alright," he whispered and Alice smiled into the window, feeling his warmth.

"Alice!" Her mother's sharp voice broke her reverie with a start, "Mrs Hesketh just asked you a question." Barbara Mclean sighed and turned back to speak to Eliza, "She's always been a bit dreamy, airy-fairy like, but she is a good girl." Turning back to look at Alice, she said, "Mrs Hesketh asked you if you were alright, not feeling sick or anything."

Alice managed a peek at the fading outline of her father's spirit before giving her mother a quick glance. Seeing that Barbara's famous powers did not seem to have detected her husband's spirit, she bowed her head to look down at the bag on her lap and shook her head.

"Alice!" The warning of irritation in her mother's voice made her shuffle back in the car seat, her little legs sticking out and almost touching the back of the seat in front where the lady in the fur coat sat.

"Not feeling sick," whispered Alice, her voice rising an octave to manage the expected, "Thank you, Mrs Hesoo," at the end.

The woman in the fur coat bent around the seat to look at her and made her red lips into a big smile.

"That's good Alice. Hesketh is a hard name to remember so I want you to call me Eliza. Can you do that?"

Barbara tried to interject here but the lady lifted her black-gloved hand and insisted. Alice felt the warm breath back on her ear and she nodded and said, "Eliza."

Twenty minutes later the light grey Hillman Minx passed through the gates of the house and swept up the drive, pulling to a stop in front of lawn at the side of the house. Alice looked in earnest at the large pile of soil and pieces of corrugated iron that covered the lawn. The man with the hat got out of the car and opened the door for her with a kind smile. As she stepped out, she could hear the lady with the fur coat talking.

"It's a real mess and it's not as if we need an Anderson shelter. The house has got a big cellar that will give us much better protection than that heap of rubbish but Tommy thinks he knows better." She laughed a pretend laugh, "Anyway, come on, let's get you inside. This is Sunny Bank." She waved her hand in a large sweeping gesture and Alice faulted as she took her first glimpse of a house that looked to her like it was made of gingerbread and cake.

Chapter Nine

Pip – 1960's

The next time Kitty had one of her 'funny turns', I was thankfully at school and so completely absolved from any responsibility for her over-excited state which Eliza kept adamantly insisting was the cause of them. In fact, I had some issues of my own to deal with on that day.

It was six months after the over eventful birthday tea and a very cold Wednesday in January and there was snow on the ground. Even though I was almost ten, Mum would walk up to school to collect me each day, much to my annoyance, and she and Kitty would be waiting outside the gates to walk me home. On this afternoon, John and I were amongst the first out of the doors and, ignoring the gloves we both had in our pockets, we began picking up snow to make into balls. We'd been in trouble for throwing snowballs at the afternoon playtime but as we bundled out of the old double doors, the sight of the whole of the front entrance covered over with fresh, gleaming white snow was too much to resist. Not a teacher in sight as we elatedly fought our snowy battle with each other, ignoring the other kids as they passed to leave the school yard. John caught me with an ambushed strike to the side of my face that made me stop sharp. There must have been grit and stones inside the compacted snow as it really hurt and I fell to my knees clutching the impact point. John's jubilant laughter stopped suddenly, realising I was really hurt and he ran over.

"Are you alright?" he started to say but was interrupted as Mrs Thackeray strode over to us.

"John Rogers, what did I tell you earlier about throwing snowballs?" She grabbed hold of him by the shoulder, "Now look what you've done." She pointed down at me. I started to stand up and was about to say we were only playing when I noticed the blood on my hand and felt it dripping down my face and suddenly I was really cold. Luckily for him, John's mum came running across to us at that moment. She had apparently been outside the school gates watching us play and was hoping to speak to Mum when she arrived. Mrs Thackeray was then forced into a quandary. She obviously relished the idea of taking us both back into school and really tearing us off a strip. She was generally happiest when she was cross, but she didn't really want the responsibility of dealing with the nasty looking cut on my face.

"Something must have delayed Mrs Hesketh," John's mum said, firmly stepping between the teacher and John. I could see the teacher's hand twitching and knew she wanted to clip him behind the ear again like she had at lunchtime. "It's not too far out of our way to take Philip home and get this cut cleaned up." She bent down slightly and looked at my face before getting a lovely white hanky out of her hand bag and started dabbing the wound, "It doesn't look too deep but we'll let his mum check it out." She put the handkerchief in my hand, "Press that on the cut Philip." Then with a nod to Mrs Thackeray, she said, "Come on boys let's get going." With a hand on my back, she steered us both towards the gates and out onto Midland Road.

For most of the journey we were all fairly quiet apart from John saying how sorry he was and his mum saying he needed to be more careful in future. I said it was alright, I knew he hadn't meant to pick up stones as well but I was really feeling cold and my face was really stinging. I was trying hard not to cry. The hanky felt wet and sticky but I kept the pressure on and even though I had pins and needles in my freezing fingers, I dared not move it to see if it was still bleeding. I was worried that Mum or Eliza would want to call Dr Freeman out and that I might need stitches but Mrs Rogers said she didn't think that would be necessary.

As we walked towards the front door, it opened to reveal Mum with her coat half on looking really flustered.

"Oh Pip, thank goodness, sorry we weren't there, Kitty is poorly, I was...Oh..." catching sight of my hand on the side of my head and the redness of the white hanky.

"It's alright, Mrs Hesketh, it's just a cut. The boys were having a snowball fight." Mrs Rogers sounded nervous and put her arm around John as she spoke.

"It was an accident Mum," I managed to say through chattering teeth and then added unnecessarily, "I'm really cold."

"Of course you are, you all must be, come on in and get warm." Mum held out her arm to usher us all in.

"Well if you are sure, I think we could all do with a bit of a warm." Mrs Rogers's relief was obvious.

The small cut on my temple did produce a lot of blood and left me with a small scar that faded to nothing eventually. Mum cleaned it up while she waited for the kettle to boil and then made Mrs Rogers a cup of tea. John and I got a cup of warm milk and a Milky Way but we weren't allowed to go up to the playroom. Instead, we had to stay at the kitchen table with our two mums while they chatted about school and shops and baking. Just before Mum had finished her tea, Eliza came in and the niceness of the teatime chat evaporated in her chill.

"Eliza, this is Mrs Rogers, she kindly brought Pip home from school." Eliza said nothing but I felt her sharp eyes on my face. Mum added, "Pip fell over and cut himself but it's not deep."

Eliza stepped closer to me to look at the wound but still said nothing. Mum stood up,

"There is some tea in the pot if you'd like some."

"No thank you," she said at last, "Kitty is awake now and I've put the television on for her in the sitting room. You should go and sit with her."

Mrs Roger took the hint and stood up quickly,

"Thank you for the tea Mrs Hesketh, we'd better be getting off home now, it's getting dark already."

"You are welcome and please call me Alice," Mum said with her lovely smile.

153

"Betty," Mrs Rogers smiled back with a small nod.

"And thank you for bringing Pip home. It's been a bit of a day." Mum saw them to the door but not before I saw the narrowed-eyed glare she gave Eliza.

As the front door closed, I went into the sitting room to see Kitty but left the door open so I could clearly hear Mum tell Eliza that she didn't think it was necessary to be so rude to John's mum. Eliza said she wasn't rude, just letting the woman know what she thought of her and her Salvation bloody Army.

Kitty was lying on her side on the sofa watching television. It was Boss Cat, one of our favourite shows that we usually watched and sang along to the theme song together but that afternoon she just laid there so still and quiet. I sat in the chair nearest the fire and left her alone. Kitty's little turn had happened at a quarter past three that afternoon. Mum had been ironing in the back kitchen and Kitty had been with Eliza in the garden. After a little walk around Eliza's vegetable plot, knocking snow from the herbs and plants, they had come in for a warm. Eliza had gone upstairs to write something in her garden book leaving Kitty sitting on the floor in the kitchen. She was playing with her tea set and chatting away to one of her teddy bears and Pearl, who sat beside her. She had, apparently, suddenly gone quite and started shaking before falling sideways in some sort of a fit. I discovered this via Mum's conversation with Dad as I hovered in the hall when he got home. I had intended to make a big thing about my cut, which both Eliza and Mum had insisted didn't even need a plaster, when he and Grandad came home, but Mum looked so worried I decided against it and went back into the sitting room.

I crouched down in front of her intending to ask if she felt better but saw her eyes were closed so I gave her a little nudge and her eyes shot open and I let out a yell. I thought she must have gone blind and yelled for Mum to come quickly. I fell back onto the rug saying "her eyes, her eyes..." as Mum and Dad bent to look at my baby sister. Her normally light blue irises were almost completely obscured by the dilated pupils as she blinked and screwed up her face in an effort to focus.

Eliza appeared in the doorway with a glass of water and edged Dad out of the way, "Come on now Kitty, have a sip of this and let's get you sitting up, you've given us enough of a fright."

"I'm fetching the Doctor," Dad said, standing up and making for the door.

"There is no need for that," Eliza said sharply, "There, that's a good girl," addressing Kitty who was taking little gulps from the glass, her small fingers around Eliza's as she tipped it over her lips. I shuffled forward and could see Kitty's eyes focused directly on Eliza as she drank and the darkness of her pupils faded.

Eliza sent Dad to get a cold flannel from the bathroom and sat Kitty up properly once she'd drunk the whole glass of water. The panic in the room began to recede as Kitty seemed to be getting back to normal. Mum and Dad were still uneasy so Eliza said she would sleep in Kitty's room that night, just in case she took bad again, which went some way to appease them. Although she was a little quiet for the rest of the evening and didn't have any tea, she picked up a little. Mum spent a long time putting her to bed and reading Peter Rabbit stories to her. Although she didn't do all the silly voices like Dad did, she still made Kitty giggle. I lay on my bed pretending to be reading my book, listening through the wall. Something seemed wrong, out of kilter, but I didn't know what it was. I was worried about Kitty and knew that Mum was too and I was embarrassed by the way Eliza had been with John's mum. I didn't understand why grown-ups had to be so horrible and wondered if Mrs Thackeray would be horrible to me and John at school the next day.

As I pondered over these worrying thoughts, feeding a growing anxiety and feeling impending doom, I heard the front door slam and went to the window. Eliza was walking down the drive in her dark coat and hat. The snow was still coming down and her footsteps were disappearing behind her as she hurried down the path. Thinking she must be going to get the doctor, I dashed down the stairs to ask Dad. He said she had gone round to see Miss Freeman as she wasn't very well but said Mum was getting Dr Freeman round in the morning if Kitty still wasn't herself.

"So she's not going to stay in Kitty's room tonight to keep an eye on her?" I asked, feeling a mixture of concern and confusion. Why would Eliza go round to see old Fanny Freeman while Kitty was so poorly?

"No, I think me and your Mum will take it in turns checking on her but I think she's on the mend now."

I got up in the night to use the bathroom and noticed the light was on in Kitty's room. The landing light was always left on and neither of us liked having the door closed so I pushed her door gently. She was sound asleep and looked her normal pink self, lying on her side facing the door, both her hands as if in prayer, under the side of her face and Pearl was tucked in beside her. I watched her for a few minutes before pulling the door to. When I went back to my own room, my feet frozen from the cold oilcloth on the bathroom floor, I went to the window. The whole of the drive was white with untrodden snow, glistening with reflections from the massive moon and the orange street light down by the gates. I felt some of the anxiety dissolve at this site and breathed a sigh of relief before getting back into bed.

The next morning, Kitty seemed fine and so the doctor wasn't called but Mum did take her to the surgery a few days later. Dr Freeman listened to her chest and took her temperature and said she was perfectly healthy. Later, as Mum spoke quietly to Dad in the kitchen, she wondered if they should take her to a different doctor. Dad said what he always said when Mum suggested doing something he knew would upset Eliza, "Let's just wait and see how things are for a bit."

Miss Freeman died a few weeks later and Mum and Eliza went to the funeral. Grandad claimed to be too busy and Dad said he couldn't take time off work. Both of these excuses were seen as completely lacking in respect by Eliza but as always, Mum smoothed things over. It was a Wednesday and I would normally be at school but someone needed to look after Kitty. There was a terrible moment when I thought we were going to be made to go too. Eliza had said it would be good for us but Mum had one of her rare flashes of temper. She said she was putting her foot down; funerals were no place for children.

The service was in the morning but it was Aunty Peg who met me from school that day at four o'clock. She said Mum wasn't very well and Eliza was still at the funeral tea. Aunty Peg stayed until Dad got home from work and then Grandad drove her home. The house was very quiet that night, Mum stayed in her bedroom and Eliza didn't come home until after I'd gone to bed. I heard her shouting at Grandad and Grandad shouting back that she was drunk. It went on for quite a while until Dad went down and told them to shut up. He said he and Mum had enough to worry about just now and the pair of them should have some consideration for the rest of us. I had never heard Dad so angry and certainly never heard him so much as raise his voice to his parents before, let alone yell at them in this way. I laid awake and listened for a bit longer after he'd come back upstairs but the only sound I thought I heard after that was Mum, crying in her bedroom.

In January of 1964, John and I joined the four other boys and two girls in our class who had their name called out in assembly to be congratulated by our teachers for passing our eleven plus. It was a brilliant moment for me as I stood there beaming. The headmaster was telling the whole school about how, because we had worked hard, we would be successful and happy in our lives to come. We would not end up going down the pit or working in the foundry or doing any other menial manual jobs because we were clever and had made our school proud. I took a quick glance at John who looked as happy as I felt and I knew that it wasn't what the headmaster was saying that was making him smile. He was thinking, as I was, about how we were going to be rewarded by our families.

The next day I was given a brand new red Falcon EC72 racing bike with five gears by Grandad and Eliza. John's parents bought him the same model in blue. We had both been so excited and fuelled with the praise of our families and rode around Royston with beaming smiles, laughing and joking and thinking we were the luckiest kids in the world. We would ride through the park side by side, pretending to be cowboys on the prairie, whatever the weather. Kitty's funny turns became just something that happened; obviously they usually created a bit of a fuss but by and large we came to accept them as something that she got over fairly quickly. Eliza insisted that she was highly strung and that they happened when she got over-excited or upset.

Life went on without much drama, well none that I was aware of anyway, until one morning in early December when Kitty got so upset she cried practically all day. She had started school then and Mum let her stay at home. The cause of the distress was Pearl, who had mysteriously disappeared in the night.

There was chaos in the kitchen when I went down for breakfast that Tuesday morning in the last week of term before Christmas. Mum had been searching the house since Kitty had woken her at 6am when she had realised the doll was not in her bed. Dad and Grandad had checked the garden on Mum's insistence, even though everyone knew the doll had been tucked up in Kitty's bed with her the night before.

"She has to be somewhere!" Mum declared, with a wobble in her voice.

Everyone in the house understood the importance of Pearl to Kitty; she had never gone to bed without her but we also understood that this old and tatty doll was important to Mum too. Pearl was one of the few things from her life before the Germans killed her dad. I went up to the play room to have a look round, not really expecting to find the doll but keen not to see Mum cry.

Dad called me down, telling me I was going to be late for school. I passed Mum on the stairs on her way back up to search Kitty's room for the umpteenth time. I felt tears well up in my eyes seeing her so upset. I plodded downstairs taking big gulping breaths and quickly wiped my eyes on the sleeve of my grey school jumper. Kitty wasn't in the kitchen but I could hear her crying. I went to the back door to see her in the yard with Grandad looking in the big boot on her bike.

"You need to eat something, do you want some toast?" Eliza's voice behind me made me jump. I turned around and she smiled, "I've just done some but no one seems to want it."

"No thanks," I picked up one of the Tupperware bowls and poured some cereal and splashed milk on top, "I'll just have these."

Quickly wolfing down my Rice Crispies, I wiped my mouth on the back of my hand which I then wiped on my shorts before picking up my bag and running to the door.

"Straight home from school tonight Philip - don't you be messing around with that Rogers boy," she called after me but I didn't look back.

Even though we searched everywhere; Mum was detailed and thorough, retracing steps and journeys, we could not find Pearl and her disappearance remained a mystery. Every now and again, Kitty would shed a few tears, even though she acquired several more dolls, none of which she ever wanted in her bed. After a few days even Mum stopped looking and didn't mention the impossibility of the disappearing doll again. But I knew, even though I never dared voice it, that she felt the loss as much as Kitty and it marked some significant change in Mum, and as a consequence, the whole family.

Chapter Ten

Alice - 1941

On that first visit to what was always referred to as Eliza's home, Sunny Bank, Alice felt like she was in wonderland. Her life, even before the Germans dropped their bombs, was not what anyone would describe as homely. Her mother's important work with the church and her father's two jobs, not to mention his extra marital activities, left little time for them to interact as a family unit. Alice was instantly beguiled at the warmth and the light and friendly chattering, not to mention the wonderful aroma of baking, as she walked into the house, all the stories her father had shared with her forgotten.

The Hesketh children, James, Margaret, Dorothy, Jack and William were instantly besotted with the small blonde child with the big blue eyes. She emanated frailty they had never experienced before and they were all instantly drawn to her. To the ten year old twins, Dotty and Peggy, she was like a little doll for them to dress up and cuddle. Eleven year old Jimmy saw her as a delicate little thing that needed protecting from his boisterous younger brothers while the younger brothers, Jack and Billy, became even more animated and loud whenever she was around in order to catch her shy glances and giggles.

It was a massive relief to Mrs McLean that she and her daughter were so warmly welcomed in to the Hesketh family. As the horrors of the terrible war were taking their toll on so many families, her work had never been more important. She thanked God and all her spirit guides that had brought about such a fortuitous meeting with Eliza at the hospital. Yes it was true that she had lost her home and her husband and all the unpleasantness of where and how he was found but Barbara consoled herself with her own theory of why this had happened. The destruction of her old life and the accompanying pain had been necessary to propel her into this new world and the next phase of her work.

She was delighted that Eliza was so interested in hearing about her gift and understood how it could so often be a huge encumbrance, a burden even, but a burden she was happy to bear, as it enabled her to help and bring comfort to so many people. Alice heard her mother make this little speech often, to anybody and everybody, whether or not they asked. She listened as her mother had told Mrs Williams about how Eliza had been so kind that first meeting and how, as they parted, she had asked for an address to write to her to continue their conversation.

"There's a higher meaning to this chance encounter, you mark my words," she said, nodding her head sagely. When a letter arrived a week later with the offer of a few days away from the little room in Armley, an offer of a little holiday and stay in Eliza and Tommy's lovely home, it seemed that Barbara's ability to predict the future, had been spot on. That night at the chapel, she had told everyone about how the generous and welcome suggestion had not come as such a surprise and she had felt the warm bond the moment Eliza had held her hand when they had spoken.

Although she had never heard of the Hesketh family, she had guessed that they must be fairly wealthy, but the sight of house and grounds exceeded all she had imagined.

On the second night of their weeklong stay, Eliza asked Barbara about Alice and if she too was gifted with second sight. Barbara explained that it had been her dearest wish that her daughter would also have the ability to communicate with the spirit guides but so far there had been no indication.

Barbara had realised that her husband was not a believer as soon as she met him but back then he had seemed interested in her work and was keen to support her. However, that had changed very soon after they had married and he became indifferent. When Alice was born he actually became difficult. Although he never openly disagreed with Barbara taking their daughter to the meetings, she had been very aware of his disapproval and he seemed to be constantly trying to fill the child's head with fairy tales. In fact, the week before the Leeds Blitz, Barbara had confided in two of her close friends that she was convinced that it was Albert's influence and these silly stories that were blocking Alice's ability to communicate with discarnate humans. She told her friends that she was trying to work out a way to put a stop to him filling her head with such nonsense. Having said these things out loud, she had thought that she ought to feel some remorse for the way in which Albert had been prevented from reading to his daughter. However, Barbara Mclean was a big believer in fate and was happy to admonish herself of any guilt – it was unfortunate but all-in-all, probably for the best.

Chapter Eleven
Pip – 1960's

The Christmas of 1966, the last one before Uncle Jimmy died, was not a jolly time at Sunny Bank. As always, Grandad opened his betting shop on Boxing Day and Dad generally went to help him. So Christmas day was the big family day when Eliza held court, playing queen of the castle. It was always a big thing for her, she planned and decorated and cooked, all done in her way. Her children and grandchildren were bit players in her drama while she had three roles, producer, director and main character.

Thinking back to my 12 year-old self, I can see a sulky and irritated child who was not looking forward to spending a day with cousins I didn't like very much while the so-called grown-ups drank too much and quarrelled. As my mind wanders back to the few days before that Christmas, although I had not yet started to worry about my little sister, I did register that she seemed to be withdrawing even more into her own world. She spent hours on her own talking to her dolls and, even though I would not have admitted it at the time, I missed her sitting opposite me at the desk in the playroom. She would come up occasionally but generally only when someone else insisted, preferring her own room where she now had a bookcase and growing collection of Enid Blyton books.

On the Saturday morning of the week before Christmas, I came downstairs to find Mum on her own in the kitchen sitting at the table with her hands over her face.

"Mum, what's wrong?" I asked, making her jump. She quickly wiped her eyes on the back of her hand and stood up.

"Oh Pip, take no notice of me, I'm just a bit tired."

"Are you poorly?"

"No love, I am just worn down by your Granny and Grandad, always at on at one another."

"What's happened now?" I asked, not sure I really wanted to know.

"Your Uncle Henry, well Aunty Grace really, has asked us all to go over to Burntwood for Christmas day. She's invited all of us, your Aunty Dot and Peg as well and their lot. They're really keen to go...."

"Blimey, I bet Eliza's gone mental!" I cut in. Mum shot me a look and opened her mouth, I knew to tell me off for calling Granny Eliza, but then closed it with a sigh.

"Yes, Pip," she said resignedly, "Eliza has gone mental, especially since your Grandad has said what a great idea it is."

I kept out of the way for the rest of that day. Wrapping up warm, I cycled round to call for John and we went to the park where a couple of other lads asked us if we wanted a kick about. They were slightly older than us and made no allowances for our size in a physical and competitive game and I forgot my angst as I charged around, skinning my knees and splattering my clothes with the saturated soil. When they had scored their eighth goal, they lost interest and abandoned us to go off somewhere else. It was only half an hour later when John said it was nearly one o'clock that I realised one of them must have taken my fairly new anorak that had been on one of piles we used for goal posts.

"Will you get into trouble?" John asked as I wiped my nose on the back of my hand. I shrugged and said probably but didn't trust my voice not to give away my upset. Keeping my head bowed, I mumbled that I'd better get off home.

When I got back, I'd been hoping to sneak in and get cleaned up before anyone saw me. I was unsuccessful.

"Philip Hesketh!" Eliza's angry voice stopped me in my tracks as I tried unsuccessfully to dash from the back kitchen into the hall. Turning, I walked like a condemned man towards the kitchen. My Granny's anger at the state of me was, I know, just an outlet for the fury she felt over her Christmas plans being challenged. She had never raised her hand to me, or as far as I was aware to anyone, but it seemed to me she came pretty close to it that afternoon. Luckily for me, Mum came in just as her rage reached its climax.

"Eliza! What in God's name is going on?" Mum's presence jolted Eliza out of the disproportional frenzy and she staggered back but not before Mum and I had seen the semi-raised hand and acknowledged what almost happened.

"Go upstairs and get yourself cleaned up, Philip, and don't get mud on the towels." I didn't need telling twice, "And get a proper wash." She added as I shot back out into the hall. Breathing a sigh of relief as started to climb the stairs, I heard Mum's annoyance as she said,

"This has got to stop Eliza, you and Tommy need to sort something out. I am fed up of living in the middle of a battle field."

That evening, Kitty made one of her rare appearances in the playroom. We sat opposite each other talking about what we wanted for Christmas and what it would be like at Burntwood. Neither of us had ever been to the big house so the thought of finally seeing this place, talked about and described in some many family stories, was absolutely thrilling to us. Eliza always made it sound creepy and bleak and as we talked about some of the things she'd said, I saw Kitty glance up at Mum's book.

"It might be alright really," I said quickly, "I mean, it's really Uncle Henry and Aunty Grace that are scary and it's Christmas so they'll have a tree and decorations so it'll be alright."

"We won't have to stay there at night time will we? She asked with a little catch in her voice and I knew what she was thinking about.

The week before had been Grandad's birthday and Mum had gone to the pub on Saturday night for a couple of orange juices and to spend an hour with Dad. Dad, Grandad and Eliza went most Saturday's but Mum generally stayed in. With instructions to go straight to bed at nine, she had trusted us to be good and given us both a Cadbury's Flake. I hadn't been able to believe my luck as John and I had been talking that day about a horror film being on TV that night. Dracula, a Hammer Horror, film was on after the news at quarter past nine. We had agreed that it would be brilliant to watch it but agreed that it was unlikely either of us would be allowed. Completely forgetting the disaster of frightening Kitty on her birthday, I was excitedly planning out our evening as Mum was putting on her coat. It never occurred to me that I should watch it on my own and send Kit to bed, well maybe it did but I dismissed it as perhaps I was not as brave as I would like other people to think. Walking upstairs to bed on my own after watching the Prince of Darkness wasn't something I thought I'd like. And so my selfish twelve year-old self, in what I think was a feeling of rebellion, cajoled my sensitive nine year old sister into sitting up with me. I let her lay on the sofa while I sat in Grandad's chair to watch the totally unsuitable film in all its Technicolor glory.

When Mum and Dad got home, leaving Eliza and Grandad to a lock-in, every light in the house was on and Kitty and I were huddled together on the sofa. We were looking at the Woman's Weekly magazine that had been on the side table and had the radio on playing the Light program. I knew I was going to be in big trouble and no matter how much I had told Kitty that I didn't know it would be that frightening and I was sorry, I knew it wouldn't help me. Mum burst into the sitting room first and a mixture of panic and confusion passed over her face.

"I wasn't feeling very well," Kitty blurted out in a voice full of emotion, "We were just going to go to bed and I felt all funny and thought I was going to have one of my turns," she finished.

"Oh God!" Mum exclaimed, lunging forward to the edge of the sofa to cuddle her. "Did you black out?" She put her hand on her forehead to feel her temperature. I edged to the bottom of the sofa feeling a bit funny myself now. The Northern Dance Orchestra were playing a really jolly rendition of 'On Ilkley Moor bar t'at' on the radio and sudden relief swept over me, I had to stifle a giggle in what I hoped sounded like a cough.

"I don't know, maybe a bit, I had all these bad things in my head and

I was really scared." Kitty's eyes brimmed over with tears and Mum hugged her tighter. Dad appeared in the doorway and I stood up.

"I wanted to come and find you but Pip said we shouldn't leave the house so he looked after me 'til you came home." Kitty dropped her head into Mum's neck.

"Well done, Pip, good lad," Dad said, going over to turn the radio off, "Are you feeling alright now Kitty?"

"I think so," she murmured, lifting her head slightly.

"Right, well let's get you two up the wooden hill then, it's gone 11 o'clock." Dad's words were a bit slurred and he staggered a little as he leaned down towards Kitty, "I think a fireman's lift is in order."

"Billy!" Mum snapped, "Go and put the kettle on, I'll take them up." Dad looked like he was about to argue but then shrugged and staggered out of the room. Mum pushed Kitty forward, holding her at arm's length, looking closely at her face as if she was searching for something. Then she pushed her back on to the sofa, stood up and went over to the TV and put her hand on the top. Narrowing her eyes, her mouth went into a tight line and she looked at me. I lowered my gaze hoping she didn't see the guilt which I knew would have been plastered all over my face.

"Right," She said quietly but definitely in her no nonsense voice, "I know exactly what went on here and I am not pleased with either of you." I tried to glance across at my sister but could only see the top of her head. "You especially, Philip," I raised my head and shifted from foot to foot, balling my hands at my side. "Anyway maybe you realise now why you are not allowed to watch these silly films." She sighed loudly, "Go on both of you, get up to bed."

A quiet night passed and the next day I asked Kitty if she'd had any bad dreams. She said she hadn't had any dreams and felt fine. It seems the drama of getting caught out by Mum was enough to settle both our disturbed thoughts and the worry of how a stay at Burntwood would affect Kitty was one none of us had to face.

On Monday morning as I came downstairs, I could hear Eliza singing along to the radio and felt the relief of a frost-free atmosphere.

"Morning, Pip, would you like some dippy egg and soldiers? Me and Kitty are having some." I looked over at Kitty, who was sitting on the floor by the back kitchen door, stroking Pal, but she just shrugged so I said yes please.

"Here's some good news," Eliza said, beaming one of her over-the-top smiles, which was usually a precursor for one of her rages, "You two won't have to worry about having to go to the big house and having your Christmas spoilt after all," she concluded, putting the bread board and well buttered bread soldiers down on the table with a flourish.

"Oh that's good," I said, picking one up and putting it all in my mouth. I knew what was expected of me.

"Yes it is, Come on Kitty, leave the dog alone now and get your breakfast. Do you want me to take the top off?"

"No thanks Granny, I can do it." She wiped her hands on her dress and sat down beside me. "I wouldn't have minded going to see the big house," she said, picking up her spoon, "And Daryl says the garden is as big as Royston Park." She tapped at the top of her egg and began picking off the shell. "Why aren't we going Granny?"

"We always have Christmas here, that's why. Now you just eat your breakfast and think about how lucky you are to have this lovely home." Eliza slapped her hand on the table as she finished speaking and I was praying Kitty would realise she should just get on with her egg and not keep on about it. But she was either being really dense or deliberately trying to make Eliza mad.

"Will Aunty Dot and Aunty Peg still come here or will they go to spend Christmas at Uncle Henry's? Grandad said he and Uncle Jimmy were looking forward to us all being there as they've got so much more room than us." Kitty rubbed her hands together to dispel the little bits of shell from her fingers before reaching for a toasted soldier. I was holding my breath, waiting for Eliza to explode. I chanced a little glance up at her and saw her face was red with anger.

"Did he indeed?" She said through gritted teeth, "Well they can just think again, all of them, because we are having our Christmas day here and that is the end to it." She slammed the spoon she had been holding down hard on the table and stormed out of the back door just as Mum came in from the hall.

"Let me guess," she began, "You've been talking to Granny about Christmas."

"It wasn't me!" I exclaimed quickly, "Kitty just told her that Grandad and Uncle Jimmy wanted to go to Uncle Henry's for Christmas cos it would be better than being here."

"I didn't," Kitty spoke over the toast and egg in her mouth, "I said they had more room there and they do. Daryl says there's 100 rooms and it would be brilliant to play hide and seek there. Why can't we go Mum?"

"It was very kind of Aunty Grace and Uncle Henry to invite us all to go to Burntwood for Christmas but after talking it over with Grandad and Granny, we have all agreed to have our normal Christmas Day here but..." holding up her hand to Kitty to stop her mid whine, "We will all go over to the big house on Boxing Day instead."

"Granny didn't tell us that," I said.

"Well she is still not happy to do that but she will come round. Now you two better get on with your breakfast, I have some baking to do and I need the kitchen to myself."

Our Christmas Day was really great that year, Eliza made it so. Nothing was too much trouble, everyone was treated to her smiles and nodding fondness which reached new heights when Aunty Peggy arrived with a thickly coated chocolate log. Normally, Eliza would at best have been scathing or at worst furious about anyone bringing food to her home so her smiling gratitude was an unexpected and pleasant surprise. After a day of jollity and excesses, it was a very happy household that finally retired to bed at just after midnight. Kitty had been allowed to stay up until ten when Uncle Jimmy and the aunties and cousins had left. After lots of cries of see you tomorrow at the big house and thank you, I had been allowed another half an hour playing with my Scalectrix on my own in the dining room before Mum finally packed me off to bed. I put my head round Kitty's door to see her fast asleep before finally settling down to sleep myself.

I was pulled roughly and quickly from a deep sleep as pandemonium erupted on the landing outside my bedroom door. Grandad was calling out in pain and banging on the bathroom door. Eliza was shouting at him to go downstairs to the outside toilet and Mum suddenly appeared carrying Kitty and asking Eliza to get her some clean sheets. As I stepped onto the landing a sour smell hit me and sent a ripple down my throat. I managed to swallow it down initially but lost the battle seconds later when Grandad threw up all down the bathroom door. My hands over my mouth did nothing to stop the projectile vomit from spraying the landing. It took quite a while for Mum and Eliza, the only ones not sick, to clear up the misery and left the rest of us feeling wretched and exhausted and so there was no Boxing Day trip to Burntwood for us. Aunty Dot was also incapacitated, along with her husband and, although Aunty Peggy was alright, Daryl and Lizzy were both struck down in the night with a violent sickness. Later that day, as things were just about returning to normal, I heard Eliza say to Mum that it was a good job they had not had any of that revolting chocolate concoction Peggy had brought.

"She has always been a bit gormless but really, giving half the family food poisoning – well I won't be encouraging her again that's for sure."

Mum didn't say anything but I definitely think she was very cross. I wasn't sure if it was because of Eliza being unkind about Aunty Peggy or because she had been looking forward, as I had, to a day at the big house.

Chapter Twelve
Alice - 1941

That first stay at Sunny Bank heralded the start of a very different world to Alice. A world full of laughter and games, of playing outside in the early sunshine, something she had never been allowed to do before, and inside the large warm playroom when it rained. The old monochrome life she had lived as a bit player in the soap opera of her parents' marriage was smashed along with their terraced house. The drabness of their previous hand-to-mouth existence was gently disappearing. Something far more colourful was developing as she was welcomed into this strange and boisterous family.

Once out of the car, they went into the biggest kitchen she had ever seen so her mother could have a cup of tea and the warm smell of baking floated towards them. Alice was offered a glass of milk which she gratefully accepted, her eyes like saucers as she noticed the large bowl of jelly with tinned peaches and chopped up banana beside two large apple pies on the window ledge. Eliza opened a door at the back of the room giving her a glimpse of floor-to-ceiling shelves full of tins and jars. She brought out a large milk bottle and poured some into a jug and then, smiling at Alice, she half filled a crystal beaker and passed it to her. It felt cold in her hands as she lifted it towards her mouth.

"Don't bite the glass Alice," her mother said sharply. Alice, who had not considered biting the glass until her mother made this comment, instantly bit in to the rim inside her mouth breaking off a piece of crystal into her mouth. She didn't feel the sharp pain from the laggard fragment but the shock of what she had done, along with the rough way her mother grabbed her and forced her head over the sink, made her start to cry. Eliza was calm and gentle, telling them that it didn't matter at all, as Barbara spilled out her apologies and rinsed away the blood swirled milk and shards of glass.

"We are not short of glasses here Barbara," smiling as she spoke,

171

"Let's just make sure Alice is alright." She stroked Alice's blonde hair.

The Hesketh children continued to treat her like a princess, taking her up to the playroom and introducing her to Coolean the rocking horse, Dotty and Peggy taking it in turns at holding her on the dark red leather saddle and swaying her.

The bedroom that she and her mum were given during their stay was at the back of the house and looked out over the garden and towards the trees that lined the banks of the canal. Unlike at the Williams' house, she did not have to share a bed with anyone other than Pearl and the teddy bears that the twins had put in the bed for her to cuddle. Alice loved this room, despite it being sparsely furnished; just the twin beds and a small wardrobe and chest of draws. Its pale yellow wallpaper made her think of sunshine and the rose patterned eiderdown made her smile as she ran her hand over the silky surface. They stayed for three days in the end and Alice slept and ate well. She became so entrenched in the light and space of Sunny Bank that she forgot the dark shadows that had been filling her thoughts. Eliza said she had roses in her cheeks at the end of the second day. This made Alice smile as the image of the lovely eiderdown flashed up in her mind and when Eliza said they must come for a longer stay next time, Alice beamed at her.

The little girls head was full of the happiness and opulence of Sunny Bank and the fun and niceness of being there. There was little room for anything else in her young and impressionable mind and so her father's voice faded and his words of warning became a faint nebulous memory, dissolving in this shiny new world.

Chapter Thirteen

Pip – 1960's

When Uncle Jimmy died, things got a bit crazy for a while, even by our families weirdness standard. Thinking back, there was a lot of stuff happening during the months before his death and of course, knowing what I know now and the things that I see, well, hindsight is a wonderful thing; it was mainly about dwindling fortunes and Eliza's refusal to be poor.

Grandad Tommy was probably the worst businessman in history - how many bookmakers have you ever heard of going bankrupt? Although to be honest, I think his bankruptcy was fairly low down on the family's worries. The year before his insolvency was formalised, he embarked on a path that almost cost him his freedom. As I mentioned before, he made some terrible decisions about his business. When he bought his own shop in 1961, it seemed like he had finally made it and the money poured in for a few years but there was little or no record keeping and certainly no reinvesting or putting money aside. Then word started to spread amongst the punters that Grandad Tommy was a bit of a soft touch and could be talked into tearing up some I.O.U's. Things started to slide and he went from one poorly judged, bad decision to another. However, never was his judgment more in question than when he took on a business partner at the start of the year in 1967. David Murphy was a salt of the earth type, an all round great bloke who everybody liked, especially as he appeared to always have a lot of cash and was very generous at buying drinks. He was, however, also a con man with a string of other identities and a trail of ruined businesses and broken families behind him. The good news for our family was that the police finally arrested him in June of that year, early enough in the partnership for him not to have cleaned Grandad out completely. But the bad news was that he implicated Grandad in his scam. The police had been after Murphy for a while as they knew he had been involved in a robbery at some stables near Leeds where one of the stable lads had been killed. The only thing that saved Grandad from prison was that he wasn't previously known to them. He was held at the police station initially and re-interviewed a number of times but, according to Daryl, who always seemed to know everything that was going on, "he squawked like a canary," and was the prosecution's star witness in the trial a year later. Even though Grandad wasn't charged until September, rumour spread very quickly about dodgy dealings after Murphy was arrested and most days, throughout that summer, the only customers in the shop were there to claim some past grievance or that they had been short changed or miss-sold a transaction. Although Kitty and I were not really aware of what was happening, it was clear that something bad was going down and Sunny Bank stopped being quite so great a place to be.

While I am in this memory of that troubling time, I recall Eliza's voice criticising Grandad at every opportunity and on one evening in particular, I think it was the Saturday after the July race meeting at Newmarket when she had spent the afternoon at the shop. I remember her being particularly viscous. She had gone along to supposedly help out but I think it was more to fend off the difficult customers. Kitty and I were in the playroom out of the way as one look at Eliza's face when they came back was enough for us to know there was going to be a row.

"You are a weak and pathetic excuse for a man, a total failure, I rue the day I married you!"

In September, Grandad was charged as an accessory in the illegal betting scam. The whole case against him seemed to centre on a race at the Ebor Festival in York when a horse called Ovaltine won at 100-8. Murphy was no longer at the shop although he was out on bail. Grandad had sworn to the police and the family that he had no contact with him but I saw them both out of Kitty's bedroom window, down the bottom of our garden, the night before the race, talking and laughing just outside the pigeon shed.

Kitty and I were at school when the police came and took him away and, of course, we weren't told anything, just a 'never you mind and go and play' whenever we asked where he was in the couple of days that he was helping with inquiries.

Mum and Dad went over to beg Uncle Henry to pay for a lawyer and bail him, which he did, but there was a period of around two weeks when there was a real possibility that Grandad would go to prison. Mum and Dad were really upset and Eliza was furious with everyone, including me and Kitty, so we were careful to keep well out of the way. But one Sunday night, around the end of October, Uncle Jimmy came round quite late. I heard the front door open and close and hearing his voice I got out of bed. I was just about to go downstairs, pretending I wanted a drink of water, when I heard Grandad say quite loudly,

"Not all this bloody nonsense again!"

"Nonsense is it?" Eliza responded with fury, "You're a bloody liar and a fool and I certainly won't be shedding any tears when they lock you up. I hope they throw away the key!"

I crouched in the corner at the top of the stairs and listened as they continued their shouting match, occasionally hearing Mum or Dad or Uncle Jimmy trying to calm them both down. I moved a bit further forward to try and hear some of what was being said but it was hard because after a while they were all shouting. I glanced across at Kitty's door which wasn't properly closed and wondered if she was listening in her bed. I was just thinking about going in to see when I heard Eliza screaming at Uncle Jimmy, calling him selfish and heartless. Uncle Jimmy shouted back that she was a fine one to talk about being heartless and that he was sick and tired of all her scheming. There was a sound like someone getting a slap and Eliza yelling that he had abandoned his family and broken her heart. There was a slight pause before I heard Grandad say in a much calmer voice,

"Don't you dare talk about family? You are the one that has

destroyed this family with your nasty and deceitful ways and you never had a heart to break." There was the sound of scuffling then and Mum's voice was pleading with all of them to stop as it was getting them nowhere.

"Alice, if you know what's good for you, you'll get Billy to take that job in Leeds and take Pip and Kitty as far away from here as possible." Uncle Jimmy wasn't shouting but he had moved nearer the hall.

"Alice and Billy are going nowhere," Eliza shouted, "This is their home and don't you come round here with your lies and stories!"

"But they're not lies are they mother?" Jimmy shouted, in a voice so full of anger I held my breath. Uncle Jimmy never lost his temper or raised his voice. I felt my eyes starting to prick with tears of shock and I stood up. There was a thud from Kitty's room and suddenly Mum was running up the stairs. She paused slightly, seeing me on the landing and pointed towards my bedroom door before going into Kitty's room. I went back to my bed and waited there. It had gone quiet downstairs but I sat in complete silence waiting. Mum came in a few minutes later to say Kitty had fallen out of bed but she was fine and had gone straight back to sleep. She told me that everyone was really upset about that horrible man who had got Grandad into trouble with the police and I wasn't to worry about what I'd heard. It would all be alright in the morning when everybody had calmed down.

"Will Uncle Jimmy stay tonight?" I asked.

"No, he needs to get back to Burntwood, he'll be off soon. Come on now you need to get into bed." She told me not to talk to Kitty about it as the last thing she needed was for her to have one of her funny turns. I said I wouldn't but asked if Grandad would go to prison.

"No, he won't go to prison but he will probably lose the shop," she said, in a quite matter of fact way, "There will be some changes over the next few months but we will all be alright so no need for you to worry."

"Will we be moving to Leeds?" I blurted out."My my, you have been ear-wigging haven't you?" Mum said, frowning as she ran her fingers through her hair and sat down on the edge of my bed.

"It was hard not to hear, everyone was shouting so loud."

"Well, we haven't decided yet about Leeds but we might have to consider it. All this business with the shop and police might mean that Grandad has to sell Sunny Bank."

"No!" I yelled. Mum held up her hand.

"We don't know yet but it's something we all might have to face. Uncle Jimmy has found a job in Leeds and it comes with a house so Grandad and Eliza wouldn't need to worry about us." She looked down at her hands and paused a little before adding, "But like I said, nothing has been decided yet, we'll just have to wait see what happens over the next few weeks." Pulling my eiderdown up to my chin she smiled at me, "Anyway you need to get some sleep now, I'm going to make Uncle Jimmy some cocoa before he goes home." She ruffled my hair, "Night, Pip."

I fell asleep soon after that and didn't hear Uncle Jimmy go. Mum told me later that he had popped upstairs to see me before he left but I was asleep. I never saw him alive again.

The day after this outburst, Grandad cut a deal with the police. He agreed to tell all he knew and the charges against him were dropped. Tommy Heskeths betting shop, against all odds, managed to survive the scandal and keep going for a little while longer. However, it was still in dire straits, not helped by a massive outbreak of foot and mouth disease that had started in October in the farming community. It was so severe and the virus spread so rapidly that the government brought in an embargo on all animal movement. Even though horses are not susceptible to the virus, they were included and movement of racehorses was also prohibited when they introduced a ban on all race meetings for the last two months of the year, despite the suspension costing government about £1m a day in lost taxes. Luckily, there was still greyhound racing and people still wanted to bet. Grandad opened the shop between eleven and three during the day but stayed in the back room for most of the time while Mum and Eliza manned the counter. He opened up again at five and Dad went there straight from work and stayed until half past seven while the evening meetings were on. They all worked hard over those months, despite all the other stuff that was going on, or maybe because of it. No one ever mentioned the job in Leeds again and, for a little while, Grandad became solvent. I buried the notion that Sunny Bank might have to be sold deep in the back of my mind and convinced myself that everything was alright. That lasted for about a week.

It was just before eight o'clock and I was in the hall putting my coat on, ready to go to school. It was Monday 6th November and Mum and Eliza were in the kitchen. Grandad was down the garden with the pigeons and Kitty was coming downstairs. The telephone started to ring, making me start a little bit. I turned round quickly to pick up the receiver and almost fell over Pal who was standing in wait for my sister. Trying to remember what Mum and Eliza had said about how to answer the phone properly, I said,

"Hello, Philip Hesketh speaking. Who is calling?"

"Philip, please can you put your Grandad on the telephone," Aunty Grace's clipped voice sounded a bit shaky.

"He's down the garden with his pigeons," I told her, "Granny's in the kitchen, shall I get her?" I asked.

"Good God no!" came her answer quickly, "Please go and get Tommy and tell him I need to speak to him urgently." I was about to tell her I didn't have time when she hung up.

"Kitty, run down the garden and tell Grandad he has to call Aunty Grace on the telephone and tell him it's urgent, I've got to go now or I'll miss the bus."

"What's going on Pip, who was that on the phone?" Mum came into the hall.

"It was Aunty Grace; she wants to talk to Grandad. I have to go or I'll miss my bus." I moved towards the back door and Kitty followed me. I walked quickly round the house towards the gate and saw Mum on the door step watching Kitty running down the garden.

When I got home from school that night, Mum was in the kitchen standing by the sink, holding the tea towel to her face.

"Mum, what's wrong?"

Aunty Grace had found Uncle Jimmy dead in his bed that morning. Normally an early riser, she had thought it was odd that he hadn't come down for breakfast and then didn't get an answer when she'd knocked on his door. She had called an ambulance even though she could clearly see that it was too late, he was already cold. His dead body was taken to the hospital for the doctors to establish just why a seemingly healthy 37 year-old should have passed away in his sleep. Grandad had gone over to Burntwood and Dad had come home from work early. Eliza was in her bedroom and Mum told me to look after Kitty, who was in her bedroom, and that we should not bother anyone. I went straight in to see Kitty after putting my satchel in my own room. She was sitting on the wide window ledge looking down the garden.

"Hiya," I said softly, "Mum's just told me about Uncle Jimmy, it's really sad."

"Yes it is," she answered without looking round, her voice a bit odd, "It wasn't his time."

I walked over to her to look at her and to see what she was looking at. I bent my head as I touched her shoulder and she started and let a sudden yelp.

"Pip! You made me jump!" she said with her normal voice.

I looked at her for a second, worrying she was going to have one of her little episodes, but she looked ok.

"What are you looking at?" I asked.

179

"I was watching Grandad down with the pigeons; he's just sitting on the bench looking really sad." I looked down the garden.

"You can't see the bench from here; it's round the other side of the shed."

"Is it?" she frowned, "Oh yes, course it is, oh well he's very sad. We have to keep out of the way. Do you want to go up to the attic?

Chapter Fourteen

Alice - 1941

It was the September of that year, six months after Alice's father had been killed, that they finally moved out of the William's back bedroom and into a house of their own. Even though it was considerably nicer than the one they had on Model Road, Sunny Bank remained an oasis to Alice. The new house was on Theaker Road near to the Spiritualist Church and Barbara now had a special room at the front of the house that she used to talk to the many visitors who came for the hour of hope and consolation she offered, for a small donation. If Alice was not at school during these sessions, she was told to stay in her bedroom and not make a sound. She would lay on her bed clutching Pearl to her chest and thinking about the Hesketh family and their enchanted home.

The long weekends and school holidays she spent there as she grew up were all glorious and happy, all except one. It was the third visit and this time Tommy and Eliza did not come to collect them in the car, instead they made their own way there, on a long slow train ride from Canal Road station, Armley, to Royston with three changes. Alice had noticed her mother's irritation that the previous chauffeur service was not available this time. Alice had not enjoyed the trip either but had remained quiet, not wanting to add fuel to her mother's annoyance. On the last train, she had listened with her solemn eyes darting around the sad faces of the other people in the crowded carriage, as Barbara muttered her displeasure at the inconvenience, completely disregarding the fact that the country was at war and others were making much bigger sacrifices.

They were met at the station by Thomas who took the suitcase from Barbara and smiling his greeting, asked how the journey had been.

"It was terrible, Tommy, we had to change three times," she began, taking hold of Alice's hand, "And the trains are so dirty and expensive," her voice raised to emphasise the fact that she had had to pay for the

181

travel. Tommy said nothing and Alice saw her mother's shoulders droop a little on realising he wasn't going to offer to reimburse her. They walked on in silence for a little until, begrudgingly, Barbara added,

"At least we had a carriage to ourselves on that last train, which was something I suppose."

"Mum," Alice said, suddenly startled at her mother's lie, and let go of her hand. All three of them stopped and Alice felt a flush as both adults looked at her.

"Alice, what have I told you about interrupting when grownups are talking." She took hold of Alice's hand again, tugging her a little, and resumed her one-sided conversation.

Alice smiled at the sight of the house as Tommy opened the gates and they had only taken a couple of steps on the drive when Peggy and Dotty came tearing towards them calling her name. Parked in front of Thomas's grey car was a bigger black car. The driver's door was open and an old man was sitting sideways on the seat with his legs out of the car and smoking a cigarette. Thomas nodded at him as they passed.

"Oh Tommy, do you have visitors?" Barbara asked.

"Yes," he replied with a sigh as he opened the front door, "My parents are here for a short visit."

"They didn't have any trouble getting fuel for their car then?" she muttered her question at the floor.

Clara and William Hesketh had arrived only half an hour before Tommy had left to meet Alice and Barbara from the train. They had arrived in their new Austin 12, driven by George, the family's handyman. They brought a large box of groceries, two bottles of whiskey, two bottles of gin and a dark cloud of hostility.

Thomas brought Barbara and Alice into the sitting room to be introduced. Alice could feel her legs shaking while her mother beamed at the prospect of meeting more well-to-do people. William was sitting in one of the large fireside chairs and Clara sat on the dark leather sofa at the same side of the room. Eliza sat at the other end of the sofa, a hard smile on her face. The short visit seemed to last rather a long time to Alice and although it wasn't dark when they left, it certainly felt like it should be. Light and happiness seemed absent for the rest of the visit, even though Alice was aware of everyone trying hard. Her mother and Eliza spent a long time chatting quietly on their own and, although this was how previous stays had been spent, there was something really different about this one. Alice felt tearful and strange and so when two days later Eliza walked them back to them station to begin their homeward journey, Alice felt a surge of relief. That was until they walked into the carriage and she felt a low down tremor in her tummy as she saw the all sad faced people sitting in the same place. Her mother sat by the window, oblivious to the lost and tortured souls.

Chapter Fifteen

Pip – 1960's

The next few days were quite tense and Kitty and I adhered to the rules of the time about being seen but not heard. To be honest, I'm not that sure that we were even seen most of the time. All the grown-ups in the house seemed to sleep walk their way through the time they were there, except for when they were on the phone or when the police came round.

Eliza had gone to the police station the day after Uncle Jimmy died to tell them that Great Uncle Henry and or Aunty Grace had murdered her son. She was demanding an investigation and, according to what I heard, listening from the top of the landing that night, she was brought home in a police car after losing her temper when she thought they weren't taking her seriously. A policeman came back the next day to tell her that the hospital had concluded Uncle Jimmy died of natural causes. Apparently, it was discovered that he had always had a weak heart and it had just given up. As soon as the policeman left, Eliza went straight up to her room but half an hour later when Uncle Henry and Aunty Grace arrived, she charged back downstairs. Kitty and I were immediately sent up to the playroom.

We sat at the top of the stairs for a while waiting for Eliza to explode but it didn't happen, even when I clearly heard Uncle Henry saying that Eliza's hysterics had prevented him from making the proper funeral arrangements. I was sure that Granny would start saying she wasn't having him involved but she didn't. I actually didn't hear her say very much at all. She was totally compliant with everything Henry said about Uncle Jimmy having a proper Hesketh burial.

"Would you like him bringing home?" Aunt Grace asked.

"No!" she said loudly, "I want him laid out at Burntwood, open casket, and the wake there afterwards."

"Right," said Uncle Henry with surprise in his voice, "Well if that's what you want, we will be happy to arrange all that."

"Are you sure about the open casket Eliza?" Mum asked.

"I am certain. We all need to say our goodbyes properly. Yes, yes, that's what we will do." We heard her voice get louder and realised she had got up and walked to the door so we ducked up into the attic so she didn't see us as she came upstairs and went back to her bedroom. Once we were sure she wasn't coming out again, we snook back towards the first floor landing to hear better. They were all commenting on their surprise at Eliza's calmness but Mum was still unsure about the open casket.

"I am not sure I want to go through all that saying goodbye ritual," she began, "And Pip and Kitty are definitely not doing it."

"I agree, Alice," Aunt Grace said, "It's not something I'll relish but we all know, if Eliza sets her mind to something....."

"Maybe we can change her mind," Dad said and Grandad cleared his throat as Grace let out a loud laugh.

"We are talking about your mother Billy. Anyway, I think her wanting us all to say our proper goodbye's is really about her making amends for what happened on the night he died."

"What do you mean?" Mum asked.

"All that unpleasantness last Sunday, goodness me, the things she said! She's probably mortified now that that was the last time she saw him."

"Never mind all that now Grace," Great Uncle Henry cut in, "What's done is done and now we have to give him a proper send off with all the dignity of a Hesketh."

"I can't pay for it," Grandad's voice was high and panicked.

"No need to worry about that, Thomas, I'll take care of it all," Uncle Henry spoke in a kind, warm voice I'd never heard before. Kitty nudged me and made to move back up to the playroom. I followed her up and we both sat on the old sofa silently processing what we had heard.

The days leading up to the funeral were quiet ones as we were all wondering how the day would pan out. Granny spent a long time in the garden on her own or in her bedroom. The whole house seemed restless and I woke up most nights to hear footsteps out on the landing as one or another family member paced around.

The aunties and their entourage came round on the Sunday before the dreaded event and, of course, Daryl was full of it. At one point, as he swayed backwards and forwards on the rocking horse, even though he was really way too big for it, I thought his head would explode, he was so excited by it all.

"Grandad's probably going to prison and Mum says Granny will probably get locked up as well if she doesn't stop accusing Uncle Henry and Aunty Grace of murdering Uncle Jimmy....."

"That's rubbish!" I interjected.

"No it's not! She went round to the police station shouting and carrying on and they had to bring her home in a police car."

"She was upset that's all and she's not shouting and carrying on now is she," I countered.

"Maybe but Mum says Granny is like a time bomb and...."

"Really, is that right Daryl? It seems your Mum's got a lot to say about me and your Grandad," Eliza said as she stepped up to the attic floor.

"You're in trouble now," I muttered with an internal satisfied smile.

"Come on then Daryl, don't go all quiet on us now. What else does your Mum say?" she asked, walking right up to him.

"Nothing." He was looking at the floor but I could see how red his face and neck were. He slid sideways off the horse, putting it between them and shuffling a little towards the sofa where his sister was. She was also a bit red in the face but managed a glare at him before saying,

"Mum's upset at Uncle Jim dying and she's knows how sad you are. She's worried about you Granny. Daryl's just an idiot who listens at doors and only hears half the story."

"We are all upset about Uncle Jimmy but not all of us are making up stories or spreading nasty lies. I'll be having a word with your mother Daryl." She gave him one of her looks, "And you are far too big to be on that rocking horse so keep off it." She turned to look at the rest of us, "I came to see if anyone would like some cake, if you can pry yourselves away from listening to Daryl's made up stories." She turned and went back downstairs as quietly as she had arrived.

The funeral was awful. I had asked Dad beforehand about the open coffin thing and how we would have to say goodbye but he had said Kitty wouldn't do this. He said she was too young. Eliza, however, insisted. She and Grandad had gone over to Burntwood the night before and had taken Mum to one side, telling her that it was really important to her that Kitty did it. I heard her say something like, "She has your mother's gift," and it was the only way to stop her from having bad dreams. She said Kitty was such a fragile soul and it had to be done – and Mum fell for it.

I suppose with all the highly charged emotion bouncing around the hard stone walls of Burntwood, it's not surprising that Kitty had one of her funny turns. Aunt Grace was vile about it of course but Eliza took charge and sorted it out quickly. But tensions rose again as we were all ushered into line outside the best sitting room by Great Uncle Henry. Mum and Dad had been talking in the car on the way there about how he would be desperate to take control and how Eliza would react to that. It looked to me like Great Uncle Henry was really struggling not to yell at Granny but he was just about holding his temper. Then everything was interrupted again when Uncle Jack turned up.

Although I had never met him, I knew the story of Uncle Jack. He had gone off to do his national service in the early 50's and, apart from one fleeting visit, never came home again. Daryl, of course, had lots of theories about what had happened to him. Most of them devised from his various keyhole listening and stories he had read in Eagle and Valiant comics. My aunties, Uncle Jack's sisters, always referred to him as the black sheep of the family but Mum and Dad always smiled and joked about what he was up to and what a great time he must be having when his postcards arrived from various places all over the globe. They were few and far between but Eliza had kept them all in the little letter rack in the hall and Kitty and I had often looked at them and wondered about him. Then suddenly, there he was, standing in the hall of Burntwood with a little coloured boy who he said was his son.

After the funeral we didn't stay too long, Kitty had fainted a second time while we were all bending over the coffin. To be honest, I almost passed out myself, it was a really scary thing to do and to this day it still makes my nerves raw. But the funny thing was, it was after she'd done her bit. She'd past the coffin and was standing with Eliza, watching, as Aunt Grace bent to say farewell, a fact that Eliza made a big about the next day but it took Kitty a long time to come round after this. She had already had a bit of a funny turn when Aunt Grace had spoken to us in the kitchen. So after the second time Mum was really worried. Dad carried her to the back sitting room sofa and said he was telephoning for an ambulance but then the undertaker and limousines arrived. Eliza and Mum were leaning over Kitty and I was standing in the door way watching as Uncle Henry led the pallbearers in and then out of the house with the, now closed, casket. As the coffin left the house, Kitty opened her eyes. I heard her mutter something, but didn't catch what it was, although it sounded like *gingerbread man*. Eliza held her up by her shoulders, her face really close, asking her what she'd said but then Mum got really cross and I was shocked to see her almost push Eliza out of the way. She said that Kitty needed some air and she had better go and bury her son. I saw the sharp flash of anger on Mum's face and clearly Eliza did too as she nodded and walked out of the room.

Mum stayed at Burntwood with Kitty and her newly acquired nephew, Raymond, while the rest of us went to the church for the service and burial. I only found out a couple of days later that when everyone had gone, Kitty told Mum that Uncle Jimmy had told her that they had to be careful. Mum told her that she had just had a bad dream and she should not to be upsetting Eliza by saying that sort of thing to her.

Uncle Jack refused the offer of accommodation at Burntwood, choosing instead to come back and stay at Sunny Bank with a beaming Eliza and care-worn Grandad. Just before we left, I went down to the kitchen to collect a tin of butterfly buns that Aunt Grace had told us to take home. As I came back up the stairs, I overheard her talking to Eliza.

"I don't know why you have to be so cruel all the time. Tommy is such a nice man. He doesn't deserve the way you treat him."

"Being nice is all you have left after you've failed at everything else," was Eliza's reply, "And I don't need someone like you to question the way I behave. I know you murdered my son."

"You can say what you want Eliza, we both know who killed James."

I stayed behind the door for a few more minutes before I heard them both walk away. I hugged the tin on my lap the whole of the drive home, sitting in the back of the car with Mum, Kitty and Raymond.

Our new cousin was a bit weird. He hardly said a word in the week they stayed with us after the funeral and he looked terrified of all of us and everything around him. He was quite scrawny too but then I didn't see him eat anything. I was relieved when I discovered that they wouldn't be coming to live with us all the time like Eliza wanted but once Uncle Jack bought his house on Alfred Street and Raymond started school in Royston, he seemed to be a bit less scared of everyone, well of everyone except Eliza.

After a slightly more subdued Christmas that year, when no one suggested we go to Burntwood, we discovered that Kitty had failed her eleven-plus exam. On hearing the news, Mum was really mad but when Kitty told her that she'd failed because Uncle Jimmy had distracted, her she went crazy. Since the funeral, Mum had been acting really odd and

189

was on edge almost all the time. When we asked him, Dad told us that she was still grieving over Uncle Jimmy and was a bit tired. He said they all had a lot on their plates just now, what, with Grandad's business and the court case coming up. He said we were just to keep our heads down and let the dust settle.

The trial of David Murphy was at the end of April 1968, just after Easter, and was at Leeds Crown Court. A police car drove up to our door at seven o'clock that morning to pick up Grandad, dressed in his best suit and heavily shined shoes, to present him as their chief witness. I don't actually know if he really was the chief witness but I do know that no one else from the family went along to support him. Despite this, cousin Daryl had plenty to tell us about what had happened when we saw him two weeks later. The trial was expected to last a week as Murphy and the three other men had all pleaded not guilty but instead, it ended after only three days when the two other men took a plea to a lesser charge and heaped the blame at Murphy's feet. In return for their cooperation, they were both fined and all three were banned from British race courses for ten years. Murphy was found guilty of conspiracy to defraud, fraud and theft and sent to jail for five years. Grandad, whose evidence was, according to Daryl, the final nail in the coffin, was presented on the second day and Murphy glared at him the whole time he spoke. At the end of his testimony, he made a throat slitting gesture as he nodded his head slowly. Grandad asked the police for protection but they told him that if you play with the big boys you should expect to get hurt.

It may be the things that happened later that have affected my memory and perception of the events but I am fairly sure that Grandad never properly recovered from the trial. Even the Brill Cream he applied liberally each morning could not control the wiry greyness of his hair. He suddenly looked old and frail. His business lasted another thirteen months before the full extent of his poor acumen and inability to control his own gambling habit became apparent. He was declared bankrupt at the end of May 1969 and the sale of the shop and other business assets went a small way to settling some of his debts. Terrible as all that was, we were all soon to realise that the nightmare was far from over.

Chapter Sixteen
Alice – Mid 1940's

In the following four years, Mrs McLean continued to enjoy long weekends at Eliza's home with Alice. She had begun to take an extra bag to bring back little bits of this and that, given to her by Eliza to help eek out her rations. Barbara knew that Eliza grew fruit and vegetables and that she had an ice house at the bottom of the garden. However, she had no idea where the sausages, bacon and tinned goods came from and quite frankly didn't care. She told herself that she was just being too polite to ask. She knew that the dresses and cardigans that came Alice's' way were clearly from the Hesketh twins but as for the endless supply of sherbet lemons and jelly babies? "Ask no questions get told no lies," was Barbara's philosophy.

On Wednesday 8th May 1945, bonfires were lit across the country in celebration of the previous night's radio broadcast. After almost six years, the war in Europe had ended. The following Saturday, Alice and her mother arrived at Sunny Bank to continue the VE Day festivities. It was particularly exciting for Barbara as this was the weekend she finally got to go to see Burntwood.

There was a garden party in the grounds for all the factory workers and their families and Eliza had insisted that Barbara and Alice go along with her, Tommy and their five offspring. Alice, now ten years old, was both excited and terrified but the Hesketh children were looking out for her as Eliza had instructed, surrounding her for most of the time and attentive to her needs and concerns.

It was the first time Barbara had met Henry and she shook his hand when Eliza introduced them. A little later, Alice saw the two women talking animatedly by one of the big hedges, glancing over at Henry from time to time. Her mother then closed her eyes and touched both her temples and Alice knew Eliza was asking about her brother-in-law's aura.

Alice looked at him, watching a grey sad light dancing around his shoulders. Then it changed to the pinkish red of shame as a girl approached him. Even though Alice had not seen her in four years and she seemed to be quite grown up, she recognised her as the girl from the hospital. There was a stiffness about both of them as they spoke but Alice knew their connection. She was close enough to hear snippets of their conversation. He was annoyed that his parents were taking the glory and thanks for the garden party when it had been his idea and he had done all the organising.

"That girl over there, is she called Grace and is she your Uncle Henry's daughter?" She asked Jack who was closest to her.

"Well, Mum calls her his bastard daughter and Dad says she's his adopted daughter." He quickly looked round to check no one had heard him, "But whatever, we don't like her. Mum says she's evil."

"I don't think she's evil," Alice spoke softly, "She's just sad. And I don't think she's adopted either." Her second statement was drowned out by boisterous laughing to the other side of Jack as Billy ran up to them.

Alice continued to take stock of her surroundings and as the festivities continued and cakes and sweets were distributed, her little band of protectors dissipated into the throng, all except Billy. He stuck to her like glue.

"Who is that silvery lady over there?" she asked him, pointing towards a frail looking woman dressed all in black by the rose gardens.

"That's Aunty Martha. She doesn't speak; she's a bit funny in the head."

"Oh no, she's not funny, she's just really sad." Alice tilted her head and lifted her hand to wave at the woman. Martha stood stock still for a moment then lifted her hand in return and gave a half wave before turning round and disappearing into the landscaped gardens.

"I think she's had enough, she's leaving," Alice said softly.

"Probably, she doesn't like being around people, she's used to being on her own in the garden." Alice smiled at him but didn't tell him that

193

that wasn't what she meant.

Two days later on the 10th May, Clara Hesketh found her daughter dead in her bed.

Chapter Seventeen
Pip – Late 1960's

As two studious and relatively shy grammar school boys, the violence of the argument between John and me shocked our teachers so much we were both given the cane and although we were made to shake hands afterwards, we never spoke to each other again. The argument started on the bus on our way to school the first day back after the summer holidays of 1969.

It had been a really odd summer full of difficult silences, punctuated by slammed doors and unpredictable outbursts of shouting and or crying. Kitty and I were more or less ignored as we made ourselves as scarce as possible. The weather wasn't great and we spent hours on our own either in the playroom or watching TV. As a fifteen year old, I had started to take an interest in the news and found plenty of distractions that summer to take me away from the issues in our household. The troubles started again in Northern Ireland, a pregnant actress, Sharon Tate, was massacred along with several other people by the Charles Manson's 'family' and man landed on the Moon. The radio seemed to only have three records to play and I got sick to death of hearing Rolf Harris singing Two Little Boys, Lulu belting out Boom Bang a Bang and the new bubblegum sound of The Archie's, Sugar Sugar.

I hadn't seen much of John at all and so was a bit excited at catching up with him. I was late to the bus stop that morning and only just managed to jump on before it left. John was already seated near the back and in conversation with Terry, a lad who was in the year below us and lived near him. Up until that moment, I had never seen him even acknowledge this boy and so was a bit put out. I walked down the bus and sat on the seat at the other side of the isle to them.

"Hiya," I smiled and nodded at him as I sat down. John glanced at me with half a smile but said nothing. Terry made a smirking noise and nudged John.

"You'd better be careful what you say to him, John. His granny might turn you into a frog or somat if you upset him." And they both started to laugh. I just stared in front of me for the rest of the forty minute bus ride as the pair of them sat with their heads together whispering and sniggering. I let them both get off the bus first before walking calmly down the aisle. I had intended to just ignore them until I had a chance to speak to John on his own but just as I got inside the school gates, I could see John and Terry with a group of other lads by the entrance to the cloakrooms. They were all laughing loudly and I just saw red. I have no idea what I said but I know I used some choice profanities and I know I was the one to throw the first punch. I discovered a little later that John had actually called for me a couple of times over the summer holidays and had been sent away by Eliza quite rudely, even though I had been in. She had never told me. John's father was among the ring leaders of the locals who had bad-mouthed Grandad, saying he was lucky not to have been locked up. There had also been an altercation in the Co-op the week before we went back to school when Eliza had shared a few choice words with John's mum, calling her a hypocrite and making her cry.

The school sent both of us home with a letter saying how we had been disciplined for the fight and how they never wanted any repeat of such an incident. That was when Mum and I both heard about what had happened at the Co-op; Eliza seemed to think it would make me feel better. Mum was mortified and I made a hasty retreat as she started to tell Eliza a few home truths.

I kept my head well down at school after that and spent all my spare time in the library swotting up for my exams. There was a great expectation on me to be the first Hesketh to go to university. This was something I had always known and accepted as my fate and so had never considered any other possibility. I knew I needed to get good grades in my O'levels and then stay at school for another two years for A 'levels.

The prospect of another two years at school with no friends and where kids sniggered and whispered about me, not always behind my back, suddenly seemed too hard for me to take. I was relieved when we broke up for the October half term but the night before I went back, Mum came into my room. I tried to wipe my eyes and not let her see I'd been crying but she sat on the edge of my bed and took my hand in hers.

"Life is really tough sometimes and it seems like there is no end to the pain we feel but I promise you there will be an end to it. Things will get better, these silly boys will soon move on to talking about some other poor soul and being horrible to them." She stroked my hair with her other hand. "In fact I would not be at all surprised if tomorrow when you get to school, all this talk about us is forgotten and replaced with some other bit of gossip." She smiled at me with her misty-eyed look that always made me smile back and I said a silent prayer that she was right.

The next day, the bus ride to school was ok. I didn't see John on the bus but noticed Terry right at the back so I sat on an empty seat near the front. A girl called Julie Harrison, who I knew only vaguely and had never spoken to, took the seat next to me and after giving me a brief smile took a book out of her bag and started to read. When we got off the bus, we walked towards the gates together in silence, but just before we parted ways to go to our own single-sexed parts of the building, she smiled and said, "See you on the way home." That was the start of our special and beautiful friendship.

A couple of weeks later, it all came out about John's dad being a bigamist and having run off with the Salvation Army funds and although I felt sorry for him, I could not forgive him for the things he'd said about my family and the way he had made me feel for the those weeks at the start of the term.

Julie wanted to be a teacher, had plans to go to teacher training college and took her school work very seriously. She was impressed when I said I wanted to be the first in our family to go to university and when I

197

said it out loud I knew it was true. In July 1970, I was delighted to show my parents and grandparents the letter showing that I had passed all ten O'levels, nine at grade A and one, French at C. It was the week of Kitty's birthday and there had been no party that year but Mum made a massive cake for both of us. Eliza wanted to make us one each but Mum had got quite funny about it and so Eliza had gone off in a sulk, taking her coat and handbag. I think that was the day I realised how much happier Sunny Bank was when Eliza wasn't there. It was a Friday and although she stayed out all day and no one had any idea where she was, none of us were concerned or had any thought of checking to see if she was alright.

I heard her come in really late that night, after eleven. Mum was watching TV and Grandad and Dad were at the pub. Kitty had gone to bed early and I'd stayed up until ten but had gone up to bed to read. The front door opened and closed quietly and I heard Eliza and Mum exchange a few words before she came upstairs. Grandad had been sleeping in the spare room ever since the day he'd first been arrested so Eliza's room was now just that. Although she kept the door locked when she was out, that was the first time I'd heard her lock it once she was inside and, for some reason, it made a shudder run down the back of my spine.

Wherever Eliza went on that day and whatever she did seemed to have had some sort of calming effect on her. She was nicer and less waspish, even with Grandad, and even wandered down the garden a couple of times to see the pigeons and ask him about them. I won't say that summer was a happy one but it was a big improvement on the two that had gone before. It was as if we all relaxed a little and the house became an easier and more companionable space, although I have to admit that my perception of how things were at that time was probably coloured by a serotonin overload from my first close relationship with a girl, a girl with whom I was completely besotted. Also, of course, I was out a good deal, doing my courting of Julie either at her house or at the cinema, at the library or just while walking around holding hands. I have no idea what Eliza thought of Julie and I really didn't want to know. It was enough for me that she smiled pleasantly and made herself scarce whenever Julie came round. Mum and Dad liked her and always made her welcome. Her parents seemed to approve of me although she was on a strict curfew and on the odd occasion when we were in their front room alone, the rule was that the door stayed open. Kitty loved Julie too and she was always trying to get us to go up to the attic to play board games with her. Kitty had settled in well at the local comprehensive school and made some good friends too. Although she had never invited any of them home, she did quite often spend long days and evenings at their houses. This was the only thing I remember that caused any friction between Mum and Eliza at that time. It was a Saturday at the end of September and I was doing some maths at the kitchen table when Eliza came in from the garden. She was carrying a washing up bowl full of blackberries, telling Mum she was going to make some jam and had thought Kitty was going to help her. Mum said she was out with her friends.

"She's never at home these days, running around Royston with these rough types and probably getting up to all sorts, it's about time you put a stop to it." Eliza seemed incensed. I started to pack up my stuff, sensing that I should make myself scarce.

"She is growing up and doesn't need to be hanging around here all the time. I'm really happy she's got some new friends and they are not rough types at all. I would have thought you would have learnt to hold that sharp tongue of yours, Eliza, and keep your unkind comments to yourself." Mum did not raise her voice but the harshness in it left no ambiguity about how annoyed she was. Eliza didn't answer, she just put the bowl on the draining board and went back to the garden.

I don't remember much of the Christmas of that year, except it was quite a low- key affair. Uncle Jack came round for a bit in the morning but left before dinner and the aunties and their entourage only came round in the afternoon for a couple of glasses of beer and some Christmas cake. Everyone was, of course, walking on egg shells, which was always the case when Eliza was on the sherry, but I know now that on that particular occasion, everyone was being very careful for another reason. Dad and Grandad had shared a secret with Mum who had insisted that Jack and the twins were also told, to give them plenty of time to prepare for the inevitable. I had not specifically been told but I had overheard a couple of conversations and saw it as my brotherly duty to tell Kitty. So that Christmas everyone in our family, everyone except Eliza, knew that due to Grandad's substantial debts, Sunny Bank had to be sold and there was no way round it.

It was two days into the New Year, 2nd January 1971 that Mum finally broke the news to Eliza. They were all in the dining room. Kitty and I were in the kitchen but I had pushed the serving hatch open slightly so we could hear how it went. Dad and Grandad said nothing as Mum outlined the reasons. Whatever any of us had thought Eliza's reaction to be to this news might be, it was not a sad smile and a slow nodding of her head. Everyone had expected tantrums and tears but she just continued to nod her head when Mum explained, her mouth set in that odd half smile she had recently adopted. Then she stood up and calmly walked upstairs to her room, closing the door quietly and turning the lock. This outward display of acceptance was so welcome, there was almost a communal exhale of breath. She had seemed so calm and completely compliant to all that was being said and done around her that we didn't stop for a moment to remember who we were dealing with. If only we knew of the hot rage that had burned deep inside her, we might have realised how it was completely twisting her mind and destroying any bit of reason she may have had left.

Chapter Eighteen
Alice – Mid 1940's

The year after the war ended, Alice had a problem. It was November, she had just turned thirteen and her body had begun the transformation into adolescence, which in itself was frightening but even more frightening was the attention these changes had brought from some of the gentleman callers who came to consult her mother, Mr Williams in particular. He was constantly popping in, without Mrs Williams, on every pretext he could find. He never said much to Alice but she felt his eyes running slowly up and down her body, making her shudder inside. Alice knew exactly what he was thinking and when she told her mother she felt uncomfortable with the way he looked at her, Barbara dismissed her with a slap and told her Mr and Mrs Williams had been good to them and she was not to start making things up and upsetting them.

A week later Alice was experiencing stomach cramps so didn't go to the Friday meeting at the church but staying at home instead, lying on the sofa and listening to the radio. Forty minutes after her mother had left, Alice suddenly felt the air in front of her change. Sitting up and putting her feet on the floor she was just about to push herself up when she felt a compression on the cushion beside her. She turned her head to look at the sad face of her father who just managed a smile.

"Go and bolt the doors Alice, both of them. Go on, be quick." She sprang to her feet and went to bolt both the front and the back door. When she came back into the little parlour, she was disappointed that she could no longer see her dad. She sat down heavily next to where she had last seen him, her eyes glistening with tears. Seconds later there was a loud knock at the front door. She sat rigidly still, hardly daring to breath. On the wireless, Billy Cotton and his band were playing 'S Wonderful and she felt her heart beating manically to the quickstep beat. She began to feel light-headed as she heard the sound of keys in the lock. A cry rose in her throat but she managed to suppress it as a warm breath on the back of her neck whispered, "Shhh my little girl. He can't get in now."

"Alice, Alice are you there?" Mr Williams' voice came through the letterbox, "Your mum says you're not well so I've come to see if you're alright." He tried the key again then knocked again before lifting the flap again, his voice not quite so friendly this time, "Open the door Alice, come on you silly girl, let me in." Still getting no response, he dropped the flap and Alice leaned back on the sofa and closed her eyes. Without the need of sight, she watched him walking round the house to the back and trying to peer in through the small kitchen window before trying the back door. Finally after a good half an hour, he gave up.

Alice did not tell her mother, she didn't fancy another slap, but she did tell Eliza the following weekend when they were at Sunny Bank. She had chosen her moment, getting up really early on the second day of their visit, knowing Eliza would be alone in the kitchen. She spoke quietly, explaining what happened on the night she was home alone and how scared she was of the way Mr Williams looked at her. When she had finished, Eliza nodded and put a hand on Alice's arm, the closest Eliza ever got to emotional attachment, and said,

"Well we can't have that sort of carry on. You just leave it with me Alice love. I'll see what I can do."

Later that day, as it was raining, Alice was in the playroom with Jack and Billy, playing monopoly on the floor. The twins, both of them now engaged, were out with their boyfriends and James was down at the pigeon shed with his dad. As usual, Jack was the banker, surreptitiously embezzling money, which Alice ignored and Billy was completely unaware of. As Jack landed on Go to Jail for the second time, he flicked the racing car across the room cursing the stupid game.

"Anyway, no point in playing anymore, Alice is going to win, she's got the spirits helping her so no point in carrying on," Jack laughed getting to his feet.

"Shut up, Jack," Billy blurted out, flushing and standing up.

"Don't tell me to shut up - you were the one that said she could see the future, that she was a medium like her mum." Jack pushed Billy in the shoulder. Alice looked at Billy.

"That's not what I said, I just said that I thought that you might see things sometimes....."

"Well I don't!" Alice snapped in alarm, glaring at Billy.

"Well you said...," he began. His gaze flickered from her to the floor and over to his brother. He was saved from having to explain what she had said that had prompted his belief by a shrill and affected voice resonating up the stairs.

"Alice, Alice," Mrs McLean's piecing cry penetrated the friction in the playroom. "Alice come down here, I need to talk to you."

It had been decided that after Christmas, Alice would come and live at Sunny Bank. Barbara told her daughter, as if it had been her idea, that she would be better off there. Even though the war had been over for five years, there was still rationing, although that didn't seem to affect the Heskeths and it would give her mother more time to peruse her good work with all the poor bereaved. And that was exactly what happened and although Alice never saw it, she was fairly sure that her mother was compensated financially as part of the arrangement for handing her over.

Chapter Nineteen

Pip

It was the end of April 1971 that Grandad and Granny moved out of Sunny Bank. Mum, Dad, Kitty and me had moved out four weeks earlier at the end March, at the start of the Easter holidays, although we didn't move to the same place. My parents and Kitty moved to Farsley, near Leeds where they took up the positions of steward and stewardess of the working men's club. The job came with living quarters over the club which were, as Mum said over and over, 'really nice' and 'perfect for us', in her attempt to convince herself as well as the rest of us. I moved into the small box room at Julie's parent's house so I could stay on at Normanton where I was now in the lower sixth form.

I had thought that leaving Sunny Bank would be hard for us but it wasn't. The events of the previous few years had overshadowed the happy memories and so the prospect of starting again, on what Dad kept calling a great adventure, was a welcome relief. I went to Farsley with them on the day they moved out and I had my own bedroom in the upstairs flat. It was the second biggest of the three, much to Kitty's annoyance, but Mum was keen to make it clear to everyone that my staying at the Harrison's house was very much a temporary thing.

My grandparents left their family home for the last time on Friday 23rd April 1971. They used Archer's removals, a local firm, to move their things the few streets away to Alfred Street. Gilbert Archer turned up with his big van and was surprised at how little the Heskeths were taking. Most of the big items of furniture, the solid oak dining table and chairs, matching sideboard and display cabinets, four of the six bedroom suites and a desk and leather chair were being left behind, all sold separately to the new owner. Grandad had tried to say it was because they wouldn't have room at Uncle Jack's small semi-detached house but he was fooling no one. Mum had packed up most of the stuff from the attic the month before and taken it to Leeds with them. This task seemed to have really upset her. I wondered if it had anything to do with the fact that the three largest items were left behind, the sofa, the large oak book case and Coolean, the rocking horse. Kitty and I had begged to have it although we knew there was no room. Aunty Grace had offered to buy it and keep it at Burntwood, to keep it him the family, but Grandad Tommy, after a quick glance at his wife, had sadly declined. He wasn't sure just how long the calm and accepting version of Eliza would last and was keen not to do anything to bring this phase to an end.

When he'd been told about the imminent sale of Sunny Bank, Uncle Jack had helped Grandad move his pigeons to the much smaller sheds in the garden of his Alfred Street house and told them of his plans to go back to Birmingham with Raymond to start another business venture. He said he had planned to keep the house on anyway so it made sense for Eliza and Tommy to live there. I don't know if there had ever been an offer for them to go to Burntwood but I cannot imagine anyone thinking that would be a good idea so I guess not.

As I wasn't around when they left, I can only tell you what I heard, via Dad, who had gone over to help. He called that evening from the phone box on Midland Road on his way back to the station to get the train back to Leeds. Eliza had been quiet, subdued was the word he'd used. Grandad was upset but tried to make light of it and Jack and Raymond would be there for another couple of weeks until he'd finished his wheeling and dealing.

As soon as the sale had been agreed, Eliza had started moving the plants and shrubs from her garden in quiet preparations which has puzzled everyone but, what seemed like her total acceptance of the situation was a welcome twist in the episode.

Although it was a bit sad for Granny and Grandad, they had a roof over their heads and at 60 and 63 respectively, although Granddad did look much older. They were at an age when they should just be pottering; Eliza with her garden and baking and Tommy with his pigeons. And so that should be where it ended with new starts for us all, but of course it wasn't.

Sunday 24th October, was Uncle Henry's 70th birthday and there was a party to celebrate at the big house. Mum and Dad had got cover for the club I had been at home with them all week as it was half term. Aunty Grace had said it was ok for Julie to come too and so we picked her up on the way over in Dad's new car, a Singer Vogue estate that he was as proud as punch of. The party started at 6.30 and the plan was for us to leave at 10.30 and drop Julie and me off at her house ready for school the next morning. All the family were there along with some friends and business associates of Uncle Henry. Uncle Jack had come back for the weekend and drove Grandad and Eliza over with Raymond. The four of them were going to spend the night and go home the next morning. It had been a couple of weeks since we had been to Royston. Mum and Dad were really busy running the club and Kitty had made lots of new friends and seemed to be excelling in her new surroundings. She made a bit of a fuss about going at first, saying she didn't want to go, that Burntwood was too scary. Mum assured her that they would only be going to the party and would be coming home afterwards, even though Aunt Grace had said we were all welcome to stay over. She and Dad had already had a conversation with Dad pointing out that, as the driver, he would prefer to stay over and drive back early the next morning but Mum was having none of that. This seemed to placate Kitty a little and when I told her that Julie was going too, she cheered up a bit.

On the way there, Mum and Dad were wondering how Eliza would be. They had hardly seen the move from Sunny Bank. Despite Dad offering to collect her, she had declined to come and see our new home, saying she was not a fan of Leeds so Mum had stopped mentioning it on her weekly phone calls.

Even though we had left in plenty of time to be there for the planned 3.30 start, we were the last to arrive at 3.15. The weather was grey and drizzly, making the house look as dark and formidable as my memories told me. As we got out of the car, I saw Kitty shudder as she looked up at the blackened stone. Mum was busy helping Dad get the two crates of beer and bottles of spirits from the back of the car and hadn't noticed. I was just about to move across to her to help as Julie grabbed my hand.

"You weren't kidding when you said it was like something from a horror film," she giggled, pulling me towards the front door.

"Philip, give us a hand with these," Mum's voice had a sharpness to it and I flinched. Julie blushed and, letting go of my hand, went to the back of the car with me, saying,

"Can I carry anything Mrs Hesketh?"

"Billy, Alice, thank god you're here!" Uncle Jacks booming voice vibrated with his wide fast strides toward the car, "Eliza is driving me nuts."

The hall was busy with people spilling over from the sitting room and Aunt Grace was standing in the doorway to the dining room in discussion with Aunties Dot and Peg and I almost gasped out loud as I saw all three women laugh. Grace turned towards us as she heard the front door close.

"Alice, Billy, how are you?" She smiled as she strode over to us, a beaming smile still radiating on her face as she hugged and air kissed them both and I wondered if she might have started on the sherry.

Eliza stayed in the sitting room, holding court from the high winged chair by a fireside. When I took Julie over to say hello, Mum, Dad and Kitty were there and the look on Mum's face told me Eliza had been giving them a hard time. As we got near, Mum smiled and mumbled something about helping out in the kitchen before putting her arm around Kitty and guiding her away. I got a couple of glasses from one of the silver trays for Julie and me and then took her for a quick tour of the grounds. I wanted to walk right down to the fountain screened by high hedges where there was a covered bench but Julie said her shoes would

207

be ruined walking that far down the garden so we found a seat in the rose garden where we couldn't be seen from the house and had a quick kiss and cuddle. I was a keen to make a bit more of this intimacy but Julie complained of being cold, confirming the statement with a chattering of her teeth, so we went back inside.

The rest of the afternoon flew by in a whirl of introductions and polite conversation about my future and rude jibes and insinuation from Daryl about me and Julie. Mum had said we could have a couple of alcoholic drinks but not to get silly but the crazy surrealness of the afternoon made me feel like a character in an Agatha Christie plot and the fancy crystal glass of sparkling wine in my hand seemed like a necessary prop. As the darkness descended outside, the yellowness from the electric lights did little to brighten up the rooms, creating dark shadows around the edges. Julie whispered to me that she'd love to see the rest of the house and asked me to give her the tour. I explained that I didn't really know my way around so it would be like the blind leading the blind. Julie said it would be fun and leaned into me giggling as we walked from room to room on the ground floor. As we left the sitting room we passed Uncle Henry as he unsteadily came in. He grabbed at the door frame with one hand to steady himself, spilling a little of the amber coloured liquor he had in a tumbler in the other hand. I heard Eliza say,

"You should be careful Henry; that brandy will be the death of you one day!"

Uncle Henry didn't say anything but went over to French windows where Edward, Uncle Malcolm and Grandad Tommy were standing looking out at the muddy walkway that led down to the ornamental garden. Henry patted his brother on the back, leaned forward and mumbled something quietly in his ear which made them both laugh really loudly. Malcolm turned round and nervously looked across at Eliza before turning back to talk to his son.

"Come on, let's get some food," Julie said, pulling at my hand. The food in the dining room was being replenished as a dozen or so people chatted and grazed. I topped up our glasses as we ignored the food and went across the hall into a room I'd been told was the library but was actually another sitting room with just one wall of books. Both aunties were amongst a large crowd of people standing around a piano. They were singing along to "It's a long way to Tipperary", which was being played enthusiastically but not that well by a heavily made up woman with very big hair. Julie started to giggle loudly so I guided her back into the hall. The door to the best parlour was closed and I had to blink away the vision of Uncle Jimmy's open coffin as we walked towards it. I was relieved to find it locked.

"What's in there?" Julie asked, pointing to the open round-topped oak door to the side of the stairs.

"It's the kitchen and the back door that leads to the vegetable garden. It'll be full of old crony friends of Aunt Grace. Come on, I'll show you the bedrooms..."

We were just about to go upstairs, somewhere I'd never been, when Mum stopped our progress, asking where we were going. I mumbled something about wanting to show Julie around and Mum said I should show Julie where the buffet was and we should both get something to eat to soak up the alcohol. We retraced our steps downstairs and Mum pointed over to the dining room.

"You have no business upstairs, Pip, there is a toilet downstairs behind the scullery if you need it." I nodded. Julie just looked down at her shoes.

"Soft drinks from now on please. Ok?" said Mum, raising her eyebrows.

"Ok," I answered. As we walked towards the dining room she asked,

"Have you seen Kitty anywhere?"

"No," I shook my head, "Not for ages. Last time I saw her she was by the French windows in the big sitting room with Raymond but that was ages ago." Mum looked worried as she nodded slightly then went towards the sitting room.

We filled some large white china plates with sausage rolls, devilled eggs, vol-au-vents and mini sausages and took them, along with two glasses of dandelion and burdock, over to one of the side tables by the window.

"I've never seen so much food," Julie commented before biting a sausage in half, just as Aunty Peg and Aunty Dot appeared in front of us.

The time melted away again as Julie and I spoke to family and other guests and I had just got up to go and use the lavatory when I realised people were starting to go home. I glanced at the big grandfather clock in the hall to see it was almost ten o'clock. I was only a foot or so away from the door to the kitchen stairs when Raymond shot out shouting for his dad. He was making so much noise and I was suddenly part of a small group trying to see what was going on. I heard him say Kitty's name and point back to the doorway and I shot down the stairs, Mum right behind me.

My sister was lying on the floor at the bottom of the stairs, her arms above her head and her legs curled underneath her.

"What happened?" Mum was shouting, "Did she fall?"

"I don't know, I came down and she was standing at the table, she was upset, then she moved to the stairs and just fell over," Raymond was choking on his words, standing on the second to bottom step. Uncle Jack suddenly appeared at the side of him. Raymond turned to him, "She said 'It's started', Dad we have to go, we have to go home now."

"What did she say?" Eliza's sharp voice echoed down the stone stairway. I stepped slightly away from Mum and Kitty and saw her standing in the doorway, her hand to her mouth.

"She's having one of her turns that's all," Mum said, not looking up from stroking Kitty's face, "Philip, get me some water."

Dad was suddenly there along with Grace who effortlessly dispelled the crowd explaining that Kitty was a little unwell and just needed to lie down. Uncle Henry suddenly clapped his hands and announced that everyone should go with him to the dining room for a nightcap before they hit the road. I followed him to find Julie who, much to my annoyance was being entertained by Daryl. I stood by the door balling my hands into fists as I saw her laughing at something he said.

"Not worth it, Pip," Grandad Tommy's voice made me turn round, "The lads an idiot and she's a bright enough lass to see it." He patted my hand before moving toward the sitting room.

Dad came up from the kitchen carrying Kitty and crossed the hall to the staircase with Mum just a step behind carrying a glass of water and a towel. Eliza and Grace followed. As they reached the bottom of the wide staircase, Mum turned and mumbled something, pointing to the sitting room, Grace nodded and started to walk away, I noticed she looked worried and was rubbing her temples. Eliza said something to Dad and made to move forward but Mum put her hand out and physically pushed Eliza back. I stood frozen, watching this confrontation. Eliza's hand went up to where Mum's was and seemed to hang there for a second. I couldn't see either of their faces but I could see they were looking at each other. Eliza dropped her hand, turned and walked towards the sitting room. I stepped quickly over to Mum and followed her upstairs.

Grace had told Mum to put Kitty in one of the guest rooms and, although she did start to come round after about twenty minutes, Mum decided she would take Grace up on her offer to stay there over night with Kit and get someone to drive them both home the next morning. I was sent downstairs to let Aunty Grace know and to tell Julie we were leaving in ten minutes. The noise level had dropped and most of the guests had left, leaving only family. They had all moved into the sitting room and I was furious to see Daryl sitting on one of the sofas rather too close to my girlfriend. Stepping angrily into the room, I was stopped by Grace putting a hand on my shoulder.

211

"How is Kathryn, Philip?"

"She's come round but Mum's worried that the car journey won't help so she's going to stay here with her tonight, if that's alright." The distraction helped me swallow my temper.

"Of course, that's fine. I'll pop up and see if she needs anything." She smiled at me and moved her hand but stayed where she was.

"Dad's taking me and Julie back to Royston now," I said, looking across to the sofa, "Better get your coat as we have to go now," I added with an unnecessary firmness on the now, "He needs to get back to the club." Julie stood up quickly and came towards me. Grace gave me one of her odd smiles before turning to the rest of the room.

"Well yes, it is getting quite late so perhaps it's time you were all making a move." She turned slightly to address her son, "Edward, help people find their coats, I'll just go and speak to Alice."

"Yes, I agree Grace, I think I'll take myself off to bed shortly too, it's been quite a long day but I might have a cup of tea first." Grandad stood up and walked with Grace into the hall. Eliza watched him go but made no move.

Julie took my hand as we left the room and Dad waited at a bend in the staircase for Grace to pass him as he came down. She touched his arm and said something I didn't catch and Dad replied and nodded his head. I was just about to ask if everything was alright when I heard a yelp from the dining room. Uncle Jack and Raymond are in there having a heated discussion and Raymond looked really upset as his dad spoke to him in a low voice. Suddenly, Raymond was shouting that he wanted to go home, "Please Dad, please, we can't stay here tonight, we have to go!" his voice high pitched and desperate. Uncle Jack was saying they had to stay as he'd had too much to drink but they would go first thing in the morning.

"Come on you two, let's get going," Dad ran his fingers through his hair as he looked round the hall. Then Raymond, spurred into action, was pulling Uncle Jack towards Dad.

"Please Uncle Billy, can we come with you? We need to go, we need to go now." he started to sob. Edward appeared with a pile of coats and put them on the chair by the clock as he stood awkwardly, unsure what to do. Dad quickly changed his baffled expression to a warm and friendly smile answered,

"Course lad, you can both come home with me." He looked at his brother, "You can stop at the club with me, in Farsley. Me and your Dad can have a nightcap and I'll fetch you back tomorrow to get your car when I come back for Alice and Kitty."

"Aye, alright then," Uncle Jack said, looking confused and concerned. Raymond looked like he was about to collapse with relief as he wiped his eyes on his shirt sleeve. Julie and I took our coats off the pile and we all began to say our good nights. Eliza was out in the hall asking if anyone was going to make a hot drink before bed as she waved us out of the house. The five of us stepped outside, closing the big oak door behind us and crunched over the gravel drive towards the car.

The last bit of this story is fragmented because I only have it second hand, and from a number of different people who all have their own version, but this is what I know happened. At 4am on the morning of 25th October 1971, a fire started in Great Uncle Henry's study at Burntwood. It took almost twelve hours to get the fire out and the house was almost completely gutted and three lives were lost.

Chapter twenty

Family History

Alice was thirteen when she came to live permanently at Sunny Bank. It was early January 1950 and she was enrolled at the local secondary school for her last two years of her school life school. She made a few friends there but generally continued to spend most of her time with Billy who she walked to and from school with. Jack had left school a couple of years earlier and had tried a number of jobs including butchers boy, window cleaner's assistant and shop assistant, all of which were short lived as, according to his father, he didn't have the temperament to do as he was told. At the start of 1951 he was called up to do his national service and two weeks later set off with his small brown suitcase to the Somme Barracks in Sheffield for an initial two weeks training with the 1st West Riding Divisional engineers, after which he was shipped off to Cypress where he found a life and camaraderie that he absolutely loved. His place in the Hesketh family saga as the middle son with no purpose became a distant memory and the army became his wonderful adopted parents; he found his place. He made good friends and learnt useful practical skills and his pragmatic approach along with a knack for tactical thinking was recognised early on, making him popular within his ranks and with the sergeant major.

The twins had married in 1948 in a double ceremony, although not looking quite as identical as normal. Dorothy had a much bigger bouquet than her sister in an attempt to hide the fact that she was nearly five months pregnant but of course no one was fooled. Both girls moved in to Sunny Bank for the first few months of their married lives but the house was way too small for so many personalities and so by the end of the year, Margaret and Ronald had found a house of their own and Dorothy, John and their baby girl Christine moved in with John's parents at the other side of the village.

When Eliza wrote to Jack in November 1951, asking him if he would be able to come back for a family Christmas, he didn't hesitate with his reply. He was really sorry to miss it but they wouldn't give him leave to come home. In fact, he had volunteered to stay and run the officer's bar over the Christmas period. He was having a brilliant time and was in no hurry to go back to the family squabbles and politics, something he tactfully didn't mention.

Three months later, in early February 1952, he found himself unexpectedly back in Yorkshire when he accompanied an injured serviceman back home and decided it was time to go and show his family how well he was doing. He hadn't told them he was coming, imagining their surprised faces as he walked in the door. However, after sauntering down the drive, he was slightly put out to find no one home and the house locked up. It was a cold but bright afternoon and so he fetched one of the deckchairs from the shed and sat at the side of the house enjoying a cigarette. Squinting up at the sky, he turned his head to the side when he heard footsteps and through the haze of smoke from his Players full strength, he saw Alice. It actually took him a couple of seconds to realise that this vision floating towards him was the serious and uncertain child he had grown up with and when he did, his heart began to speed up. Her smile, the way her hair floated and danced around her face, her every movement, caused his breath to catch in his chest and he felt suddenly giddy. When she called out his name, showing her delight at seeing him, a surge of euphoria swept through him, pushing him to his feet.

"Jack, Jack, oh, you're home." She stood right in front of him and held her arms out, "When did you get back?" Her voice washed over him like a soothing balm as he gave her a tight squeeze and he laughed out loud at the pleasure he felt at her being so close.

"I've just got here, I'm on leave. Where is everyone?" As she stepped back he took her in, drank her in almost. She was the most beautiful thing he had ever seen in his life and he knew he loved her.

Timing is of course everything in life and Jack was about to realise his was out by two weeks. He had to dig down deep into his inner strength to keep the smile on his face as they walked toward the house just moments later.

"What do you think to this?" she asked him, holding out her left hand to show him three tiny diamonds on a yellow gold band. He had tried to keep the laughter in his voice as he congratulated her and, as he saw Billy coming down the path behind her, all smiles, he felt something break inside him.

Although he had a ten day pass, Jack told his family that this was flying visit, he only had forty-eight hours before he had to go back, but it was still a long forty-eight hours. Eliza was keen to show off her boy in uniform to her parents-in-law and insisted that Thomas drove the three of them and James, to Burntwood. It was a stilted two hours in a very crowded sitting room. Henry was there along with twenty-three year old Grace and her forty-five year old husband, a business colleague of Henry's and their six year old son Edward. Clara and William sat in state over the assembled family, asking the odd questions through the general chit chat about Cyprus and the army.

Shortly before they left, Jack managed to ask Henry about the two large greenhouse structures he had noticed at the bottom of the kitchen garden. Henry was pleased to talk about a new area the business was exploring and the two of them, along with James, went out to have a close look at the structures. Jack listened intently as Henry spoke and chain-smoked his way through four cigarettes before going back to join his parents who were just getting ready to leave.

The next morning, he got up early and found Eliza, as he knew she would be, alone in the kitchen. He told her that he loved the army and that he didn't feel there was much of a future for him in Yorkshire and so he was planning on staying on once his national service ended. Eliza demanded to know what Henry had said to him in the garden but Jack just shrugged and muttered that what Henry had said to him had nothing to do with his decision. He had laid a false trail as to the reason he would not be coming back, he knew he could not tell anyone the truth about how he felt about Alice. An hour later, he left, whistling as his boots crunched down the drive not to return again for another ten years.

He did not come back for Billy and Alice's wedding later that year, although Eliza sent him a photograph, also telling him what a lovely day it had been, despite the death of her old friend, and Alice's mother, just a month before.

Neither did he return to see any of his nieces and nephews born or for the large almost state funeral of his Grandfather William in 1955, a lavish and completely over-the-top display, with the coffin on a four horse carriage leading a massive procession and that after 5 days of laying in state at Burntwood, or Clara's funeral, just a year later, with a much less showy or costly send off once Henry was in sole charge of the family coffers.

Jack remained in Cyprus and in the Army until 1959 when he returned to England to be demobbed in Andover, Hampshire and it was from there that he sent his last letter home. He told Eliza that he had a taste for seeing more of the world and planned to travel a bit and they were not to worry. After that, they received the odd sparsely worded postcard form far flung places but had no idea where he was or what he was up to.

Indigo Children

Part Three

Indigo Children

Chapter One
Kathryn

I have a very clear recollection of the day I finally got out of hospital, the day I left the last of the wards and solitary rooms with their differing lights and their mood altering medications. This was the day I began the mammoth task of picking up my life.

The memory plays out like this; On that morning, Janet, the nearest person I had to a friend, smiled warmly at me as our paths crossed in the corridor. Like all the other nursing assistants, she was generally busy dashing up and down but she always found time to talk to me.

"Are you ok?" she asked and I nodded my mute smile, "I know it might be a bit scary but you will be fine." I nodded again and opened my mouth but didn't trust myself to vocalise the expected response so closed it again and tried for what I hoped was a more convincing smile instead. Moving forward, she reached out and put her hand on my arm, "It's a big thing and you're bound to be a bit anxious but you are ready." Her extra warm smile lit up her face briefly, her eyes twinkling as she gave my arm a squeeze before braking contact and whispering, "Honest." I managed a nod of acknowledgement in her belief in me but could already feel myself being overwhelmed by the bright, unreal quality that was filling the corridor, sensing the greyness lurking on the edges of my periphery.

'Please don't let me wobble' I was incanting in my head as I glanced at the door of my room fifty or so yards ahead then looking back at Janet to see if she'd noticed. She was turning to walk away, her professional smile returned along with her singsong tone of voice,

"I'll pop in and see you before you go." I watched her walk away, focusing on her wide, confident steps, looking for calm mundane thoughts to fill my head and push away the creeping darkness.

Back in my little room, I noticed the sunshine seeping in round the edges of the closed blinds. When the nurse had come in earlier, with her beaming good morning smile, she had swished open the curtains to 'let in the day'. This upbeat kindness had made my eyes sting and I asked her to leave the blinds closed. Now I opened them slowly, seeing the garden lush and colourful, bathed in early morning sunshine and I felt my mouth twitch as it tried out a smile. I'd been a voluntary patient at Middleton Hall for nearly three and a half years and I guess as madhouses go, it wasn't too bad and, as someone who was declared mentally insane and committed at the age of thirteen, I have seen a few, so I feel I am in a position to know.

The first place they took me when my mental capabilities failed me and I descended into madness was not so nice but it took me a little while to realise the full extent of the horror. There had been an incident, a fire, and people had died and I had been hurt. I was found unconscious near the bottom of some stone steps with my left arm limp and broken in three places. I knew nothing of the ambulance trip, lights flashing and sirens blaring, to Pinderfields Hospital in Wakefield, or of the first few days being treated for the head injury and suspected smoke inhalation. Apparently, I was so out of it, there was some concern about whether I was going to make it; that perhaps I would be the fourth member of the Hesketh family to die as a result of the fire. But after three days, I began to wake up. The concern was then focused on my inability to remember anything about what had happened. The police had been waiting, along with my parents and brother, for me to come round and tell them what I knew about the incident. They were none too pleased when I couldn't help them. According to my brother, I could barely string more than a couple of words together and was 'quick to tears' according to the notes at the bottom of my bed. I probably drooled a bit as well.

When they moved me from intensive care, there was no bed available in the children's ward and anyway at aged 13 it was considered that I'd be better off in an adult ward. That's where I first came round properly, in a bed next to the nurses' station. I was in quite a state and perversely, these first moments of complete consciousness have stayed with me, occasionally haunting my dreams, ever since. I was frightened; no, actually I was terrified. There were voices in my head, whispering and calling my name, telling me things I didn't want to hear and shapes and shadows flitting around the ward, not coming too close but hovering, watching me. They weren't there all the time; when Mum and Dad came, or Pip, they stopped for a bit but they always came back. Pip showed me the earphones above my bed and tuned in Radio One for me and they helped but even in the spaces when I couldn't see or hear the apparitions, I was petrified with the terror of their return. My state of high anxiety and inability to communicate was diagnosed by a forward thinking junior doctor who went on to make quite a name for himself in later years as an eminent child psychiatrist specialising in schizophrenia and psychotic behaviour. A day later, still with my arm in plaster, I was transferred round the corner to Stanley Royd Hospital, previously known as the West Riding Pauper Lunatic Asylum, and part of the mental health facility in Wakefield.

I have no idea what was said to Mum and Dad about the state of my mental health, all I know is that short move, one third of a mile, from one bed to another was the most terrible thing that ever happened to me. I was prescribed Largactil, injected every six hours, which made me catatonic but at least it stopped the voices. I was in a small ward with only eleven other beds and fairly close to the front of the hospital. I mostly slept my way through the days that turned into weeks and then months. My medication only reduced for the weekly visit from Mum and Dad. Pip wasn't allowed to come.

When I saw them in the day room, I was disorientated and confused. I think I'd stopped crying so much by then but I was vacant, bewildered and totally lost. At the end of each of these visits, Dr Arnold, the one in charge of my treatment, tried to get Dad to sign a consent form for me to have Electroconvulsive therapy, or ECT. Dr Arnold didn't like Mum; he thought she asked too many silly questions so he ignored her. Dad, though must have looked like he would defer to the doctor's expertise and knowledge but, thankfully, he was programmed to defer to Mum and so refused consent. I cried when they left me each time, sobbing so loudly I was given a double dose to calm me down. I was set adrift in a drug-fuelled haze of sadness and loss with the sting of their abandonment, unable to understand what I had done for them to have left me locked up in this place.

The doctor's patience with my parents' inability to understand the severity of my illness ran out just before my fourteenth birthday. I'm not too clear about the timing or even if I have the series of events right, but I think it was a Friday because we had fish for our midday meal and I had been taken for a bath and had my hair washed. Once back on the ward, the orderly plaited my wet hair and told me to sit quietly on the chair while she got all my things out of the locker. I watched her as she folded my few clothes and belongings into a cardboard box, my hair brush the last thing to go in, her expression pursed and unfriendly as she closed the lid. After a second's pause, she gave me a quick glance before filling a glass of water and handing it to me and turning towards the wheeled cabinet parked at the end of my bed. Using one of the large bunches of keys clipped to her belt; she unlocked it and collected the three pills, two yellow, one blue in her hand. Then with her mean little smile, she held her palm out to me and watched me take them, one at a time, with a large gulp of water between each. I was well rehearsed with the drill and obediently opened my mouth afterwards, moving my tongue up, down, right and left so she could check I had swallowed them.

"Right then your highness." This one always called me this - I'd heard her saying my family were stuck up although they had no cause to be, "Come on then, your chariot awaits," and she gave a nasty laugh, pleased with herself. I followed her out of the ward and down the corridor.

"Am I going home?" I asked, feeling something flutter in my chest.

"Oh no, you're not well enough to go home yet, you are going to a much grander hospital, one where they can give you the care and help your family think you need." She laughed again and the flutter turned into a twisting pain of panic.

"Kitty!" Mum's voice was like a salve around my heart as we stepped into the large entrance hall. She hugged me and I wanted to hug her back but my arms felt heavy and my emotions were all over the place. Dad was beside her. Both their faces showed worry and concern and something else. I was starting to feel dizzy and the scene around me seemed to jump. I was sitting on a chair and Dr Arnold was talking to Mum and Dad about a long term prognosis and medical imbalance but his voice was distorted and I could see Mum opening and closing her mouth but I couldn't hear her voice. I closed my eyes and when I opened them again I was lying down. It took me a few minutes to work out I was in an ambulance but the effort of thinking wore me out and blackness filled me up again. The next thing I knew I was being wheeled down a long wide corridor, full of echoing sounds and shapes that may or may not have been real, by a strange looking man with long white hair. When he saw my eyes were open he laughed and leaned over me.

"Hello sleeping beauty, you've woken up before I've given you a kiss, that's a shame." He started singing, "Any little girl, that's a nice little girl, is the right little girl for me," as he wheeled me towards a barred gate. A nurse appeared with a large bunch of keys and unlocked the gate.

"Can she walk?" she didn't sound too friendly.

"Dunno, she's only just come round, I'll wheel her in, which ward's she going on?"

"She's not on a ward, she's only here for assessment. No need for you to trouble yourself, I'll take her from here." I felt a rush of something course through my body like an electric current and a familiar voice in my head whispered, "Get up Kitty, get off the trolley and stand up." I twisted my shoulders in panic as the man said,

"Ah well, you see I can't leave the trolley, I have to take it back with me so I might as well go all the way with her."

"I'm alright," I said suddenly and began to shakily push myself up, "I can walk, I am alright," my voice rising in panic, "Please let me walk!" Completely awake now, I was gripping the raised side of the trolley. The nurse gave me a slim smile as she took my hand and released the guard rail and I lunged forward. She steadied me with her firm, cool hand and I took a step closer to her. I could feel bile rising in my throat as I got my first proper glimpse of this man. He was wearing a green porters coat, open at the neck showing a thick gold chain. He reached down and picked up the box with my belongings in and held it out to me. My eyes were drawn to the wide gold bracelet he also wore.

"Here ya go then, Princess," he winked, "Catch you another time." He started to whistle as he retreated back down the corridor with his trolley and the nurse took me inside. It was July 1972 and I had just become a patient at High Royds Hospital in Menston, just outside Leeds. It had been decided by doctors and communicated to my parents that a few months rest and specialised care in there was the only way I was ever going to get better.

Those few months turned into almost four years and the 'specialised' care was more drugs. However, after eighteen months of no real improvement, according to my new, arrogant and bullying psychiatrist, Dr Hurst, my parents, well actually my Dad, agreed to a course of ECT.

I know a lot about High Royds now, too much actually, but it wasn't all bad, just most of it. However, the only memory I will share with you of that place, is of the last few days I spent there. Dr Hurst was on the verge of insisting that an operation, normally used to suppress aggression, of which I had none, was the only thing that would rid me of the apparitions that were destroying my sanity. Psychosurgery was a manipulation of the brain cells and was the next logical step, he explained, and gave Mum and Pip examples of similar cases where this small operation had been successful, careful not to mention the ones that hadn't been. At this point, I was seventeen and Mum wasn't doing too great herself. It was just over a year since Dad had died and she wasn't coping. She had asked Pip to go with her for the meeting with Dr Hurst, explaining that she felt intimidated by him and needed moral support. When Mum insisted that she needed a little more time to consider the operation before giving her consent, Dr Hurst exhibited traits that might suggest he himself would benefit from a similar operation. Pip had stood up and stepped a little in front of Mum to shield her from the doctor's aggressive tirade. He was demanding to know if she remembered the reason I had been hospitalised in the first place, suggesting I was not only a danger to myself but also to the other patients and his staff. I sat very still at the other side of Mum, feeling as broken and wretched as she looked.

"I need to take my mother home now, Dr Hurst," Pip said in his newly acquired grown up voice. Bending slightly to touch her arm, "As you can see, she really isn't very well. I'll think over what you've said and discuss it further with her and we will get back to you in a couple of days." Mum shakily got to her feet before moving to the side of the desk while Pip held out his hand which the doctor shook with a satisfied smile.

Mum leaned over and kissed me lightly on the cheek and my brother did the same before putting his arm around her and guiding her out of the office. The two nurses who had stood just behind me throughout the whole discussion were suddenly at my side, pulling me roughly to my feet. As I walked back to my solitary room, I thought my fate was sealed but I was wrong, I was about to be rescued by the last person I would have thought would help me.

Two days later and three days before my eighteenth birthday, my Aunt Grace's big black Daimler swept down the main drive of the hospital and she and Mum strode confidently into Dr Hurst's office. Aunt Grace had secured and agreed to pay for me a place, in Middleton Hall, a small private nursing home in Meanwood, just outside Leeds, specialising in mental disorders. An hour later, I walked between them down the long, ornate corridors of this grade II listed facade and stepped out of the front door, leaving, escaping this horrible place. I could feel something rising inside. Blinking back my tears, I climbed into the back of the big black car. Mum held my hand as we drove towards the end of the drive and out of those bleak and terrifying grounds. Just before we passed through the gate, I felt an immense surge of adrenalin and turned to see the huge gothic clock tower looming in the darkening afternoon light.

Chapter Two
Alice - Now

Alice is an old woman now and she knows her time is almost done. She's not sad, well maybe a little. She would quite like to enjoy a few more years with her family. She has two great grandchildren now and would love to see them grow, see what wonderful people they will become, and of course she would like to be there a bit longer for Kathryn. She would like to be sure that all that digging up of the past, therapy she'd called it, didn't make everything worse. In her experience, the truth very rarely sets anyone free.

Alice wants to be sure that her fragile and damaged child, who she still sees from time to time behind the facade of the woman she has become, is really strong enough to deal with what she uncovered. Kathryn has been diligent in her research of the family tree even though she didn't need to go too far back to find it was rotten. She doesn't blame Grace for what she did. She wished that she'd had the strength to break the silence herself and not been such a coward. Even now, all these years later, she cannot talk about and if she was truly honest, there were some things she would have preferred her daughter not to know. How she'd failed her, her culpability, her collaboration – unintentional but nevertheless, that is what it was. Kathryn felt she needed to know and she had a right to know but Alice knows the harsh truth is not for everyone. She also knows that, however hard she would like it to be otherwise, the past cannot be changed. So she has spent the last forty years trying to create a better life for her and her children and she believes she has done a reasonable job. She allows herself a smile as she thinks of Kathryn and of the woman she has become, against all the odds. She will be alright, they all will be, the fear has passed, the witch is dead.

Alice has led a full life – a fairy tale life in fact. Not the sanitised Disney version where only the bad people come to harm and everybody lives happily ever after. No, her life has been a very modern day version

229

of a tale written by The Brothers Grimm.

She still has the book her father gave her all those years ago. She knows now why he gave it to her and why her instincts were to treasure it. It was a reminder of all the things he had taught her, in the short time they had been together, to help her prepare for what lay ahead. He had known that he wasn't going to be there to see her grow up and protect her. She also realised that he had known, had seen on the first moment he held her, that she was special. He had looked into that tiny pink face, her baby blue eyes, focusing far too soon, looking back at him, his own eyes filled with love and fear. She was a mini version of her father; everyone commented on the resemblance but Albert Mclean knew she had not just inherited his looks. She had his gift, the one he hid from his wife, the gift his wife pretended to have. And he knew he would have to do everything he could to stop others, especially his wife, from seeing it too.

He need not have worried. Barbara soon tired of her new 'mother' role, finding the requirements of a newborn baby too much of an inconvenience. Albert had done as much as he could for Alice, including enlisting the help of the elderly widow from next door. She had helped with the basic care and attention his little girl needed while he was at work for the first few years, leaving the famous Mrs Mclean to get back to her work in the church.

It was easy to make Alice understand that she must not tell her mother about what she felt or heard. The voices and shadows she saw were their secret. She was barely two years old when he told her that her mother pretended to talk to spirits; she did it to make money and spent so much time pretending, she didn't see what was actually happening in the real world and Alice, even at that young age, had understood.

Things came to a head one evening when he came home from work late to find Alice cowering in her room, hungry and scared. Her mother was giving private readings to a group of people downstairs. Alice had never heard or seen her daddy this angry before. It was the week of her third birthday and the third day in a row that he had come home to find strangers being entertained and his daughter neglected. He called her downstairs before announcing that the readings were now over and any further appointments would be at the church and not in his house. He had then picked up his daughter and carried her into the kitchen where he made her bread and dripping and poured her a big glass of milk before stepping back into the living room, half shutting the door. There had been a lot of shouting. Her mum was really cross too and said her work was important and she could not help it that Alice had been burdened with her gift. Albert had laughed at this and called her a 'bloody charlatan', a word that Alice had not heard before but she liked the sound of. She whispered it into her drink and echoed it around in her head. It sounded such a pretty word but she knew her mother didn't think so. She had gasped as she heard the slap of her mother's hand as it struck her dad's cheek. Alice's eyes were as wide as saucers, even though she was still looking down at her glass of milk. She saw her mother, livid with anger and resentment, storm out of the room and heading upstairs, taking her tin of money with her.

Now at the end of her life, Alice thought about the things her father had taught her. The insight she was given about the wickedness that lived in some people and vigilance she would need to defeat it. But the turmoil of war and the loss of the person who loved her most had left her vulnerable and she struggled with what was real and what was imagined, never talking to anyone about what she saw or heard. Her inner sight faded as she grew and she lost her child's perception - no she didn't lose it but allowed the feelings and whispered knowledge to melt into the background. This made her easy prey to the 'kind' old woman in the gingerbread house. Not all evil witches are old and ugly.

On the day Alice was preparing to welcome her daughter home, a warm bright June day in 1979, she placed the inscribed copy of Grimms'

231

Fairy Tales on the book shelf in of the newly decorated room, Kathryn's room. She could no longer call her Kitty; after all that had been said she could not use that name. Kathryn was finally being discharged from Middleton Hall and coming home and it was to be just the two of them in the small red brick terraced house in Armley, just round the corner from Model Road. Alice had gone full circle.

Her girl was thin and pale, her eyes like saucers taking in everything as Alice led her round like an over enthusiastic estate agent, praying that she would like it, that she would be happy. In the bedroom, Alice held her breath as Kathryn reached out and took the book and hugged it, her eyes moist with the tears she was holding back.

"You kept it safe," she said as she blinked quickly. Alice nodded before turning her head slightly to look at the lilac covered single bed where Pearl lay on the pillow.

"Oh Mum," she sobbed as she reached out for her long lost favourite doll, "Is it really her?" Alice was only able to nod, the emotion robbing her of speech as she watched her beloved girl clasp the doll to her face. "Where did you find her?"

Using all the reserves of strength she could summon, Alice swallowed and took a deep breath, still battling with the internal machinations between the truth and a gentler fiction.

"She was hidden in a box in Eliza's wardrobe; Grace found her when she helped clear out her things." Alice decided on honesty, there had been far too much lying and pretence. They sat together then, on the small single bed and as a twenty year old Kathryn cuddled the doll that had been her childhood comfort and security object. Alice put her arm around her daughter and their thoughts mingled in the silence. There was no need for words, Alice knew Kathryn was clinging to her story; she remembered nothing of the night of the fire. As they hugged, heads together with Pearl still against Kathryn's chest, their separate memories began to weave in and out like wool on a loom, creating a tapestry of the past, like a graphic fairy tale illustration.

Now, nearly forty years later, these homemade histories have faded slightly as the new generations have been making their own, happier scenes but to mother and daughter, although the darkness is gone, the memories and verbal overshadowing of what it brought are still there, hovering in their peripheral vision. So, maybe the one persistent regret Alice has at her imminent passing is leaving the burden for Kathryn to bear alone.

Chapter Three
Kathryn - Now

My brother called me today to talk about the arrangements for Aunt Grace's funeral. We'd spoken about it earlier in the week when I'd told him I wanted to do a reading or a poem. It had stopped him in his tracks. He is trying to be the calm and helpful organiser and still treating me like his fragile little sister, like I'm made of glass; even after all this time.

I try not to be too hard on him when he gets like this around me, which is pretty much every time he sees me lately. I know it's his way of coping, getting on with life without having to talk about the past, which is of course, the exact opposite of my coping strategy. So I try and play the role he has cast me in because, when all is said and done, I suppose his nervous concern is to be expected. I am after all, very much a bi-product of Hesketh Glass and although I have always been a little sub-standard, there are cracks running right through me; they are letting the light in.

It's going to be a humanist service at the crematorium, *'none of that mumbo jumbo god stuff'* Grace had declared. *"You all know I'm not a believer,"* she'd said with a chortle before turning her head so no one saw her wink at me.

I've spent a long time looking on the internet for something appropriate. I'd really like to write something but have found myself floundering in the emotions and memories. After an hour, all I have managed is this,

For many years I didn't really know my Aunty Grace and as a small child I was terrified of her, which now all seems quite preposterous as I now know that she was the one that saved my life...

I know of course that I can't really say that. I must not let the room full of mourners and the local dignitaries who will want to be seen there know about how she saved me from the clutches of Dr Hurst, the butcher surgeon. How she sprung me from High Royds in the nick of time, preventing him from performing an operation that would most probably have killed me. No, this is definitely something that they don't need to hear. Although I am sure there will be a few people there wondering if I might mention Burntwood and the fire but as I am sticking resolutely to my story of my mind being a complete of that fateful night and I shall say nothing on the subject.

I am not being totally deceitful – it really was a blank for a long time and let's be frank here, the amount of drugs, prescribed and otherwise, not to mention the ECT were probably enough to have completely scrambled my brain. It's a wonder I can remember my own name. At various points over the years, fragments and chunks have floated back and forth in my head. These were usually triggered by what I learnt from my research and now I believe I know exactly what happened, but it has taken me most of my adult life to piece it together.

My cousin, Edward, will be here tomorrow, his flight, the one he calls 'the red eye', gets into Heathrow at 6 am. He is still a bit bossy and at times obnoxious but I have come to like him, perhaps mainly because we now live on different continents for most of the time. He is upset that he didn't get to say goodbye to his mum.

"If only I'd known," I had heard a stifled sob in his voice, "She seemed so well when we spoke." She had seemed well, very well in fact. We'd had a Skype call with him the day before she had died; Aunt Grace, as always in charge, had hired a girl from a top beauty salon for a home visit to do her hair and make up to reassure her boy.

"Image is everything," she said looking at herself in the mirror and testing her smile before the call.

His flight was booked for him to come home in two weeks time and she didn't want him changing his plans. He was still her pride and joy and the successful life he had; CEO of large IT Company, an American wife and a son at Yale, was a credit to her selflessness.

The final act, of which I and my Mum were conspirators, was to convince Edward to remain in Boston and conclude one of his biggest

235

deals, even though we all knew she had only a few hours left. After the call, she gave Mum an envelope with her legal documents and her modest funeral instructions.

'Just something simple. No over-the-top Hesketh family display' she had declared with one of her rare smiles. The only thing she stipulated was the date, three days after Edward and his wife and son arrived for their pre-planned holiday. *'Give them time to acclimatise before the sad stuff.'*

Pip and his wife Karen had been keen to help, take over is what they actually meant, most of the funeral arrangements and Mum and I were happy to let them. Mum's not been herself since Grace died. She seems to have taken it pretty hard. They had been so close over the years and the secrets they shared bound them to each other.

Karen is a very practical woman who relishes an event to organise, always has apparently. I missed their wedding, being in the care of Dr Angel, that really is his name, in Middleton Mad house but I have seen the pictures in a beautiful white and gold leaf album. By all accounts, it was a wonderful and much needed happy event in my family and I am sorry to have missed it although I recognised the scenes in the photographs from a very vivid dream I had had.

The other day, I was round at Pip's house with Mum and, as an antidote to their glum faces, I mentioned a thought that had occurred to me a couple of days earlier. I said maybe I should contact Richard Curtis and ask him if he'd like to make a film about my lost years and the things I'd missed.

"He could call it four funerals and a wedding." I laughed as I delivered my punch line, no one else did. Mum rolled her eyes and sighed and Karen got up and started clearing away our tea cups. I could see Pip was a bit cross but he managed a weak smile as he argued,

"Shouldn't it be five funerals? That's not got the same ring to it."

"Oh no it was only four, although technically one was a double funeral." I gave him my smug, I knew you'd fall for that, face and he glanced quickly at Mum before shaking his head and asking if anyone had heard anything from Raymond lately.

After the fire, the consequences went deep and hard. My remaining family members were left shattered and desperate to find some anonymity. The Hesketh name can still raise eyebrows in some quarters even now and people remain curious about the infamous family and the triple murder for which no one was ever tried. In fact, the fire caused two further deaths, Uncle Malcolm, Grace's husband who died three years later from complications caused by burns and damage to his lungs, and my lovely Dad who died of a broken heart once he finally understood the truth of what had taken place.

Grace and Mum were the only ones who had been at Burntwood that night who didn't sustain any burns or injuries. Something the police had found quite suspicious to begin with. They were also the ones who arranged for Eliza to be cremated instead of being buried in the family plot with only immediate family present and no service, Mum insisting it was what she had wanted in spite of Dad's objections.

Edward was badly burned on his back and arms but was considered very lucky by the doctors and apart from some bad scaring, went on to make a full recovery. It's been said it was the making of him; every cloud and all that.

Even though he and Aunt Grace lost everything in the fire; all they had left were the night clothes they were wearing when they escaped the fire, they both managed to salvage their determination and ambition. Aunt Grace was never one to be beaten and like a phoenix she rose from the flames and maybe, because she was no longer in the Hesketh shadow, her business acumen and strong will came to the fore. In the year after the fire, she presided over the sale of Hesketh and Sons Glass Company with the full agreement and co-operation of the remaining Hesketh heirs. Her savvy and confident manner completely wrong-footed the vultures waiting to profit from Henry's demise, ensuring a nice little windfall to all of Tommy and Eliza's offspring. She also took over Malcolm's failing brewing company while he was ill, completely turning it around and then selling it for a considerable sum in the mid 1980's. She worked hard and she worked smart and, although it was her that enabled Edward to set up his own business with her money, his success was then his own.

What was left of Burntwood was demolished once the police investigation was concluded, albeit not to everyone's satisfaction. The land was eventually sold and a hotel with business and conference centre stands on the spot today. A very light and airy design with lots of glass I am told but I've never had any desire to see it. I don't even go there in my sleep, it's always Sunny Bank that I wander around in dreams, it remains my nearest faraway place.

I have decided to read the Maya Angelou poem, 'When Great Trees Fall', at Grace's funeral. I think it says everything that needs to be said about the amazing person she was and how she should be remembered.

"Are you sure you are up to it Kathryn?" Mum asked me just now when I told her. Everyone always calls me Kathryn now, no more Kit, Kitty, poor little mad Kitty.

"Yes I am sure, it's the very least I can do and I want to."

"Well then that's a lovely tribute and I know Edward will appreciate it." She smiled her lovely faraway smile and I had to look away and bite back the emotion. I could see the edges of her fraying.

So much of my life disappeared, my childhood memories coloured over with a black wax crayon, it took years of scratching away to gradually disclose what had happened. Researching our family tree was great therapy. Mum and Pip, he is still Pip, worried I was becoming obsessive but it was important for me to know why and how things went the way they did.

"Knowing what happened isn't the same as understanding," my very clever brother told me, "I doubt I'll ever understand it. I think it's best just forgotten." The catch in his voice tells me it's time to change the subject. At 65, I know he's too old to cope with the fallout of emotions. I need to let him be the strong and practical big brother. I need to let him keep the shutters down and locked on the terrors of our past but I know that would never work for me. I had to get the bolt cutters on the padlocks of my childhood, snap the shutters open and let in the light.

I had spent years in the dark. Left alone and afraid, you lose track of time. I lost eight years. I thought I was so lost, there would be no way back and yet here I am in my sixth decade looking back at a life that seems now to belong to someone else.

Chapter Four

1971

On the night of the fire, Grace had woken Alice from a sleep too deep to be natural. The urgent shaking followed quickly by tugging as Grace and Edward pulled her from her bed and dragged her from the crackling and smoky room. Out on the landing, as her wits started to return, she had called out her daughter's name reaching back towards the now closed bedroom door. Grace had pulled her back,

"Eliza's taken her," she said, pulling her along the landing towards the stairs and pausing to say to her son, "Edward, go and help your dad get the others out." Edward ran towards the bedrooms at the other side of the house. As Alice watched him through unfocused eyes, she saw the smoke swirling out from under the door of the bedroom and heard something crash.

"Come on Alice, you have to help me," Grace spoke urgently as they started down the stairs.

"So tired, my legs..." Alice was struggling. "I can't stop her, please, save Kitty."

"She drugged the tea, I was stupid not to realise she'd not given up. Here," Grace waved something under Alice's nose which brought her a little more clarity. They reached the bottom of the stairs as the door to Henry's study cracked and buckled, drawing their attention to the fire behind it. Alice stood up a little straighter as her senses became clearer, "The kitchen," she whispered and Grace nodded as they moved towards the closed door and paused as Edward came up behind them.

"Grandad and Uncle Tommy and Eliza's doors are both locked and we can't wake them. Dad's phoning the fire brigade before he tries again but he says I have to take you outside now." He had his hand on his mothers arm. She shook it off saying,

"You and your dad go out of the front door, go now and let the fire brigade get the others out. We're going through the kitchen to get Kitty;

we'll get out that way. Go!"

As soon as he turned, Grace took hold of Alice's shaking shoulders and whispered, "You need to be strong, just follow me but be as quiet as you can." Alice nodded in response and Grace slowly turned the brass knob and pushed the door silently open. They shared one more glance before Grace stepped forward and started to carefully ascend the stone flagged steps, Alice right behind her, all the time aware that they were walking straight into the source of the black shadows that had dominated both of their lives.

It was later confirmed that there were a number of other fires around the house, but fiercest and the heart of the fire was the empty room between Alice's and Eliza and Tommy's rooms and so Alice knew that she was meant to die that night, she had outlived her usefulness. She had been drugged, along with everyone else; all of them intended victims of a completely deranged mind.

The first fire engine arrived about twenty minutes after being called and an ambulance and second engine a few minutes later, followed by another ambulance and a police car. Despite their best efforts, all the firemen could do was to attempt to contain the blaze and it would be sometime before they could send anyone inside to check for survivors. Edward and Malcolm were both taken to hospital in the first ambulance, their burns apparent, but Grace stayed with Alice, still searching the grounds for Kitty. One of the two policemen who had arrived in the first car joined the search with an almost hysterical Alice while the second one radioed for advice on how to handle the situation. The Heskeths were, after all, still a big name in the area. He was struggling to understand the two women's insistence that the child was not in the house and the odd things they had been shouting as he tried to get them to tell him who was still unaccounted for.

"It's all a bit funny Sir, one of them was saying there was no point going into the house. When I asked her if Henry Hesketh had got out, she said no, said him and his brother are both dead, then she says that somebody was trying to kill them all and why am I wasting time asking her questions and not looking for her daughter." A further two police cars were quickly dispatched to the scene.

The sun rose at around 7.30 the next morning and with daylight came a very sorry vision of the smouldering ruins of Burntwood and the story of the events of that night began to unfold. There are two versions of what had happened, the official one, which Alice and Grace gave to the police in their statements, and another version. A version of what they really saw and did, a version that neither of them discussed with anyone else until Alice finally had to tell Billy five years later. However, neither of these versions can account for a small window of time that remained locked in Kitty's memory for over forty years.

In the official version, given by both women identically, Grace had been woken by noise on the landing. On climbing out of bed she had seen the smoke under her door. She woke her husband and son, asking them to wake Henry, Eliza and Thomas while she went to rouse Alice and Kitty. Alice became hysterical when she realised Kitty was not in bed and so Grace called to Edward to telephone for help and went downstairs with Alice to search for her. They noticed the kitchen door open and a light on as they came into the hall. Edward was just behind them and had just picked up the phone as Grace and Alice descended the steps. Eliza was standing by the sink looking shaken and worried. She had heard a noise and got up to investigate but seen nothing other than the door to the kitchen wide open and a light on. Alice told her that Kitty was missing and Eliza seemed really concerned and had sat at the table with a glass of water. Grace told her there was a fire upstairs and they needed to leave the house. Eliza sad she would follow them and to go and find her granddaughter.

The back entrance to the kitchen was indeed wide open and calling back to Eliza once more to leave the building, both women took coats from the hooks by the door and went out to look for the girl. Grace and Alice insisted that Eliza was fine and was about to follow them once she had put on her shoes and coat.

Once outside they had split up to look for Kitty. Alice had gone first to check in the kitchen garden, shed and greenhouses while Grace went round to the front to check her husband and son were out and safe. She told them that Eliza was safe but Kitty was missing. Malcolm was sitting on the floor half way down the drive. He had some bad burns and his breathing was laboured. Edward assured her he had alerted the emergency services and asked them to contact Billy. As she left them to go back to help search the grounds for her niece, she could hear the sirens of the approaching vehicles.

Grace found Kitty quite a way from the house, at the bottom of the steps to the ornamental garden, unconscious and practically naked in just her pants, her right arm at such a twisted angle there was little doubt it was badly broken. An x-ray would later confirm that all three of the bones were fractured, the break to the humerus being the worst and the joint to the elbow completely shattered. Grace had covered her niece with the old coat she had picked up as she had left the kitchen, before shouting for Alice, who had arrived, followed shortly by one of the police constables. Edward had stayed with his father and helped him move further down the drive as the house was now fully ablaze. It was only a few minutes after Grace had left them that the first police car and ambulance arrived followed swiftly by three other emergency vehicles.

It was only then that Grace realised that Eliza could still be in the house and told one of the policemen. He alerted one of the firemen who went to check out the kitchen door at the back of the house. At this point, the fire was mainly confined to the front and on upper floors so he was able to easily get in.

Billy arrived in his dark red estate car with Jack in the passenger seat at the same time as the second police car. They had been woken by a policeman's knock and the initial state of panic in both brothers had been further fuelled by the hair-raising journey from Leeds. They had passed the first ambulance, carrying Edward and Malcolm, half a mile from the drive, making Billy push down harder on the accelerator again and having to floor the brakes to stop in a swerve in front of two police cars by the gates. The two constables were on the verge of blocking their entry to the drive when Jack explained quickly that his wife and daughter were inside. When they finally got through to the back of the house, Kitty was being stretchered into an ambulance. She was floating in and out of consciousness but her distress was palpable to all the concerned onlookers. Jack's car which had been parked at the front of the house, in front of the study window, was completely destroyed. Billy gave him his car keys as he followed his wife into the ambulance with their daughter. Alice had hesitated before stepping in but a reassuring hand on her arm from Grace and a slight nod gave her the strength to climb in and sit by Kitty. The second ambulance passed the third police car, carrying the senior officer, at the end of the drive. Alice felt a surge of something as she saw the blue lights go by and prayed that Grace would not let them down.

When interviewed by the detective in charge, Grace had spoken at length about recent prowlers in the grounds and when he checked, Detective Inspector Barry Fields did indeed find two reports of phone calls from the house about suspected intruders. On both occasions, a car had been sent but no one or anything suspicious had been found. Alice had been near to hysterical when questioned briefly at the hospital and refused to leave her daughters side. Kitty was still unconscious and the doctors were concerned about a head injury.

When Eliza's body was found in the kitchen, a full scale man hunt was launched to find the arsonist and murderer.

Chapter Five

1971

In the real version of what happened on that fateful night, the sight that confronted Alice and Grace as they stepped down into the kitchen was very different to the scene they had both described in their statements to the police. It was actually the scene that the first fireman was confronted with when he went in to the house via the back door almost forty minutes later, apart of course, for the changes made by the two women.

Eliza's body was in front of the huge cooking range which was still hot, the oven door was wide open and Eliza's head was leaning in onto the bottom shelf, cooking slowly, as she lay half propped against it. Her dressing gown fully open, revealing her white cotton nightdress, stained dark red around the stab wounds which had pierced her heart. Alice opened her mouth to let out a scream but Grace stopped her, grabbing her shoulders and shaking her. The two women locked eyes as thoughts and images flowed between them before Alice blinked and stepped back and with a nod from Grace both of them began a fast and coordinated staging of the crime. Grace bent down and carefully felt in the pockets of Eliza's robe. She pulled out two keys and small dark blue book. She put the book in her dressing gown pocket and the keys on the table. Alice picked up a glass from the draining board and half filled it with water before placing it on the table. Grace picked up a large kitchen towel and wet it under the tap. The back door was open and blood smeared over the handle, she wiped it clean before putting the towel in her dressing gown pocket. She took her car keys from her handbag on the small table in the alcove and then both women took two coats each from the hooks by the door and went outside, leaving the door open.

They found Kitty almost straight away and while Alice unfastened and took off her daughters blood stained nightdress and placed it on the ground, Grace wiped the blood from the girl's hands and arms with the

245

towel. Alice stoked her daughter's hair after covering her with the second coat she had taken from the kitchen. Grace picked up the nightdress and wrapped it tightly in the stained wet towel. Kitty had hardly stirred. The two women exchanged a look before Alice nodded and moved from her crouched position to sit at the side of her daughters head. Grace walked briskly to get to the front of the house to get to her car, leaving Alice with her daughter. She needed to check on Malcolm and Edward and tell them she had seen Eliza alive. She also needed to hide Kitty's night dress and the tea towel under the spare wheel in the boot of her car before getting her keys back into the house and put them next to her handbag just inside the kitchen door. It didn't take too long and in less than ten minutes she was back.

Alice struggled to leave Kitty, hysteria was kicking in but she managed to pull herself together knowing how important it was to sully the waters. The women did an excellent job of creating a smoke screen and adding weight to the intruder theory and keeping Kitty in the clear. It was a well executed bit of theatre and it almost worked.

It was later confirmed that Henry and Thomas were both found in their beds and after a thorough and detailed examination of their remains, their cause of death was established. Henry died from smoke inhalation which had most probably occurred in his sleep. Thomas's post mortem revealed a slightly more alarming fact. Although both bodies were badly burnt, the fact that someone had caved in half of Thomas's scull before hand was still very much apparent. The two separate fires in both rooms were initially accelerated by Henry's excellent brandy but had not burned for long. Both doors had been locked, according to Edward and Malcolm's testimony, presumably from the outside as no keys were found in either room. Two keys were found on the large oak table, next to a half full glass of water, down in the kitchen, the only room that remained almost fully intact and barely touched by the fire.

Thirty-six hours after the fire, Police Inspector Barry Fields was under pressure to close the case and let the family grieve – Henry had been a magistrate and had friends in high places. Fields sat at his desk rereading the reports and statements and felt the disquiet he always felt when something just didn't seem right. He rubbed his eyes and stretched before picking up the two witness statements again and placed them side by side on the desk in front of him. He was certain they were lying about something but no matter how many times he went through it, he got nowhere. He had questioned both women again and their testimonies were word perfect, answering all his questions with confidence but his uncertainty remained; they were not telling the whole truth or withholding something. He didn't believe the story about an intruder, it was all too pat, there was something they were hiding he was sure. However, after a phone call from his superior, which he was sure was instigated by the family, he was told to back off, the conversation leaving no doubt that his gut feelings or intuition were of little interest when a family like the Heskeths were concerned, so he launched a hunt for the reported intruder, telling the newspapers that this was the line of inquiry they were following.

When Alice saw on the front pages of the newspaper that the police were looking for an intruder or intruders in connection with the Hesketh House massacre, her hand went involuntarily to her heart. What she didn't know was that a small chain of events that were happening back at the South Yorkshire Constabulary Headquarters would lead to an unravelling of the story that she and Grace had concocted.

A bloody kitchen knife that matched Eliza's stab wounds was found in the shrubbery, close to where Kitty had been found, by an eager young constable as daylight had broken on the morning after the fire. He had found it just after the unmarked police car carrying Inspector Fields had left the scene. He had given it to his sergeant who had been about to go off duty and so had left it in the glove compartment of the police car. It was more than forty-eight hours later before he remembered and retrieved it, finally handing it in to be logged as evidence. When news of this reached the detective inspector, a further twelve hours later, he immediately put on his coat and set off for Pinderfields Hospital to question the teenage Hesketh girl. Feeling sure he was finally getting somewhere, he was disappointed to discover that the girl was not fully conscious and it also appeared she was being guarded by her mother and aunt; his two unreliable witnesses. Noticing the blood leave the mothers already pale faces when he mentioned that the murder weapon had been found close to where her daughter had fallen, he felt sure he was on the right track.

The next morning before setting off for work, he was called again by his superior and told to stop harassing the family. By the time he finally got the go ahead to interview the girl and went back to the hospital, on the Wednesday morning four days after the fire, he was told by the forward thinking doctor who had been treating her that Kitty Hesketh had been transferred to Stanley Royd as she was suffering from paranoid schizophrenia. It was all he could do not to shout "Yes!" as the policeman put two and two together and came up with his child arsonist and murderer.

Chapter Six

Kathryn - Now

There is a large sliver birch tree outside my kitchen door that whispers about the life I might have had. A husband maybe, and children... and there is sometimes a flicker of regret deep within my thoughts but it never catches. I know too much about grief and loss to allow that thought to gain any purchase. Grief is a many layered and complicated emotion that takes its toll in lots of different ways.

As I stepped back into my life as a confused twenty year old, I knew the wife and mother role was one I would never play; I dare not be responsible for anyone else being touched by our family's curse. Finally, I got to make a decision about how I would live my life.

Immediately after the fire, the confusion and pain experienced by the surviving members of our family was immense. I think it must have been particularly hard for Pip, not helped by the fact that he seemed to become a bit-player in the family drama and no one ever took the time to explain anything to him. Although, even if Mum or Grace, the people in the know, had taken him to one side to fill in some of the blanks, I doubt it would have made any difference, he would not have believed it. He would never have been able to comprehend how the people he knew could have behaved in such a way or the sheer madness of it all.

He was told the official version of course and, had he asked, I am sure he would have been reassured that all the talk and silly rumours of my homicidal madness were ridiculous but I doubt he asked. He is after all, his father's son. I have no animosity towards my brother for anything that happened, even though I am certain he suspected things weren't right a long time before anyone else and well before Mum forced our move away from Eliza and Tommy. To be fair, I guess there was a timing issue here, what with his own struggles, internal and external, as he passed through puberty with the burden of perceived expectations, courtesy of the Hesketh name, I certainly do not begrudge him the happy life he has now. After all, he and Karen, his wife, have given me the closest thing to what was lost to me.

The first time I met my sister-in-law was two days after I came home from Middleton. She had been married to my brother for three years and was seven months pregnant. Pip had visited me at Middleton quite a few times over the previous year and things had been good and easy with him. He had also phoned on the night of my repatriation, suggesting that I go over to their house with Mum for dinner.

"It would be great for you to see our home, we've done loads to it and I'd love to show you the baby's room – which I have decorated single-handedly." he laughed.

"Well, yes, I'd love to see your house but..."

"And Karen is a great cook, she does a brilliant chicken a' la king and her black forest gateau is incredible," he cut off my objection and I felt my hand starting to shake.

"Hang on a minute," I said, putting the phone receiver down on the window ledge and walking towards the closed kitchen door. Mum, who had answered the phone and then left me to talk to my brother, was sitting at the small kitchen table looking though a copy of Woman's Realm magazine. She looked up with alarm as I came in.

"Pip wants me to go and see his house and his baby's bedroom and have dinner with his brilliant wife. Tell him, Mum." At this point I started to sob, "Tell him I can't, tell him Mum, please."

She got up and made to step towards me but stopped and took a deep breath before giving me the slightest of nods, turning towards the hall and moving quickly across to the phone. I wiped my face on the sleeve of my cardigan and got myself a glass of water.

"No problem," she said breezily as she came up beside me, "They are going to come here on Sunday for a cuppa, you can meet Karen then." She gave my arm a squeeze before turning back to her magazine and adding, "You'll like her, she's a bit bossy but she's a nice girl and she makes your brother happy."

I nodded and sat down opposite her, scraping the chair on the autumn leaves lino as I fidgeted myself into a comfortable position. I placed my palms flat on the table and addressed them rather than my mother.

"I do want to see his house and what he's done to it and of course I'm going to like Karen and I am happy and excited for him, for them, to be having a baby. I'm going to be an aunty," I lifted my head to look at her, "But I just need a bit more time to settle in here first."

"I know and you are absolutely right, there is no rush," she put her hands on top of mine, "We are all just so glad to have you home."

I woke up early on that Sunday morning and like the previous two days, I was jolted awake by a soundless scream, wondering where I was. The house was silent and warm and the sun was barely over the horizon but the thin unlined lilac curtains were no barrier to its message of a new day. I sat up slowly and smiled at Pearl who was watching me from the top of the bookshelf where she sat, leaning against the other family heirloom. I got washed and dressed quickly before going downstairs to make a pot of tea and then take a cup back up for Mum.

"Good grief, Kathryn," she exclaimed as I stepped into her room after a small knock, "What time is it, it's still dark outside?"

"No it isn't" I said, putting the mug down next to her bed, "You just have heavier curtains than me." I swished open her thick brown drapes to reveal a bright sunny morning. "It's half past seven."

"Half past seven on a Sunday morning!" Mum protested, pulling herself up a bit.

"Yes, well I haven't quite got the hang of days being different yet," I stayed at her window taking in the houses opposite and glancing down the street, "And anyway I thought you'd want to get up early and do some baking, you know, for the afternoon tea"

"No!" she said quickly and a little forcefully, "No baking. I don't do that anymore." She blinked herself more awake and her everyday smile banished the flash of anxiety from her features, "I have three boxes of Mr Kippling French Fancies in the cupboard and an Arctic roll in the freezer. I think that will be more than enough for the five of us."

I had asked Mum to invite Aunt Grace to come round as well. During my time at Middleton she had visited me every week, mostly with Mum but also sometimes on her own. Along with Mum, she was my therapist of choice.

Pip and Karen arrived first, unfashionably early, and Mum and I both went to welcome them through the door, wearing our very best smiley faces. Nobody hugged or kissed or invaded anyone else's personal space but it was all good, everyone keen for it to go well. Karen had brought a box of Milk Tray chocolates that she handed over to mum saying we should have them one night while we watched TV and Mum said that was very thoughtful and we would. Still smiling, we all walked the eight or nine steps into the knocked-through lounge diner where it all suddenly became slightly awkward. The room was light and cheerful as sunshine freckled its way through the nets in clear shards, giving testament to how well the house had been cleaned and dusted. Pip and Karen sat on the dark red draylon sofa, Pip leaning back and slightly tilted towards his wife who was perched upright on the edge, her heavily pregnant belly resting on her upper thighs. Mum looked really nervous, her wide eyes sweeping around the room before she announced in a pitch much higher than her normal voice that she would put the kettle on and left the room.

"How much longer do you have to go?" I asked from one of the armchairs, mirroring her uncomfortable position.

"Seven weeks," she replied, pushing her chest out slightly as she rubbed her back with the knuckles of her right hand.

"First of September," Pip informed me, "I think it's a boy," he added proudly.

"So long as it's healthy," Karen said smiling at him and he beamed back at her, "We have decorated the baby's room with some lovely wallpaper of sunshine and rainbows, even though Phil wanted footballs and racing cars." She rolled her eyes in a pretended despair at her husband.

"Phil?" I asked without meaning to.

"Are you sleeping alright Karen?" Mum asked quickly, having just come back into the room carrying a tray loaded with her best china and a cake stand adorned with the highly coloured French Fondant Fancies.

"Not bad thanks Alice, a bit of heartburn sometimes but that's all," she answered before turning to look at me, "Sorry, Kathryn, I know you call him Pip, I'll try and remember but he never shared that nugget of family history with me until a few days ago. He has been Phil or Philip to me since we met." Her smile was warm and friendly and I really wanted to like her and I wanted her to like me but there were words flying around in my head and I could feel the blood flushing my neck and cheeks. I was on edge and feeling excluded and distant. Even though I was now a woman, my emotional maturity was still that of an adolescent.

"Right, well as long as he shared the important bits with you, the fire, the madness, the killer sister."

"Kit." My brother almost said my name, my family name, but couldn't manage it, "Don't be so ridiculous and rude." He had sprung forward and was on the verge of standing up. I felt my eye leaking and the room became over-bright. Mum had been midway on her return trip to the kitchen to collect the tea pot. She let out a gasp at my words and turned back towards me. Karen burst out laughing.

"Goodness me, you don't pull any punches do you. Well it's not often that I'm lost for words." Turning to Pip, she added, "Your sister isn't being rude, she's just saving us all from skirting around stuff." She laughed again as she pushed him into the back of the sofa. I felt stupid and kept my head bowed a little, trying to work out what I should say or do. Karen leaned forward and took hold of my hand.

"I have really been looking forward to meeting you Kathryn. Phil, Pip, has told me so much about you, the important stuff about what a lovely person you are. Of course I know about all the rubbish written in the newspapers and the terrible things that happened to you but that's all in the past." She squeezed my hand and I lifted my head slightly to look at her. "I hope we will be great friends," she concluded. I managed a smile and Mum let out the breath she had apparently been holding and gave a nervous sounding laugh, just as the kettle in the kitchen started to whistle.

"Right, I'll get that tea mashed then," she said, quickly retreating to her domestic duties. I sat back a little and asked if they had decided on any names yet. Karen beamed at me before giving Pip a quick, sly glance and said,

"We like Jessica for a girl."

"But of course, as I said, we're having a boy and he's going to be called James," Pip added quickly.

"After your Uncle Jimmy?" Mum asked, sounding a little alarmed as she hovered in the doorway.

"No Mum, after James Bond of course," I answered, feeling a rush of nostalgia for the brother of my childhood. Karen did another mock eye roll,

"Absolutely right Kathryn. Still, it's not such a bad name," she smiled at Pip.

"I would probably call him Jamie," I said and turning back quickly to look at me, she nodded and said, "Me too."

There was a quick rap on the front door which then opened and an immaculately presented Aunt Grace, dressed in a beautifully cut black dress and a bolero, entered the conversation.

Mum brought in a second tray with her best teapot with matching milk jug and sugar bowl. Grace greeted us all with a smile and a hello before taking a seat on the sofa at the other side of Karen. Placing her black patent handbag next to her matching sling-back shoes, she eyed the cakes.

"Good God Alice, what on earth are these?"

"They're Mr Kipling French Fondant Fancies," Mum said smugly with a little nod, "The white ones are for you, I know you can't be doing with anything colourful."

"And he does make exceedingly good cakes," Pip said, leaning forward and taking a yellow one.

My brother met his wife at the University in Birmingham during fresher's week. It was the end of September 1972 and, although they became very close very quickly, I doubt that it was then that he mentioned his sister was in a lunatic asylum and suspected of trying to wipe out her whole family. Well of course he wouldn't as he didn't believe any of that then. In fact, for quite a long time he believed the intruder story that Mum and Grace had sold him but of course, Dad's death, in October 1976, just three months after Pip and Karen were married, changed everything.

Pip had been intending to go to Leeds along with his then girlfriend Julie but the repercussions of our family notoriety made him seek refuge in a place where the Hesketh name might not be so well known. Julie fell by the wayside very quickly too, her parents deciding they wanted to distance themselves and their daughter from any connection to us. Mum has said many times over the years that she never really liked Julie, she was a bit shifty, and Mum would not have put it past her or her mother to have told the newspapers some of the terrible lies they printed about the family - about me.

I didn't have much of a memory of Julie and am not sure if I ever even spoke to her much. Mum says I must have but she clearly wasn't that memorable for me and once I had met Karen, I couldn't imagine Pip with anyone else.

On the night Pip, or Phil as he had started calling himself, first met Karen, she asked him what he was studying and when he said engineering she laughed and said,

"Yesterday, I couldn't spell engineer and now I are one!"

"Ok smart lady and what are you studying?"

"I'm doing a combined degree in English and History."

"Ah right, is that because you can't make up your mind or because you're just hedging your bets?"

"No, it's because I'm brilliant at both subjects."

"Right, so while I'm helping to provide the world with roads, bridges and towns you will be able to go around correcting everyone's spelling and telling them stories about the past that may or may not be true."

"Wow – I think we should get another drink and continue this debate over there." she had responded, her face lighting up with a beaming smile; and that was it. The dye was cast and their love began but although they were almost inseparable for the next three years, Pip didn't tell her anything about our family until they had both done their finals. Karen was going on a three month working holiday in France with one of her girlfriends and was disappointed that Pip wasn't up for a bit of travelling.

He told her the night before she went, asking her not to interrupt or say anything until he'd finished his narrative and then at the end he told her he wanted her to enjoy her French adventure. He said he really loved her but it would be good for them to be apart and give her time to consider how she felt about him, especially now she knew about his family and background. She listened without saying a word and as he stopped speaking, an unusual silence fell on them both before he stood up, gave her a peck on the cheek and squeezed her hand. He said again that he loved her but understood if she felt their relationship had run its course and he left, driving back to Leeds in his Austin 1300.

Thank goodness that even though he'd never brought her home to meet Alice or Billy, or told her much at all about his family, he had told her that they ran the Farsley Working Men's Club, which is how Karen managed to find him when she turned up on the door step two days later; all thoughts of France forgotten.

Karen became the sister I had never had; such a wonderful, calm and patient friend. I know there have been times over the years that she has been uncomfortable with things I've said and done but she has taken it all in her stride. She was the one that helped me work out what I was going to do with my life.

I had six GCE's and three A'Levels gained after private tuition, paid for by Aunt Grace while I was at Middleton. I am sure that my physician at that time, Dr Angel, had quite a crush on Aunt Grace but he also seemed genuinely interested in making me better. After the previous ghost years, he had encouraged the studying as something to fill my hours with, giving me a purpose and helping me find a way to express myself.

Once I was released back into the community, I could have floundered, Mum and Pip thinking I needed protecting but Karen, after Grace's initial suggestion, was keen to help me enter higher education and with their help I went on to do a degree in English literature and an MA in creative writing, both through the Open University.

It was a good job Karen had insisted on the neutral colours for the nursery. Their beautiful baby girl arrived in the early hours of Friday 7th September at Leeds General Infirmary. I went with Mum the next day to see mother and child who were both doing well and I thought my heart would melt at the sight of the tiny little six pound seven ounce ball of love wrapped in a pink blanket. My brother and sister-in-law looked exhausted but deliriously happy as they fussed over the clear plastic crib containing their daughter.

"Do you want a hold, Mum?" Pip asked and I thought Mum's nod of response was because she was too emotional to speak but watching her carefully as Pip placed her granddaughter in her arms, I saw the truth of it. I saw her look down, moving the blanket slightly to look properly into the tiny baby face and I watched the relief as she saw nothing but a beautiful baby girl and heard the catch in her voice as she pronounced,

"She is just perfect," she cried with happiness.

"Yes Mum, she has all her fingers and toes and is absolutely the most beautiful baby I have ever seen," Pip agreed with pride as he leaned down and gave Karen a kiss.

"You clever, clever girl – thank you."

After a few minutes of watching Mum, I got my first cuddle too and thought I was doing great at keeping it together. That was until Pip said,

"Here you go, say hello to your niece, Jessica Kathryn."

Chapter Seven

Kathryn - Now

As a patient of the various institutions, sedated and chemically controlled for most of it and separate and isolated for all of it, I was unaware of the circus that was going on out in the real world. No one was caught for the murder of my grandparents and Uncle Henry or for starting the fire that burnt down our ancestral home and so no one was charged or tried and punished. The case, I believe, is actually still officially open but no one will ever waste any time re-examining this crime. Not even the diligent and tenacious Inspector Fields who believed he knew the perpetrator and had, what he considered, evidence to back up his theory which probably would have been enough to get a prosecution. However, when the case was presented to them, the powers that be would not allow the prosecution and his theory was quashed along with any conviction.

I am not sure whether it was my name or my age that they struggled with or the fact that I was diagnosed as being as mad as a bag of frogs, or even perhaps the pleas and remonstrations on my behalf from Aunt Grace, Uncle Jack and my Dad. Whatever the reason, it was decided that, as my parents had agreed to my treatment and incarceration, there would be no further investigation into my involvement in the event. Mum and Aunt Grace, still the only witnesses, stuck to their story of Eliza being alive in the kitchen when they went out to look for me. The autopsy on Eliza could not give any accurate time of death as the heat from the oven and kitchen door, being left open and letting in the cold night air, played havoc with the body temperature.

Inspector Fields may not have agreed with the decision but he was not foolish enough to risk his career and so he kept up the pretence of looking for person or persons unknown, while moving on to other cases. However, he might have let it slip to one or two of his cronies about Killer Kitty, the mad teenager responsible for trying to massacre her whole family, and how it had been hushed up because of the family name. He could also have been the one who leaked the information to the newspapers that I had been sectioned and put in a padded cell where I would stay, no doubt, for the rest of my life.

This is a matter of supposition on my part; I don't know for sure that he did this but I'm sure Grandad Tommy would have made him odds on favourite as the snitch. I thought about trying to find out for sure as part of my research but soon realised that it would be hard, if not impossible, for me get any information about a still serving police officer who had since moved up the ranks and what his relationship with the press was. And anyway, it didn't really matter – it wouldn't really change anything. The names they called me and the things that were said couldn't hurt me and the newspapers very soon became chip papers as new stories and scandals made new headlines. As I've got older, I've realised I was lucky that I had my flirt with notoriety back in the early 70's and not twenty or thirty years later when the press would indeed have had a field day with my story, not to mention the stuff that would have been on the internet. So I confined my research to what I really wanted to know, filling in the blanks that led us to that fateful night.

I am not sure how I'm going to cope, losing Alice. This is how I think of her now. I know her, I know all of her. Not just the Alice who struggled to keep me safe or the one who fought for my freedom and then continued my stability. I know the Alice from before I was born, Alice the small child who coped with the loss of her father and the neglect of a selfish and delusional mother. The confused but hopeful teenager sold a dream of a perfect life. Alice the young wife and mother coming to terms with her surrounds as if waking up from a dream.

But the Alice I like best is the one I have now. The one I have got to know in the last forty years of her life. My brother and his wife went on to have two more daughters in the next two years, Helen and Megan. All just as beautiful as each other and equally perfect, bringing much joy to

Alice and me. I relished my role as an aunty and was only too happy to help with babysitting as and when required but what made me happier was watching Mum with them, seeing the love she felt radiate around her like a halo.

I got a job at Pudsey Library while I did my OU courses and absolutely loved it. It was only part time which meant I had some daytime hours free to help Karen with the girls and also talk through some bits of my course with her.

When I had completed my studying, I continued with the library service and in 1987, when I finally passed my driving test, I worked at various sites around Leeds and occasionally drove the mobile library to cover sickness and holidays. I enjoyed the work but never committed to full time. The money I had inherited, not a fortune of course but more than enough, had been put in trust for me and so I have been financially comfortable all my adult life, meaning I could pursue writing as a hobby. I started to have some success back in the early 90's with a series of children's books, which my publisher marketed as modern day fairy stories, and my three nieces became my biggest fans.

The series consisted of six books following the trials and tribulations of five children with extrasensory perception, born into normal families, whose parents are unaware of their ability. The first five books are stand alone stories of each of the children and titled only with the child's names; Jasmine, Matthew, Shelby, Nicholas and Jack. I wrote them so they didn't have to be read in any order but the sixth book, the last one, tells the story of what happens when all five children meet and is called 'The Indigo Children'. I have a pen name of course although, in this case, not to protect the innocent.

The success of my scribbling was a real big deal for me, I had had the initial idea for these stories during my last few months in hospital but it did take me nearly ten years to write them. Although I found it cathartic to put my thoughts into words, I found it emotionally draining, especially the last part and so, despite the disappointment and pleas from my agent and publisher, I refused to continue the series. I said I wanted a break from writing and would come back in a year or so with another project.

I had first heard the term indigo child, or something like it, when I was in Stanley Royd back in 1971 as a frightened thirteen year old. Two nurses were having a conversation close to my bed about another patient, a girl, Jasmine, who was a bit older than me whose parents, according to them, were 'feckless hippies' and completely to blame for the girl's madness. The girl I saw was quiet with large vacant eyes, circled with bruise-like dark rings and bore no resemblance to the aggressive and feral child they were discussing.

"The mother keeps insisting that she's one of them Indigo kids, you know with special powers and the like," one of them scoffed, "But of course, Dr Adams soon put her straight." They both looked across the room to where she sat on the floor, her arms round her knees and rocking gently.

"He said the term Indigo child is a made up thing, being used by ill-informed or bad parents who had failed their offspring. These children were not gifted or special in anyway other than they needed medical intervention to make them normal."

I filed away these words in the drug-proof tin I kept in the back of my damaged brain, knowing that there would be a time that I would need to retrieve them and examine the possibilities that they suggested. I watched Jasmine for the rest of that day and a few more days after that. I am not exactly sure how long after this but one night I woke up suddenly and she was standing at the side of my bed.

"Why are you staring at me all the time?" she had asked, quietly, with nothing more than curiosity in her tone. I wasn't afraid and as I sat up I saw it, the light all around her, a cool blue indigo haze emanating from her like she was bathed in a coloured spotlight.

"You're an indigo child," I said and she smiled at me and leaned forward.

"And so are you," she whispered, nodding slightly before turning around and going back to her own bed.

I didn't see Jasmine again the next day or for a few days after that but when she was back on the ward she looked even more absent. She had started ECT and between sessions, her Largactil dosage was increased to keep better control of her. I only saw her once more after that; well actually, I don't know if I did see her again or if I dreamt our meeting. I have some vague and almost illusive memory of sitting with her on a black and white tiled floor, our legs stretched in front of us, our feet bare. Feeling happy and safe. She was telling me something but I have never been able to catch the thread of what it was even though I am sure I was nodding.

For the first few weeks after I came out of hospital, I woke up with this massive anxiety that there was something I had forgotten, feeling as if I was being interrupted from searching for something. It would take most of the morning to calm these fears, to feel that it was just a dream. It wasn't like waking up from a nightmare, my dreams are never scary, it's the waking that shakes me and there is always the echo of Jasmine's pale and frightened face as my consciousness returns. I still get this feeling from time to time, not too often but more so just recently since Grace died. It had been her idea to write Jasmine's story, the one I had made up in my lost years, the one where she had a good life, as a way of either capturing or dispelling the anxiety I sometimes felt.

When my books became a success, Grace had been delighted for me, in her way, and said maybe one day I would have the strength to write my own story. I had laughed and said that would be difficult as there is so much of it I don't remember, not to mention understand. She had smiled and raised her eyebrows before suggesting that my memory was not as vague as I liked to pretend – 'You can't kid a kidder' - and maybe I should do a bit of research into the family history. If I didn't like what I found, perhaps I could just write my own version. I had said I liked that idea and maybe I would do just that. She had got up to leave then but as she leaned in for a hug she'd said,

"Do your research, make your notes but please wait until me and your mother are gone before you tell the world about our complicit silence."

It's Grace's funeral tomorrow and since my waking at first light this morning, I have been full of the aching pain of loss. It's taken me by complete surprise; I thought I was prepared, ready and able to cope with the inevitable sadness of the official goodbye. Perhaps my grief has been hiding behind my annoyance that this small family funeral which Grace had requested now looks like being a massively oversubscribed event, one to be seen at. There was a large quarter-page notice about the service in the local paper yesterday and Mum has been inundated with sympathy cards, mostly from people she doesn't know, saying they will be coming to say their goodbyes to a wonderful lady.

I phoned Pip last night, furious and ready to give him a piece of my mind for turning our goodbye to Grace into a three-ringed circus. I know – a ridiculous thing to say but I was cross. Once I'd finished blustering, Pip responded with bewilderment, saying he doesn't really understand how things have got so out of hand. It started with one or two of Grace's friends from the Women's Institute asking if there was anything they could do to help and then telling him to leave it with them to make sure everyone knew the details of the arrangements. They had, it transpired, placed the death notice in the Yorkshire Post giving details of the funeral. I had burst out laughing, my anger completely displaced with the hysteria of my brother and his wife being ambushed by the W.I.

Mum also laughed when I told her but later. As we sat together, I wondered out loud if the high profile of the service would set the rumour mill off again and maybe I should speak to these busybodies about their interfering. Mum sighed and put her mug down on the coffee table before taking two Hobnobs from the open packet in front of her. She started to nibble one before telling me I needed to stop being manic and hiding my sense of loss behind a grievance I didn't have.

"What does it matter who comes and who doesn't come?" she asked, pushing the packet of biscuits towards me, "Gracie was an extraordinary woman and she was liked and respected by a lot of people. No matter what she said, I think she'll be touched that so many people are making the effort to come, even if some of them will only be there to do a bit of networking over the bun fight." She took a sip of her Ovaltine, "I think she'll even like that, it will put one of those rare smiles on her face."

I acknowledged that she was probably right but felt uneasy at the way she referred to Grace in the present tense and the way she looked to the empty seat next to me on the sofa as she spoke.

"Is she here Mum?" I asked, my voice cracking with emotion. Her eyes glanced quickly to the empty seat, then to me before she looked down at her steaming mug. She took a another sip then put her left hand on her chest and said,

"She's in here love, where she's been for most of my life, even if I didn't know it." Seeing the tears in her eyes, I didn't respond. I knew she was lying. Grace was there and I knew why.

Chapter Eight

1971

It was teeming with rain as Alice and Jack left the Stanley Royd Hospital in the early afternoon of Wednesday 28th October 1971. Despite the downpour, Alice walked slowly, her head slightly bowed, while her brother-in-law walked besides her trying to nudge her into a faster pace. By the time they got into the car, they were both soaked. He wound his window down slightly to help clear the windscreen as he started the engine of his brother's car.

"Do you want to go straight back to the club or do you want to go and see Grace?" he asked her as he turned the windscreen wipers to full speed. Grace had moved into Jack's house on Alfred Street as she literally had nowhere else to go. Edward and Malcolm were both still in hospital.

"I need to talk to Grace," she mumbled, her words as if in her sleep. The two women had not had any time to speak since leaving the scene of the fire, having given their statements separately.

"Ok love," Jack answered, unable to think of anything else to say and set off towards Royston. Alice sat rigid in the passenger seat, staring in front of her, her eyes following the hypnotic whooshing and scraping of the wipers. She was willing her mind to disengage from the utter despair that was smashing into all her senses. How could this have happened, they had been so careful, how can things have played out like this. She had a sudden image of Eliza smiling triumphantly at her and a sob of rage and despondency burst from her. Jack automatically hit the brakes but eased off slightly only slowing the car as he glanced at his sister-in-law.

"You alright Alice?" he asked, feeling the stupidity of his words. Of course she wasn't alright. An arrogant and smarmy copper had just told her they were bringing charges against her thirteen year-old daughter for torching Burntwood and murdering her granny. He stole another quick glance before flicking on his left indicator and turning off the busy A road and into the car park of The Castle public house. Alice's whole body was shaking as she sobbed into her hands. Pulling the hand brake on, he turned in his seat and lifted his hand to touch her but quickly pulled it back up to his own face and raked his fingers through his hair.

"Jesus, Alice I have no idea what these bloody idiots are thinking. Anybody with half a brain could see that Kitty is just a kid and can't possibly have done this."

Alice continued her weeping, the noise she was making becoming louder. Jack could contain himself no more. He leaned towards her, engulfing her in his open arms and she melted into them. On the moment of their touch, she let out a howl of desolation and Jack held her head to his chest, trying to absorb some of her sorrow and ease her pain. He rocked her gently and they stayed like this for a good five minutes, Jack stoking her hair as her sobs subsided. His emotions were all over the place, he tried to control his breathing but the smell of her hair was driving him crazy. He was trying to engage his brain, to think of something to say when he felt her become rigid and pull back from him, her hands on his chest.

"Raymond!" she yelled, "What did Raymond say when he wanted to go home? Pip said he was scared of something, what was it, what did he say?"

"Alice..." putting his hands on her shoulders, "Ray is a sensitive lad, he gets these odd moods sometimes."

"He knew! Jesus – why didn't I see it before? Oh My God, why didn't I see it?" she exclaimed, banging the bottom of the palm of her hand on her forehead, "I need to talk to Grace, she can come back to Farsley with us and talk to Raymond, she'll know if he saw it." She was suddenly animated, her eyes wide and wild, "Come on Jack let's get going."

Jack pulled his arms back as she turned to face front again, reaching down in the footwell for her handbag. He was trying to process what was going on and felt suddenly cautious as he turned the key in the ignition.

"Alice love, this isn't something to do with your mother is it, this seeing and not seeing. Ray's had a rough time losing his mother and then moving about. What happened at the house, well I don't think Ray knows anything about that, he just wanted to go home." He tried to keep the panic out of his voice as he moved the car into gear and edged towards the exit of the car park. He turned the heater fan onto full in an attempt to demist the windows.

"Don't worry Jack; we won't upset him I promise." She was suddenly calm and blew her nose loudly before adding, "And my mother was a charlatan who only saw pound notes and gullible people."

"Right," he said, nodding uncertainly, "Can you wind your window down a bit 'til the windows clear?" Alice wound the window down fully and gulped in a couple of big mouthfuls of the cold damp air. The rain had eased off a little but was still heavy and blowing into the car. She took another breath through her nose before winding it up to a within a couple of inches of closed. Half an hour later the VW Passat Estate pulled up by the curb in front of the semi-detached house Jack had bought when he had actually considered returning to the family fold. Jack thought he would laugh at the irony if it wasn't all so bloody terrible.

Jack put the kettle on to make the three of them a cup of tea while Grace took Alice up to the bathroom to 'sort out' her face and hair. He leaned against the back door and watched the gas jets dancing under the black kettle that had come with his mother from Sunny Bank. He was trying to get everything straight in his head. Raymond's insistence that they leave Burntwood, saying 'something bad was going to happen', well that had been a bit odd but he'd put it down to his natural shyness and, let's face it, he thought to himself, that old house, even with all its lights on was a dismal and creepy old place. The only other time Ray had been there was for Jimmy's funeral and there had been a dead body in an open bloody coffin. It was no wonder the lad didn't want to be there. These had been Jack's unspoken thoughts on the night of the party, as he had sat, in his semi-drunken state, next to Billy on their drive back to Leeds. Raymond had been silent for the whole journey and once they got to the club, he had not said much then either but seemed a lot calmer. Billy told them to use Pip's room and Raymond went straight to bed. Jack had another couple of drinks with Billy before going through to join him. He was still awake, lying on his back looking at the ceiling. Jack took off his shirt and trousers and, as he pulled back the covers, he saw his son was still fully clothed.

"Didn't you feel like getting undressed son?" he laughed.

"It'll save time in the morning," he answered and then he turned on his side. Jack switched off the light, wishing again that Delores was still around to explain how he was supposed to understand and parent this strange lad of theirs.

The next morning they were woken at 5.30 by a banging on the door to the flat. As Jack opened his eyes, he saw his son at the window looking down into the street.

"What's going on?" he asked, holding his throbbing head, the combination of too much brandy and too little sleep.

"It's the police," said Ray, moving away from the window to sit on the chair in front of the desk to put on his shoes, "You'd better get dressed; we'll have to go in a minute."

"What...Ray..." he suddenly felt sick as he tried to twist out of bed, one hand over his mouth, the other on the side of his throbbing temple. The banging had stopped and he was aware of voices, then Billy shouting. Jack forced himself to his feet and went to the window. A BMW police motorcycle was parked in front of the door, its headlight and rear blue light still flashing. Jack watched the rider turn and start to walk away as the door slammed and he heard his brother running back upstairs yelling,

"Jack, there's been a fire, at Burntwood, it's bad, really bad, we've got to get back there now!"

Billy had managed to calm down enough to call the club secretary and explain that he wasn't going to be around to open up while Jack had thrown up the top layer of semi-absorbed brandy that had been fermenting on top of his stomach. He was standing at the kitchen sink gulping down a second glass of water when Billy picked up his car keys. Raymond was already standing by the door with a totally unfathomable expression.

"You all right son?" he asked, trying to sound a lot calmer than he felt.

"Yeah, I think so," he replied nodding, "Shall I stay here to hand over the keys for Uncle Billy?"

"Yes!" Billy shouted, "Yes Ray me lad, that would be a big help, me and your dad can get off now. Mick Wellard will be here in about half an hour, he'll knock at the door. Tell him I've taken the alarm off and I'll let him know what's happening when I get back. Ok?"

Raymond nodded his understanding as Billy thrust a large bunch of keys in to his hands and grabbed his jacket from the hooks by the door.

"Get some breakfast, Ray, I'll be back soon." Jack forced a smile and reached out to ruffle his son's hair. Although it was a forced and unnatural movement and the thick black curls hardly budged, Raymond gave his father a small smile, letting him know he understood the gesture. It was only as he was sitting in the passenger seat as his brother drove along the Stanningley bypass, well in excess of the speed limit, that he remembered Raymond's words about 'something bad' happening at Burntwood.

Five days later, standing in the kitchen of his Alfred Street house, he could feel a dull ache in his stomach and terrible sense of foreboding.

The boiling kettle brought him back to his overcrowded surroundings. He reached up for the tea caddy, his hands brushing a jar of his mother's homemade strawberry jam which toppled from the shelf. His sharp reflexes kicked in and he caught it. He replaced it further back on the shelf and flexed his shoulders to try and calm the adrenalin rush. Turning off the gas from the whistling kettle, he was aware of the women's voices upstairs. He could hear Alice, still clearly distressed, and Grace, her tone calm, but he could only catch the odd word. He put the tea leaves in the pot and drenched them with the boiling water, all the time trying to blot out a feeling of dread that was growing within him. After allowing five minutes for the tea to mash, he poured out three mugs before going to the bottom of the stairs and calling up, "I've made you both some tea."

Not waiting for a reply, he collected his own mug and went to sit in the living room with it, trying to fill his head with thoughts of his uncomplicated life with Delores. His drink was finished slowly but the other two mugs remained untouched. It was nearly an hour before Alice and Grace came back downstairs, both seeming subdued and thankfully, Alice was no longer crying.

The three of them set off back to Leeds, Grace following in her own car as she wanted to visit her husband and son later. Raymond had been making himself useful over the last few days, helping Billy stock the bar and washing glasses as well as keeping the bar clean. Pip was off school and back at home but had been given some work to do to keep up with his studies. When Alice and Jack had left that morning to go and see Kitty in Pinderfields, they were all feeling that things were bad, what with three members of the family dead, and Kitty, Malcolm and Edward in hospital but he had thought they were all pulling together and the worst was behind them. Now he realised there was more to come.

When they pulled up in the car park, Jack took a breath to prepare himself for what was to come. The club was closed but Alice let them into the flat entrance and then opened the internal door where they saw Billy and Raymond in the bar restocking the shelves. Alice had been quiet for most of the journey and Jack had hoped that whatever Grace had said to her when they talked upstairs had calmed her down. But as she entered the bar area, pushing open the door fully with a sudden violent force, he realised it hadn't. Billy stood up in alarm at the crash from the door but seeing Alice, his face softened,

"Ay up, you frightened the life out of me," he laughed, "How's she doing today?" He came out of the bar walking towards his wife. Alice met him halfway and thumped him hard in his chest with her fist bawled.

"Why did you tell that doctor about her episodes, calling them fits and funny turns? You might as well have just said she was crazy or not right in the head, you bloody idiot, you've made it worse!" She spat the words at him and was bringing her other hand up to join in the onslaught. He grabbed at her wrists,

"Alice, what are you talking about, what's happened?"

"What's happened is that the police think that Kitty is crazy, that she killed Eliza and burnt down the house, thanks to you and that jumped up bloody doctor. They've moved her to Stanley Royd, the bloody lunatic asylum! Our daughter is now locked up in a mental hospital because you told that doctor that she's crazy!"

Chapter Nine
Kathryn - Now

Jasmine's face was on the back of my eyelids as I blinked awake this morning and I knew I would need to dig deep to keep calm. It's this feeling of everything ending that I am struggling with. This complicated, multifaceted feeling of loss and helplessness seems unshakable and I think I might drown in these breaking waves of grief. I know that I have to try and control myself, get these multilayered emotions back under control.

Some people, well mainly Pip and Karen, think that I never actually grieved for Dad. Assuming, because I wasn't around - I was in the Menston Mad house at the time - I was oblivious to his death. Also, because I wasn't well enough to go to the funeral - it's amazing what barbiturates and ECT do to the physical health of a teenage girl - I never got to engage in the family grief or say goodbye. However, my brother and sister-in-law are mistaken.

My father died in the October of 1976 and three days after I had the sixth and final session of the course of ECT. Dad had finally been persuaded by Dr Hurst to give his consent two weeks before. Dad was told that it was better for him to agree as I was now seventeen and if there was no improvement before my next birthday I would probably be in the hospital for the rest of my life.

Mum and Dad visited me the day after the last session, in the morning. I had been really out of it, feeling my eyes rolling around in my head and unable to control my limbs. I also think I wet myself, I have a small flash of recall of Mum trying to get me to go to the lavatory with her and Dad being embarrassed but it's disjointed and bitty. What I do remember - I think it's a memory but it could be a false one created from what I learnt later - was Mum screaming at Dad, telling him this was his fault, screaming and asking why wouldn't he didn't listen and why had he let it all happen. Then they were both gone and I was alone again in a dark room watching shadows moving around the walls.

The next night I woke with a start, struggling to get my breath. As I opened my eyes I could see unfamiliar walls, rough brick and metal, and suddenly I wasn't in bed. I was standing in the corner of the garage in Farsley and looking at Dad through the windscreen of a car. There was smoke circling around him from the hosepipe wedged through the crack in the passenger seat window and even over the noise of the engine I could hear his sobs, begging for me to forgive him and I could feel the pain of his heart breaking. I tried to move forward only to wake up again, back in my lonely bed, with the taste of carbon monoxide in my throat and the demons of the past swirling around me.

I didn't cry out or cause any sort of fuss, that sort of thing never ended well, I just lay there and waited for morning. When it came, it brought no news, instead the day passed slowly, following the normal routine. I rolled up the painful stabs of grief I felt, rolled them up tight into a ball and forced them deep inside the damaged bits of my brain, knowing I would only survive if I kept it hidden until I got to my safe place.

When Mum came to see me, two days later, I put my finger to my lips as she started to speak and leaned forward to hug her, whispering into her ear, "I know."

My brother and sister-in-law are worried about how I am going to behave at Grace's funeral. They have voiced their concern to Mum. Will the emotion make me wretched and inconsolable and unable to do my reading? Or will I become hysterical during my tribute and say things that should not be mentioned? Or perhaps I'm going to be manic and overly jolly, making bad taste comments about how we Heskeths do love a funeral and thank goodness we all look good in black. Or perhaps make some reference to the Burntwood fire as the coffin goes behind the curtain at the crematorium.

I won't do any of these things of course, and I am sure they know that but then again, perhaps they aren't completely sure; people who have had their brains fried can be a tad unpredictable from time to time.

Mum chose the three pieces of music for Grace's funeral at Edward's request and suggested that I do my tribute near the beginning, before the middle track, which she thought I might find too emotional. We will be walking into the crematorium, behind her coffin to Nina Simone singing 'Don't Let Me Be Misunderstood'. When Mum told me this, I spat my tea out. Apparently, Grace herself had requested this particular opening track. She had given Mum a list of half a dozen others saying she could chose the rest.

"I decided not everyone would appreciate 'Happy Days Are Here Again' or 'Always Look On The Bright Side Of Life'," she told me, "Or even Frank Sinatra's 'I'm Gonna Live Till I Die." She handed me a napkin and picked up her own teacup, "So actually there was very little doubt what music she wanted."

Once we have got to our seats, the celebrant will tell us about Grace's life, the edited version of course, and all the wonderful and philanthropic things she has done, before asking me to come to the lectern. I have rehearsed my bit several times in the sitting room at home. The bit I am most scared of is the actual walking to the front and standing up there, looking out over the sombre and respectful faces, terrified of who I might see. So I shall keep my eyes lowered, I will smile at the light oak veneered coffin as I pass and blink back the sheen of tears as I nod to the celebrant. I will have the words of my tribute typed in nice big letters on a piece of paper and place them in front of me as I swallow hard to compose myself. Lifting my head only slightly in my shaky but best articulated voice, I will tell the assembled congregation just how wonderful my Aunt Grace was. How she was there for me, my mum and my brother at the lowest points of our lives and I will tell them what she said to me as she drove me home from the hospital nearly forty years ago.

"You are braver, stronger and cleverer than you realise. You have

275

a whole happy life ahead of you and you are going to achieve so much, you have so much to give." I will have to pause here to take a breath and fight back a sob before my final statement.

"My Aunt Grace taught me to believe in myself and she became my best friend and mentor for the rest of her life." Then I will read the poem 'When Great Trees Fall' and even though I have memorised it all I will still look down at the lectern. I will not dare to look across the sea of faces, just in case I catch a glimpse of the past and my demons smiling their acknowledgment.

We will then all pour out our grief to the recording of Sarah McLachlan singing 'I Will Remember You' and despite what Ms McLachlan sings, I will weep for the memories. Finally, after more tributes from the celebrant, there will be an invitation to all the assembled to join Edward and the rest of the family at the Old Black Mill pub for a buffet lunch and a chance to share stories of Grace and the legacy she has left. The celebrant will then step away from the lectern as the final piece of music starts and we will all leave the crematorium to 'Star Man' by David Bowie; it appears that Aunt Grace was a big fan – who knew?

Then as we walk out, despite Mum and I promising ourselves that we will be strong for each other, we will have to be helped out of the crematorium by Uncle Jack and Pip. Edward will be looking helplessly on, immersed in his own grief and trying hard not to crumble, his American wife and son by his side, bewildered at this very un-British show of emotion. Karen will follow with Jess, Helen and Megan and their respective families who will be smiling and acknowledging cousins and other family members they have not seen for quite some time. Aunties Peg and Dot, both widows, will not be there of course, as their health is poor. They live together now, sharing a ground floor flat in a warden-assisted complex in Wakefield, not far from where Daryl lives with his third wife. He has promised to go and see them straight after the bun fight to tell them who was there and take them some of the cakes, homemade of course by the wonderful ladies of the W.I.

I know all this, how it will be, what will happen because that's who I am; sometimes, I know things. Despite the drugs and ECT, despite what Eliza did to me, I still have it from time to time, this knowing, these flashes of perception. You would think that it would help me prepare for these times of sorrow and loss but if anything it makes them worse. I understand now that they are generally a fixed forward memory and I can do nothing to change them.

Tomorrow will be hard but I will, we will, get through it. It's what comes afterwards that I am not sure I can cope with.

Chapter Ten

1971

Grace had been surprised when Jack had suggested that she stay in his house after the fire. He and Raymond were going to be staying in Farsley for a few days to help Billy with the club while Kitty was in hospital so the Alfred Street house was empty. She had always felt that his hostility towards her was fake, a bit of posturing to placate his mother, but his offer still took her by surprise and she felt a sense of relief and gratitude, giving her one less thing to worry about.

On her first night in the small but comfortable bedroom, she hadn't slept too badly. After spending most of her day at the hospital, she hadn't got back to the house until half past nine and having been told Edward was doing well and Malcolm had improved slightly, she had fallen into a deep sleep almost as soon as she had climbed into the cold cotton sheets. Waking suddenly, she had allowed her eyes to adjust to the dimness of the room and realising the sun had yet to rise, she made herself stay in bed for another hour, thinking through the events of the previous 24 hours.

The previous morning, as she had stood, still in her night clothes and dressing gown at the scene of the fire, Mr and Mrs Thornbury, the nearest neighbours to Burntwood, had appeared by the gates. Grace had felt such relief as they approached her. After checking with the policeman in charge that it was okay for her to leave, she had got into their car and gone half a mile down the road with them to the warmth and safety of their home. She had little recall of the few hours she spent in their home, other than the immense kindness and generosity of these people who had previously only been on nodding terms. But she did remember being alone, locked in their bathroom, in her smoke-damaged and dirty night clothes, breathing deeply and fighting to banish the flashbacks from the horrors of the previous night. Standing still, her hand gently rested on her dressing gown pocket, feeling the shape of the book she had placed in there hours earlier, not daring to take it out. She needed to have a clear head and be sure not to be disturbed for that, so left it safely where it was. She asked the lady of the house for a carrier bag to put her clothes in, refusing to allow Mrs Thornbury, who had been beyond kind already, to launder them for her.

It was shortly after 10am on that grey and overcast Sunday morning when she emerged clean and smartly dressed in a borrowed outfit, from the neighbours, carrying only a bag of her bundled up dirty clothes. Mr and Mrs Thornbury, 'please call us Ken and Marjory', insisted on driving her back to the still smouldering Burntwood, offering help and accommodation throughout the short trip which Grace politely refused. There were two policemen just inside the gate and they were not allowed past them. Grace had pointed to her car that stood just inside the gate, well away from the house and completely undamaged and explained that she needed the keys and her handbag that were in the house. The older of the two constables shook his head and said he was very sorry for what had happened but he could not let her go into the house. Ken Thornbury had stepped forward at this point and asked if the policeman knew who he was talking to before mentioning that he played golf at the same club as the chief constable and was on the verge of squaring up to him when Grace intervened. She understood fully, she said, he had a job to do, however, she needed to get her car keys and handbag. Both of these items were, she was sure, in the kitchen which was undamaged. She explained that she had nothing, having escaped the fire in her night things, and was desperate to see her husband and son who were badly injured in hospital. The policeman said again he was not to allow anyone into the building, they had been strict orders from the inspector but, he added, raising his hand to stop any further dialogue, he would go and have a look for her if she described her bag and could tell him exactly where it and the keys were. Then he allowed himself a condescending smile as he added that the three of them had to wait there with the younger policeman.

The keys to her Austin 1100 were beside her handbag on the small table in the alcove behind the kitchen door. The large black handbag containing everything she needed had been placed there before going to bed on the night of the party. The policeman brought them back with a smile and, ignoring Ken and Margery completely, handed them over to Grace, wishing all her family a speedy recovery. Grace put the bag of soiled clothes in the boot, thanked the policeman and her neighbours and set off to the hospital.

As the sun made a feeble attempt to light up the Alfred Street bedroom, Grace came out of her reverie and glanced at the small alarm clock beside the bed. It was half past seven and, sighing deeply, she pushed herself up and twisted her legs out of the soft warm bed. The house was cold but it was a different cold to the chill she was used to at the big house. She padded out of the room to the bathroom and examined her face in the blotchy mirror before getting washed and dressed back into the borrowed clothes; they would have to do for the time being, and she went downstairs to make some tea.

Once in the kitchen, she leaned against the sink waiting for the kettle to boil and glanced around at the crowded shelves and worktops. Most of the pots and pans, crockery and baking tins had come from Sunny Bank, too many for this small house but nonetheless now installed, claiming the space. Even in her absence, Eliza dominated the whole house. Jack had told her to make herself at home, use whatever she needed, and Grace wondered about Eliza's clothes. She had no plan; there was no forethought to her actions other than the possibility of some clean underwear. As she climbed the stairs, pausing only for a few seconds at the top of the landing before stepping forward, with the very tips of her fingers, Grace pushed open the door to Eliza and Tommy's bedroom.

As she walked, still in bare feet, over the linoleum and onto the large rug, she felt a tingle on the back of her neck. She stopped as her focus blurred slightly before quickly sharpening again as her gaze was drawn to the Victorian mahogany wardrobe on the far wall of the room. The double doors were closed and as she reached out to the small brass knobs, she discovered they were locked too. Removing her hand, she paused for a second before moving over to the dressing table, taking a seat on the stool and placing her hands on the glass covered wooden surface. She glanced into the mirror in front of her before closing her eyes. After a few seconds, she opened the top draw a little way and felt at the very back for the tiny hole. Placing her index finger in, she could pull out the thin piece of wood that revealed a false bottom. The secret compartment was the length of the draw but shallow and a series of books lay positioned flat, taking up practically all of the space except for an oblong near the front; one book was missing. She lifted out the one next to the gap, a small key that had been wedged between it and the side of the draw fell into the space. She picked up the key with her empty hand and closed her fingers over it tightly, pressing it into her palm as her attention went back to the book. It was almost identical to the others, all A6 sized with a year on the front, navy blue leather embossed and with a gold swirly pattern. The one in her hand was 1970 and she knew the missing one was still in the pocket of her dressing gown with her soiled clothes in the boot of her car. Carefully, she took out each of the blue journals, dated 1964 to 1970 and placed them in two piles on the dressing table before reaching right to the back to retrieve a brown leather book, slightly thicker and with no year or any other markings on it. It looked much older than the rest and had clearly been well thumbed. Opening the first page, she read the spidery handwriting that declared that it was the journal of Frances Eleanor Freeman. This book was more of a notebook than a diary. The first dated entry, which was a few pages long, was April 1947. Grace flicked through the entries which stopped about ten pages before the end. The last one, in a barely legible scrawl, was dated November 1963. Grace sat down on the dressing table stool as her

281

eyes struggled to follow the messy and smudged ink, imagining the frail and arthritic old hand as it dragged the fountain pen across the page. She closed her eyes for a second as she reconstructed an image of the Doctor's sister holding a black velvet draw string bag and something in her head shifted. A half formed thought, a thing she had known but not known was slotted into place and suddenly her knowledge, her knowing, moved forward and she was almost there.

She went out to her car to retrieve the missing journal from her dressing gown pocket to complete the set and placed 1971 on top of Eliza's diaries. Smiling, she moved back to the wardrobe with the discovered key and locked the doors. Both sections were full of Eliza's clothes. Tommy's suits had never been unpacked after the move from Sunny Bank and were still in boxes in the small attic, all except the one he had worn to his brother's party. His other few clothes had been designated to the three small draws in the chest at his side of the bed. Half of one side of the wardrobe had shelves which were all full with neatly folded clothes. The bottom shelf, slightly higher than the rest, was home to a shoe box placed long ways on. Grace got onto her knees and pulled it out to reveal a pair of smart, black patent leather court shoes, size four. They looked like they had hardly been worn and Grace saw a flash of Eliza walking into Burntwood for James's funeral, the black queen. She put them carefully back in the box, replacing the tissue paper and the lid, before bending her head and reaching into the space behind where it had been. Feeling cold metal on her fingertips, she leaned forward and, stretching her arm to get her hand into the small space, she could feel the shape of a box. Easing her hand in further, she struggled a little before finally gaining purchase of an edge and pulled it out.

It was a khaki green coloured, six or seven inches deep, oblong tin that looked well worn and battered in places. Grace opened it to see that it was divided into six sections; all were empty except for bits of, what looked like, wood shavings and soil. Crouching further down and pushing her hand back into the space again to check the hiding place, she discovered an old and dirty china faced doll and a black velvet drawstring bag.

Chapter Eleven
Kathryn - Now

I wasn't lying about not remembering about the night of the fire. For most of my time in hospital, I remembered little, just the odd flash of something buried in the shadows but they were underdeveloped images that my addled brain could not comprehend. It was only when Pip took me to Grandad Tommy's grave, a month before I was finally discharged, that I saw the events playback through my head. It was a dull day for the beginning of June but I think, even if it had been sunny, the bleakness of the grey granite and marble stones surrounded by poorly maintained paths and lawned edges could not have looked much better. The area around the Hesketh plot looked as if someone had spent a bit of time and energy on it recently and I wondered if Grace had paid someone to tidy it up, but I didn't ask.

Pip stood back as I walked towards the edging stones to the plot, my eyes taking in the array of engraved and stencilled tributes going back to the founders of our dynasty and the wheels and cogs in my head started to move. My vision became slightly blurred as the memory files were slotted into place and began to fill in some of the blanks.

They were stilted flashes to begin with, like off-cuts from an old black and white movie. Faces and expressions and unnatural movements, shuffling around, all slightly out of focus until my recall found the image it was looking for. Me, lying under heavy blankets in a big oak framed bed that I knew was at Burntwood, Eliza standing over me with her lovely smile, a taste in my mouth as she pressed the glass to my lips and nodded. Taking a few hesitant sips, I glance across at Mum, lost in a deep sleep beside me, and I know she can't help me, no one can. I let the liquid dribble from the side of my mouth onto the pillow, swallowing as little as possible. My head is hurting and my limbs are heavy but I get out of bed, taking my grandmothers hand as we walk to the door. I am not in control; it is as if I am watching myself being led from the room. This all feels strange but at the same time, oddly familiar, as a whirring sound fills my head. A chemical and adrenaline mix curses through my veins, quickening my heartbeat. At the door, Eliza pauses for a second, looking at the lock and I know she is looking for the key, which isn't there. It is safely hidden under my pillow, I know this but I don't know why. I feel Eliza breathe her annoyance before giving Mum one last glance and leading me out onto the landing. I can hear the crackling, feel the heat and smell smoke from the fires that had not yet fully taken hold and I see the manic gleam in Eliza's eyes, her tight lips curving upwards as she leads me down the stairs.

Flashes of light stopped my recall and the dedication on Grandad Tommy's headstone came back into view.

Treasured memories of
Thomas Stanley Hesketh
Born 12th January 1908 - Died 25th October 1971
A much loved Son, Brother, Father and Grandfather and forever in our
thoughts.

My eyes followed the words as images stirred in my head. I saw Grandad smiling at me as he watched me ride my bike for the first time, laughing at the dinner table when I tried to tell him a joke, ruffling my hair in the shed as I helped him with his pigeons. All bright and happy memories except for the final half-formed image of him lying against a white pillow, his face covered with blood and brain matter. I felt myself lurch forward as the image dissolved but my peripheral vision returned and I steadied myself.

Grandad and his brother were buried side by side on the Hesketh plot, just in front of the grave of Martha, their sister. Although her headstone was twenty years older, it was well tended and had a large display of fresh flowers in various shades of purple and white underneath the brief inscription bearing only her name and the dates of her short, empty life. I moved around Uncle Henry's stone, a twin to his brother's, to get a better look at the resting place of the great aunt I had never known while she was alive. As I stood looking at the recently cleaned, carved lettering, my focus became hazy again as a familiar feeling floated through me and I just caught a glimpse of her. She was only a few feet away from me, bathed in beautiful warm lilac light, her half smile made my heart flutter before she faded completely into the background. I lifted my hand towards where she had been but felt light headed again and swayed a little.

"You ok Kathryn?" Pip put his arm around me as he spoke. I nodded, leaning into to him and he gave me hug before turning to look at me, "Do you want to sit down?" He nodded towards the oak and wrought iron bench, shimmering with drizzle and cobwebs and bearing the gold plated plaque of our ancestors.

"No, I'm ok, I'm just a bit tired, it's all a bit...well you know," I said, knowing that he didn't know but he would pretend he did.

"Yes, course," he said quickly, "Do you want to go to see... err would you like to go to the crematorium?"

"No," I said, louder than I meant to, shaking my head to absolutely confirm my reluctance. I did not want to see the small brass plaque marking my grandmother's ashes, "But I'd like to go and see Mum's garden, the roses...before I go back."

"Right, come on then, we can have a cuppa as well. Mum's been a bit worried, you know, how you'd cope, so she'll be glad to see you."

When we got to Armley, Mum opened the door as we walked up the path. The tea was already mashing and there was a plate of jammy dodgers and custard creams on her small Formica table in the kitchen.

"It's like you knew we were coming," I said, looking around the small kitchen. Mum blushed as she gave me a quick hug.

"Would you like to see the rest of the house?" she asked.

"No thanks, we can save that for later, when I don't have to go back."

"Of course, yes." She had watery eyes when she smiled, "Not long now love." I smile back and was pleased she didn't hug me again and notice me shaking.

"Can I see the garden? Dad's roses..."

"Yes, yes absolutely," she said with over the top enthusiasm as she shot towards the kitchen door, "You go out there and have a minute; me and Pip will wait here for a bit." She opened the door and stepped back out of the way.

The garden is a small rectangular shape with high fences at each side. There is a crazy-paved path dividing a neat lawn leading to an even higher wall at the bottom. In the centre, a climbing rose was growing through a fanned out wooden trellis and a variety of other rose bushes blooming beautifully in front of it. At either side, the brick was only visible in patches but mostly hidden by beautiful displays of flowering plants and shrubs that went from one fence to the other. To the left hand side was a small wooden bench, set at an angle from the fence to provide the perfect view to this wonderfully devised tribute. Mum and Pip had clearly worked hard to create and maintain this small patch of remembrance and, seeing the beauty of what they and nature had created from soil and ash, lifted my spirits in such a devastatingly emotional way that I staggered the last few steps to reach the bench. I knew of course Mum had done this purely for Pip and me, for us to remember our Dad with love; a sentiment she could not share with us.

By that time, I had been three months without medication and so my head was a lot clearer. Although my poor brain had been attacked and damaged it still managed to function to some degree and so that evening when I got back to Middleton, I started to untangle the suppressed and broken memories. Over the next few weeks, I was able to use the calmness of the hospital grounds to slowly start to reassemble the puzzle.

Two days later, Aunt Grace came to Middleton to see me and as we sat by the pagoda smelling the honeysuckle, she told me I looked different from the last time she had seen me, just the week before.

"Something's happened hasn't it?" She put her hand on my arm. I didn't say anything, I just kept my focus on the middle distance and nodded a slight confirmation.

"Tell me," her voice gentle as she turned slightly to look at me. I didn't look at her as I spoke, detailing what had happened at the cemetery and in Mum's garden.

"All these years, I thought I really was mad, that my brain wasn't normal, the things I saw, the voices, I thought I was Mad Kitty." I raised my head to look to the sky as I tried to keep calm.

"You were never mad Kathryn but you were deceived and let down badly, by all of us." Grace reached out to try and take my hand.

"But I must have been mad, I saw it, I saw what I did, I saw.." I pushed her hand away but she grabbed it and held it in both of hers.

"You were drugged that night like the rest of us. Nothing that happened that night was your fault, nothing." Grace spoke quietly but with a forcefulness that overrode the panic that had been rising in me. I swallowed and took a deep breath.

"Will you tell me, tell me it all?" I looked at her, seeing her consider for a second, weighing up the pros and cons.

"I will help you fill in the blanks. I'll tell you anything you want to know but not yet," squeezing my hand as she spoke, "I want to talk to your Mum first, she's been waiting a long time to get you back."

"I know," I said with a nod.

"But what I tell you will be my version and you must compare it to your own. It's really your story, no one else's version is as important as yours."

I didn't respond, instead I let the silence rest easily between us as fragments of memory, some real some not, moved around in my head and I smiled. Grace squeezed my hand again and although I wasn't looking at her, I know she was smiling too. And she kept her word, on Friday 27th July 1979, fifteen days after I had been released back into the community, she told me everything I needed to know.

Chapter Twelve

1971

Grace put the journals back in the hidden compartment of the dressing table draw, leaving the 1971 diary and Frances Freeman's note book out on the bed, returned the tin and velvet bag to the wardrobe and relocked it, all thoughts of using some of Eliza's clothes completely abandoned. She placed the key in her handbag along with the two books. She put the only surviving clothes of her own in a bath of warm soapy water and spent a therapeutic few moments rubbing and scrubbing at them as she tried to order her thoughts. Finally, she put the borrowed clothes back on and brushed her hair before picking up her bag and a borrowed coat and left the house.

After a short stop-off at Marks and Spencer's to buy new underwear, a pair of slacks, two blouses, a cardigan and some grapes, she drove to the hospital to see her husband and son. Malcolm had shown little improvement and was barely conscious, his breathing was laboured and his distress was apparent. His age, a doctor untactfully informed Grace, was against him. At 62, twenty-one years her senior, she knew they were right. He had never been a particularly healthy man and so the smoke inhalation he'd suffered escaping the fire had done real damage. The burns to his body were superficial but the ones to his hands and arms were deep and extensive, third degree she heard a nurse say as she sat by his bedside. They were doing all they could, she was assured, but the next few days would be critical to any hope of recovery. It was better news about Edward. He was doing well; although he had serious burns, the prognosis for him was good. She had steeled herself for his inevitable questions as she left the intensive care unit to go and see him. He told her he was comfortable and not in any pain, which she knew were lies, and so began to answer his questions, creating lies of her own.

After leaving Edward with the official version of what happened, along with the grapes, Grace wondered along the chilly high ceilinged corridors until she found the noisy, florescent tube lit canteen. She bought herself a cup of tea and sat on a hard-backed chair at one of the slightly grubby Formica tables, in a room full of strangers, and started to read through Frances Freeman's notebook and Eliza's 1971 journal.

When Alice and Jack arrived back at Alfred Street two days later, Grace was sitting by the fire in the back sitting room. Watching the flames, she was trying to get her thoughts in order. After a restless night with only small snatches of fitful sleep, she had decided not to visit her husband and son that day. She had been reading through and cross-checking the journals with events she was aware of for most the last two days and she was now trying to quell the full horror that had been revealed in Eliza's scribblings.

Hearing the car turn onto the small drive, she blinked hard and stood up to make her way to the kitchen door. It was still raining hard and on opening the door, she was brought up sharp at the sight of Alice, wet and shivering and almost on the verge of hysteria. Jack looked miserable and not for the first time, Grace wondered how Alice had ended up marrying the wrong brother, but of course she knew the answer, Eliza.

"Grace, the police....." she managed before her voice broke. Rushing forward and flinging her arms out in total despair, her sobs wracked her body. Jack closed the door and stepped into the kitchen wearing a feeling of helplessness as he shrugged and gestured with his hands for a few seconds before finding his voice.

"Kitty's been moved to Stanley Royd, the doctor thinks she's mad, mentally ill! That jumped up bobby thinks she stabbed Mum and set fire to the house."

"It's Billy's fault!" Alice shouted, "He started telling the doctor about her fainting and her funny turns. I kept telling him to shut up, they had nothing to do with any of this and then he goes and tells him that she hears voices." Her anger had risen as she spoke, along with her voice and her arms. When she stopped shouting, she looked suddenly surprised at where she was, looking quickly round the room as she dropped her shoulders. Jack was standing in the doorway to the kitchen, his face ashen, blinking away the moisture in his eyes.

"Will you come back to Leeds with us, I want to talk to Raymond, I'm sure he knows something. He was with Kitty for a lot of the time and then he didn't want to stay, do you remember?" her voice shaking again with the emotion that was keeping her afloat, "He was desperate to leave, he knew something bad was going to happen, he knew..."

"Alice love, he doesn't know anything, he's a sensitive lad and that bloody house is, was, enough to put the willies up anybody. Sorry Grace but it's always been a creepy old place." Jack's voice gave away his fear.

"You'll get no argument from me about that house." Grace gave him one of her half smiles and then addressed Alice, "Come on upstairs, let's get you dried off a bit then yes, I'll come back with you and talk to Raymond but I don't really think he knows anything. Like Jack says, he's just a very sensitive boy."

"I'll put the kettle on." Jack turned quickly, wanting to busy himself, and didn't notice the way the two women looked directly at each other before moving towards the other door and going upstairs.

The old brass bedstead creaked as Alice perched on the end of the large and lumpy mattress that had once been in a much larger room at Sunny Bank. Grace had handed her a towel to rub her hair before unlocking and opening the wardrobe and crouching by her feet to retrieve its secrets.

It had been hard for Grace to keep Alice calm as she told her what she had discovered. She began with the three main points and tried to do this as calmly and as gently as she could. She held both of Alice's hands in her own as she told her, firstly; Eliza had killed James. Secondly, she had intended them all to die in the fire but particularly Alice, - Eliza and Kitty were meant to be the only survivors. Finally, Eliza had been systematically poisoning Kitty since she was three years old.

Alice did not shout and scream or even cry at this revelation. She remained still, staring past Grace into middle distance, her mouth slightly open. She no longer saw the room or Grace. Playing out before her were her memories of the times she had known things were not right, of the times she had refused to see what was going on right under her nose. Alice did not respond to what Grace told her because it was not a revelation, Alice knew that Eliza was bad, she had always known it.

Grace said nothing and they sat in silence for a short while, giving Alice time to take in what she had been told. After a few moments, Grace noticed the tears flowing silently and she hugged her tightly as Alice then began sobbing into her shoulder.

"I knew, I always knew she saw it in Kitty, I should have seen what she was doing."

"She manipulated you, Alice, practically all your life," Grace said softly, stroking her hair, "You were only a baby yourself when she first got her claws into you."

"She was so nice to me and my mum; I thought she was so kind."

"She knew from the onset that your mum was a phoney, she was interested in how gullible people were to begin with. Your mum made a very good living from her 'gifts'." Grace pulled herself away a little and put her hands on Alice's shoulder, "But she knew you were the real thing - that you felt and saw things."

"I tried to hide it, from the beginning I had this feeling... something...oh..." Alice broke off and fished a tissue out from her sleeve to wipe her nose, "Mum always went on about what a good friend she was and how lucky we were that Eliza had taken us under her wing, I thought she cared about me but there was always something nagging at me, like a small voice in my head telling me to be careful." Alice sniffed loudly and Grace pulled out a handkerchief from her cardigan pocket and passed it to her as she said,

"She always hated me because she knew I could see her darkness. When I was little, I thought she was an evil witch."

"Turns out you were right." Alice lowered her eyes and swallowed before saying, "It's my fault Eliza killed James..."

"NO!" Grace held her hand up, "It's not your fault. She was nasty, sly and selfish, all her life, but I think sometime over the last few years she went mad, totally insane. She was on some sort of a quest to see the future, to know things." Grace stood up and pointed to the journals, "It's all in there. It started with her friendship with that mad old woman, the doctor's sister..." Grace stopped mid-sentence, shrugging first before moving over to the pile of books, "Take them back to Leeds, read the madness for yourself."

"No," Alice said quickly, shaking her head, "I will read them, but not in Leeds. I don't want anything of hers in my house."

"Ok, I'll put them back in the false compartment of the draw." She went back to the bed and sat beside Alice, "Eliza killed James because he was helping you and Billy to move out of Sunny Bank. He suspected something wasn't right with her."

"Did he tell you?"

"Not exactly, I was always close to him you know, despite Eliza. He had worried about what she was capable of when she didn't get her own way. He told me that the way she had looked at him when he told her he was moving back to Burntwood had made his blood run cold." Grace paused and rubbed her temples, "But no one could have guessed just how far she would go."

"Except, perhaps...Kitty..." Alice spoke softly, her voice trailing away. Both women sat in silence for a minute before Alice exclaimed, "Did she do it? Did my little girl stab Eliza and position her in that way?"

"I don't know Alice but I do know that she ended the evil, she was stronger than you and me and now we have to protect her as best we can."

"What can we do?"

"I don't know," Grace shook her head, "But I think if the police saw these journals it wouldn't help. Eliza's ravings about Kitty talking to the dead and experimenting on her with drugs and potions." She inhaled deeply through her nose and gave her temples another rub, "And to be honest, I'm not sure they would believe any of it, or us." She stood up, "Anyway we should get going, I'll get in touch with Reg Draycock, he's the assistant chief constable. He was a good friend of Henry's, a fellow mason." She gave a half laugh, "He might be able to help."

"Yes, oh yes, please can you talk to him today," Alice said quickly.

"Yes, I'll telephone from the club as soon as we get there." Grace took a comb out of her bag and handed it to Alice who took it and automatically and began to tidy her damp hair. Then she also stood up and said,

"We can't tell Billy about the journals," adding as if just making up her mind, "He won't know what to do but he will want to do something, he's ....."

"I agree," Grace cut in, saving her from saying out loud something she might regret, "We shouldn't tell anyone else about them." She held out her hand to take back the comb, "Billy was always Eliza's favourite and she has manipulated him all his life but he loves you and both his children; don't forget that." She touched Alice's arm and treated her to one of her rare smiles. Alice nodded her head and gave a small return twitch of her mouth. Grace walked to the bedroom door, speaking over her shoulder,

"I think we should still talk to Raymond, you are right, I think he is a little like James, he senses things."

Jack looked up as they walked in. He was sitting by the fire leaning forward slightly, his hands resting loosely on the arms of the big arm chair that had been his fathers.

"You two alright?" he asked tentatively, "The tea's probably cold now, I couldn't find the cosy." He stood up, his arms dangling at his side, looking ill at ease.

"No problem. I'm impressed you found anything in that kitchen there's so much stuff and clutter. Anyway, we should be off, it's starting to get dark. I'll follow you in my own car and I'll need to leave shortly after six to get to the hospital for visiting time." Grace was back to her efficient self, in full control.

Jack tried a couple of times to engage Alice in conversation on the journey back to Farsley but realised her mind was somewhere else so turned the radio up. He glanced at her as he indicated to turn into the car park of the club and saw that she looked angry again, her thoughts had clearly been building up despite the lively pop music Terry Wogan was disc jockeying on Radio One. She got out of the car without a word and strode purposefully to the back door entrance to the club. "Billy boy you're for it now lad," he said quietly to himself as he locked the car.

Chapter Thirteen
Alice

Over the years, Alice has played out scenarios of how she could have done things differently. She could have questioned more, not been so naive and she should have trusted her instincts. She relives all the times she had the opportunity to speak out and she is wretched as she accepts her culpability. This guilt has eaten away at her, no matter what Grace said to excuse it, and although it has mainly been about Kathryn, just recently, as she nears her own demise, she has been thinking about James. She knows his death was her fault, if she had not told Eliza about him helping Billy get a job in Leeds, a job that came with accommodation, then maybe... but all the ifs and maybes would not bring him back or change the terrible things that followed. She has realised that if there was a time to have changed things, it was years before Jimmy died and her memory flicks back to 1952.

The recall of her wedding day is grey and full of shadows. It should have been the happiest day of her life but was instead full of uncertainty and doubt. She spent the night before in a fitful nervousness, worrying if she should be marrying Billy. She had an overwhelming feeling that she was trapped, but tried to rationalise her feelings, to get a different perspective. She was an orphan with no money or friends; her only family were Eliza and Tommy. They had looked after her when her own mother couldn't, wouldn't. They had provided for her and treated her as their own. Sunny Bank was her home. But something felt wrong.

The romance and engagement had happened so quickly and her mother and Eliza had been so delighted, as was she, but her initial happiness had been short-lived as the doubts began. She was only just sixteen and had lived such a small, sheltered life but the biggest uncertainty she had was about Billy. Did she really love him? She had grown up as one of the family and was really close to him and she knew he was kind and gentle but was this really why you married someone? In a few moments of clarity, six weeks before the wedding, she had admitted to herself that she had thought of Billy only as a brother. She did not love him and actually wondered if he had only asked her to marry him to please his mother. As her doubts grew, she knew she had to voice them to someone and so when her mother arrived two days later, she confided her worries. They were in the bedroom and Barbara was unpacking and hanging up her clothes. Alice sat on the edge of the bed and attempted to tell her mother how she felt. Barbara was distraught and annoyed at the prospect of Alice 'jilting' the son of her best friend.

"This family has been good to you. Eliza has been good to you and they are good and wealthy people. You have to stop this silliness." Barbara glanced at the bedroom door as if worried that someone might be listening in.

"But I don't think I love him," Alice had said quietly.

"What has that got to do with anything?" Barbara snapped, "You just make yourself love him. Good grief, Alice, you have nothing else, you are not very clever and I have no money to give you. What else are you going to do with your life?"

This response was not unexpected. Alice had known her mother shared Eliza's view about the coupling of her and Billy, that she had been just as pushy in putting them together.

"Can I come back to Leeds with you, just for a few days? Maybe being away from here I might stop panicking and I'll realise that I am just being daft."

"Well I don't know. I mean, what will Eliza think to that?" Barbara worried.

"I don't know but I am sure she will understand if it's just for a couple of days. She was talking about having a day out in Leeds soon so maybe if I come back with you we can meet up with Eliza at the end of the week and I can come back with her."

"Well I don't know," she repeated, her concern at this turn of events making her clearly uneasy.

"I'll ask her what she thinks," Alice said, getting off her bed and moving to the door. As she turned she saw her mother sit down heavily on the bed hugging a black and red chiffon dress to her chest, eyes down and deep in worried thought.

Eliza had been surprised at Alice's suggestion but after a few moments agreed it was a good idea. She suggested that she and Alice get the train to Leeds the following week; they could meet Barbara and do a bit of shopping, Alice still needed some wedding shoes, and the three of them could have a meal. Then Alice could go and stay with her mother for a week perhaps, before coming back home.

Alice felt a stab of disappointment about having to wait but thought it was a good result. Barbara agreed and the rest of the weekend went well as her mother and Eliza continued to plan the wedding. When she told Billy, he looked confused. Why would she want to go and stay in Leeds even for a few days and what did his mother think to this idea. When she told him it had been Eliza's idea, he looked relieved.

Alice and Billy walked Barbara to the railway station on Sunday evening. Alice was feeling a lot happier than she had for weeks. Billy carried her small suitcase, which was much fuller than it was when she arrived. Eliza's generosity knew no bounds, Barbara had said to her daughter as she struggled to close the lid just before they left. On the platform, Billy stepped back as mother and daughter embraced and said their goodbyes. He carried her suitcase on to the train for her and then resumed his place at Alice's side as they waved the train out of the station. That was the last time Alice saw her mother. The planned shopping trip never happened as Barbara died in her sleep four days later.

Alice had burnt her wedding photographs on a slightly ritualistic fire in her garden three days after Billy had killed himself. But she can still see a couple of them in her mind's eye and she sees it clearly; the madness glinting in Eliza's eyes as she stands triumphantly centre stage beside her and Billy.

There was another bonfire in her garden the month after Kathryn came home. Alice never read Eliza's journals or Frances Freeman's book. It was a step too far for her and she didn't need to read them to know that her mother-in-law had been totally insane, her madness intensifying as the family fortunes declined, raging against the world, consumed by fury. Grace kept them; she said it was important that Kathryn had the chance to read them if she wanted. And of course she did. Kathryn spent a week reading them, cross-referencing the dates, with her own truths which finally allowed her, she claimed, to understand. Frances Freeman's battered old notebook began with a story of a young nurse caught up in the Spanish civil war. How she fell in love with a Spanish fighter of Mexican origin who was also a botanist and how their shared interest in plants for use in medicine became an obsession. Long after her lover was killed, she continued to collect and research the effects of herbs and other vegetation. Half way through, her little notebook became a poison diary, chronicling her experiments with Seer's Sage, Nutmeg and Mushrooms. Once she had finished reading them, Kathryn had phoned Grace and asked her to come over. The three of stood in the middle of the garden and watched the flames consume the books.

Alice brings her wallowing to an abrupt end and makes herself get up from the sofa. Kitty will be home soon, she dashes her hand to her mouth at this thought. For years she had not called her that or even thought of her with that name. She goes to the kitchen and gets herself a glass of water. She is determined to spend a pleasant evening living in the present and counting her blessings. So she presses the pause button on her regrets and hopes that the misery of her guilt will allow her to get through her last few weeks. Glancing at her watch, she realises she has about half an hour to do a little job she has been putting off for a while. Watching the second hand counting down the time, she decides she must do it now. She goes into the small dining room that doubles up as a study and pulls the down the flap on the bureau. Taking out a set of Basildon Bond writing paper and envelopes and a gold tipped fountain pen, she pulls up a chair and begins to write.

My darling girl,

I am sorry that I let you down and that I never had the courage to talk to you about what happened, about what I allowed to happen. I know that Grace told you all she knew and explained what she found but I was so very scared of losing you a second time, I didn't dare. Your memory was incomplete and I wanted it to stay like that, for us both to forget it all and start again. I am not sure this has been helpful to either of us but I hope you know that it was because I love you.

I am fairly certain your memory is complete now – I think you know it all but I want you to leave it all where it belongs now. The past can be a trap; let it go.

The future is yours to do with what you will so don't look back Kathryn; you are not going that way.

In our little world of contradictions, you have always been consistently extraordinary.

All my love

Alice xx

Chapter Fourteen

1971

Once Alice had calmed down, mainly due to Grace's intervention, she and Billy went upstairs to the flat so she could tell him exactly what had happened at the hospital. Billy sat down heavily on the couch, staring straight ahead into a chasm of despair.

"But how can they think that, how could anybody think that Kitty was capable of any of those things?"

"This detective, this Barry bloody Fields, well he's just looking for a quick result. Now this stupid jumped up doctor has decided she is mentally ill, it's an easy solution for him."

"I'm sorry love, I just thought maybe the doctors needed to know that she's had some problems, I wanted them to make her better that's all." He buried his head in his hands and began to cry. Alice took a deep breath in through her nose, she wanted to tell him to stop it, to man up and help her. She stood there knowing he wanted her to comfort him, wanted her to tell him everything would be alright. She wavered, raised her hand slightly and was about to speak when he said,

"It's the shock of it all, losing Mum and Dad in such a terrible way," he let out a sob and raised his head, "Christ, Alice, my poor mother, who would do such a thing." And Alice knew Grace had been right, she could not tell him and in that moment she hated him. She said nothing but walked towards the small kitchen area.

"She must have been protecting Kitty from the intruder. She must have heard them getting in through the kitchen and gone downstairs." He stood up and pulled his handkerchief from his pocket and wiped his nose as he continued to create his own acceptable narrative of the night's horrors.

"Once Kitty is properly conscious, she can tell us what happened, it's going to be alright. The police will catch the bastards that did this. I can talk to the doctor tomorrow, I'll come with you to the hospital and we can get this all sorted out, we can...." He walked towards his wife as he spoke. She had been trying so hard not to lose it again but reserve was failing.

"Stop!" she yelled, holding up her hand in front of her, "Just stop talking". Billy flinched as if she had slapped him. His eyes wide, his face pale, he had never seen her like this before. They stood staring at each other. The telephone rang, slicing the silence and bringing them both back from the edge, saving them from words that could not be unsaid.

Alice sidestepped her husband and pick up the phone. It was Pip. The conversation with her son helped take her back into the role she had played for most of her life. As she glossed over the facts for her first born, Alice focused on the orange and yellow geometric patterned wallpaper and tried to convince herself that what she was saying was true.

Kitty was still very ill but out of danger. She was in a lot of pain from the breaks to her arm and the concussion caused by the bump to her head was giving them a little concern, so they were transferring her to Stanley Royd for a few days where the doctors could give her better and specialised care. Pip repeated the name of the hospital in a higher pitch but Alice did not let him ask the question. She said Kitty was poorly and the doctors were doing everything they could to make her better and he should not worry. He asked when he could go and see her and Alice promised they would take him at the weekend. All the time she had been speaking, she had stood with her back to Billy. As she replaced the receiver, she turned to see he had not moved. He was still leaning against the doorway to the kitchen staring at nothing. She took a deep breath and walked towards him. He turned towards her, his eyes red and full of tears and held his arms out. She stepped in to his embrace, her own arms hovering for a second before she allowed them to rest lightly around her husband.

"It's going to be alright love," he spoke into her hair, "You'll see, we'll have her home in a few days." If he felt her body stiffen he showed no reaction and even when she pulled her arms up between them and pushed herself away from him, his expression didn't change.

"Please don't tell that policeman that Kitty has any sort of mental illness. She had allergies that made her sick and dizzy. That is all you need to say," she said coldly before turning to go back downstairs. She paused in the doorway to tell him that Grace was going to try and call in some favours with the assistant chief constable so he should wash his face and then get back down to the bar to get ready for opening time. She wanted to have a word with Raymond so told Billy he should get Jack to help him. She left the door open as she gripped the banister and carefully walked downstairs. Billy followed his wife back down to the bar a few moments later, still looking upset but trying to act as normal as he could. His brother had patted him lightly on the shoulder as he passed him and nodded in an act of allegiance. Grace went up to the flat to use the phone while Alice went to change her clothes. They both returned to the bar fifteen minutes later. Grace hadn't managed to speak to the Reg Draycock but she did get an appointment to see him the next day. She was having lunch with him at Painthorpe Country club in Crigglestone. Both Jack and Billy thought this was a brilliant result, Jack nodding as he thanked God for the old boys' network. His smile faded slightly when Alice asked Raymond if he'd come up to the living room with her and Grace, just to talk to them about what Kitty had said to him that night. They wanted to talk to him before the police did.

It was a surprise to both women that Raymond nodded and although he retained his normal serious expression, his eagerness to talk to them was apparent. He followed them upstairs and Alice made two mugs of tea for her and Grace and placed the requested glass of water on the coffee table in front of her nephew.

"Kitty weren't happy when she got there. I could see it straight away," he began. "She had that sad smile, like she was scared, like she used to get when she lived at Sunny Bank." He was looking from one to the other of the women as he spoke, with concern hooding his eyes. Alice felt a cold pain in her chest as she visualised the small upturn of her daughter's mouth and the hint of unease in her eyes.

"I was in the dining room when you were all taking off your coats then you and Uncle Billy went into the big room to see Eli... Granny. Pip brought his girlfriend in to the dining room to get them some drinks but Kit stayed in the hall. She was standing by the bottom of the stairs looking up. I went out to talk to her and look at what she was looking at." He swallowed hard and looked down at his hands that were clenched on his lap.

"What did you see?" Grace asked gently.

"I don't know...there was something...someone...I felt her, I didn't see her, a grey lady," he raised his head quickly, looking right at Grace, "But Kit saw her, she nodded and then her face changed and she stopped looking scared."

"What did she do then?" Alice prompted.

"She was just normal again then. We went into the big room and she said hello to her Granny. Then we went over by that big sideboard thing and talked about school and stuff and Slade, that's a pop group we both like." He looked again from one to the other. They both nodded encouragingly. "So we were there for ages just talking a bit; she really likes her new school and she's got loads of new friends. People were coming in and out." He paused to take a gulp from his glass of water. Retaining the glass in his right hand he glanced up and slightly to the left as he accessed his memory.

"I think you came in and said there was some hot food," looking at Grace who nodded, "Lots of people went out, I think Pip and his girlfriend were over by the window with Daryl, he had just got them some more Champagne and was talking really loud. Pip was looking annoyed. Kit stood up and went over to them and said something, I didn't catch what it was, then Pip and his girlfriend went out, Daryl stumbled a bit, I think he was drunk, anyway he asked Kit if she'd..." he looked down again before taking a breath and continuing, "He's not very nice..."

"It's ok Raymond we all know what a horrible boy he is," Alice said.

"He asked her if she'd been with a lad yet, he used some other words...."

"We can guess," Grace said, breathing out heavily through her nose.

"Well, then Kit leans forward and whispers something in his ear and he steps back like she's hit him. He looks a bit mad but also really shocked and scared. Kit then just told him he'd better keep out of her way or she would have a word with his mam."

"Did you hear what she said to him?" Alice asked.

"No, but I asked her, she said she thought he should start behaving a bit better if he didn't want everyone to know that he had been stealing money from his mam's purse for weeks and she had seen him dipping his hand in his auntie's handbag not half an hour earlier."

"Where was Eliza while this was happening?" Alice asked.

"She was sitting in that chair over by the fire, she was watching. She had gone out for a bit but had come back and was just sitting there and smiling. Daryl looked over at her and she laughed out loud at him. I had stood up and he pushed me out of the way, he didn't need to, and went out."

"What happened then?" Grace asked.

"Eliz – Granny called Kitty over to her, there was a bottle of champagne and some glasses on the little table by the bookcase. She got up and poured out some glasses. I went over to the French windows. I didn't think she wanted me, just Kitty." He frowned as he tried to find his words, "I just felt itchy everywhere, like something wasn't right, so I just stood there and watched through the window."

Alice and Grace could almost see it too. They watched Raymond as he recounted what he saw reflected through the leaded glass panes. He saw Eliza pass one of the heavy crystal champagne glasses to Kitty and heard her say she shouldn't tell her Mum as she would just spoil the fun.

She said she deserved a nice glass of fizzy after dealing with the likes of Daryl.

"She called him a nasty little toe-rag." he said flatly.

"I think that's how we all think of him." Alice smiled and nodded.

"I saw Kit put the glass to her lips but then Eliza asked me if I would like a glass. I said no thank you and then someone else came into the room, I don't know who but it was a man. He sat in the other chair and started talking to Granny. I saw Kit standing just slightly behind the chair, edging backwards; she still had the glass in her hand. Then more people came in the room, most of them had plates in their hands, and Dad came in and asked me if I was alright. I said I was but then when I looked over again Kit was gone."

Alice and Grace exchanged a look as Raymond again picked up his glass but just before it got to his lips he suddenly said,

"I didn't see her drink it and I think that's important, I did see her look at me, like she wanted me to notice as she moved the glass away from her mouth."

"Why do you think that?" Grace asked.

"I don't know, I just think, the way she looked at me, I don't know..." He lowered his head.

"It's alright Raymond, we know what you mean, sometimes you get a feeling and it's hard to explain." Alice smiled at him and he smiled back, "What happened next?"

"I didn't see her again for a bit. I went into the dining room and stood with Dad. He was talking to Uncle Billy about the troubles in Northern Ireland. Dad was saying he was glad he was out of the army." He put the glass of water back on the table without having taken a drink and then sat forward.

"Then I saw her in the hall, she was walking towards the dining room but stopped in the doorway and waved for me to come over. She was acting a bit weird saying she had something really important to do

307

and needed my help."

Both women leaned forward, Alice rubbed her temples to try and reduce the tension growing behind her eyes.

"She asked me to go and stand at the top of the stairs to the kitchen, while she went down there. She said she had to sort something out. I was to talk loudly if anyone looked like they might be coming down." His arms were straight in front of him one hand resting on each knee. He looked ahead as he spoke, "No one came but I'm sure I heard her talking to someone down there."

"Did you hear the other voice, was it a man or a woman?" Grace asked.

"I could only hear a murmur, it might not have been anyone, I just heard Kit's voice. She might have been talking to herself." His worried expression returned.

"So what happened then?" Alice asked, rubbing her eyes.

"She came back up, she seemed... she was like...I can't explain but she wasn't like Kit. Her voice was a bit different and her eyes looked strange."

"What do you mean strange?" Alice asked quickly.

"I don't know, sort of bigger and a bit black I think but they made me nervous. She was talking quietly but she told me I needed to get Dad to take me home. That it wasn't safe, she said something really bad was going to happen. She wouldn't let me speak to ask her anything. She just said again it wasn't safe and I had to make Dad understand we must not stay there over night."

"But she didn't tell you what it was?" Grace asked.

"No," shaking his head, "She just got me to say I would make Dad take me home and we wouldn't stay there. Then she went back through the kitchen door, she said for me to go with her. When she got to the bottom of the steps she...." His voice broke and he looked like he was about to cry.

"It's alright Raymond, really, you can tell us." Alice went over and sat next to her nephew and placed her hand on his arm.

"She said she didn't feel well and she sat on the floor. I asked her if she wanted some water. She shook her head and she said..." a sob stopped him and both his hands went to his face. Neither women spoke.

"She said something, she said..."

Another long pause as he wrestled for control of his emotions.

"She said 'It's time she learned that the victims can sometimes be the dangerous ones'." He wiped his nose on the sleeve of his jumper and sniffed loudly, "Then she told me to go and get you, to say she had fainted, so I did."

Alice moved closer and hugged him and he folded himself into her, accepting her comfort.

"Thank you, Raymond," Grace said, "You have been really brave."

"Yes," Alice said softly as she stroked his hair, "You have, thank you."

The boy pulled away, and Grace passed him a handkerchief. He blew his nose loudly and then asked,

"Will Kit be alright?" His voice was quavering with concern and his brown eyes wide and begging to hear positive news.

"Yes, I think she will but it will take a little time." Alice spoke with a certainty she was not feeling.

"I'm not going to tell anybody else about what I remember," he said suddenly, "If the police ask I am going to say she was fine until she fainted."

"Yes that's probably the best thing," Alice nodded.

"And Dad," he said, "Dad wouldn't understand, he wouldn't like it if I said any of this to him."

Alice nodded again and Grace stood up.

"Have you eaten today, Raymond? You look a bit pale. Shall I see what I can rustle up from your Aunt Alice's fridge?"

And while Alice went to her bedroom to take some time to think, Grace started to cook bacon, eggs and tinned tomatoes.

Chapter Fifteen
Kathryn - Now

Initially, as I thought back to life at Sunny Bank, the memories were coloured with the warm sepia softness of nostalgia, the inner smudging of my perception of the life of our extended family, the home baking, the family meals and garden picnics creating an impression of a quaint and idyllic time. Only as my world expanded to give me reference points did I realise just how askew things actually were but the shock of this revelation then became compounded as I realised that no one else seemed to have noticed, or if they had, they just allowed it to continue.

I have a pocket of a memory of sitting at the table in the kitchen of Sunny Bank on the morning of my thirteenth birthday. Eliza was standing at the window watching a solitary magpie hopping around the lawn. Dad was there too and it was just the three of us. Glancing up from his newspaper to see what she was looking at, he made some comment about one magpie being unlucky and Eliza nodded her head sagely without taking her eyes off the bird, her words clear despite her back to me.

"They're wicked things but they have to be, they kill other birds to protect their own," I went over to the window to look as she added, "They're attracted to badness, that's why they're here."

"Don't start all that rubbish again Mother," Dad said with a sigh, "We have enough going on now without that."

Once I was away from Eliza and the thrall of the world she had created in Sunny Bank, something altered inside my head. I slotted so neatly into our new life in what finally felt a normal family unit and the ordinariness of our new daily routine was blissful. A few days in, as I walked to school on my own, I had an overwhelming feeling of realness and it was with that clarity that I understood just how wrong my life had been up to then.

The first night in my new bedroom, I slept deep and long and woke

311

the next morning, without screaming and alerting anyone else, with a feeling of happiness and safety as I emerged from a heavy dream. For as long as I could remember, my dreams had been large and frightening and although this one had been both of those, it had ended better. It was full of strange but familiar people, pushing and pulling me through mazes of sharp and stinging walls that moved and blocked me. I knew I was in danger and was scared but I could see a way out and I used a strength I didn't know I had to free myself. The state of my bed as the sleep left me was a testament to my nocturnal struggle and, as I picked up the eiderdown from the floor, I smiled at my achievement. Perhaps it was the onset of the chemical imbalance of my adolescence; I was told and it was noted in my medical files that I was very late to puberty, my arrested development providing further confirmation to the mad Kitty theory, but then my medical records were created from asymmetric information and were full of lies and omissions.

Whatever the reason, I am certain of that feeling of liberation as Mum, Dad, Pip and me began our new life in Leeds. So as I felt myself emerging from this strange past, I straightened the bottom sheet and began remaking my bed.

My feeling of realness, normality and happiness lasted for just over six months until it was shattered by the invitation to Uncle Henry's birthday celebration. The events of that night are well documented even if there is some ambiguity and economy of truth, well you must remember a lie is a created thing - it's the art of survival.

There is only one part of the story left to tell, the gap in my memory, the missing piece.

Well here it is and it's a proper fairy tale ending.

After all the guests had left the party, I continued to feign the drowsy sleepiness as I listened to the others getting ready for bed. It took a little while but I kept my eyes closed and my breathing light as I waited for Eliza. I could hear her moving around the house, she didn't feel the need to be quiet; she had made sure no one would hear her, or so she thought. She left the bedroom door open as she stepped towards my side of the bed. I lay as still as she would have expected from the valium she had put into my drink earlier that evening.

Mum lay beside me in a deep and unnatural sleep. Poor Alice had been so concerned, I know she had felt the unrest in the house, the feeling of foreboding, she knew something was coming but she let her guard down after putting me to bed. She had gone back down stairs and taken a cup of tea from the large silver teapot in the dining room. Thomas had told her Grace had made it, but it was Eliza who had told Thomas this. Alice was so tired and keen to get back to bed she had poured herself a cup; everyone else was drinking it. No one noticed that Eliza's cup was empty and unused.

As soon as Mum came back to the bedroom she struggled to take off her clothes she was so tired. She stroked my hair and whispered good night as she climbed in beside me and within seconds was asleep. I waited a few more moments, listening to her breathing deepen before I got out of bed and took the key out of the lock in the bedroom door. I placed it under my pillow before resuming my position.

I could see the smoke seeping under the closed doors of Uncle Henry's bedroom across the landing as Eliza guided me down the big staircase. I maintained my pretence of semi-consciousness, ignoring the crackling noise as the fire was taking hold in the front of the house. As we got to the kitchen door she laughed, her madness in full control of her as she said,

"You were meant to be with me Kitty, you were born to be mine and now no one will ever take you away from me again." Her arm was around me as she walked me down the back stairs, my feet cold on the stone flags of the kitchen floor, but a newly acquired energy allowed me to externalise these sensations. As she pulled me past the large oak table, I took in a deep breath that made her pause and turn to look at me. I retained my trance like appearance but I felt her sudden wariness. We took another step and I let my foot catch on one of the chair legs and pretended to trip. I lurched forward pulling myself out of her grasp and heard her gasp as I knocked her off balance. I fell to my hands and knees and retrieved the large kitchen knife I'd placed on the seat of the chair earlier. She grabbed the back of another chair to steady herself, looking confused, and tilted her head to try and see what I was doing but she wasn't quick enough. I sprung to my feet, the knife in my hand and her confusion turned to alarm as I stepped towards her. My vacant expression was gone, replaced by something she had never seen in me before and she let out a scream, her hands to her face, unable to comprehend what was happening. Her dressing gown fell open exposing her white cotton nightdress and she stepped back but her head leaned forwards slightly, her mouth moving as if she were about to speak. I lunged at her, plunging the knife deep and hard, knowing I had found the organ that pumped blood around her evil body – she had no heart.

I pushed her as she started to fall, both her hands were around the embedded knife, and I stepped around the blood that was already pooling at her feet. She fell back on to the range, in a seated position, her legs in front of her. Her face was a picture of bewilderment as her mind caught up with what was happening to her body. She was still holding on, her mouth twitching, her eyes searching as I pulled her forward from the shoulders. I opened the large oven door and let her head roll back into the still warm dark void before standing up and looking down at her.

I watched the red stain on her nightdress get bigger as her hands fell away from the knife. Bloody bubbles were forming around her mouth and her eyes were fixed on me and I saw a flicker of recognition. Perhaps she saw the light change beside me or maybe she recognised a shape or heard a whisper of a voice she'd thought was long gone. The trace disappeared, moving silently back into the house and up the stairs to wake up Grace. I nodded as I leant forward and pulled out the knife, keeping eye contact and smiling. The knife was still dripping a little as I stood, watching the last few seconds of Eliza's life fade away. Once I was certain she was dead, still with the knife in my hand, I left the kitchen by the back door and started running.

Indigo Children

Post Script

It's hard to know where the story really starts, where the rot first set in, maybe it was always there but the ending is easy – it ends with me.

Kathryn Elizabeth Hesketh

12th July 1957 – 1st February 2021

Indigo Children

ABOUT THE AUTHOR

A.K.Biggins grew up in Yorkshire but now lives in Hampshire with her photographer husband. Although she has been writing stories and poems all her life it was not until she reached a significant age that she published her first novel - Losing Jane, in 2017.

More information can be found on - AKBiggins.com

Indigo Children

Printed in Great Britain
by Amazon